IT WAITS

IN THE

FOREST

IT WAITS IN THE FOREST

SARAH DASS

HYPERION

LOS ANGELES   NEW YORK

First Edition, May 2024
1 3 5 7 9 10 8 6 4 2
FAC-004510-24080
Printed in the United States of America

This book is set in Baskerville/Monotype
Designed by Phil Buchanan

Library of Congress Cataloging-in-Publication Data
Names: Dass, Sarah, author.
Title: It waits in the forest / by Sarah Dass.
Description: Los Angeles : Disney-Hyperion, 2024. • Audience: Ages 12–18. •
Audience: Grades 7–9. • Summary: Inspired by Caribbean folklore, eighteen-year-old
Selina gets pulled into a string of mysterious murders on her island home.
Identifiers: LCCN 2023035537 • ISBN 9781368098335 (hardcover) •
ISBN 9781368098724 (ebook)
Subjects: CYAC: Supernatural—Fiction. • Murder—Fiction. • Rain forests—Fiction. •
Families—Fiction. • Interpersonal relations—Fiction. • West Indies—Fiction. • Mystery and
detective stories. • LCGFT: Detective and mystery fiction. • Thrillers (Fiction) • Novels.
Classification: LCC PZ7.1.D33552 It 2024 • DDC [Fic]—dc23
LC record available at https://lccn.loc.gov/2023035537

Reinforced binding

Follow @ReadRiordan
Visit www.HyperionTeens.com

® SUSTAINABLE FORESTRY INITIATIVE   Certified Sourcing

www.forests.org
SFI-01681

Logo Applies to Text Stock Only

To my sister, Rebecca. Thirteen months younger but much wiser. I have too much to thank you for, so this one's for you.

THE GHOSTS OF ST. VIRGIL

You picked up this book. You looked at the title. And if you're like me, your first question was: What waits in the forest?

Are you sure you're brave enough to find out? Oh-so-many things await. The central mystery of the novel, yes. That is terrifying enough. But the ghosts of the past also lurk in the shadowy trees—broken hopes and dreams, the secrets of a whole community that may tear Selina DaSilva's life apart once and for all.

Sarah Dass invites us into a world of magic and murder. She imbues the sunny island of St. Virgil with a dark, sinister mood as effectively as Walter Mosley did for 1940s Los Angeles. This is a novel that will keep you turning pages as layer upon layer of mystery is peeled away, slowly revealing the truth behind the strange goings-on in this supposedly sleepy Caribbean hideaway. What really happened when Selina's father was murdered? What did her mother see that left her unresponsive and bedridden? Is witchcraft just superstition, or is it something more? And who—or what—is killing people on the island?

Our hero, Selina DaSilva, is the perfect companion for this journey. She is savvy but melancholy, resilient but hurting, jaded but hopeful. She has an impossible legacy to live up to. Her father was a police investigator until he himself was murdered. His unsolved death still haunts Selina. Her infamous mother was the island's most prominent woman of magic—both feared and respected, although ultimately scorned—but she left Selina none of her magical gifts . . . or at least, so it seems. Selina will have to be both detective and magician to find the truth and stay alive.

As compelling as the plot is, what I really love about Dass's novel is the way she conjures up an entire world of complex and sympathetic characters. We are thrust headlong into a living, breathing network of friends, family, rivals, enemies, frenemies, lovers, and exes. The emotional investment is immediate.

It Waits in the Forest is a love letter to life on a Caribbean island: the tight-knit, small-town dynamics; the double-edged sword of tourism; the sense of isolation but also local pride; the dissonance of living in paradise while struggling with poverty, lack of opportunity, claustrophobic relationships, and the weight of your family's reputation. But these are characters any reader can relate to, no matter where you live. I found myself reading for the interpersonal drama as much as the action. Sure, I want to know what force is stalking victims on the island. Is there actually a serial killer on the loose? But I also want to know why Selina and Gabriel broke up. I want to understand why Janice is so mean to Selina, why Allison really came back from the mainland, what Edward wants in a relationship, and whether or not I can trust Muriel, or Dr. Henry, or . . . well, really any of these wonderfully crafted characters.

At its core, this story is about overcoming the past. Is it ever possible? Can we embrace and accept where we come from, deal with all the baggage of our families and our personal relationships, and somehow manage to become more than our history? Are we controlled by destiny, restrained by our roots, or can we make our own fate?

Waiting in the forest are the answers. But you'll also find many ghosts . . . unresolved traumas, hidden tragedies, ruined lives, and dreams of what might have been. It's a potent brew. It will haunt you long after you finish reading. But to tell the truth? I wish I could read this book all over again for the first time. Now I feel like a ghost myself, waiting in the forest, hoping for another chance to step into the sunlight of St. Virgil. Sequel, anyone? I'm ready!

CHAPTER
ONE

My mother always said that guilt had a scent. That it was as acrid as unripe akee fruit and just as toxic. She claimed she could smell it on a person like the tang of unwashed skin. That it hung in the air like the scent of oncoming rain, suspended overhead like a threat.

Then again, my mother lied about a lot of things. I learned at a very young age not to believe everything she said.

"Look how the sky set up again," Edward said, facing the shop-window. He had his back to me, the lines of his broad silhouette blurred against the sullen gray clouds. Outside, the colorful buildings cast gloomy shadows on the almost-empty street. The bad weather seemed to have deterred the day's tourists from venturing beyond the pristine shops of the town center to our little souvenir store, which was tucked like an afterthought at the end of Main Street.

"It's Sahara dust," Edward said confidently. "That's what have it looking like that."

"It can't be," his sister, Allison, said. "If it was, I'd be coughing down the place." She sat with her feet propped on the counter, snacking on a brown bag of honey-roasted cashews. She'd bought them from Cliff, the nuts man, whose cart rolled past the shop a few minutes earlier. Her eyes never left her iPad, an American dating show playing on the screen. "Selina, tell my brother he's wrong."

"You're wrong," I said, dusting off the postcard display, only half-listening to the siblings' disagreement.

From time to time, particles of Sahara sand swept across the Atlantic Ocean, darkening the skies of the small Caribbean island of St. Virgil. It coated our land and our lungs and left a hazy, hazardous mess in the air. The sunsets were stunning, though, the skies streaked with brilliant reddish hues.

"Ha!" Allison said. "There. Selina knows."

"Selina works for you," Edward said dryly. "She's not going to disagree with you while she's on the clock." He drew closer to me. "Besides, I know what I'm talking about. They mentioned it on the radio last night. Said it might last a few days."

Allison tucked her long twisted locks behind her ear. "Who listens to radio anymore?"

"I did, last night." He rested his chin on my shoulder. His warm, minty breath brushed against my cheek. "In the car. Selina can vouch for me."

In my memory, the radio had been background noise. At the time, I'd been too distracted by the feel of his lips and his hands to listen to any reports, and honestly, I was a little offended to learn that he hadn't been. But still, he wasn't wrong. We'd been together last night, and for many of the nights before—a part of an unlabeled relationship that had bloomed between us over the past few months.

Edward wrapped his arms around my waist. I reached up to dust the highest row of postcards—scenes of Crimson Bay at sunset, an ibis bird perched in a frangipani tree, the mountains that stood like sentinels on the northern end of the island—all of them faded and yellowing with age. In the seven months I'd been working in the shop, we'd sold maybe three in total.

"Ew," Allison said. "If you two start kissing in front of me, I will vomit."

"We won't," I assured her.

Edward drew me even closer. "Well, let's not completely close off the possibility."

I pulled away to rearrange the carved figurines in the window—some were dancing, others playing drums or steel pans. Overhead, wooden and bamboo chimes hung from nails in the rafters. Over the past few weeks, Edward had become bolder with his public displays of affection, as if he no longer cared what people thought about our association. I found the notion as tantalizing as it was worrying.

Edward sighed dramatically. I continued to ignore him. He might have been pouting, but I knew he wasn't actually offended.

Early in our relationship, I'd learned he enjoyed my seeming indifference. It was all part of my *mystery*, as he called it. Honestly, it was more like my *weird*, though he was too tactful to say that. Everyone on St. Virgil knew about my family, what my mother had done, and what had happened to my parents.

Edward, like his sister, had a slightly morbid streak—perhaps a result of a very comfortable life? Not that I'd ever be foolish enough to call him out or criticize him for it. Not when it was that same streak that attracted him to me in the first place. And I'd be a hypocrite if I denied that it was his distinct *lack* of weird that made me like him back. I'd had enough weird in my life already.

Besides, Edward was movie-star gorgeous, with luminous brown eyes and rich dark brown skin. Apparently, he'd liked me since we were in secondary school, him two years ahead. He said that's why he used to tease me so much.

Even if he had made his crush obvious in the past, I wouldn't have noticed. Yes, he was smart and charming, and the son of the revered chief of police—but none of that mattered. Back then, I'd only had eyes for one person, and it wasn't him.

An argument broke out on Allison's dating show. The shop filled with voices raised in anger, occasionally undercut by the sound of a bleep censor.

"Can't you watch something with a bit more substance?" Edward asked, returning to the window. He'd studied filmmaking for only a year before dropping out to take a job at his mother's real estate firm. And yet, he considered himself the local authority on all forms of visual entertainment media. "There's so much better content to spend your time on."

"How is this any different from those documentaries you're obsessed with?" Allison pointed at her screen. "This is about real life, too. Except, you know, not boring."

"No, documentaries are about finding and presenting the truth. The trash you're watching—"

A thunderous hammering from next door cut him off. It rattled the walls and shook the glass windows.

"What the hell?" Allison rocked forward, raising her voice to complain over the noise. "Not again! It's after six. The construction should be done for today."

"It's only five to six," Edward interjected, but either Allison couldn't hear or she didn't want to listen.

"I'm sick and tired of it," she said. "First, it was the bakery across the street, now it's the jewelry store beside us. Here I am, just trying to watch this cinematic piece of art—"

"No," Edward said.

"—without feeling like I'm being repeatedly punched in the ears."

The hammering stopped.

"Thank you!" Allison said, when the silence persisted. Her chair creaked as she kicked back again. "I swear, if it's not one thing—"

"Incoming!" Edward announced, sounding a little too excited.

"—it's another." Allison sucked her teeth. She paused her show. "Tell me it's not Miss Heather again. No way she burned through all that incense already. We're almost out of stock."

"No, it's someone else." Edward leaned closer to the window. "Older woman. White. A tourist, probably. I don't recognize her."

"Well, don't stand there gawking at her." Allison tucked the iPad under the counter. "That's not a one-way mirror, you dodo. Your face will scare her off."

Edward approached the counter, reached across, and swiped the nuts from her. "Better my gawking face than your ugly one."

"Hey!" Allison tried to retrieve her snack from him.

Edward held on to the brown bag, twisting the top to seal it. He threw me a smirk and started to back away. The door opened, triggering the chime that hung over the top.

"Oh, *thank you*," Edward said, clutching the bag to his chest like it was some great prize rather than an oversweetened street snack. He did this sometimes—pretended to be a customer, brimming with awe and gratefulness. No one asked for this performance, but he seemed to enjoy it.

"I can't tell you what this means to me. I didn't know what else to— Oh!" He backed right into the new customer, then made a show of recoiling in surprise, as if just noticing her for the first time. No doubt he'd formulated some story in his head. Perhaps he was pretending to be a farmer who needed a charm to cure blight, or a new homeowner who asked for a talisman for protection from evil jumbie spirits. A future Best Actor winner, he was not.

Thankfully, Edward did not stick around, promptly exiting the scene after chewing it up.

The newcomer paused in the center of the shop. She looked the way most people did when they came to us: Nervous. Suspicious. A little thrown by the innocuous decor. From the outside, our shop was no different from the eleven or so souvenir stores she'd have passed on her way here. But almost everyone who came to this shop came for a specific reason.

"Can we help you?" Allison asked not too kindly, when the silence stretched.

I continued to clean the other side of the room, sneaking glances at them from the corner of my eye.

"I'm . . . uh . . ." The woman hesitated. "I'm looking for someone. Someone who can . . . help me."

"Are you sure you have the right place, ma'am?" Allison's tone was dry. Dismissive. "They have an information booth on the port and a health center down the street. Maybe one of them can help you?"

The lady rocked back on her heels, indecisive. Allison's tone was a bit rude, and there was always a chance the customer would leave, but we had a system. A routine. A show that had started the second she'd stepped inside the shop.

Step one: Establish an antagonist.

"I . . . I heard about you from Mikael," the lady said, cautiously stepping forward. "He told me to give you some . . . password—some phrase—but I can't remember it. Maybe you know him? He works as a waiter on my ship."

Ah, *Mikael.* It had been a while since he'd sent someone our way. Not as prolific as some of our other referrers, but he had a talent for sniffing out the right kind of person to send.

"I'm sorry, ma'am," Allison said, not sounding apologetic in the least. "I think you have the wrong place." She left the counter, crossed the room, and pulled the front door open. The lady flinched as she passed.

"Gloriosa superba," the lady blurted out, startling us and herself. "That's it. That is what he said to tell you. Gloriosa superba."

Allison's eyes narrowed. She said nothing, the door still open.

Step two: Establish an ally.

"You heard her," I said without turning to face them. "She said the magic words. She can stay."

Allison waited a few beats, then appeared to reluctantly relent, shutting and locking the door. She turned the sign so that it read CLOSED to anyone passing by.

"Is that . . . necessary?" the lady asked.

"You know where you are?" Allison asked, but gave her no room to answer. "If you did, you wouldn't ask them kind of questions."

"Oh—yes. Of course." The lady's polite tone strained with false confidence.

I waited, listening as Allison revealed the cost and took payment. There was a rattle and clip as Allison unlocked the safe behind the counter, then said, "Please empty your pockets and place all your things inside."

"What?" the lady asked. "Why?"

"They can be distractions."

"I won't be distracted."

"It's not for you," Allison said. "Everything you own carries a psychic history of touch and use. Everyone who held it. Every place it's been. Leaving it behind will allow for a clearer, more focused reading."

The lady shook her head. "I'm sorry, I don't feel comfortable leaving my things. I don't know you."

"Well, these are our rules," Allison pressed. "If you don't want to—"

"We can give her the key to the safe," I interjected. "If it will make her feel more comfortable. She can be the one who holds on to it."

Step three: Build trust.

Allison's eyes widened. "But we only have the one key. We can't just give it to her. What if she loses it?"

"I won't," the lady said quickly. "Yes, I would feel better about it."

"Well then . . ." I said with finality, my back still to them.

Allison muttered something I did not hear, nor did I particularly want to. Even though it was all an act, her tone was not pleasant. The safe shut and locked with a snap and click.

"This way," Allison said, and the sound of their footsteps crossed the floor.

The door to the back room creaked open. I turned just in time to catch a glimpse of the lady's stunned expression as she took in the room before the door shut.

Step four: Research.

From this point, I had to move quickly. I dropped the duster on the counter and retrieved the extra key for the safe from under the register. Because of course there was an extra key. Why wouldn't there be?

It was a constant surprise to me that no one ever suspected. Then again, the people who came here tended to believe what they wanted.

After unlocking the safe, I pulled out the contents.

There was a saying: *A woman's life was in her purse.* In my experience, this was true. A wealth of information could be learned from a person's most mundane possessions. Yes, there were the obvious ID cards, address books, and phones—if you were lucky enough to get an unlocked one. But there were also the receipts and wrappers and ticket stubs. Sometimes even novels and bottles of medication.

You just had to know what to look for. And I always did.

———

A few minutes later, I opened the door to the back room, instantly assaulted by the stench of heavy incense blending with the large cinnamon candle burning in the center of my reading table. I made a mental note to remind Allison to light one at a time. I knew the idea was to confound the guests with an influx of stimulation to the senses, but if we couldn't breathe, that could be an actual problem.

The rest of the setup was flawless—the air slightly warm but not hot. Nonsensical geometrical shapes had been chalked onto the floor. Oddly assembled bundles of feathers, leaves, and dried sticks hung from the rafters above.

Several glass bottles filled with dyed liquids glimmered on the shelves, sitting next to books with dead languages carved into their spines. Jars had been filled with dried petals, roots, seeds, painted stones, and plastic gems. And two dozen white and red candles had been strategically set out for both ambiance and to flicker or extinguish when a series of hidden fans or the air conditioner's swing function was activated.

But that wasn't all.

No, then there were the real showstoppers. The props that looked like they were plucked right out of a Hollywood movie—because they were.

A few months earlier, a popular Indiana Jones rip-off franchise decided to film their newest movie on St. Virgil. They constructed a few set pieces on the northern coast. This included a hut for a local witch. While they never used the term *voodoo*—having recognized how problematic it was to misrepresent and demonize a whole religion—it had all the trappings of the old stereotype.

While they were filming, a lot of props were stolen. It was a huge deal at the time, and even made international news. Chief Montgomery had vowed to catch the culprits, though he never did. I wondered what he would do if he ever found out his own children had been a part of it.

Nevertheless, our pilfering did provide the most interesting additions to our back room decor, including all manner of fake animal parts preserved in glass jars, a black cauldron made of plaster and paint, and a charred skull that Allison had named Eddie just to piss off her brother.

After Allison left the back room and shut the door, I took the seat across from Louisa—that was her name, according to her driver's license. At sixty-one years old, she'd recently sold her house and moved to Florida with her daughter and her daughter's family. She liked historical romance novels and badminton, and went to the cinema every Tuesday. She'd been an English teacher before retiring, and she lived with both chronic back pain and insomnia. Her husband had died just over a year ago. His name was Steve.

It wasn't hard to work out why she'd come to us.

Four minutes into the session—a new record for me—Louisa's eyes welled with tears. "So, he *is* here?" she said. "I was worried he wouldn't show up. He's mad at me, I know."

"You've been having nightmares about him," I guessed. It would explain the bottle of sleep medication she carried around with her.

Her eyes widened. "How did you— *Yes!* Except, sometimes, it doesn't feel like a dream. I wake up and he's standing there. At the edge of my bed. Staring at me. He says nothing, but his expression—I know he's angry."

"Does this have anything to do with selling your house?" I asked.

"You're very good." She nodded frantically. "It took us twenty-five years to pay off our mortgage. He renovated it himself. I shouldn't have sold it. But it was too big and I hated living there without him."

"I see."

"Every room had some reminder of him. I couldn't . . ." She dissolved into choked sobs, muffling the sound behind her handkerchief. I waited for her to recover.

My mother used to talk about guilt as if it were a real, living entity. Something she could sense, capture, manipulate, and dissipate at will. I saw it as something profoundly human: regret for the things we did or didn't do, said or didn't say. For some, it became the ugly chair in their home, always present, but they learned to live with it. For others, it was a weight strapped to their back, dragging them down, dangerously overwhelming in their most vulnerable moments. The latter I knew from experience.

If someone threw me a lifeline, I'd want to grab it in an instant. But belief didn't come easy to me. Not like it did for the people who came to this shop.

"Listen," I said, holding her gaze. "That isn't Steve you're seeing. That was just a dream. And I know that because he's in the room with us now."

She blinked rapidly. "He is?"

"Yes. And he wants me to tell you that he's not mad about the house. He's glad you're not living alone. He wants you to be surrounded by people who love you."

Tears welled in her eyes again. Her lip curled into a sad smile, and for a moment, I wondered if it was possible I'd said the right thing. That I'd actually helped someone, without resorting to theatrics for once. That I wasn't just lying for profit. A con artist, who sold fake spells and charms that were no better than placebos, only successful in situations where belief was already enough to fix it.

"No." Louisa sniffed, wiping her cheeks. "I know what I've seen. It's him. I know it." She lifted her chin, a hint of steely stubbornness behind her gaze. "He's there. Every night. I haven't slept properly in months. How do I make him stop?"

Oh right. Of course. How silly of me.

For a second, I'd almost forgotten who I was and why she was here.

"Like I told you, that's not Steve," I repeated. "Steve isn't angry at you. What you've been seeing is a spirit who's taken on your husband's face to try to trick you."

She frowned. "What? Why?"

Good question.

"Because some of them like to cause mischief. It's what they do." I lifted a hand to my head. A signal. A cue. "I sensed a dark presence the second you walked into the shop. But now it's clear to me. This is what has been haunting you."

A cold wind swept through the room. The lit candles flickered.

"Yes, there it is," I said.

Louisa sat up and glanced about. She wrapped her arms around herself. "What do I do?" she whispered, as if afraid the spirit would overhear her.

"I will give you a list of ingredients. When you return home, you are to boil them together, under the light of a full moon. Strain out the water and let it sit in a bowl that has been blessed in the waters of a sacred stream until the next new moon. You will then take the water and wash the floor of your house."

"Where do I get a bowl that's been blessed in the waters of a sacred stream?"

"You know what?" I said, after pretending to think about it. "We may have one in stock."

Louisa nodded, completely taken in. Her faith in me held for the rest of the session. It wasn't until we returned to the shop, and she saw my face in better lighting, that it faltered a little.

She paused, in the act of stuffing her purchases into her purse. "Aren't you a bit young to be doing this?"

It was not an uncommon question. Most people expected an elderly woman with a face that betrayed decades of experience and wisdom. They did not anticipate a fresh-faced eighteen-year-old with unruly curly black hair, and a slightly crooked nose that resulted from a tree climbing accident. For some reason, this tended to throw off customers. That was why I tried to keep my distance from them before the session started.

"I know what I'm doing," I told Louisa. "Age is irrelevant. I have been preparing for this since I was a baby. My mother taught me everything I know. My grandmother taught her before that."

Of all the lies I'd told her that evening, this one skirted closest to the truth.

"And your mother is okay with you doing it on your own already?" Louisa asked.

"My mother is dead," I said, which tended to prevent further questions.

Two seconds after the chime of the door announced Louisa's exit, Allison pulled out all the cash and started counting. "Good job today. I thought we'd never get rid of that ugly bowl. It's been sitting there for years."

"Thanks." I stood before the storefront window, watching Louisa disappear around the corner to the Amber hotel.

"I'll admit it," Allison said, "I freaked out when my parents cut me off. But there *is* a thrill to making your own money. A couple more weeks of this and I'll have enough to get my own place away from them."

I almost told her not to exaggerate. That her version of being cut off consisted of living in a massive house with a closet full of imported clothes, prepared meals, and a live-in maid. What she *meant* was that she didn't have pocket money anymore. Everyone should be so lucky to have parents who'd give us a shop to manage as punishment for dropping out of university after a month.

"Happy to help," I said instead, because, despite everything, I did like Allison. Over the last year, she'd proven to be a good friend, taking me under her wing. During my worst days, when the nights felt endless, my memories had teeth, and silence was treacherous—she had been the one who pulled me out of my head. She'd dragged me to parties and given me this job, providing distraction so I could temporarily forget.

As I stood at the window, a pair of workmen from next door walked into view. Their navy-blue overalls were sweat-stained and dusty. As they crossed the storefront, one caught my eye. I watched as he stopped, a flicker of recognition transforming into lip-curling disdain. Before I could move, blink, or breathe, he drew back and spat. The glob splattered against the glass in front of me.

I flinched, then silently chastised myself for reacting. I'd given him exactly what he'd wanted. But no matter how much time passed, the depth of their hatred was still startling.

"Do you think it'll work?" Allison asked, her voice breaking through the silence and causing me to flinch again.

The man smirked. Apparently satisfied, he jogged off to catch up to his partner.

"What'll work?" I asked. She clearly hadn't seen what just happened. It was for the best. There wasn't anything either of us could do about it. Just another day on St. Virgil.

"Do you think she'll stop seeing him at night?"

It took me a second to realize Allison was talking about Louisa. When I did, I threw her a judgmental side-eye. Even though I'd repeatedly told Allison that I made it up, sometimes I got the feeling she didn't quite believe me. "Do I think the demon version of Steve will leave her alone?"

She rolled her eyes, tucking the money into a gray pencil case that she kept under the counter. "You know what I mean. Will she stop imagining him or whatever?"

"Maybe." Hopefully. "Belief is a powerful thing. My mother used to say a ritual is only as powerful as the intentions behind it."

Make sure they're good, she used to tell me, with all the gravity required of a warning. *What you put in is exactly what you get out.*

"And what about our intentions?" Allison leaned against the counter, smirking. "Do those factor in, too?"

I seriously hoped not.

For a few seconds more, I lingered at the window, the spit sliding down the glass. The sun had begun to set on St. Virgil, the sky painted in a brilliant, awful red. It looked like Edward had been right after all.

If I were a different person, I'd have seen the bloody sky and read it as a sign of something sinister on the horizon. Instead, I turned away from the window and returned to dusting.

CHAPTER
TWO

My parents met on the job—at the gravesite of a woman who'd been missing for eleven years. He'd determined the sex and age; she'd divined that the death occurred near a body of water with pressure crushing her neck. After that, they were inseparable for almost twenty years. That was not to say they always got along; they were too different to coexist easily. But they made a good team, each filling in the gaps the other missed.

Mummy believed trauma left a mark, not just on people but on places, too. Not like a splash of paint on the wall, but something deeper, embedding itself into the foundation and reverberating for years to follow. She used to claim she caught these reverberations and experienced every emotion like they were hers.

On the other hand, my father, a forensic investigator, experienced scenes of trauma very differently. To Daddy, the marks left were fingerprints, fibers, hairs, DNA, and blood spatter. He believed every contact left a trace and he'd been excellent at finding them.

In the aftermath of their attack, people would remark on the irony that they might've been the only ones capable of solving their own case.

———

I set off early the next morning, while the world was still silent but for the whistling birds in the trees and the rustling of fowls in the bushes.

A walk from the main house took about ten minutes. I had to cut through the edge of the rainforest to get there.

Since moving to the main house, I had not stepped foot inside the guest cottage, where it happened—where one part of my life was crudely separated from the other. But I still visited Mummy's garden from time to time, the herbs thriving despite the encroaching weeds and her long absence.

After Elizabeth Alleyne's murder, when the harassment turned dangerous, we took refuge in this small bungalow for almost a year. It stood a good distance from the road, isolated and hidden from those who did not know where to find it.

When I arrived at the garden, I got to work quickly. Clipper in hand, I snipped and collected what I needed to replenish the stock at the shop, as well as supply a few of my experiments.

The garden was the only place my mother and I held a common interest. She'd taught me the plants and their uses. I'd learned that a poultice of wonder of the world was good for treating cuts and bruises. A bit of aloe could stimulate hair growth. A tea made of lemongrass boosted immunity. Plants had the miraculous ability to heal and hurt, as close to real magic as I'd ever believe in.

I placed the cuttings into my basket and tucked my umbrella under my arm. The sky was still so very gray, and even with the confirmation that the cause was Sahara dust, it seemed impossible that it wouldn't break into a downpour at any moment.

When I was finished with the garden, I walked around to the back of the house. Before I left, I wanted a clipping from the flame lily—scientifically known as *Gloriosa superba*—which crept along the wall and clung to the ledge of the back window. Mummy had brought it home one day, after one of her random excursions into the rainforest. When she'd shown me the tuber, it had looked like a weird emaciated yam. She'd held it cradled in the fold of a banana leaf.

The day it first bloomed, I'd been fascinated by the strange yellow-red flowers—the thin rippling petals and the clawlike shape. I'd ripped one off to study it, not as gentle as I could have been. The next day, the plant had rotted and withered away.

Mummy had been livid—though not for the reasons I'd thought. Within weeks, the lily had regrown, a sensitive but resilient thing. No, her anger stemmed from fear. She didn't want me to experiment with it. It turned out every part of the plant was poisonous. Especially the root tuber from which it grew, where the toxins were highly concentrated.

The night my parents were attacked, the culprit—or culprits— crushed the flame lily beneath their shoe. On the scale of destruction inflicted during this awful visit, this wasn't rated particularly high on the list. And yet, when I'd spotted the familiar sprout reemerging from the soil weeks after, I'd sunk to the ground and wept for hours.

Over the last two years, the creeping plant had flourished. The last time I visited, it had almost reached the roof, sprawling and undisturbed.

Or so it had been.

I stooped beside the spot where the plant lay on the ground. It was brown and starting to shrivel, the faint edge of a shoeprint pressed into the soil. This had to be relatively recent.

I briefly entertained the thought of birds or some other aspect of nature being the cause, but I knew from experience it took a heavy-handed touch to do this much damage.

I drew closer to the wall, inspecting the back window. Scratches marked the ledge, but that could've been there for ages. Hell, I might have even made them myself, back when I used to sneak out of the house.

As I stared at the shriveled lilies, a chill skated down my spine, and I was gripped by the sudden certainty that someone had been here. Someone had crushed the creeper on their way through the window and into the house.

Was it thieves? Vandals? Pranksters?

Or was it the bullies? The people in town who'd harassed us. Who still whispered *witch* and *demon spawn* behind my back. The ones who taunted my family in our lowest moments and made us retreat into the forest like hunted animals.

Some of my family's belongings were still stored in the cottage. What damage could they have done inside? I needed to know.

As I shoved the window upward, all I could think about was their lies. I'd heard what they said. Heard them whispering in their little clusters, talking out the sides of their mouths. Rewriting my mother's past. Changing the history of our island's celebrated psychic into the legend of a witch who'd made a deal with the devil and gotten exactly what was coming to her.

I'd heard it all.

They wanted to spread lies and fear about my family, so I'd decided to play into it. After years of schoolyard teasing and taunts, I'd learned my best defense was to pretend to be the monster they thought I was, then scare the hell out of them.

I shoved the window again. And again. It creaked in protest, then flew all the way up. After setting down the basket and leaning my umbrella against the wall, I hooked my arms over the edge and hauled myself through the opening. I hadn't done this in ages, but my body knew the routine on reflex.

Unfortunately, someone had shifted the love seat below. My left hand slipped off the edge of the armrest. I managed not to fall on my face, but I clipped my chin on the back of the chair, my teeth digging into my lower lip. The sharp pinch of pain was followed by the metallic taste of blood.

I swiped my thumb across the broken skin. My fingertip came away bloody. It hurt quite a bit.

I sat there for a moment. The act of breaking in had cooled my head a little. I should've returned to the main house for the keys. Or asked someone else to check inside the cottage for me. There was no reason I should be in here on my own. But I hadn't been thinking clearly.

Part of me still felt protective of this place—the last place we'd been together as a whole family.

Whatever. I was already inside. I might as well check it out so I hadn't busted my lip for no reason.

Besides, there wasn't exactly much ground to cover. The whole cottage consisted of one floor with a joined living room and kitchen, two bathrooms, two bedrooms, and a small storage cupboard. I walked through most of it in seconds, lingering in my old bedroom for a little longer than necessary. It had been my sanctuary in what I'd thought was the worst time of my life.

My favorite feature was the desk beside the window. I'd used it as my workstation, my texts on botany on one end and space for any ongoing projects on the other. The rest of my books were packed into shelves, mostly fictional tales of mystery, adventure, and fantastical escapes. Because my father had kept his shelves alphabetically organized by author's name, I'd done the same.

I dragged my fingers along the spines, tempted to take a few, but I knew I'd never read them again. They'd only make me sad, reminding me of a time that had passed. A time when escape seemed possible.

My hand paused over my copy of *The Voyage of the Dawn Treader.* It was out of place, nowhere near the rest of the series. I pulled it off the shelf, confused by the mistake. Through the open space, I spotted something wedged into the back. Curious, I leaned in, trying to see what it was. More novels had to be dug out before I could pull it free.

It was a notebook. Right away, I knew it wasn't mine. The burgundy cover was worn, the spine repeatedly cracked with use. It wouldn't close properly because of a few papers folded and tucked inside. I carefully unfolded one. My curiosity twisted into shock as I recognized Ken Thomas's beady eyes staring up at me.

LOCAL MAN CHARGED WITH THE MURDER OF

18-YEAR-OLD ELIZABETH ALLEYNE

I set the newspaper clipping aside, my hands trembling. A quick flip through the book revealed page after page covered in my father's familiar writing, every word about the case that ruined our lives. The case that made it necessary for us to banish ourselves to this cottage. It was all there. Dates, names, places, pictures. *Ken, Elizabeth, Maeve, Mom . . . murder . . .*

I barely blinked, my eyes burning as I took in the morbid contents, but I couldn't stop flipping through the pages. I didn't understand. Elizabeth's murder was solved. The case was long closed. Why would Daddy have had this? And more importantly, why was it tucked into the back of my shelf? Had he meant for me to find it?

A soft thump startled me.

I looked up from the notebook, toward the open bedroom door. The hall beyond appeared empty, but that did nothing to ease the sudden flash of fear that rooted me to the spot. I'd forgotten why I'd come in here.

Slowly, I closed the notebook and tucked it under my arm. I approached the door and peered into the hall. It was as empty as the rest of the house so far.

There was just one place left to check: my parents' bedroom.

I hadn't been the one who found them there, for which I should've been grateful. And I was, but I still wanted to know what happened. Especially because the attackers were never found.

I'd read all the reports, all the articles. Even though I had no forensic training like my father, he'd told me all about his work as I was growing up. He explained how he examined a scene, recorded the layout, and took note of every detail no matter how small. I'd become convinced that the police must've missed something. Maybe, if I'd been there, I'd have found the truth. I knew it made no sense, but that didn't change how I felt.

I shut my bedroom door, and I heard it again—the thumping noise. Not like a lock snapping into place. This was something heavier. Like the sole of a shoe against the tiled floor. It reminded me of the sound my father's favorite boots made when he wore them inside. I opened my bedroom door and closed it again, repeating my actions to see if I'd somehow triggered the noise. But when I did, there was nothing.

Halfway to my parents' room, I heard it again. Two thumps. Louder and closer this time. Right behind me. I whipped around. Nothing.

I clutched the notebook, holding my breath, listening, and waiting for a repeat.

Nothing happened. Not after ten seconds. Not after twenty. Thirty. All I saw were three closed doors and an empty hallway. No one else was here.

I needed to get a grip.

Approaching my parents' bedroom door, I drew a fortifying breath. All I had to do was peek inside and make sure nothing was missing or vandalized.

There was no reason I couldn't do this. It had been two years. The room had been cleaned, the traces of what happened long gone.

I reached out, the knob oddly cold in my hand. I pulled the door open and looked inside.

The symbol appeared first—a huge red circle, crudely painted onto the wall over the headboard. Within, it contained smaller markings that I didn't understand. Then there was my father sitting on the very edge of the bed, his shoulders slumped, his head tilted to the side. Blood spilled from the gaping wound on his head, soaking his favorite blue T-shirt and pooling on the bedsheets. The longer I stared, the more details appeared: the ransacked drawers, the smashed lamp, the red splatters on the walls, and the smears on the floor.

My father lifted his eyes to look at me.

A sudden terror gripped me—not mine. *His.* Somehow, I knew it was his. It burned in my chest, and in my lungs, as if he'd breathed it right into me.

At a point in the police investigation, they'd considered me a suspect. *Me*, the rebellious sixteen-year-old daughter. The only one in the family not home at the time, though I should have been. People had heard us arguing the day before. I'd yelled. I'd told them that I hated them. Told my mother she was ruining my life, and Daddy was letting her do it.

But I loved my parents and missed them desperately. Seeing my father now, like this, it felt like my insides were being carved out. The notebook slipped from my hold, smacking against the floor.

I stumbled backward, away from the room, out of the hall. Bile rose in the back of my throat. Fear choked off my screams. All I wanted to do was get out of there, but when I got to the door, it did not open. I gripped the handle, pulled, and pulled, but it did not budge. Then I remembered the padlock on the outside.

I realized the futility of what I was doing, and a sliver of sense cut through the panic. The lock was still intact. It was unlikely anyone was in the cottage. Realizing this calmed me down a little, but I still wanted to get out.

On shaky legs, I returned to my parents' bedroom. It took everything I had to look inside again.

The room was empty now. Stark white sheets stretched across a queen-sized mattress. The windows were closed and covered by heavy curtains. There was no sign of my father. No symbol. No blood. Just a bit of dust and neglect.

See? I told myself. *This is what came of reading all the articles, all the reports.* How many times had I dreamed about a gruesome scene just like that? When I'd flipped through Daddy's notebook, I must have triggered something in my head. My mind imposed a nightmare scenario into reality. Clearly, I was still more affected by the attack than I'd realized.

And yet, even armed with this explanation, fear and doubt clouded my thoughts. All traces of my nostalgic mood from earlier had evaporated. Now the cottage felt too enclosed for comfort.

I snatched the notebook off the floor, my hands trembling. The image of my bleeding father burned at the back of my mind. I tried to block it out, returning to the love seat. My exit through the window was far clumsier than my entrance.

The second I landed outside, my skin flared with the prickly sensation of being watched. I gathered my basket and umbrella. My every move was measured in a forced nonchalance, even as my heart thundered in my chest.

I tucked the notebook into my basket, covering it with the herb clippings. My father had hidden it for some reason. Until I figured out why, I had no plans to share it with anyone.

Perhaps I was just being paranoid, but I still felt unsettled. Despite the intact padlock and the lack of proof, I still suspected someone *had* been in the house. A nosy child or an annoying prankster—or someone whose intentions had been more nefarious. As the implications of that set in, I realized how foolish I'd been to go inside at all. Even for my typical self-destructive tendencies, this was extreme.

I picked up my pace, following the path from the cottage to the main house. I refused to run, even as the feeling of being followed persisted. If I ran, they might chase me. They'd know I knew. If I pretended nothing was wrong, maybe they'd let me go.

I'd almost cleared the forest when a crunch of footsteps caught my attention. A figure emerged from the shadows of the trees, heading toward me.

I screamed.

CHAPTER
THREE

"Wait!" Gabriel held out his hands. "Selina, it's only me."

"What the hell?" I hunched forward, my hands braced on my knees. I breathed. He was the very last person I wanted to see. But in my panic, still afraid of being followed, I welcomed the familiar face.

"Are you all right?" He drew closer, steps light despite his tall stature. "What happened?"

"The cottage . . ." I said, still trying to catch my breath. "Someone . . ."

"You were at the cottage? Why?"

"I thought . . ."

Thought what? I glanced back, toward the path behind me. I hadn't seen anyone. And I couldn't tell him that I'd had a feeling that someone had been there. Not because I thought he wouldn't believe me. I knew that he would. It was I who doubted myself.

"Are you sure you're okay?" Gabriel grimaced. "I knew seeing each other again would be awkward, but I didn't expect screaming."

I straightened up, the reality of his presence dawning on me. "You're here?" I took an involuntary step back. "How are you here? When did you get back?"

Why did he come back?

His eyes darted away from me in a sudden show of nerves.

Gabriel looked good. Really good. A healthy golden hue warmed his brown skin. His jet-black hair was disheveled and long enough to curl right above his ears. The plain white T-shirt he wore might have hung a little looser on his wiry-muscled frame, but the change was unsurprising considering what he'd been through.

"I just got here this morning," he said, rubbing the back of his neck. "I finally got the all clear to travel. Janice is here, too, for the school break. She wanted us to surprise Ma together."

Oh.

"I'll be here for the next few weeks," he said. "I've got an internship at the newspaper. Something to keep me busy until university starts."

I couldn't speak, even as he left the open space in the ensuing silence. The shock of his presence wiped out every thought.

For the most part, he looked the same. A few raised scars marked his skin, including one that nicked the corner of his jaw. The upper muscle of his left arm appeared slightly smaller than the right—which I might not have noticed if I hadn't known to look for it. From what I'd heard, his left hand had not healed as miraculously as the rest of him.

"What happened to your lip?" he asked me.

"What?"

"Your lip. It looks swollen."

My skin warmed as his attention focused on my mouth. Tendrils of awareness snaked beneath my skin. "It's nothing."

The wind picked up, snatching at our hair. I tucked mine behind my ear, while he ignored his. Overhead, the sky still glowered down at the earth in miserable shades of gray.

Gabriel's hand lifted and then dropped in an aborted gesture. He'd been about to reach for me. I was certain of it. It hit me then, all at once—every latent emotion he unearthed. The disappointment, anger, longing, guilt . . .

For two days he'd balanced on the precipice of death. The doctors had warned us, trying to prepare us. It could've gone either way. But he was alive.

And now he was *here*.

I started toward the house. Holding my basket to my chest, I hoped to hide my shaking. "Can't talk. I'm going to be late for work."

"Work?" Gabriel followed. Together, we broke free of the tree line, entering the open field that surrounded the house. Rosy periwinkle clustered alongside the walking path. "You have a job?"

"I have a job." My voice was surprisingly level. "Some things changed since you left," I said, then winced. We had not spoken in so long; I was not sure how much he knew. As cowardly as it was, I didn't want to have to be the one to tell him about Edward and me.

"I'm aware." His caustic tone made me flinch.

So he did know.

I shouldn't have been surprised. Of course his sister would tell him. I bet Janice couldn't wait to spill the news. She'd never approved of me or my relationship with Gabriel.

"We need to talk," he said.

"I disagree," I said without breaking my pace. Had he come to the forest looking for me? I suppressed a thrill at the thought that he'd felt the need to seek me out. It was foolish and fruitless. After all this time, I shouldn't be so affected by him. "We said everything we needed to say before you left."

"You can't be serious."

I did not answer, practically jogging past the open gate toward the front door. He passed me on the steps, blocking my path.

"It's been a year, Selina," he said, his chest rising and falling with uneven breath.

Ten months actually. Ten months and twenty-eight days since he'd left the island. Ten months and twenty-nine days since we'd last spoken. Not that I'd ever admit to counting, but when the boy you love nearly dies, the dates tend to stick.

The door opened. Muriel smiled at us from the other side.

"There you are, Gabriel." My godmother's words curled with a slight accent—a remnant of her years living abroad. She wore a loose linen dress, her straightened gray hair styled in a layered bob. "We were wondering if you'd already left. Are you staying for breakfast?"

Over Muriel's shoulder, her daughter, Janice, appeared. "Oh, you must. I'm showing Ma this amazing crêpe recipe. I learned it from one of my roommates. She's French, so this is the real deal."

Gabriel shifted to face his family. "I've seen you burn water, Jan. Threatening me with your cooking is not the way to get me to stay." And yet, when Muriel stepped aside, he entered the house.

I was still a little wary of being trapped in conversation with him, but seeing no alternative, I followed them inside.

"Au contraire, mon frère," Janice said with an exaggerated French accent. "This will be très délicieux." Then she reached out, drawing me into a hug, wrapping me in her sugary, fruity perfume.

To say I was surprised by the embrace might've been an understatement. She was the same person who'd persuaded most of our secondary school to randomly hiss at me for the better part of a year. The fact that she'd acknowledge me at all was a bit bizarre.

I itched to check Gabriel's reaction to his older sister's warm greeting. Maybe we'd share our silent disbelief, then come together and laugh about it later. Except he and I didn't do things like that anymore. I had to remember that.

"Selina!" Janice said, pulling back. She tucked her sleek, black hair behind her ear, and adjusted the strap of her butter-yellow A-line dress. Somehow, she did not have a single wrinkle on her outfit despite her travel.

After two years of university, she looked the same as she always had—prim, pretty, and perfect.

"So good to see you," she said. "I was just telling Ma how surprised I am that you didn't peace out the second you graduated. I thought for sure you'd leave and take your rightful place among the other science nerds at some big university abroad."

"Yes, well . . ." I forced a smile, biting back the words I would've said if Muriel wasn't there. Clearly, my plans had changed. She already knew why.

"Don't get me wrong," she said. "I like that Ma has company."

"And I love having her here." Muriel hooked her arm through mine, leading us into the kitchen. "It can get lonely in this big house."

"I should go," Gabriel said, echoing my own thoughts.

Not only was I beginning to feel like an interloper amid this family reunion, but Gabriel's presence was overwhelming. It took everything I had not to stare at him.

After finding my father's notebook, and my strange hallucination at the cottage, I couldn't handle this. I needed space to think. To assess the situation.

"Already?" Muriel let go of my hand and approached him. "But you just got here. After a long trip, too. You need to be careful. You're still recovering."

"I'm fine, Ma."

She shook her head. "Are you sure? You look tired. Doesn't he look tired?" she asked us.

He did look tired. And stressed—which was only exacerbated as we turned our collective attention to him. He clenched his jaw, the muscles of his face already drawn so tight they should have snapped with the movement.

Our eyes met, and I felt a punch to the gut. I looked away.

"Stay," Muriel urged him. "Have breakfast. We can catch up."

"Okay," he said, hesitating on the threshold. "But only for a few minutes. I've got to organize my apartment. And check in with my boss at the paper. I'm supposed to be starting my internship tomorrow."

Muriel shifted, a new stiffness to her posture. "So nice that you were able to get your old apartment back," she said, while sounding like it was anything but. "I can't say I'm surprised it was still vacant, though, considering its location. . . ."

"Ma, where do we keep the frying pans?" Janice opened one cupboard, then the next, progressively moving farther away from the correct one. "Ideally, we'd use a crêpe pan, but we'll work with what we have."

Gabriel sighed. "Please, Ma, don't start. I'm only going to be here for a few weeks."

"I'm not starting anything. I only feel that now that you're back, and you've reached the point in your recovery that you're ready to work, we should be discussing your role in the family business."

"I'm not seeing them, Ma," Janice said. She was making quite a racket. I didn't know if she was being deliberately obtuse or trying to derail their conversation. As much as I hated giving Janice the benefit of the doubt, it was probably the latter. Even I could tell, from the tight set of Muriel's lips, things were about to take a turn.

For as different as Gabriel and Janice were, they had always been very close. Perhaps because they were only a year apart. I used to be jealous of their connection. Then again, I used to be jealous of anyone who forced me to share Gabriel's attention.

"All I'm saying is that we have internships at VE, too." Muriel's shoulders squared as if preparing for a fight. I wasn't surprised. While Muriel could polish up as well as any society lady, my godmother was not raised nursing a silver spoon.

Mummy once described her childhood friend as scrappy, single-mindedly determined to claw her way to her best life. This started with a sparkling tennis career, which led to medals, scholarships, and low-level fame. Then she met her husband, Donovan Pierre, the richest man to ever settle on St. Virgil.

After the tragedy of Mr. Pierre's passing five years ago, no one would have faulted her for selling off his company, Virgil Enterprises. Instead, she'd taken control of the business, not only holding it together, but exceeding expectations by leading it to new heights. She was not the type of person to let go of what she wanted easily.

Gabriel leaned against the wall, his head tipped back to face the ceiling. "I just got here. Do you have to start already?"

"And when would you prefer that we talk about it?" Muriel asked.

"Can I opt for never?"

"Excuse me," I mumbled, retreating from the room. I'd heard

versions of this argument before. Once Gabriel started whipping out sarcastic one-liners, the argument would quickly go downhill.

As I slipped past Gabriel, I made sure not to look at him, wary of what I might find in his expression, and terrified of what might slip through mine. In the past, I might've stayed at his side in silent support. But it wasn't my place anymore.

At the bottom of the stairs, I stepped around the pile of Janice's paisley-print suitcases and made my way to my room on the second floor. There, I hid my father's notebook under my mattress, then dressed quickly. All the while, I kept an eye on the time.

When Edward sent a voice message to let me know he was almost here, I grabbed my handbag, and checked my reflection.

I wore a short-sleeved white blouse, dark jeans, and sandals. Simple silver studs adorned my ears. My curly hair was brushed into a tight ponytail, my makeup limited to a few pats of face powder and a swipe of lip gloss. Over the last year, my style had simplified, veering away from the bright colors and costume jewelry that I used to love. It drew too much attention.

The only exception I kept was my mother's long gold chain. The attached pendant—an inky-black obsidian stone locked within an intricate pear-shaped lattice—settled just above my navel. I'd been wearing it since my parents' attack. I tucked it under my clothes and hurried downstairs.

I had to be quick. The last thing I wanted to do was give Edward a reason to come inside. Navigating a face-to-face between him and Gabriel would be a minefield that I wasn't prepared to handle.

"What is your plan exactly?" Muriel's voice floated over from the kitchen. "Be honest—what do you hope to get out of playing errand boy at the newspaper? Living in that tiny rathole of an apartment?"

"Oh, come on, Ma," Janice said. "It's bigger than a rathole. Slightly."

"Thank you for your support, Janice," Gabriel said. "Truly."

With the argument still in full swing, I tried to slip out unobserved. I'd gotten mere feet from the door when a honk blared. I winced. I looked out the front window and spotted Edward's silver car rolling through the main gate.

"Selina?" Muriel called out.

"Just leaving!" I yelled back, then fled.

"What happened to your lip?" Edward asked in place of a greeting.

I sighed, slipping into the passenger seat, and shutting the door. "Good morning, Edward."

"Good morning," he amended, then without missing a beat, asked, "What happened to your lip?" He tucked a finger beneath my chin and lifted my face for a better look.

"It's nothing." I drew back from his touch, desperate to get going. "I fell and accidentally bit it."

"You fell? It's not like you to be so clumsy."

"Yes, I know it's hard to believe, but I'm not without some flaws."

He wrinkled his nose. "Impossible."

Even though I made a show of rolling my eyes, I was pleased by our light back-and-forth. It felt so mundane. Simple. Being with Edward was easy—this thing between us shiny and new, detached from my past and the darkness that came with it. Unlike being with Gabriel, whose very reappearance seemed to coincide with everything I'd been trying so hard not to think about.

I buckled my seat belt. Edward hooked his arm around the back of my seat and stretched over to kiss me. My lip stung.

"There," Edward said, pulling away. "I've kissed it better."

"It's a miracle," I said with exaggerated wonder.

He laughed, steering the car into a U-turn.

As we peeled away from the house, I looked back and caught movement in the front window. My stomach twisted. I told myself that Gabriel couldn't have seen the kiss from that angle. And even if he did, I shouldn't care. He'd broken up with me after all.

And yet, the feeling of guilt lingered long after the house disappeared from view.

CHAPTER
FOUR

Natalie knew her first night at the Amber Oceanside Hotel would be her last. And the second the booking website loaded, she planned to write a review stating just that.

She sat against the wooden headboard, lifting the phone higher and higher, stretching this way and that, desperately trying to reconnect to the hotel's feeble Wi-Fi. The condition of the room was pleasant enough, if a little small, but the internet services left much to be desired.

After a minute passed with no success, Natalie slumped into the sheets, staring at the whitewashed ceiling. She could not say why she was here. Only that when the time came to board her flight back to Miami from Jamaica, she could not do it. She could not return to the relentless routine of school, tutoring, eat, sleep, and repeat. Instead, she bought a ticket to the cheapest alternative. Then, after spending a night on the much larger sister island, she'd taken the ferry over to St. Virgil that morning.

She had wanted remote. Boy, had she found it.

Every now and then, she'd entertain herself by thinking about her parents' reactions. Wish she could've seen their faces when they realized what she'd done. How long had they waited, fruitlessly scanning the faces of arriving passengers only to realize that she wasn't among them? Had they panicked? Argued with the ticket agents? At what point did the truth sink in?

They deserved it.

They were the ones who'd sent her away, saying she needed a break, then subjecting her to a mind-numbingly boring stay with her great-aunt in Kingston.

She wished they'd be honest. *They* were the ones who'd wanted a break, quick to ship her off, as they did every school holiday.

Natalie flipped onto her side, closed her eyes, and tried to sleep. Silence smothered the hotel like a weighted blanket. For someone used to the steady hum of city noise, it was almost suffocating. It reminded her of the summer she'd turned thirteen—this time, shipped off to her father's family in Indiana. Another forced vacation, this one after her first school expulsion. Her father insisted that she'd like it. *All that fresh air and open space.* He'd said it would feel like freedom.

Natalie disagreed. Standing on the edge of the cornfields, watching the endless sea of stalks swaying under that bright open sky, the nearest neighbors miles away, she'd felt trapped. Isolated.

Inside the house was even worse, her tiny bedroom a little more than a closet with a single window too high to reach. The wood was rotting, the roof leaking, windows and doors creaking on rusted hinges. The scent of something stale lingered in the air. Dust layered every surface.

Her uncle was boorish, and her aunt severely judgmental. They didn't allow locks on bedroom doors or idle time. There was no space to be alone, nowhere to seek comfort.

And then there was her cousin Benny. Her aunt and uncle's only child. Their golden son. At seven years old, he still spoke with a baby voice that seemed to grow cutesier in proximity to his parents. In their eyes, he could do no wrong.

Natalie hated Benny and his little games. Especially the ones he'd play at night.

It would start with the creak of her bedroom door, the patter of tiny feet, then the drag of a small body against the floor.

The first time it happened, Natalie awoke to the sound of high-pitched giggles in the darkness. She bolted upright, disoriented, and terrified. She shifted to the edge of the bed, stretching for the light switch just out of reach. The second her feet touched the floor, a pair of clammy, stubby fingers snatched her ankles.

Got ya!

She screamed.

Her aunt and uncle rushed in. After assessing the situation, they were angrier at her for waking the house, dismissing their son's little prank. The next morning, they sent Natalie to remove the vines that grew on the barbed wire fences. She couldn't find gloves and no one helped her. By mid-morning, her hands were pink and scraped raw.

Benny's pranks continued over the rest of the summer. Not every night, but often enough. She'd lay awake, listening for footsteps. The sound of giggles filtered into snatches of sleep, permeating her dreams and nightmares. Sometimes he'd whisper to her or talk to himself. Other times, he'd carry on one-sided conversations as if speaking to someone else.

Natalie didn't scream. Never again, after the first night, too afraid of the fallout. The cries locked in her throat, caged behind her teeth.

A few months after Natalie's visit ended, the roof gave in, collapsing on everyone inside. If her parents regretted making her stay in that ticking time bomb, they never said. The next time she got expelled, they sent her to a different set of relatives.

She still heard her cousin sometimes. On late nights like this one, when the line blurred between sleep and waking. When she couldn't tell if she was dreaming.

First came the creak. Then the footsteps.

Then the screams.

Natalie opened her eyes and stared into the darkness. She didn't move, afraid to look over the side of the bed, sure that if she did, she'd see her dead cousin crawling on the floor. She waited for the giggles and the whispers.

A thunderous knock startled her. It did not sound like a fist against wood, but something heavier. Like a body slammed against the wall. Voices rose. More shouts and a scream so raw it almost didn't sound human. The urgency of their tone finally broke the grip of Natalie's longtime fears.

She jumped out of bed and sprinted to the door. Blinded by darkness, every second it took to find the lock, to turn the knob, she anticipated the feel of tiny hands snatching at her ankles.

She opened the door, and the room flooded with light. After looking back at her empty hotel room—just to be sure it was empty—she stuck her head into the hall. A broad-shouldered man in a navy-blue uniform hammered his fists against the door beside hers.

"Open up!" he called out. "This is hotel security. We've had noise complaints." He continued to knock and shout, all the while casting furtive glances toward the end of the hall where the elevators led to the lobby. Every now and then, he'd try the doorknob. It did not open, but other doors along the hall did. More guests peeked out, curious, searching for the cause of the commotion.

Natalie's lips parted, about to ask what was going on, when the security guard stopped. His entire body froze in a picture of confusion. Slowly, hesitantly, he leaned in, his ear angled toward the wooden surface.

"Hello?" he said, far too softly.

Natalie stepped into the hall, too concerned to care about her pajamas or bare feet. The guard leapt away from the door, stumbling, arms flailing as he fell onto the carpet.

Natalie rushed forward to help. "Are you okay?"

He ignored her, scrambling backward until he hit the wall. His wild eyes never left the door. Another guard came sprinting from the direction of the elevators. The keys in his hand jingled with each step. When he noticed Natalie and his colleague on the ground, he slowed but did not stop.

At the door, he inserted the key. The guard on the floor gasped as it opened.

At first, none of them moved. None of them wanted to go inside.

Without a doubt, this would be Natalie's last night at the Amber Oceanside Hotel. It was also the first night, in a long time, she screamed.

CHAPTER
FIVE

Despite the persisting gloomy weather, it was a pretty busy day. I'd had five customers—three tourists and two locals—which was high traffic for our little store.

For the most part, the visits were typical—insomuch that these kinds of visits could be typical—including a second session with Miss Aubrey, an art teacher at the primary school. She continued to insist that her elderly neighbor not only broke into her house regularly but did so in the form of a soucouyant. However, her version of the flying fireball folk legend didn't engage in the traditional blood-sucking behaviors so much as steal food and shift items around the house.

The last time she was here, I'd tried to hint toward the possibilities that she might've been sleepwalking, or—more likely—the wayward son she'd kicked out a few weeks earlier still had a key. Miss Aubrey had walked out mid-session.

This time, I decided to keep those theories to myself. Though, in addition to recommending the known deterrent to a soucouyant, which involved scattering rice outside the house so the creature would be compelled to count each grain (a lengthy task that should keep them occupied all night), I also tactfully suggested that she get her locks changed as well.

"Why?" she'd asked me, the lines of her face hardening with suspicion. "It's not going to matter. They can slip through keyholes."

Right. I'd forgotten about that.

"Well, that is true, but I've been working on a new protection charm. It only works on doors that have not been tainted."

At just minutes to seven, I showed a satisfied Miss Aubrey out of the store. The sky reddened with another bloody sunset. "Should we close up?" I asked, exhausted. Pretending to solve supernatural problems all day took a lot out of a person. "I don't think we'll get any more customers."

"Hold on, nah," Allison said. She'd placed her chair near the window that morning and barely moved for most of the day.

Since we'd opened, there had been a steady stream of police in and out of the hotel. Rumor was someone had died there the night before.

"We've got a few more minutes left," she said. "Might as well wait it out."

"All right," I agreed, though I knew her adherence to the open hours had not been inspired by a sudden burst of work ethic, and everything to do with morbid curiosity. I joined her at the window, peering through the thick pane of glass toward the building a few doors down.

The Amber Oceanside Hotel was neither amber nor oceanside, constructed out of blue limestone and a ten-minute walk from the coast. It was pretty to look at, but it always gave me the creeps. It was the only building on Main Street to somehow survive the hurricane of 1938. With its iron banisters, plate-glass windows, tall doorways, and quoined corners, it stood out among the more modern store facades that surrounded it.

"Anything interesting?" I asked Allison.

"Nothing." She pouted. "Nuts Man said they definitely took a body out—they made him move his cart so they could bring the ambulance. Dad is keeping it all hush-hush. But before I left the house, he did ask if I saw anything strange while we were closing yesterday."

"Did you?" The day before I'd been more than a little distracted by Gabriel's return to notice much of anything.

She shook her head. "It must be a murder, right? They wouldn't be doing all this if it wasn't."

"Must be," I agreed, though my stomach churned at the thought.

Murders were rare on St. Virgil. Each year, we had about a dozen fatal accidents—drownings, car crashes, people who got irrevocably lost or injured in the forest—but hardly ever murders. The last case would have been my father.

While I knew the chances were low that this was the same person responsible for what happened to my parents, I was haunted by the small, awful possibility that it could be.

It had taken me months to work up the courage to leave the house or walk outside alone without the constant fear of someone coming after me. Of someone tracking my mother or me down to finish the job. But after two years of nothing, I'd accepted that, whoever they were, they'd gotten what they wanted.

Still, at the mention of murder, all those old fears came creeping back, like a parasitic vine twisting across my skin. We had ten minutes left before closing time, but I desperately wanted to go home now. The shop no longer felt safe.

The chime over the door rang.

We both turned to the man standing on the threshold. I hadn't seen him approach, my eyes on Allison and my mind circling terrible possibilities.

The man seemed to loom there for a moment, unspeaking. He held the door open, his chest rising and falling with heavy breaths. His lanky silhouette appeared as a dark shadow against the red glow of the sky.

There was something not right about him—I knew that immediately. Something off in the way he held himself: the rigidity in his shoulders, how his eyes darted about the room. He reminded me of a house lizard, ready to hide at the first sign of movement. Like he knew he shouldn't be here.

"Gloriosa superba," he said without preamble.

Okay, so maybe he was supposed to be here.

He checked over his shoulder once. Twice. Three times.

I followed his glances to the street and saw no one, only our reflections in the darkening glass. An indefinable fear burrowed into my chest and clawed its way up my throat. It seemed to originate somewhere outside of myself, like it wasn't mine. It reminded me of the feeling of fear I'd had upon hallucinating my father in the cottage the day before.

If only we'd closed when I'd wanted to. I could've been on my way home now.

"Can we help you?" Allison rose to her feet. From her hesitance, I could tell she was as thrown by his appearance as I was.

Strangely enough, under different circumstances, he might not have been threatening at all. He was not as old as I'd first thought. Maybe only a few years older than us, and good-looking in a lean, pretty-boy sort of way.

"Gloriosa superba," he repeated, louder and impatient. "Is this the right place or not?" He glanced over to the street again.

Allison held out her hands in a placating gesture. "Sir, what exactly—"

"Yes or no?" He slammed the door behind him. The chime rattled so hard it fell from the hook. It crashed onto the floor, breaking apart in an awful cacophony. Immediately, the stranger dropped to his knees to pick it up. Apologies spilled from his lips as he collected the parts.

While he was distracted, I met Allison's eyes and shook my head.

He needed to go.

"Sorry, sorry, sorry," the guy said, rising to his feet. He held out the broken pieces like an offering. "It's been a long day and . . . and I need help." He raised his head, his brown hair falling back to reveal wild gray eyes. "Can you help me?"

I shook my head. "I don't—"

"How much is it?" he asked. "I've heard what you can do and I'll pay you. It doesn't matter how much."

"Yes, of course," Allison said, stepping forward to take the broken chime from him. "You have come to the right place."

Uh. No, he had not.

What the hell was she doing? I tried to catch Allison's attention again. Clearly, this guy needed real help from a trained medical professional. Not cheap tricks and spells from a fake teenage psychic.

She wouldn't meet my eyes. Instead, she led him over to the counter and named some absurdly high price—more than double what we usually charged for a single visit.

The guy agreed easily, his expression lightening with something like hope. Then he checked over his shoulder and it darkened again. "Do you have somewhere we can talk away from the window?"

"We do, actually," she said, pointing toward the back room door.

I watched, a sinking feeling rooting my feet to the ground.

"What's your name, sir?" she asked.

"Just call me Len."

"Len," she repeated, stopping in front of the safe. "We do not allow any recording devices into this sacred space. Please empty your pockets. We'll store your belongings in this safe until we're done."

He hesitated, as most did. "You want me to give you my phone?"

"Not just the phone. Everything in your pockets, sir."

For a second, I thought he'd resist. That he'd say no and leave, and we'd be done with it. But then he reached into his pockets and pulled out a phone and a wallet. He held them out to her, and she took them.

"It's through there." She opened the back room door.

In a true testament to his desperation, he didn't even wait to make sure she'd locked his things away—much less ask for the key—before he walked inside. She placed his things on top of the safe, waiting a few beats before following him and shutting the door behind her.

I didn't act immediately. Precious seconds ticked by as I remained frozen to the spot, refusing to accept that this was happening.

But it *was* happening, regardless of my objections. And even though every cell of my body rejected the idea of going through with this, I needed to be as prepared as possible before I got into that room with him.

I checked the wallet first, surprised to find that his name really was Len. Well, actually, *Lennard* Bisson. I'd suspected he'd lied about that but apparently not. American—which I already knew from his accent. At twenty-three years old, he lived in Florida but carried a mix of currency that indicated a lot of recent traveling. In addition to the expected US cash, there were a few dollars of our local currency, Chilean pesos, Guyanese dollars, and British pounds. He was rich, probably. Though I'd already guessed that from the way he'd paid Allison's exorbitant price without blinking.

As I dug deeper into the wallet, something pricked me. I yanked my hand out. A fine bead of blood was welling at the tip of my index finger. Carefully, I widened the mouth of the wallet and peered inside. There was a small red pouch tucked into the corner; the pin that held it closed had opened during my riffling. A few dark strands of hair peeked out from inside. It felt too stiff to be human. Horsehair, maybe. It could be some kind of charm. I did not want to touch it. But I had to replace everything as it was.

I closed the wallet and placed it into the safe. There wasn't much to go on. Women with purses were so much easier, and since most people who visited us were women with purses, this usually wasn't a problem.

A part of me wanted to just skip the phone. I almost never guessed the PIN right. But I tried his date of birth anyway. When it worked, my knees almost gave out.

I'd only correctly guessed the PIN a handful of times before. Quickly, I pulled up his photo gallery, my hands shaking with a mix of excitement and dread. Normally, I would have felt at least a little apprehensive about going through a phone, but this time it wasn't just the invasion of privacy that made me nervous; it was something more.

I scrolled through the pictures, surprised to find that instead of typical vacation material—lush landscapes, beaches, cocktails, selfies in front of landmarks—all the most recent photos were . . . odd. The corner of a room. A dim hall. An empty doorway. Most were too dark or out of focus. There were too many to all be taken by accident.

What had he been trying to do?

It took a bit of scrolling to get to a point where they started making sense.

Lennard Bisson definitely liked how he looked. He'd taken quite a few bathroom selfies, a handful of photos with friends, and *tons* of pictures of a freckle-faced auburn-haired woman. She had to be a girlfriend, judging from how intimate they were. They seemed mutually smitten, heads bending together over a shared drink, exchanging wrapped Christmas gifts, kissing in the driveway of a house. Almost every photo was of her or them together.

Then something changed.

As I continued to scroll back through time, in many of the pictures she no longer engaged with the camera, her gaze distant. With a pang of alarm, I realized this was because she wasn't aware she was being photographed. In the most chilling shot, the auburn-haired woman sat on a couch watching TV, a hooded figure's reflection in the window through which the photo was taken.

The skin of my scalp tightened. Every pore on my body raised in alarm.

"I'll be one second," Allison said.

I lifted my gaze to find her inching out of the back room.

She shut the door and glared at me. "What the hell are you doing?" she whispered. "Do you know how long I've been stalling?"

"Allison, we've got to get him out of here." I held up the phone to show her. "I knew there was something wrong with him. He's a creep."

"Don't wave that around." Allison snatched the phone away. She cleared the screen without looking at the contents, then shoved it and the wallet into the safe. "Look, I know he's a little weird, but he already paid, and he paid well. So, get in there, tell him what he wants to hear, and we can send him on his way."

I shook my head. "You don't get what I'm saying." She needed to listen to me. She hadn't seen what I'd seen on the phone. She didn't understand the full scope of the situation. "He needs help. Real help. We might need to call the police."

"And let it get back to my father?" She laughed incredulously. "No way."

"Allison, I think he stalked his girlfriend—"

"If we called the police, we'd blow our whole operation. If my parents ever found out, they'd kill me. Then they'd take the shop away, and you'd be out of a job."

"I know, but—"

"Not to mention I'm pretty sure what we've been doing might actually be illegal. Using the stolen props and taking money under the table, if nothing else."

The protests died on my lips.

She was right. We couldn't call for help.

Allison folded her arms. "I mean, you can try to kick him out now, if you want." Her tone held a condescending edge. "But he seems determined. I doubt he'd agree to leave quietly."

"This isn't a joke, Allison."

"I know. So just do the session for him. Then he'll leave and be someone else's problem."

Did she hear what she was saying? Did she not see how messed up this was?

This guy could be dangerous. He clearly had a temper, and he might've been a stalker. Even if I got through this session without a hitch, did she think I could just carry on with the rest of my life, knowing what I knew, and doing nothing about it?

But what else could I do? She was right. There was no other choice.

"Fine," I said, then caught her arm as she tried to walk past me. "Oh, no. You're coming in there with me. I'm not staying alone with him."

She sighed, exasperated. "I'm going to be watching anyway."

"I don't care. You're staying in the room."

"Who's going to run the fans and everything?"

"I do not care," I said, through clenched teeth. "We're keeping this simple. No theatrics. We're getting him out of here as soon as possible."

"Okay." She shrugged. "If that's what you want. It seems unfair, though. He paid so much and he's not even getting the full show."

I had nothing to say to that. Instead, I opened the door and not-too-gently nudged her into the room. After throwing her one last glare, I approached the table, and dropped into the seat across from Len.

He frowned. "You're the one doing the—"

"I'm young. Yes. I'm aware." No need to waste time on this. "I'm all we've got at the moment, so tell me what you want."

"Why do I have to tell you?" His lips curled into a sneer. "Can't you already tell? Isn't that what you do?"

So he wanted to test me first. Okay. Fine.

"You think you're being followed." That much was clear from his actions—the constant looking over his shoulder and insisting that we move away from the window.

"I *think*?" His tone hitched with incredulity and panic. "What? You don't believe it? You don't . . . see it?"

"See what?"

"Come on, it's right there," he said, voice breaking. "I can see it in the corner of my eye." He lifted a hand and held it beside his face as if to illustrate where *it* stood in his vision. The nails of his long, bony fingers were bitten to the quick and rimmed with dirt. "Even now. It's right there. Watching. Waiting."

I traced his gaze to the edge of the room. Nothing but shelves of bottles and dusty books.

"What is *it*?" I asked, then quickly amended, "I mean—what does it look like to you?"

"You really can't—" He glanced around as if taking in the back room for the first time. "What is this?" He shot to his feet. "Is any of this real? You're a fake, aren't you? I've visited enough places like this to spot a con artist."

"Wait, wait." I held out my hands in a staying gesture. For all that I wanted him gone, I couldn't have him going around and telling people that I was a con artist. It might affect the business. For better or worse, I was in this now. "Just because I don't see it doesn't mean I can't help you. You seek protection, yes?"

He shook his head. "I've tried protections. Charms. Talismans. It doesn't work. I need something more." His eyes watered as he stared at me, unblinking. "I need to be washed. Cleansed of it."

"Purified?"

"Yes," he said, slipping back into his seat. "My soul renewed. Then I'll be alone. I'll be free."

I exhaled slowly, relieved that he was no longer standing over me. Gently, I pointed out, "If it's just watching you, then it's not hurting you, is it?"

"No," he said. "Not yet."

A tear slipped down his cheek, and I felt goose bumps rise along my arms. He might be a total creep, but his fear was genuine.

I stood and retrieved one of the lit candles, a notebook, and a pen. After setting them on the table before him, I retook my seat.

"Write the name of the person . . . or whatever on the paper."

He stared at the notebook as if it offended him. "Why?"

"We'll burn it, collect the ashes—"

"I can't." He looked up, horrified. "What if it gets angry?"

"You can. Names have power, Lennard. We can bury the ashes, say the right words, cover it in layers of protection—"

"And what if it doesn't work?" he said, then recoiled as if he hadn't wanted to voice the thought aloud. "I don't know what else to do. I've traveled to so many places, spoken to so many people, and none of it has worked. All this because of one mistake, and now it won't go away."

A mistake?

Did he mean the stalking or something else? Something worse?

I should've realized this came down to guilt. Again. It almost always did. I was beginning to think all ghosts were regrets, and we were the ones that haunted ourselves.

"You know, the only real way to cleanse yourself completely is to take responsibility." I held his gaze. "Face the consequences for your actions and seek forgiveness from the ones you've hurt. Once justice is done, then, and only then, you'll truly be clean."

Another tear fell from his eyes. And then another. He did not try to stop or hide them. Instead, he pulled the notebook closer, opened it, picked up the pencil, and started writing. When he was done, he ripped the page free.

I held out my hand.

He hesitated, then folded the paper and gave it to me. On his upturned wrist, I noticed a tattoo of a spider, the black ink a stark contrast against his pale skin.

I dragged an empty candle holder closer, prepared to collect the ashes. "Now, focus on the name," I said, dipping the end of the paper toward the flame. "Repeat it in your mind. Picture it as the flame erases it from your life."

Across the table, Len closed his eyes and breathed.

The flame flickered, casting long shadows against the walls. The bitter scent of burning tickled my nose, and I was hit by a memory of another burning paper. Of watching as the torn edges blackened and disintegrated into ash. Of moonlight on a house consumed by vines, and the stooped back of a small gray-haired woman standing over a makeshift altar. Of my startled cry as someone tightly gripped my arm and dragged me away, the memory so tangible that I could feel the fingers digging into my flesh. I froze, overwhelmed by an all-consuming dread.

This was a mistake.

The lights overhead went out. The back room descended into weak candlelight. I dropped the singed paper onto the table.

Len opened his eyes. "No, no, no, no . . ."

"What's going on?" Allison demanded as a cold wind swept through the room. The candles extinguished as if on cue, including the one in front of me. I'd watched this happen dozens of times before. Except, this time, it couldn't be Allison operating the air conditioner and fans.

When the last flame extinguished, we plunged into complete darkness.

I stood, blinking, waiting for my eyes to adjust. The air chilled quickly, goose bumps blooming along my skin. "Allison? What's going on?"

Len's chair scraped against the floor as he stood, too. "I knew this would happen."

"Relax," I told him while trying to hide my alarm. "The power's gone out. It happens sometimes. It's just a coincidence."

"No." The sound of his footsteps filled the air. He must've been pacing. Because of an echo in the room, he sounded everywhere, all at once. "It's too late. There's nothing anyone can do."

"Allison!" I called out again. What the hell was she doing?

"I'm looking for the door," she said.

Looking for the door? "What do you mean? It's right there!"

"You can't help me," Len said, sounding much closer than he should.

I took a step back, stumbling over the seat behind me. Pain shot up my backside as I hit the floor, but it paled in comparison to the cold spot I'd plunged into. It was freezing to the point of pain, like a thousand tiny needles driven into my skin. The atoms in the air vibrated with a furious buzzing, and the walls rattled with pounding and scratching, as if something was desperately trying to claw its way inside. I recoiled, covering my ears in a futile attempt to silence it.

"I need to get out!" Len shouted.

Finally, Allison got the door open. The last light of day poured into the room. Len sprinted out in a blur, the angle of the lit doorway making it look like he had two shadows chasing him.

I pulled myself up, using the chair for balance. Apart from a dull ache around my tailbone, I wasn't hurt. My breaths came hard and fast, my knees unsteady. The air around us warmed with the door open.

"What the hell was that?" I asked Allison, meeting her in the doorway. She and I peeked into the shop, unsurprised to find it empty, the back door wide open. As quickly as Lennard Bisson entered our lives, he'd left it.

"You don't think—" Allison started, only to be cut off by a knocking sound.

Now that we were in the front of the store, the pounding sounded slightly softer, and more familiar. It sounded like hammering.

The lights came on.

"It was the construction next door," I said, my back bowing under the weight of relief. "They must be working late."

Allison burst into panicky laughter. "You know, I thought, for a second there, when I couldn't find the door—"

I straightened up. "What do you mean you couldn't find it?"

"I have no idea. I just . . . couldn't."

While she went to lock up the shop, I returned to the back room. With the lights on, the space looked the same as it always did, except for Len's overturned chair and the items we'd left scattered on the table. The AC *was* on, somehow. Probably triggered by a power surge, or something like that.

"You're not going to believe this." Allison ran into the room. In her hands, she held a pair of familiar items. "He left so fast, he forgot his phone and wallet."

"That's not all he left behind." I showed her the piece of paper. The one I hadn't had a chance to burn completely. In the center, scribbled in barely legible cursive, was the name he'd written.

Lennard Bisson.

CHAPTER
SIX

"You seem distracted," Edward said.

I startled out of my thoughts, lowered the bottle from my lips, and turned to look at him. Moonlight spilled through the open car window, illuminating his expression. His lips were pinched, his dark brows furrowed in concern. One of his hands rested against my bare hip, warm and impatient. I got the impression he'd been trying to get my attention for some time.

"Something on your mind?" he asked.

"Not really." Despite the warm back seat, I shifted closer to him. Salt-scented sea breeze filtered through the car, the day's heat lingering in the night air. His thumb drew soft circles against my sweat-damp skin. I twisted my head to kiss him.

He pulled away. "Something is wrong?"

"Nope," I said, then closed the gap between us.

He sat back against the door. For some reason, he seemed upset.

I sighed. "I had a weird day, okay?"

"How was it weird?"

I stared at him, disbelieving. Frustrated. Warm beer sloshed in my stomach, making me nauseous. "A strange customer came in today."

A bit of an understatement.

"It was nothing," I insisted, slouching against the seat. I lifted the bottle to my lips and let the last of the drink slip past my tongue and down my throat. I'd been hoping there'd be a party tonight. A lime. Something with people and noise and music.

Instead, Edward and I ended up parked near the beach, the only alcohol a single bottle of beer that had been left in his back seat for who knew how long. It was nowhere near enough to get me buzzed, much less try to blot out everything I'd been trying not to think about.

Lennard's face . . . scratching against the wall . . . the cold spot . . . Gabriel . . . the cottage . . . Daddy's notebook . . .

Every time I thought I'd finally shaken the choke hold of the past, it caught me again. Like an insidious creature shadowing my every step, I couldn't shake it.

Over the last two years, I'd tried to drown out the darkness with parties, the shop, and now Edward. But it didn't seem to be enough anymore.

"I'm tired. Take me home." I dropped the empty bottle on the floor and crawled into the passenger seat. If he didn't want to hook up, then I might as well be alone.

"If that's what you want," Edward said, his tone light but brittle.

Instead of crawling into the front seat as I did, he got out of the vehicle and walked around it. After dropping into the driver's seat, he slammed his door a little harder than necessary. Without a word, he started the engine, maneuvering the car off the gravel-lined path and back onto the road.

I turned my face to my open window. The quiet streets slipped past in snatches of streetlights and darkness. Swaying trees cast long shadows, marking the edge of the forest. The light of the moon blurred behind heavy clouds.

"So, you had a strange customer," Edward said, breaking the silence. "And that's the only thing bothering you tonight?"

I closed my eyes, silently willing him to let this go. I didn't want to explain what happened today. I wasn't even sure that I could.

"I spoke to Janice," he said after another long moment. "You didn't tell me she and her brother were back."

Oh.

Oh. Now I understood. The *and her brother* was less than subtle. It explained his weird mood. Or rather, what he believed was the reason for mine.

"Why would I?" I asked. "Janice has always been your friend, not mine."

Incredulity broke through his stiff tone. "And that's it?"

"Edward . . ." I gentled my voice, twisting against the seat belt to face him. "Trust me, if I had something to tell you, I would." As far as I was concerned, Gabriel's return did not change a thing.

Seconds passed and Edward said nothing. Exasperated, I resettled into my seat. I couldn't tell if he believed me. My stomach churned at the thought that he might not. I didn't want to end what we had, as superficial as it was.

Only when we almost reached the house, he spoke again.

"I think it's time for you to meet my parents."

"I've . . . already met your parents," I said, surprised. And confused. Granted, his mother and I had only spoken once in passing. But his father and I had met multiple times in his professional capacity—which, admittedly, was less than ideal.

"Yes, you've met them before," he said. "But not as my girlfriend."

"Girlfriend?" I searched his expression for any indication that he'd used the term by mistake. He seemed a bit twitchy. Nervous, maybe?

"Yes, girlfriend." He glanced over at me. "Don't you think it's time? We've been doing . . . whatever this is for months now. Shouldn't we make it official?"

I honestly couldn't say I saw this coming. What we had worked. The lack of expectations—the lack of complications—made things easy. Fun. Distracting.

"Do you think that's a good idea?" I didn't try to hide my skepticism. "Me, meeting your parents?"

He parked the car in front of the house. "What's wrong with that?"

I shot him a disbelieving look. Surely, it should be obvious. But if he really wanted me to say it . . . "Me. My family. Who I am. Who they are."

He cut the engine, then sat there, expectant, like he needed more of an answer.

Fine. I unbuckled my seat belt and faced him. "Your parents already hate that I'm hanging out with you and your sister." When he opened his mouth, probably about to claim otherwise, I added, "Allison told me."

He shut his mouth.

"What would they think if I'm your *girlfriend*? They'll never accept it."

He rolled his eyes. "Of course they'll accept it."

"Edward . . ."

He slung an arm around the back of my seat, leaning closer to me. "Look, I don't mean to sound ridiculously arrogant—"

"As opposed to your usual amount of arrogance?"

The corner of his lips quirked. "How dare you. I am a simple, humble guy."

"Sure."

"Selina," he said. "I'm saying they *will* accept you because you're my choice. I want you. And everybody knows I make only good decisions."

"Everybody knows? Feels like the first time I'm hearing about it."

His lips curled into a smile. Pleasant tingles bloomed across my skin. As skeptical as I was, his shameless confidence was getting to me. He seemed so sure of himself. So sure of us. It was hard to hold on to my objections.

"Is this what you really want?" I asked.

"Positive. I'm choosing you. There's nothing anyone—not even my parents—can do about it."

I found myself wanting to believe him. "You do sound sure. . . ."

"I am sure." He rested his index finger under my chin, lifting my lips to his. "You're my girl, Selina. I'll protect you. If you're with me, no one can touch you. Never again."

My breath hitched.

I knew what he meant about protection. Even though Muriel's company practically ran St. Virgil, it was widely accepted that she was a bit of an eccentric. In the eyes of the community, her money meant she'd be tolerated, but they didn't like that she was a successful working widow who'd once married an outsider. That she'd been best friends with a witch. The fact that she'd taken me in hadn't exactly hurt her reputation, but it didn't help mine either.

Edward's family was different. They'd been living on St. Virgil for generations. His father was the chief of police and his mother a successful real estate agent and an active member of the church. They were pillars of the community. Untouchable. The idea that I could have some of that power by association was more than tempting.

Maybe this was the answer. The way to finally leave the past behind.

And it wasn't like I didn't like Edward. I did. I liked his crooked smile and his relentless confidence. The way he was unabashedly physical and sometimes bit my lip when he kissed me. He was gorgeous, sweet, and smart.

Plus, what would happen if I didn't say yes? Would he still want to continue as we were? If not, how long before our breakup affected my relationship with Allison and my job at the shop?

"Okay," I said.

"Okay?" he repeated, raising a brow.

I nodded.

Edward beamed, then immediately reined it in to a smirk. In an exaggeratedly cool tone, he said, "I knew you'd say yes." •

"Of course you did."

"I did," he insisted. "That's why I got you this."

He stretched around the back of his chair and grabbed a small black bag that had been hidden under his seat. He shook out a small jewelry box and opened it. A delicate silver necklace with a small pearl pendant rested inside.

"Wow," I said, for a lack of anything better to say. It looked expensive, if not exactly my taste.

Edward lifted the necklace. The pearl glowed in the meager light from the front porch. "Here." He lifted it over my head. The cool silver settled against my skin. The pendant nestled between my collarbones.

Belatedly, I leaned forward to give him space to fasten the clasp. I didn't expect that he'd also undo the chain I was already wearing. It slipped free, landing in my lap.

"There." He flipped down the sun visor so I could see my reflection in the small mirror. "You can finally stop wearing that ugly thing."

Annoyance flared, but I stifled it. Edward didn't know the gold chain belonged to my mother. If he had, I knew he wouldn't have said that. Besides, he wasn't wrong. It wasn't the prettiest.

"It is beautiful," I admitted, though I couldn't really see my reflection. It was too dark, the mirror too small. I gathered my mother's necklace, holding it in a fist. It wasn't like I'd planned to never take it off. I just hadn't yet.

"You're beautiful," he said, then kissed me again. I leaned into it, chasing his joy, trying to keep some of it for myself.

A stray thought slid into my head. It questioned the timing of this talk, wondering if it had anything to do with Gabriel's return.

I ignored it.

———

All the lights in the house were off except the ones in the kitchen. I peeked inside to find Muriel and Janice sitting together. Papers, magazines, and binders were scattered on the surface of the dining table in front of them.

When Muriel saw me, she smiled and waved me over. She was still in a navy-blue pantsuit, her black pumps discarded under the table, like she'd gotten home from work, sat down, and not moved since.

"Perfect timing," she said. "Settle this for us. Janice is helping me finish up the preparations for the anniversary party, but we're having a disagreement." She lifted two pairs of samples. "Which combination of tablecloth and runner do you prefer?"

I examined them, having no idea which was better suited for the occasion. I'd never been to the anniversary party before. Muriel's husband, Donovan Pierre, started the tradition to celebrate the date of their wedding. The first party was held shortly after he and Muriel settled on the island as a way to introduce—or, in Muriel's case, *reintroduce*—themselves to the community. When Mr. Pierre was alive, it was an open invitation. After he walked into the forest and never stepped back out again, Muriel continued the tradition, but she'd had to limit the number of attendees to a group of specially invited guests.

My mother had gone once. She said she'd spent the entire evening performing free readings and arguing with skeptics. After that, she decided she never wanted to go again.

Last year, the party had been canceled at the last second because of Gabriel's accident. But this year, I'd finally see what all the fuss was about.

I couldn't deny my curiosity. My excitement. I'd get a fancy dress and my hair done. And now that Edward and I had made it official, I'd enter the party on the arm of the most enviable date. All the people who'd bad-talked my family and me would have no choice but to bite back their vitriolic words, their poisonous tongues caged behind polite smiles.

"This is better." Janice pointed to the bland cream-on-white combination. "It's understated and it won't clash with the decorations. Trust me, I know what looks good. I'm not doing a fashion degree for nothing."

Janice was studying for a fashion *merchandising* degree. I was pretty sure that was more focused on business and marketing rather than the art. But even if I was wrong about that, her pick was the more boring of the two options.

"This one," I said, pointing to the purple-and-silver combination.

"That's what I thought, too," Muriel said with a small smile.

There was a sound like sucked teeth, but when I looked up, Janice's face was placid. "Purple and silver it is." She slipped the samples into a binder. "I think that's the last one for now."

"Good." Muriel's lips stretched in a silent yawn. Her slender manicured hands covered her mouth. When she caught my eye, she gave me a self-conscious smile. "You're back late. Did you go to see your mother after work?"

I did visit Mummy some afternoons, though not as often as I used to. Nowhere as often as I should.

"How is your mother?" Janice asked before I could answer. "Any changes?"

Slightly taken aback by her question, all I could do was shake my head.

"I'm sorry," she said. "I'm hoping to visit her and pay my respects while I'm here—"

"Don't say that," Muriel cut her off, her tone sharper than any I'd ever heard from her.

Janice blinked, effectively silenced. Even I felt chastened, and I wasn't on the receiving end.

"*Pay your respects,*" Muriel repeated. "It sounds like you're giving condolences. She's not dead."

"Ma . . ." Janice said softly. She set down the binders. "I didn't mean it like that."

I had to agree with Janice. Muriel's reaction had been a little too much.

Muriel must've come to the same conclusion because the tension in her shoulders eased. "Of course. I know you didn't." She closed her eyes and pinched the bridge of her nose. "Sorry, sweetheart, I've had a long day. I'm not thinking clearly."

"It's okay," Janice said softly.

I wondered what Muriel would say if she knew how often I told strangers Mummy had passed. Sometimes, it was just easier. Telling the truth came with inevitable follow-up questions, and I didn't want to deal with any of it.

"I'm going to bed," Janice said, rising from her chair.

When we were growing up, Janice treated me like scum. In primary school, she spread rumors that I'd left dead animals in her desk and used mind-control spells on her brother. In early secondary school, she aggressively ignored me, and—apart from the hissing campaign—she'd made sure her friends followed suit. If she'd never left for university, Edward and Allison would've never befriended me.

I had every reason to dislike her. And yet, I felt a twinge of sympathy when she walked past, her head down as she left the kitchen.

Muriel didn't seem to notice her daughter's somber exit, resting her hands on the mostly cleared tabletop. "Do you want something to eat?" she asked. "We have some stewed oxtail and rice left over from yesterday. You could warm it up."

"No." As good as oxtails sounded, I didn't have the appetite for any food at that moment. "I'll make my tea and go to bed, too."

"That sounds like a good idea." Muriel checked the screen of her phone and winced. "I think I'll make some cocoa tea, too. It's just . . ." She sighed and slumped against the table. "I'm too exhausted to move, much less make anything right now. We had a board meeting today. I know it could have gone so much worse, but if this new resort deal does not go through . . ." She sighed again.

I tried to look sympathetic, like I had any idea what she was talking about. "Do you want me to make the cocoa tea for you?"

"Would you?" She smiled. "Thank you, love."

"No problem." After everything she'd done for my mom and me— covering Mummy's medical bills; keeping me clothed, housed, and fed—it was truly the least I could do.

I put on the kettle for me and a small pot of milk for her. My tea was a special blend of herbs and flowers that I picked and dried myself. My mother used to make it for me every night, so it became part of my bedtime routine. It calmed my mind like nothing else, the hibiscus petals giving it a bright red color and a flowery scent.

"If you need more help with the party prep, I wouldn't mind helping, too," I said.

She let out another yawn, this one louder. "Thank you, love, but the planner's taking care of most of the work. And you have a job now. Janice and I can handle what's left." She raised a brow, leaning toward me, as if sharing a secret. "I received some good news this afternoon—confirmation that our new governor is going to be attending."

"Cool," I said, trying to sound as enthusiastic as she did. I was pretty sure the previous governor had attended in the past. Perhaps this was special because this was a new guy?

"Not just cool, Selina," Muriel said, slightly amused, but mostly serious. "It's vital for the business that we foster a good relationship with him and his people. We must make an excellent first impression."

"I'm sure you will," I assured her.

"*We* will," she corrected me. "The governor is old-fashioned. He's known to advocate for traditional family standards. In his eyes, I'm already at a disadvantage as a single working woman in charge. It's ridiculous, but unfortunately, a necessary hurdle to jump through. I hope I can count on your help putting up a united front."

"You can," I agreed, hoping I sounded more confident than I felt. The fact that she considered me part of the family was both sweet and a lot of pressure.

When Gabriel and I had started dating, Muriel and my mother had been, perhaps, too approving, taken by the idea of one day becoming family through their children. Then, when Gabriel and I had broken up, I'd expected Muriel to eventually cut me out of her life, as I had done to her son, but she never did.

A few minutes later, I placed the mug of cocoa in front of her. She reached for my wrist and squeezed it gently. "You're a sweetheart, you know that? I'm not sure what I'd do without you."

I smiled, warmed by her praise. A comfortable silence filled the kitchen as I returned to the stove to finish my tea. While performing the familiar routine, my mind drifted back to the shop and Lennard Bisson. And the memory of the burning paper and the vine-covered house. Who was that elderly woman at the altar?

"Muriel . . ." I said, even before the question had fully formed in my head.

"Yes?" she prompted.

I paused, about to add a teaspoon of honey to the steaming liquid. "You and my mom were always close, right?"

"Since we were children," she confirmed. "Josephine and I did lose touch for a bit when I lived abroad, but the second I moved back we were thick as thieves again. Why do you ask?"

I wasn't sure. I already knew the answer, of course, having heard stories of their friendship since before I could remember. So, what *did* I want to ask?

I thought of the morning I'd hallucinated my bleeding father in the cottage. And the strange symbol in the bedroom. "When Mummy talked about her gift, to me, it sounded like she would know things, feel things, that she shouldn't be able to know or feel. But did she ever see things?"

"*See* things?" Muriel asked. "Like visions? Not that I can recall." She gripped the edge of the table, her eyes alight with a sudden and intense alertness. "Why are you asking? Are you finally getting the gift? After all this time?"

"No, no," I hurried to clarify before she got her hopes up. I knew she would like nothing more. She'd always been a staunch believer in my mother's abilities. I hated to disappoint her. "I'm just trying to understand the extent of . . . what she could do?"

"I don't understand," Muriel said. "You knew her. You saw what she could do."

I hesitated. Yes, I'd seen her in action. She did have a talent for reading people. But she also performed. She exaggerated and turned our lives into a spectacle. It was difficult to tell when the truth ended and the show began.

If anyone had answers about my mom, it would be Muriel. But considering her reaction to Janice's remarks about Mummy earlier, I didn't know how she'd take my questions and what they insinuated. Like: Who was the older lady at the altar? Why were they burning papers? What had my mother been involved in?

Was there truth in the rumors about Mummy that the island's people spread?

I reached up to touch my new necklace. It felt so much lighter than the old one, literally and metaphorically. I no longer had this remnant of my past sitting like a weight on my chest. Maybe that was a good thing.

"Never mind," I said. "It was nothing."

———

That night I dreamed of my parents.

It began with Mummy and me standing in the garden, beside the cottage. She had a watering can in hand, chatting with her plants as she often did, showering them with high-pitched encouragements, like they were children.

I watched, speechless as she tipped the watering can over the leafy shrubs. Instead of water, red sludge slid out, maggots wriggling in the thick, chunky liquid. They burrowed through the leaves and into the soil, the plants shriveling and rotting into nothing. My mother continued her encouragements, smiling, oblivious as they died in front of her.

My father was shouting my name, somewhere in the distance.

CHAPTER
SEVEN

"**B**ack up," I warned Nathan, then dropped another batch of dried seeds into a ceramic mortar. Pestle in hand, I carefully ground them into a fine orange-brown powder. Despite my warning, Nathan leaned even closer. I pushed the mortar away from him. "Don't you see these gloves? Do you think I wear them for fun?"

"I don't know what you do in your spare time," he said, a sparkle of mischief in his eyes.

Edward sighed from his seat in the corner of the shop. "Do you have to do that now, Selina?" He sounded irritated—had been for most of the afternoon. On another day he might've been worse than Nathan, overly curious about my experiment and constantly trying to get my attention.

But Janice was here. That changed things.

The day had started as a quiet one. We'd had only one local client, so we took inventory to fill the time. Well, *I* took inventory. Allison watched TV.

In the afternoon, Janice had shown up, followed by Edward and his best friend, Nathan. To celebrate their mini-reunion, Allison flipped the store's CLOSED sign, locked the door, then brought out the chairs from the back room.

I was a part of the group, but not really. My role varied between a wallflower and live entertainment. Janice controlled the conversation, her presence reestablishing their old dynamic, squeezing me out. I had to remind myself that this was temporary. Soon, she'd return to school, and everything would go back to the way it was.

Nathan leaned closer again. I elbowed him away.

"I know which plant those come from." Nathan pointed at the seeds. "It's the one with the spiky leaves. The fruit smells like spoiled milk."

"It is," I said, surprised he'd recognized it. The plants might have been native to the island, but they were still relatively rare. Only a few trees grew on the northside, at the foothills of the mountain range. Locals called them snake eye trees, so given for the yellow fruit they bore. They burst upon ripening via a single slit at the bottom. A person standing beneath the branches might be faced with the illusion of dozens of serpent eyes staring down at them.

"I knew it," Nathan said, nodding. "Edward, remember when Jonesy dared me to lick one of the fruits, back in fourth form? The trip was wild."

I stared at him for a moment, speechless. "You're lucky that's all that happened." While snake eyes weren't as toxic as some other local fruits, like unripe ackee or beach apples, they still had nasty hallucinogenic side effects if ingested. Especially the seeds, which were particularly potent.

"You're telling me," Nathan said, laughing. "Jonsey had a bite of one. My boy swore he was talking to God."

"What the hell are you using it for?" Allison eyed the mortar with alarm.

"Pesticide," I said. "Miss Kelvin thinks someone's put a curse on her garden. But I've seen it, and it's far more likely a particular species of whitefly. They use their mouthparts to suck up plant juices, and the substance they leave behind causes fungal diseases to grow on the leaves——"

Their disgusted protests shut me up. I went back to work, satisfied that there'd be no follow-up questions.

"Seriously, finish that later," Edward persisted. "Come over here and join us. Relax."

"You relax," Janice said, rolling her eyes. She reached for one of the steel-pan-playing figurines, looking it over. "I don't remember you being this pushy when you were with Dahlia. Then again, Dahlia wasn't exactly the type to let herself be pushed."

"Dahlia *was* something," Nathan agreed.

"Shut up," Edward said. He glared at his friends while they laughed, amused at the memory of his ex.

"Wonder what she's been up to?" Janice said, absentmindedly flipping the figurine on its head. "You two still in contact?"

"No," Edward said bluntly. His tone sounded final, but he made the mistake of glancing at me, checking for my reaction.

"He's got to be careful about what he says." Nathan nodded toward me. "It may be used against him later."

This set off another round of laughter. Edward's lips thinned into a strained smile. It seemed obvious to me that he was trying to placate them, which pissed me off.

"Don't worry," I said. "If I truly held what people said against them, I wouldn't be speaking to anyone in this shop."

Their silence was satisfying for a few seconds, before I realized I'd crossed a line, the good mood effectively broken.

Sure enough, the talk, when it resumed, was about going somewhere else. Janice decided on Blueside, a gated residential area that bordered the southern coast. It consisted of large privately owned villas, mostly holiday homes for foreigners. For most of the year, they stood vacant, maintained by a small staff. Allison had told me they sometimes snuck in to make use of the unoccupied amenities.

"We could visit the Billingsley house," Janice said. "Spend a few hours in their infinity pool. I know for a fact that the family is at a destination wedding in New Zealand. It'll be empty."

"I can't leave the store closed that long," Allison said.

"Then leave Selina in charge." Janice flicked one of the chimes. "That's what you hired her for, right?"

The tinkling chime noise filled the silence as she oh-so-nonchalantly waited for an answer. Allison and Edward shared a look, carefully avoiding my gaze.

As Janice and Nathan finalized their plans, Edward tugged me aside. We stepped into the back room. I thought he was about to apologize for Janice's attitude and his lacking defense of me. Instead, he was angry.

"Why would you say something like that?" he whispered sharply.

I folded my arms, offended. "You heard what Janice said."

"I heard. But those are my friends. *Our* friends. They weren't being mean on purpose."

I breathed through the anger. He was right. I shouldn't have said what I'd said, but hitting back was a reflexive response. It was born from years of schoolyard teasing—teasing that was perpetrated by these very same people. Sometimes it was hard to remember things were different now.

"Sorry," I said. "It's just Janice. She pushes my buttons."

He chuckled. "She is a button-pusher. Ignore it."

"Why do you put up with it?" I honestly didn't understand.

He shrugged. "We've been friends for too long. It's like a sunk-cost fallacy or something like that."

I almost pointed out that the sunk-cost fallacy was exactly that—a fallacy—but he kissed me, the argument apparently resolved.

"You going to join us at Blueside after work?" he asked, opening the door.

"No, I'm going to see my mother." After talking to Muriel the night before, I'd realized I'd been putting off a visit for too long. "I'll find my own way home."

"Just be careful," he said, as we left the back room. "That psycho is still on the loose. He could be dangerous."

"Psycho?" Allison asked before I could. She lifted her attention from the register, a tamarind stick clamped between her teeth. The rest of the shop was empty, Nathan and Janice already outside, ready to leave.

"Yeah." Edward squinted at her, incredulous. "The one the police are looking for. That Lennard guy."

I froze.

Allison choked and started coughing. She took the tamarind stick out of her mouth. When her brother moved to slap her back, she waved him off. "I'm fine."

"Why are they looking for this guy?" I kept my voice as level as possible.

"Haven't you heard?" Edward looked between us. "It's on the front page of the newspaper this morning. Everyone is talking about it. The story's gone international and you don't even know what's going on down the street?"

He seemed amused by our ignorance. It was annoying.

"Why are they looking for him?" I pressed.

"He's involved in the murder at the Amber."

The second Edward left the store, I pulled up the local newspaper website. The *St. Virgil Guardian* hosted an outdated, ugly page. The layout, when it finally loaded, came up wonky but still legible on my phone. I found the headline article quickly and opened it.

Lennard's photo loaded onto my screen. Any hope I'd had that this was some mistake—that perhaps, two different Lennard Bissons had visited St. Virgil at the same time—was dashed. It was him. The same gaunt features. The same haunting gray eyes.

I skimmed through the article.

Kyle Gordo, 20, found dead at the Amber Oceanside hotel . . . Authorities have been tightlipped about the situation . . . copious amount of blood . . . throat cut . . . not the first mysterious death connected to the hotel . . .

Lennard Bisson, 23, traveled to St. Virgil with the deceased. Authorities ask for any information . . . considered a person of interest. Bisson is believed to still be on the island. His current whereabouts are unknown.

I shoved the photo in Allison's face. "It's him."

Allison stepped around me, grabbed a dry rag, and started wiping down the counter. "Yes. And?"

"And?" She couldn't be serious. We'd seen Lennard yesterday—right here, in this shop.

"We have to tell someone. The police." From the minute he'd stormed into the store, I'd known he was trouble. He'd been behaving so strangely—begging us for a session, then running out like he did. Now we knew why.

"Tell the police what exactly?" Allison stepped around to the other side of the desk. "We don't know anything. Did you hear him mention a murder while he was here? Because I don't remember that."

"We have his phone and wallet," I said, still in disbelief at what she was saying. "The police will want those. What if they could help find him?"

No doubt the police would be monitoring the ferry. It was the only way off the island. We had no planes, and helicopters were so rare they'd be noticed. While Lennard could've hired a boat, he'd need a sizable vessel and an experienced crew to navigate the notoriously dangerous waters that separated St. Virgil from the sister island. It wasn't impossible, but it was highly unlikely that he could pull this off without being found.

Allison rested her hand on her hips. "They can only use the phone to track him if the phone is on him." She froze, then sprinted toward the safe. After pulling out Lennard's phone, and looking it over, she asked, "Can they track it if it's dead?"

"I don't know," I said, though I was almost certain they couldn't. "We should hand it in either way."

She shoved the phone back into the safe and locked it. "And how would we explain why we have his things? They'll want to know."

"We could . . ." Oh. Right. We still couldn't tell them about the psychic sessions. Word would inevitably get back to her father and land us in a world of trouble. "I could say . . . that he was in the store for some other reason. He was looking at souvenirs or asking for directions when he accidentally dropped it."

"He accidentally dropped his phone *and* his wallet? Because those are items people accidentally drop and don't notice?" She turned away from me.

"Allison, we're talking about a murder here." She must see that this was bigger than the store. A risk we had to take. "If Len is dangerous and we can help find him, then we have to."

"We don't know he's dangerous." She wiped down the shelves, cleaning more in a few seconds than I'd seen her do in the entire time I'd worked here. "He might not be the murderer. Just a witness."

"All the more reason to find him! He could be in danger." I stood beside her, blocking her progress. "Why are you so against this? You don't have to be involved at all. I can tell them I randomly picked it up somewhere else."

"My father wouldn't believe you. He'd find out that I was connected somehow."

"But keeping a secret like this—people could get hurt."

"You don't understand. There's too much at stake for me. He cannot find out about this. Selina, please."

I looked at Allison's face, her eyes bright and brimming with tears. "Is there something you're not telling me?"

She flinched.

Oh no. "What is it? Tell me."

Her shoulders slumped, her hands falling limp at her sides. "I didn't drop out of university, okay? Not voluntarily. My parents convinced the administration to let me leave so I wouldn't be formally expelled."

"What?" *Expelled?*

She returned to the counter and collapsed into her chair. "This is so embarrassing." She tossed the rag down and covered her face. "My roommate and I were at the mall, bored and a little day drunk. She talked me into swiping a few tubes of lipstick. You know, to see if we could do it."

"You stole them?"

"It was just the once," she said defensively. "For me, anyway. We got caught walking out of the store. When the police reported it to the school, the administration searched our room and found my roommate's secret stash. I tried to tell them that none of it was mine, but they didn't believe me."

Wow.

"Don't look at me like that," she said. "I know it's bad, okay? That's why my parents put me in charge of the store instead of forcing me to work for the real estate company, like Edward. It's supposed to teach me the value of money. They told me if I messed up again, they'll send me away."

I gaped at her, still trying to muddle through her logic. "Then why risk the fake psychic readings at all?"

"Well, they weren't supposed to ever find out, were they? All I wanted to do was make a little extra money." She pouted. "I think a part of them doesn't believe the shoplifting was a one-time thing. This"—she waved around to indicate the shop in general—"is a test. They're waiting for me to slip up. They're expecting it."

"Allison—"

"I'm not as smart as Edward. I have no big passion or goals to follow. Right now, this shop is all I have. If you take Len's things to the police, and they trace it back to me, that's the end of it. I'll have no job and neither will you."

My resolve wavered. Like Allison, the shop was all I had, too. I used to dream of working in a lab, developing new drugs that would save lives. But after the attack on my parents, school became less of a priority. All of it felt pointless. I'd barely scraped through exams, graduating by the skin of my teeth.

Allison pressed her hands together as if in prayer. "Please, I'm begging you."

"Someone has been murdered," I said.

"The police will find Len," she said confidently. "The island is too small for him to stay hidden for long."

That wasn't true. The rainforest covered over 90 percent of the island, some areas so dense that sunlight couldn't even penetrate it. If anyone could lose themselves, it would be here.

CHAPTER
EIGHT

That evening, we closed at seven on the dot. Allison seemed as reluctant to linger as I was, the atmosphere in the shop tense after our disagreement.

There had to be a way to get the information to the police and stay anonymous. If only Allison would listen. It didn't escape my notice that she'd kept the phone and wallet locked in the safe, both keys on her person the whole afternoon. Almost like she didn't trust me.

Fair enough.

Plans might have been percolating in the back of my mind, but I had no intention of following through. Not yet, anyway. She was my friend, and by going against her, I'd risk alienating the entire group, my relationship with Edward included.

For the moment, I put it out of my mind. That evening, I had an important appointment to keep anyway.

After Allison and I bid each other a stilted goodbye, I caught a taxi to the island's medical center. The private facility had only been operating for three years, its construction surrounded by controversy. Virgil Enterprises had built it over the remains of an old hospital, which many considered a historical landmark. Protests and petitions ensued, but construction went ahead anyway. Residents slowly accepted it, as we always did.

I held mixed feelings toward the center. Having such a state-of-the-art facility on the island proved to be an invaluable help to my family. But not everyone had someone like Muriel to cover the bill.

We could've used the regular hospital, but their facilities weren't the best. Locals told morbid jokes about perfectly healthy people walking in and never walking back out. Most who needed bigger procedures and couldn't afford the center usually had them done on the sister island instead.

It was dark by the time the taxi dropped me off. When I approached the entrance, the automatic doors slid apart to let me inside. Cold air blasted me in the face.

The facility's layout couldn't be more different from the regular hospital, everything new and sleek. The walls were white with minimal decor, the shiny floors slick with polish. The waiting rooms had cushioned chairs, stocked vending machines, and coffee makers. Large-screen TVs played nineties sitcoms on mute.

The receptionist sat behind a curved desk. She held a receiver to her ear, talking on the phone. I charged past with a wave of acknowledgment.

"Hold on a minute!" she called out.

I backed up, exasperated. Was this necessary? She knew who I was and why I was here. I visited often enough. Or, at least, I used to.

She held the receiver against her shoulder. "Miss DaSilva. You know you must check in with me first."

"Sorry," I said with a plastic smile. "You were busy and I didn't want to bother you."

"How considerate," she said, then held up a finger for me to wait as she returned to her call. For the next few minutes, I stood there as she tried to clarify the details of someone's bill. When she finally hung up, she said, "Thank you for waiting. Dr. Henry would like to speak to you. I'll tell him you're here."

Every muscle in my body tensed, all the worst-case scenarios playing out in my head.

"Good evening, Selina," Dr. Henry said, meeting me in my mother's room. He had a bald head, thick neck, and the muscle-bound physique of a gym rat. It contrasted with his gentle voice. "Nice to see you."

Honestly, I couldn't say the same. But I offered him a strained smile anyway. "You wanted to see me about something? Is everything all right with Mummy?"

His lips stretched into a polite smile—the kind meant to placate but reaching nowhere near the eyes. "More or less. I thought, since you haven't been here in a while, you would like an update."

Relief punched me in the chest, abruptly followed by shame. "I'm sorry. I've been busy."

"My apologies. I did not mean to sound judgmental." Dr. Henry stopped beside the bed. "I only meant that we've recently run some tests. Her condition remains unchanged."

"Okay . . ." So, the update was that there was no update? I suppressed a sigh. "Have you told Muriel?" She was Mummy's court-appointed guardian. If anyone needed to approve any new care plans, it would be her.

"Of course. Miss Muriel is paying for the best care. She's very invested in Josephine's well-being. We provide her with regular updates."

"Glad to hear it," I said flatly, more than ready for this conversation to be over.

He nodded. "I thought you should be aware of the situation as it stands. The chances of her regaining consciousness remain negligible."

"I understand." I'd heard it all before, done the research, read the statistics. "Thank you for letting me know."

Just before leaving the room, he turned back to me. "It's okay that you're busy, you know." He shrugged. "After two years, with no change, it's almost expected."

I said nothing.

After he finally left, I turned to the bed. For the first time since I entered the room that evening, I looked at my mother. If I tried, I could almost pretend she was sleeping, still and peaceful, tucked under the covers. But the illusion never held—she looked too unlike herself.

In the years she'd been here, she'd lost a lot of weight: her cheeks ice-pick-sharp, the skin around her eyes sunken.

I shut the door quietly, then waited a few minutes to make sure no one immediately reopened it. When no one did, I pulled the solution of ground snake eye seed from my purse. Using a cheap dropper, I carefully placed five drops on my mother's tongue.

A handful of regional folktales mentioned the seeds of the snake eye fruit. In the stories, the characters used them to wake the dead. For centuries, people dismissed it as a myth, but recent scientific studies suggested that a chemical found in the seeds did abnormally stimulate brain activity. They theorized that the rising dead spoken of by our ancestors might have been individuals waking from comas. Experimental drugs made from the seeds were currently in development, but it would be years before they were approved for medical use. I couldn't wait that long.

Was it risky to test it on Mummy? Possibly. But I'd diluted it to the point where it shouldn't be poisonous. At worst, she'd have a bad trip like Nathan.

Besides, after two years, I was willing to try anything to bring her back to me.

I returned the solution and dropper to my purse, reopened the door, then stood at her side. I waited for any immediate effects, ready to call for a nurse if necessary.

With shaking hands, I pushed the stray curls away from her face. She used to dye her hair regularly and keep it a few inches shorter than it was now. My mother would be the first to admit to her vanity, taking great care and pride in her good looks. She'd be so mad at the gray streaks that had grown in.

"Would you understand why I haven't been here as often?" I whispered, taking her hand in mine.

When I was a child, she'd make sure I held her hand when we went walking, especially while crossing the street. By the time I was eight or nine, I'd decided I was too old for it, no longer a baby. I told her as much and she seemed to find this endlessly amusing. Since then, whenever we were in public, she'd catch my eye, stretch out her hand, and wiggle her fingers expectantly. I'd roll my eyes and ignore her every time.

My grip tightened as a wave of missing her crashed over me. I stood there and held on until it passed.

My phone rang. I retreated from the bedside to answer it.

"Are you still at the medical center?" Edward asked. When I confirmed that I was, he said, "Stay there. I'll pick you up."

I peered out of the room's window. Darkness had indeed settled in, the view of the coast from the window nothing but specks of light in the distance. I wiped my tears and my transparent reflection in the glass did the same. "I told you—I'll catch a taxi."

"That was before. Now we know a serial murderer is running around."

My stomach dropped. "Serial?"

"You haven't heard? They found another body."

CHAPTER
NINE

Emma had spotted the ruins first.

The early morning hike had been a last-minute addition to their schedule. Chord told them he'd learned about the trail from some random local and decided they absolutely had to check it out. He'd spotted the ruins second, yelling back to the rest, then charging toward it. The others followed his lead, as they always did.

Emma emerged from the forest last. She hung back, filming, absorbing the shot. Mentally, she was back on her laptop, already planning the best way to edit the reveal. They'd been hiking for over two hours, lost for most of that time. Just seconds earlier, their group was a walking chorus of complaints, but all that vanished in the excitement of the discovery.

The sting of a mosquito bite brought a sharp end to Emma's thoughts. She rubbed the rising, reddening bump, and trudged up the incline to join her friends. Mitch ran straight through a large stone archway, while Chord and Angela headed for the cliffside. The couple stopped beside one of the old cannons aimed toward the sea, a relic of the colonial era, when many wars were fought over the island.

Emma had read about the battles of St. Virgil. One sea fight was reported to be so bloody that it turned the waters red. Hence the name for the beach below: Crimson Bay.

Chord and Angela stood against the wind, facing the sea. They reenacted the king-of-the-world pose from *Titanic* before Chord grabbed her hips and pretended to try to throw her off the edge. Angela spun out of his hold, shrieking, laughing, and punching his shoulder. "That's not funny!"

"Sorry, sorry." Chord grinned and ducked his head. He ran a hand through his black hair, bashful and gorgeous.

Angela's pout melted into a smile. She curled into his side, resting her head on his shoulder.

Emma filmed the whole interaction, knowing their shippers would eat it up. Somehow, she kept the camera steady, even as something inside her broke.

"Okay, you were right." Angela laughed, breaking the embrace. "This view alone was worth the visit. It is gorgeous."

"I told you," Chord said. "And St. Virgil is so far off the grid, no one else is doing it."

Personally, Emma would've preferred Egypt or Thailand for their vlog, but her opinion counted for a lot less these days.

Chord grinned at Angela, something unsaid but affectionate passing between them. They seemed to read each other's thoughts, so in sync, a stranger might be surprised to learn that they'd only met three months earlier.

In contrast, Emma and Chord met when they were children. Best friends for as long as they could remember. When he'd wanted to start a YouTube channel, she'd picked up the camera, watched the tutorials, and learned to use the editing apps. She'd been his sounding board, his assistant, his co-host, his manager, his advisor—his everything for years.

But then, a year ago, something changed. Chord changed.

His face, which Emma had always thought held a unique appeal with its irregular angles, blurred into a generic handsomeness. His charm, which had been a little goofy, smoothened into something slick and magnetic. The subscriber count jumped from hundreds to thousands to millions, the rapid growth gaining the attention of mainstream media, which only brought more views.

With the new subscribers came new opportunities. And with new opportunities came the Insta-famous aspiring actress Angela.

In the blink of an eye, they went from filming reaction videos in Chord's mother's kitchen to vlogging international vacations. But Emma couldn't deny that she missed the time when everything was small and less complicated. When it was just them.

She bit back a sigh and lowered the camera.

Chord turned in her direction. His brow furrowed, his expression strangely intense. For a brief, heart-stopping second, Emma thought he'd sensed her hurt. That he finally saw her, and understood her, for the first time in what felt like ages.

But no. His attention was focused somewhere else.

Emma glanced back, toward the trees. The forest blanketed the edge of the incline, a prettier view now that they weren't locked within its verdant walls. For a few minutes, during the second hour of the hike, she'd been gripped by a wild thought that they wouldn't get out. That they'd accidentally crossed into some dimension where there was nothing but trees and dirt and sky forever.

When she turned back to them, Chord was smiling—the too-broad, plastic smirk he'd cultivated over the past year. "You got the shot?" he asked her.

Emma nodded. "I always do."

Almost immediately, Chord let Angela go and stepped aside, the move so abrupt it bordered on callous. Angela blinked, swaying slightly, like a marionette with a cut string. Her nostrils flared, obviously irritated. Her lips parted, about to speak. But she glanced at Emma and shut her mouth.

For all that Chord might have been oblivious to Emma's feelings, his girlfriend was not. Angela's solution was to act like there weren't any faults in their relationship, as if Emma would ever use them to her advantage even if she could.

"Hey!" Mitch shouted. His flushed face appeared in one of the long, arched windows of the fort. "I found something. Come on!"

Angela looked to Chord, as if waiting for something. When he gave nothing in return, she flashed a smile as empty as his. "Let me go see what this fool is up to." Then she shouted to her cousin, "This better not be another beetle!"

Mitch's fascination with insects had been an exercise in patience for them. All trip long, he'd delay their schedule and disappear into unannounced detours just to seek, identify, and photograph various species. During the hike, Emma had learned more about golden silk spiders than she'd ever wanted to know.

"I'm serious, Mitch!" Angela shouted, marching up to the entrance.

Emma started to follow, then noticed that Chord hadn't moved. "You coming?"

Chord shook his head. "You go on." He tipped his head toward the direction of the sea. "Give me a minute. I want to absorb this view a little longer."

Emma hesitated. She wanted to ask what was wrong—because clearly something was—but the time when they could've talked to each other, openly and honestly, had long passed. The gulf between them spanned a great distance, as wide as the bay that stretched along the coast below them.

Later, she'd look back at this moment and wish she'd tried to cross it.

"Okay. Whatever." She started toward the fort's entrance, briefly glancing at the trees. Awareness tickled her skin. It occurred to her that someone could be lurking in the brush, watching them, and they'd never know.

Emma shrugged off her paranoia. That's what she got for falling asleep to true crime podcasts. She charged up the rest of the incline, stepping around the exposed rock and tall patches of grass. She passed through the arched entrance and crossed a small courtyard area.

Mitch and Angela were crouched near the farthest wall, behind the crumbled remains of a staircase. They were talking, their heads bent together, Angela's tone pitched higher than usual with agitation. As Emma drew closer, she could see what caught their attention.

Some sort of large rodent lay on its side. Its head was twisted at an odd angle, the light brown fur soaked with blood. Its throat had been cut repeatedly.

"What the hell did you do?" Emma demanded, choking on the bile that rose in the back of her throat.

"It wasn't me!" Mitch sounded on the edge of tears. "I just found it." Since he had no blood on him, she was inclined to believe that was true. It only made her feel slightly better.

"Why would someone do something like this?" Angela asked.

Emma didn't answer, less preoccupied with the question of *why* than she was with *when*. No amount of money in the world could motivate her to touch the animal, but she suspected that if she did, it would be warm.

"No flies," Mitch muttered, circling the same conclusion she'd already arrived at. "It must be fresh."

Emma met Angela's eyes, and she knew they were thinking the same thing. Whoever did this could be close by.

"Get up." Angela tapped her cousin on the shoulder. "Come on."

"Maybe we could bury it." Mitch reached out.

"Don't touch it!" Angela grabbed his arm and hauled him backward.

Emma left Angela to deal with her cousin, sprinting for the entrance. She needed to warn Chord that some sicko could be lurking in the area. Assuming it was just one person. She didn't even want to entertain the thought that it could be more. That their group could be outnumbered, two hours away from safety.

But when she emerged from the archway, Chord wasn't there. He wasn't anywhere.

They searched the ruins and called his name, their voices bouncing off stone walls and carrying on the wind. Emma, whispering a prayer beneath her breath, inched right up to the edge of the cliff and looked down. The image of Chord slipping played in the back of her head, but she only saw the churning, dark blue waters below.

The police dismissed their worries. Chord had been known to pull a prank for views now and then. The officers took the report but couldn't waste time or resources on a joke when they had a murderer to find.

"He's eighteen," one of the officers said, yawning. The skin around his eyes sagged. The unblinking, glazed look on his face spoke of too little sleep and too much caffeine. "If he wants to disappear, he can."

It didn't help that Mitch wasn't convinced it wasn't a joke. "Chord was the one who insisted we hike up there," he told them, disconcerted by Emma's anger. "He insisted we go. Maybe this was his reason."

Emma begged the police to do more anyway. An awful feeling had burrowed into her gut. Something wasn't right. But when it came to calling Chord's parents, she agreed to hold off on telling them for a day.

If this was a prank, she would never forgive him.

That night, Emma awoke to the sound of voices and rustling. She lay still, listening. Her eyes seemed to take forever to adjust to the darkness. Slowly, pieces of the room revealed itself. In this foreign place, unfamiliar shadows formed menacing shapes. She watched as one grew, elongating, moving, whispering.

"I don't want to. Leave me alone."

The familiar voice registered. Emma sat up. She threw off the sheets and flicked the switch above the headboard. The shadows retreated in the hazy orange glow of twin lamps that bracketed the bed. Chord stood in side profile. One of his hands rested on the doorknob, like he was leaving.

Later, Emma would wonder why he was in her room. And how he'd gotten in. But in that moment, she was too relieved to think beyond *He's here.*

She jumped out of the bed and ran up to him. "Where have you been? We've been looking everywhere for you."

Chord did not answer, his eyes on the door. He was shaking, his hair a nest of knots, his clothes damp and stained with mud.

Emma's relief drained away. "What's going on?" When he wouldn't speak, she stepped closer, ready to shake the answers out of him if she had to. "Do you have any idea how scared we were? You just disappeared without any explanation. I swear, if this was some sort of joke— Are you listening to me? We even went to the police."

At the mention of the police, he flinched and finally looked at her. "You shouldn't have done that."

A chill skated down her spine. It didn't sound like a threat and yet . . . "Why wouldn't we? You were gone."

She reached out and grabbed his arm. His skin was clammy, covered with a fine sheen of sweat. Her grip tightened. "What happened to you?"

He pried her hand off. "If I'm not back by tomorrow night, don't look for me."

"What?" She reached for him again, but he shook her off.

"Don't look for me," he said firmly. "I don't want any of you to find me. Especially not you."

"Why are you saying this—"

He ducked his head to kiss her cheek. His lips lingered for a moment. When he pulled back, there was a familiar warmth in his expression, a flicker of the old Chord, the boy she used to know before Angela and the fans and the views.

Then he opened the door and walked out, shutting it behind him. Stunned, Emma pressed a hand to her cheek and held it there.

His lips had been ice-cold.

She snapped out of her shock and threw the door open.

"Wait!" she shouted down the empty hall. All the hotel room doors were shut, one of the overhead lights flickering. She ran to the end of the hall, her bare feet on the coarse red carpeting. The elevator carriage was empty, the adjoining stairway silent.

She'd lost him again.

The next evening, two fishermen found Chord Grayson on the rocks of Crimson Bay. He was face down, half his body in the water. His throat had been cut.

CHAPTER
TEN

"Is this the best you can do?" Mrs. Nelson tapped her fingers on the edge of the table impatiently.

I glanced from her to the clock. I needed to wrap this up. Knowing Allison, she wouldn't want to wait around much longer. Any second now, she'd start locking up. For my plan to work, I had to help her with closing.

"It's very effective," I assured the irate older woman, nudging the pouch closer to her. The small bag had been made from a translucent green fabric. Tucked inside were a few yellow oleander seeds and a mix of dried leaves and stones. "Place this under your son's bed. He will have no problems with exams."

Luck or not, I highly doubted the poor kid would not do well. With a mother as overbearing as Mrs. Nelson, he would feel the pressure to ace everything.

"I don't just want him to do well." She rolled the gold band of her wedding ring. Throughout the session, her posture had remained pin-straight, sitting at the very edge of her chair, as if determined to come into as little contact with our furniture as possible.

"He needs to be first in his class," she said. "He deserves to. Not that new girl from the sister island. She was held back a year and shouldn't be in their grade in the first place."

Ah. I could see where this was heading. It wasn't enough to have her son thrive; she wanted his competition sunk. I had to cut this off. "I'm sure he will do fine. The charms I make are excellent quality."

"Fine isn't enough. Make one that is guaranteed to put that girl in her place."

I glanced at the clock again, frustrated as the seconds ticked away. Yes, I could've bagged a rock and called it a bad-luck charm, mumbled a curse around the intended's name. But I didn't have the time for that.

And frankly, I had no desire to even pretend to help Mrs. Nelson bring down a child.

"I'm sorry, I can't do that," I said, then proceeded to rip a few lines from one of my mother's speeches. "Magic is an unnatural tug on the balance of the universe. We must be careful of what we put into the world. You might tip the scales and find yourself drenched in the very energies you tried to direct onto someone else." I nudged the pouch back toward her. "*Fine* will have to be enough."

"Hey." Allison gently knocked on the door. "Sorry to interrupt, but I'm—"

"We're done." I kept my tone firm as I rose to my feet.

Mrs. Nelson did not appreciate that one bit. A sour expression marred her face as she paid and left the store.

"Another satisfied customer," I muttered, flipping the CLOSED sign on the door.

Allison pulled out the cash from the register, added it to the money from the safe, and started counting it. While she did that, I closed the back room.

We had not mentioned Len or his things for the entire day, but the unsaid lingered in the atmosphere. One death might've been an accident—something personal that had gone terribly wrong. But two was alarming. The latest victim, Chord Grayson, turned out to be a popular online personality. His death caused a ripple across the internet, thrusting St. Virgil further into the international spotlight.

The number of police on the island had risen, more than a dozen officers brought over from the sister island to help. Just that day, we'd seen uniformed officers pass the store several times. Instead of making me feel safer, it only reminded me of the evidence we were hiding.

Allison might have been content to ignore this, but I was not.

After shutting the door to the back room, I joined Allison. Leaning over the counter, I stretched out a hand to flip off the extension outlet. My elbow knocked into a key chain rack, which tumbled sideways, scattering all it held onto the floor.

"Shoot!" I bent down and started to pick them up. "Sorry."

She shook her head and continued to count the cash. The safe hung open behind her, Lennard's phone visible from where I stooped. Allison's grip on the keys to the safe had been looser today, the spare in its usual spot under the counter. But I couldn't have risked taking Lennard's belongings yet. I had to make sure she locked them in first.

I took my time, watching her out of the corner of my eye. She placed the cash into the brown pencil case, zipped it shut, and dropped it into her bag. The second she shut the safe, I subtly reached for the phone in my pocket and pressed call on the most recent number.

Just as Allison turned the lock, my ringtone blasted from the back room.

"Oh damn," I said. "I must've left my phone in there. Would you mind getting it for me?" I made a show of being too busy, reaching for the handful of key chains that had gone under the counter.

"Seriously?" she asked, rolling her eyes. "You're all over the place today. Mrs. Nelson did not look happy when she left."

"When has she ever looked happy?"

"Good point."

She tucked the key into her pocket, reopened the back room, and entered it.

The second she was out of sight, I stood. Using the extra key, I unlocked the safe, snatched the phone and wallet, and dumped them into my bag. Once that was done, I returned the key to its spot under the counter and shut the safe. I did not lock it.

I'd just dropped to my knees when Allison reemerged.

"It's Muriel." She held up the phone so I could see the contact I'd changed that morning. It was actually my mother's phone number. I still had her cell, which is what I'd used to make the call. "Do you want me to answer?" she asked.

"No, I'll get back to her later."

She handed it over. I swiped the screen, and the ringing stopped.

"I think that's the last of it." I stood and dumped the rest of the key chains on the counter. "Do you mind if I sort these in the morning? I'm exhausted."

"Sure, whatever." She retrieved the extra key from under the counter and pocketed it.

Behind Allison the door to the safe inched open. My heart dropped. As she started to turn toward it, I hurried around to the other side of the counter, moving quickly, and speaking loudly to keep her attention. "Hey! So, what are your plans for tonight?"

She frowned, scooping up her bag. "Janice is busy helping Muriel with the party. I didn't really plan anything."

"Oh, so we can only do things with Janice now that she's back? I see how it is." I tried to keep my tone light and amused, but some of my irritation slipped through.

She tilted her head. "It's not like that. Really, Selina. We can do something tonight if you want."

"As an afterthought? No thanks." I grabbed my own bag, backing up toward the door. "Though, I suppose I should be grateful to be invited at all this time."

She winced. "Okay, what Janice pulled with the Blueside thing wasn't cool. She's just a little territorial. She doesn't mean anything by it. Give her a chance to adjust to you being around."

"I've been around. We've known each other since we were babies. She just doesn't . . ."

The door to the safe crept outward some more. My breath caught in my throat. If Allison glanced back, she'd definitely see it.

"She hates me," I finished in a rush, then quickly flipped the light switch. The store plunged into darkness. The shadows obscured everything, including the safe. "Always has."

"Only because she's never tried to get to know you properly. Not that you've given her a chance to. You and Gabriel were always joined at the hip, off in your own world."

We stepped outside. She closed and locked the door. I exhaled in relief.

"Maybe," Allison said, "while she's here, you two can spend some time together. Then she'll start to adore you like we do." To my surprise, she pulled me into a playful hug, complete with a loud kiss on the cheek.

I laughed at her ridiculousness. My handbag felt heavier, burdened by the weight of my deception. Allison had been a good friend to me this year; I didn't want to lose this.

Still, I had to remind myself that I was doing the right thing. If everything went according to plan, she'd never find out.

"What do you want to do tonight, then?" she asked me.

"What?" It took me a second to understand. "Oh. I'm busy. I'm going to the medical center to see my mom."

She threw her hands up. "So, what was that whole guilt trip for?"

"It's the principle of the thing. Just because I won't accept the invite doesn't mean I don't want it."

"Amazing," she said dryly. Her expression sobered. "How is your mom doing?"

"The same." Unfortunately. The snake eye seeds had no effect. I'd have to take another look at the research.

"Is Edward picking you up?" she asked.

"No, I'll take a taxi."

"Is that . . . safe?" she asked, brushing against the topic we were avoiding.

"I think so. It's the medical center. Nothing's going to happen with so many people around. But please don't mention it to Edward. He likes to worry over nothing."

Allison didn't look totally convinced, but she retrieved her bicycle without argument. She used to have a car—a bright blue Beetle. It was taken away after she left school. She didn't have too far to travel anyway; her house was located a fifteen-minute ride from town.

We parted at the taxi stand. After she pedaled off, I crossed the road and ducked into the covered bus stop. A timetable plastered to the wall stated a bus would stop every half hour, but everyone knew not to expect it on time.

As more people arrived, I drifted farther into the shed. A musty odor hung in the air. Scraps of paper, snack wrappers, and plastic bottles littered the floor. A flyer stuck to the heel of my shoe. I peeled it off, my attention momentarily snagged by the printed advertisement.

Psychic Readings by Miss Claudia . . . Palm readings, tarot cards, spiritual counseling. Learn about your past, present, and future . . .

Of course. Our biggest competition. I snorted, kicking the flyer away from me.

Someone knocked into my shoulder, and I stumbled backward. I lifted my gaze to meet the unrepentant stare of a long-faced older woman. Without a word, she shifted aside to put some space between us.

She wasn't the only one at the stop looking at me. Glaring at me. I kept my head down, avoiding eye contact, but I still caught my mother's name. I was very aware that, in that moment, I was alone in an enclosed space, among people who did not like me.

The bus finally arrived and I boarded quickly. I took the first open seat at the very front, near the door. I set my purse on my lap and hugged it to my chest. Passengers shuffled down the aisle, the bus filling up. The last person to board was an unkempt older man. He had a shaved head and stout body. Patchy, graying hairs sprouted from his chin. Something about him seemed familiar.

While trying to figure out where I knew him from, I accidentally made eye contact. I dropped my gaze immediately, but I could feel his red-rimmed eyes boring into me long after the bus pulled away from the stop.

First, we passed the glossy storefronts of Main Street, then made the roundabout at the port. As we left the town center, I hoped the man would disembark at every stop, but as the number of travelers thinned, he and I remained.

The bus headed east. This was the part of town most visitors would never see. Most residents lived here, in large apartment buildings, everyone stacked on top of each other. There was no sensible layout to the streets, most of them too narrow for the number of cars on them. I hadn't visited this side of St. Virgil in ages. I hadn't had a reason to until now.

Forty minutes after boarding, the man was still watching me. I didn't have to look back to know. I twitched in my seat, uneasy. When the bus finally arrived at the stop ahead of the one I'd really wanted, I impulsively disembarked, unable to stand it any longer.

On my way out, I subtly glanced back. The man hadn't moved. There was a disturbing hollowness to his gaze as it tracked me. Even after the bus had driven off, the man gone, I could not silence the instinct telling me this wasn't safe.

But I couldn't go yet. I was here for a reason.

I slipped into one of the side streets, sidestepping around water-logged potholes and open dumpsters. The windows of the surrounding buildings lit up as night set in. Through the walls, I could hear voices, music, and TV sounds—glimpses of the lives inside.

At the end of the street, I cut through an alleyway, which spat me out across the road from Sugar's Bar. The entrance lit up the street, the inside bustling with patrons. The lights were a welcome sight. I charged forward, convinced all I had to do was get inside, then I'd be as good as invisible in the crush of bodies.

At the edge of the entrance, just when I thought I'd made it, a large hand grabbed my shoulder. It yanked me backward before I could scream.

CHAPTER
ELEVEN

I spun around to face the man from the bus.

"You." His breath stank of alcohol and must. I shrank away, but he pushed, and my back connected with the wall.

Had he followed me? No, that didn't make sense. I'd left him on the bus. It was more likely we'd been heading to the same destination all along.

"It is you, isn't it?" His chapped lips retracted in a sneer. "You're that woman's daughter. What are you doing on this side of the city? Don't you have any shame, showing your face around here?"

"I don't know what you're talking about," I said, trying to slide away from him.

"Don't try that." He gritted his teeth, his hand clamped on my arm in an iron-tight grip.

I recognized him then. Marlon Alleyne. Elizabeth Alleyne's father. He looked so different, a shadow of his former self.

"I know it's you," he said. "You look just like her. The witch. That wicked con woman."

I shoved at his shoulder, trying to push away from him. He wouldn't let go of my arm. He had me trapped. Vulnerable. My old playground instincts kicked in, prompting me to lash out. "I'm confused. Was she a witch, or was she a con woman? You can't have it both ways."

A myriad of emotions flashed across his face before his expression hardened. "You make jokes? You think this is funny? She took everything from me. I have nothing left."

My anger slipped, sympathy and guilt seeping in. "Look, whatever your problem is, it has nothing to do with me. Let go."

A young man and woman stepped out of the bar, nursing bottles of beer. They appeared to be in their late twenties, dressed for a night out. Upon noticing us, they stopped.

I caught the guy's eyes, silently begging for their intervention. "Let me go!" I raised my voice so they'd hear.

The woman whispered something to the man. He nodded and took a sip from his bottle, his movements smooth and unhurried. "Everything all right, Uncle Marlon?" he called out.

Mr. Alleyne grunted his assent. The young man took another sip, and I realized they had no intention of helping me. Once again, I was on my own.

"What is your plan here?" I asked. "You're hurting me—for what?"

"You think *this* hurts?" he said. "What do you think my daughter went through in her final moments? Can you imagine?"

I turned away from his hot breath and the images he tried to conjure.

"Because I do," he said. "I think about what she went through first thing in the morning and last thing before I go to sleep. All that pain she felt, bleeding out for hours until she died."

Tears sprung to my eyes. No, I did not know what Elizabeth went through. But I did feel his pain. His grief and his anger burned through his skin, scalding me like a brand. I rotated my arm, trying to twist out of his hold. He shoved me back again, his free hand clamped on my shoulder.

"Let me go." I kept my tone as calm as I could. "My mother didn't kill Elizabeth. Ken Thomas did."

"Thomas would've already been in jail if it hadn't been for your mother," he said. "He'd have been locked up like the animal he is. My girl would be alive today if your mother hadn't gotten him released. Ellie's death is on her hands."

"What are you doing?" someone shouted. "Hey—let her go!" And then Gabriel was there, in front of me. He had his hand on Mr. Alleyne's shoulder. "Get back!"

When Mr. Alleyne didn't listen, Gabriel shoved him, putting himself between us. Mr. Alleyne stumbled, tripped, and fell onto the pavement.

"Hey!" the young man with the beer cried out. He handed his bottle to the young woman, then hurried to help Mr. Alleyne off the ground. "Don't touch him." To Mr. Alleyne, he asked, "You okay, Uncle?"

Mr. Alleyne blinked, seemingly stunned speechless.

"Oh, so now you want to say something, Brent?" Gabriel stepped toward them. "You see your uncle harassing her and you just stand there?"

The young man—Brent—rose to his feet. He approached Gabriel, his hands fisted. "Looked like they were having a conversation to me. Not my business."

"But now you feel the need to say something?" Gabriel didn't move. Although Gabriel had a well-toned runner's physique, Brent had a slight height advantage. Gabriel was also still in recovery. I was tempted to try to intervene, but showing concern for Gabriel might imply that I thought he was vulnerable or distract him, neither of which would be helpful in this situation.

A few patrons came outside to see what was going on.

"My uncle is a member of this community," Brent said. "He lost his daughter in a tragedy. He doesn't deserve to be attacked and shoved to the ground. Apologize to him."

"Sure," Gabriel said. "I'll do that. After he apologizes to Selina."

Brent snorted. "And why should he do that?" His gaze slid toward me, lips curling with distaste. "From the sound of it, Uncle wasn't saying anything she didn't already know. It's her fault for coming around here. She knows she's not welcome."

"According to who, exactly?" Another young woman strode out of the bar. She had a hand towel slung over her shoulder. I knew her— Khadija. She'd been two years ahead of me at school. Back then, she'd been the school's best track athlete. We'd all expected her to go pro. It was a surprise when she didn't.

Khadija set her hands on her hips. "Last I checked this wasn't your bar, and I don't remember me or Mummy banning anyone." She gave him a sharp, mocking smile. "But if you want to continue being a pest, I may have to start. You can be the first."

"You saw what he just did?" Brent demanded. "He shoved an old man to the ground."

"The old man was harassing my—" Gabriel bit back the rest of that thought and turned to face Khadija. "He was hurting Selina. Brent and Lori just stood there, watching like assholes."

"You know who she is?" Brent asked Khadija, pointing at me. "This is the DaSilva girl. The witch's daughter."

"That's enough," Khadija said to Brent. "Go."

"As far as I'm concerned, your mother got off easy," Brent said, his eyes locked with mine. "The only thing a witch is good for is burning. When you least expect it, I'm going to—"

Gabriel's fist slammed into Brent's face.

Brent stumbled backward. The girl with him screamed. I caught a glimpse of blood—and what could've been a broken nose—before Khadija hurried Gabriel and me inside. She steered us through the gathered patrons, toward a back staircase.

"Go wait in your apartment," she told Gabriel. "I'll make sure they leave."

"I shouldn't have done that," Gabriel said through gritted teeth. He shook out the hand he'd used to punch Brent. "You don't have to—"

"I'll take care of this." Khadija's eyes dropped to his hand. She sighed. "And I'll bring up some ice when I'm done. Go on."

When she left, Gabriel looked at me. I stared back, immobilized by guilt and uncertainty. Mr. Alleyne's pain and anger lingered, pressing against my skin. I knew people hated me, hated my family—but what I'd felt from him was something deeper. Something dangerous.

Gabriel sighed. "Come on," he said, and started up the stairs.

I followed, sure that if I weren't here, he would've gone back outside with Khadija. Then again, if I weren't here, there wouldn't have been any punches thrown in the first place.

He led me to a door at the end of a short hallway. After unlocking it, he leaned against it, holding it open to let me inside. I passed him on the threshold, the woodsy scent of his cologne distractingly familiar.

I couldn't look at him, suddenly self-conscious. Instead, I turned my attention to the room. Despite the circumstances, I couldn't suppress my curiosity. He'd lived here before, for a few weeks before he left for university.

When Gabriel announced that he'd been accepted to study journalism in a school far away, Muriel threw him an ultimatum. So long as he lived under her roof, he'd study business in preparation for a job at Virgil Enterprises. Within a week, he moved out. The inheritance from his father provided more than enough to pay for everything.

Since Gabriel and I had broken up by that point, I imagined the fact that I also lived in Muriel's house had contributed to his decision to some extent.

"I'm sorry," I said, when he closed the door. "I didn't mean to cause a scene."

Gabriel snatched a bottle of pills off the desk. "Why are you apologizing?" He collapsed into a rolling desk chair, the cushions of which appeared to be worn by age. A bit of foam stuck out the side. He positioned himself to face me, his back to the desk. "It's not your fault he attacked you."

"That was Mr. Alleyne," I said, in case he hadn't realized. "He's the one whose daughter . . ."

"I know who he is." Gabriel shook out two white pills, popped them into his mouth, and swallowed them dry. "He still had no right to grab you like that."

"I know. But I understand why he's mad."

A few years earlier, thirty-two-year-old Maeve Downs was found, body broken against the rocks of Crimson Bay. The immediate and only suspect was Ken Thomas, a well-known local creep, who'd been stalking and harassing Maeve for months.

But Mummy believed Maeve's death was accidental. Mummy read the body and concluded that Maeve had slipped and fallen on her own. No one had pushed her. When a reporter asked Mummy her opinion on the case, she'd said as much. While it could not be measured how much effect Mummy's words had on the outcome of the case, at that point in time, Mummy's track record had been spotless. Media and the general public opinion shifted to Ken's side.

But less than a year after the jury acquitted him, Ken stalked and murdered Elizabeth Alleyne. There'd been a witness. No reasonable doubt this time.

"All your mother did was tell the truth," Gabriel said. "If she didn't see Ken murder Maeve, then what was she supposed to do? Lie? Let an innocent man go to jail?"

I rolled my eyes. Of course he'd defend my mother. Gabriel and Muriel might have disagreed on many things, but when it came to my mother's abilities, they were both believers.

"But Ken wasn't innocent, was he?" I said. "Even if he didn't push Maeve, he did kill someone later."

Gabriel stared at his bruised knuckle. "Your mom didn't know he would do that."

"No, she only knows things when it's convenient." I shut my eyes and held up a hand. "Wait, no. I didn't come here to argue with you." We'd had this same conversation many times before, almost word for word.

"Why are you here?" Gabriel asked. "I thought we had nothing to say to each other?"

When I opened my eyes, I found him watching me. His head tilted to the side, his hair falling across his brow. His expression was a mix of curiosity and condescension. Despite his deceptively slumped posture,

I could read the coiled tension in the lines of his body. In the unwavering focus of his gaze. Frustration radiated off him in waves as he waited for my answer.

I didn't know if it was the adrenaline from the fight, or the intimacy of the small apartment, but he seemed set on tackling the unsaid between us. Too bad for him, that wasn't why I was here.

A knock at the door broke our silence.

"Come in!" Gabriel called without looking away from me.

Khadija pushed the door open. She handed a blue pack to Gabriel. Just behind her, a guy about our age, dressed in striped athleticwear, lugged a silver bucket filled with ice.

"Here you go," Khadija said. "Do you need painkillers or something?"

"No, I've got it," Gabriel said, taking the pack from her. He laughed as the guy set the bucket on the floor. "That's way too much, Adrian. But thanks anyway."

"I told you." Adrian pouted and rolled his shoulders. "Am I done now? The team's going out tonight."

"Oh, baby brother," Khadija said, throwing her arm around Adrian's shoulders. "So sorry you had to take thirty seconds to help an injured friend. Did you at least empty the trash bins, like I asked you to?"

"Stop calling me a baby," he grumbled. "I'm sixteen." He stuck out his tongue at her, then left.

"So long as I'm older than you, you will be the baby," Khadija called after him. "And I noticed you didn't answer me about the bins!" She sighed, turning to Gabriel. "I'm proud but also terrified. If he does make the Olympic track team, I'm afraid his ego will be out of control."

Gabriel raised a brow. "Because it isn't already?"

"Fair enough." She adjusted the back of Gabriel's collar—the gesture, perhaps, a bit too intimate for a tenant and landlord. At least in my opinion. "But I am proud of him for getting to do what I couldn't. He was so lost when he was younger. It's nice to see that he's found some direction." She shrugged. "Anyway, how's the hand feeling?"

"I've had worse," Gabriel said. "Could you imagine if I'd injured the one arm that didn't give problems?" He flexed his fingers. "Brent is gone, right? He didn't cause you more trouble, did he?"

"I handled it." She waved him off. For the first time since entering the room, Khadija looked at me. "I'd give it a few minutes before heading out, though. They might still be lurking around."

"Okay," I said, belatedly adding, "Thank you."

"No worries," she said, then wrinkled her nose. "That being said, I'm sorry, but if you two plan to keep meeting up here, either lay low during business hours or I'll need you to take it somewhere else. I know it's not your fault, but . . . You see, ever since my mother's stroke, I've been helping her mind the bar. We don't need any trouble. We've got enough to deal with already."

"I understand," I told her. Even if I didn't make the trouble, that didn't mean it wouldn't follow me anyway. "It's not going to be a problem. I won't be around. This is a one-time visit."

Gabriel's lips flattened into a bland smile. "You heard her. One time."

Khadija's eyes darted between us. "Okay, then. I'll leave you to it."

When she started to go, Gabriel stood. The pair continued chatting in the open doorway, their voices too soft for me to hear. I took the bitter, ugly feeling that twisted in my chest and shoved it down. To distract myself, I looked around.

The whole apartment could have fit in my current bedroom. It was one combined living room, bedroom, and kitchen with a tiny bathroom attached. The yellow walls were faded in patches, the ceiling spotted with water damage. He had one small window that overlooked the street and the building next door. A single overhead light emitted a dull, florescent glow.

I was sure that Gabriel could've afforded a better apartment than this with the inheritance he got after his father's death, but he'd always liked the bustle of the city. Plus, I suspected that he was amused by the fact that the location over a bar annoyed his mother.

A laptop lay open on his desk, manila files, notebooks, and a tangle of wires scattered around it. Several books sat on a wooden shelf, haphazardly stacked to fit the space available. I walked over to them, unsurprised to find familiar names on the out-turned spines: Michael Crichton, Jules Verne, and Diana Wynne Jones, among others.

Gabriel had craved adventure since we were children. We both had. We'd spend hours pretending to be secret agents, explorers, or detectives. We'd solve crimes, search for hidden pirate treasure, and hunt for mythical beasts in the rainforest.

At its core, it was about escapism. Me, the outcast with an insatiable curiosity; him, the reticent, rebellious son who wanted to make the world a brighter place. We planned to leave after graduation. To travel. To start a new life in a place where we had no past. No expectations.

But after my parents' attack, I couldn't think long-term. All my energy narrowed to making it through one day, and the next. That's when I connected with Allison and leaned into the partying, the drinking. I learned how much less it hurt when you didn't care. Or at least pretended not to.

Gabriel had hated it. So I didn't tell him.

After the fourth time he'd caught me in a lie, and the second time he'd crashed a party to scrape me off the ground, he offered me his own ultimatum. That approach didn't work out any better for him than it had for Muriel.

I drifted deeper into his apartment. A folded newspaper lay on the edge of the bed. Lennard Bisson's printed face stared back at me. Even though I'd already read the new article that morning, I couldn't resist picking it up.

BODY FOUND ON CRIMSON BAY

"It's messed up, isn't it?" Gabriel said, startling me. "He was our age. I swear, there's something about that bay that attracts death."

I turned to find him a few steps behind me, watching the newspaper over my shoulder. He tipped his head toward the kitchen area, which I'd been blocking. "Do you mind letting me . . . ?"

I quickly stepped aside, flustered by his proximity, and trying very hard not to show it.

"Thanks." He hauled the bucket of ice and dumped most of it into the sink. "My name's not in the byline, but I contributed to that article." He scooped a few blocks of ice into the pack. "Kel, my boss, says he's willing to consider any articles that I submit. Mind you, he can be more than generous since it's just six of us working there."

He sold himself short. Gabriel was a good writer. Though his interest leaned toward journalism, I'd always suspected he had a novel in him. He'd certainly read enough of them to at least try.

"Why are you here, Selina?" he asked again.

I swallowed, my throat tight. "I need your help."

He glanced at me over his shoulder, then broke into laughter. "Oh wow. You must be desperate if you had to come to me. What about your new friends? They can't help you?" He turned and leaned against the edge of the sink, ice pack pressed against his knuckles. "Do they even know you're here right now? Does Edward?"

I said nothing, dropping my gaze. Of course I wouldn't tell Edward—especially not after our late-night car ride had revealed his insecurities related to Gabriel's return. My relationship with Edward was too new, too fragile to be testing it already.

"If this is what you're going to be like, maybe I should go," I said.

"Seems a bit late for that. You're here. The damage has already been done."

"It doesn't matter. I don't want your help if you're going to be this difficult."

"I'm difficult? Me?" His brows inched upward. "You haven't spoken to me in a year. You're hanging out with the same people who treated you like crap all through school. And you're dating Edward. *Edward?*"

Okay, I'd heard enough.

I started to leave and opened the door. A bruised-knuckled hand reached over my shoulder to shut it.

"Did I say I wouldn't help you?" he asked, right behind me. A thrill skittered across my skin. He stood so close that I could feel the heat of his body. "Like I said, if it's so serious that it got you here, then it must be bad."

I hesitated, my hand on the doorknob. A part of me wanted to go, regardless. Just being around him—this close to him—I felt exposed, shaken by how well he could still read me. Even after everything, I felt the pull to lean back and fall into him.

But I came here for a reason, and it was *that bad*.

I turned around, pulled the phone and wallet out of my purse, and held them out to him.

Gabriel set the ice pack down on his desk. He wiped his wet hands on his pants and took the wallet first. "What is this?"

"You still have friends in the police service, right?"

"*A* friend," he corrected me. "One. And to be honest, she'd probably prefer the term *acquaintance*. Why?"

"I need you to hand these in. And not tell her you got it from me."

"And why would you need me to do that?"

He flipped the wallet open. Lennard's driver's license was visible through a clear pocket.

"Right," he said after a moment. "I have questions."

CHAPTER
TWELVE

Despite my protests, Gabriel insisted on driving me home that night. After the incident with Brent and Mr. Alleyne, I understood his reasoning, but that didn't make it any less awkward.

Sitting beside him, I stole glances at his profile. More than ever, I could see the changes in him. The edges where there was once softness. A blunt detachment where there was once patience and sincerity. He used to wear his heart on his sleeve, holding nothing back. When he read a book, you could tell exactly where he was in the story just from his expression.

"I still don't understand why you can't go to the police yourself," he said, his bruised fingers flexing against the steering wheel. "Who cares what Allison thinks?"

I exhaled slowly, looking out the window. Glimpses of the town were illuminated in the orange glow of streetlights.

Somehow, he'd retrieved his secondhand Jeep. The beat-up moss-green vehicle had seen better days and worse owners, but Gabriel loved it. It had been his first big purchase, paid off with his own money. I remembered the day he'd proudly driven it off the ferry. He'd picked me up at the port. I'd never laughed so hard as I did then, watching him grow irritated while trying to figure out how to maneuver the cumbersome vehicle around the melee of disembarking tourists.

When he left for school, I'd assumed he'd sold it. But apparently not.

"Allison has her reasons," I said. "She doesn't want to get involved."

"So what? This is a murder investigation. Two people have died. If Lennard Bisson was in your store, the police will have questions for both of you. Like what time was this? What was he wearing? How was he behaving? Did he say anything odd? Every bit of information is important right now. They need to find him."

"I told you—Allison and I don't know anything that would be helpful."

Gabriel glanced over at me, clearly skeptical.

What did he want me to say? That Len believed he was being haunted by an invisible entity? How would that help? All the valuable information we had was in the wallet and phone. Once the police got those, they could work it out from there.

"Are you okay driving?" I changed the subject.

His brow pinched. "If I couldn't drive, I wouldn't be driving."

"I'm not questioning your skills. You were in pain earlier. And you took something."

"That was paracetamol," he said, the shadows melding into his face so that it seemed cast in stone. "And I'm always in pain. It's nothing new."

I stared at his profile. *Are you okay?* I wanted to ask. Just one of many questions that built over the night.

I was still haunted by the memory of that phone call—the one where Muriel told me about the crash. That particular airline had never had a flight-related fatality before. All it took was one negligent air traffic controller, and they lost one hundred and five passengers out of three hundred and thirty. It had almost been one hundred and six, but Gabriel had stubbornly clung on. Over the course of two days, he'd almost lost his grip on life multiple times, only to be revived seconds later.

When I looked at him now, I thought of the old tales where jumbie spirits intercepted bodies that were on the brink of death. Not that I thought Gabriel was possessed or anything like that. But I wondered how much of the version of Gabriel who returned was the same as the one who left.

Wrapped up in my thoughts, I almost missed the turnoff. "Wait! I need to stop at the souvenir shop for a moment."

"Now?" he asked.

"I forgot something inside. No, don't take Main Street. Take the side road. I'll go through the back."

"Okay . . ." Again, he sounded skeptical, but he did as I asked.

At this time of night, there would be a handful of restaurants and bars still open on Main Street, a few tourists lingering about, eating, drinking, and walking along the dimly lit pavement. Even though our store was mostly hidden from the nightlife, the side street behind the shop should be empty, which was ideal. What I planned to do would be best without witnesses.

"Stop over there," I said.

He slowed to a halt, parking behind the closed hardware store, a few doors down from the shop. Thankfully, the side roads weren't as heavily monitored. That wasn't to say there weren't any cameras at all, but I knew how to evade the few spots that had them.

"Do I want to know what you're doing?" he asked.

I unbuckled my seat belt and opened the door. "No."

He shook his head. "When did you get so shady?"

"Probably around the same time you got so angry." I shut the door, cutting off any response he gave, if he had any.

After hurrying into the alley between the shop and the jewelry store, I paused to make sure no one was about. The only sounds of life filtered down from Main Street, the area around me so still it was almost eerie. Barely even a breeze tickled my skin, the heat from earlier in the day emanating off the asphalt and brick.

I scooped up a discarded block of wood left by the construction at the jewelry store and smacked it against the frosted glass on the back door of our shop. Because I was afraid the noise would draw attention, my first hit was a bit hesitant. The glass cracked but did not shatter, a spiderweb of fractures blooming across the surface.

Not wanting to waste any more time, I hit it again, harder. This time the glass broke. Two more hits were enough to completely dislodge the triangular pane. The hole provided enough room for me to reach in and unlock the door. I opened it.

Tomorrow Allison would arrive first, as she always did. She'd see the back door broken and unlocked, the safe open and empty, and assume that Lennard had returned to get his things. Because she didn't want the police involved, she'd quietly have the back door repaired, and I'd be in the clear.

Allison might wonder how Lennard got into the safe. But as far as she knew, she'd locked it. The phone and wallet were in there when we left. Since she was the only one with both keys, she'd most likely conclude that she'd accidentally left it open.

Satisfied with the setup, I tossed the block back onto the pile of construction debris, then left the alley. After checking the surrounding area to make sure there were no witnesses, I returned to the Jeep.

———

"You can drop me over there." I pointed Gabriel to the bus stop at the top of our street, just out of sight from anyone at the house. I didn't know if Janice and Muriel had already returned home, but I couldn't risk it.

"What?" Gabriel asked dryly. "You don't want to be seen with me?"

I said nothing, which was answer enough.

"Right," Gabriel said, his jaw tight. He pulled over to the stop. "Well, if you're insisting on this, can you at least message me to let me know you've gotten inside safely? That way, I won't worry all night about leaving you out here."

"Of course," I said, my tone light. I ignored the flutter in my stomach at the indirect admission that he cared.

"You still have my number?" he asked. "Just making sure, since you haven't used it in so long."

The flutter disappeared.

I opened the door, started to climb out of the car, then stopped.

"Gabriel, it's really important that this doesn't get back to Allison. I know she wasn't the best person in secondary school—" Despite the laughter that burst from his lips, I pressed on. "But she is my friend. So can you please not tell anyone we were together tonight?"

"Oh no," he said in a dry monotone. "What will Allison and I have to chat about over Sunday brunch now?" He gave me a flat look. "Somehow I don't think that's going to be a problem."

"I meant don't tell Janice." He might not have any cause to interact with Allison directly, but he still spoke to his sister. Once Janice knew, Allison would very likely find out.

Gabriel looked ahead. "How about we just pretend this whole night never happened?"

"Gabriel—"

"You should get out of my car," he said. "Before somebody sees."

His derision stung, but it wasn't undeserved.

After I got out, he pulled the Jeep into a tight U-turn and drove off. The taillights retreated, disappearing in the distance. I stood there for a moment, shaking off the lingering sense of loss, the darkness of the night pressing in. Heavy clouds blanketed the stars overhead, the moon a pale sliver in the sky.

I started for the house.

Insects chirped. Wind and small animals rustled the trees and grass. I'd made this walk a million times before. It would take less than five minutes. And yet, I'd never been more conscious of how far back the neighbors' houses sat from the road. How wide the distance between each streetlight.

A chill skated along my shoulder blades and I shivered. I glanced over my shoulder, then toward the dense line of trees that bordered the rainforest. Maybe sending Gabriel away had been a mistake.

Would Mr. Alleyne or Brent follow me here? We hadn't seen anyone tailing us from the bar, but he wouldn't have to. It wasn't hard to find out where I lived. Everyone knew Muriel was my guardian, and to find Muriel all anyone had to do was look for the biggest house on the island.

I picked up my pace, my shoes smacking against the asphalt. The iron gates grew closer, the face of the house looming just beyond. Muriel's car wasn't there; no one was home yet. But a single light illuminated the front porch, warm and welcoming. I focused on it. Almost there.

I was just at the gate when something flashed in the corner of my eye. A dark figure darted out from behind the bougainvillea bushes. I turned and defensively raised my hands, but it was too late.

He grabbed my neck and pressed me against the iron bars. I screamed and a large, sweaty palm smacked over my mouth. The force of it knocked the back of my head against the gate. A spark of sharp, intense pain stole my breath.

"Don't do that!" Lennard's voice cracked, his sour breath hot on my face.

He looked awful, his hair a tangled mess. His nose and cheeks were sunburnt, his eyes bruised and sunken like he hadn't slept in ages. He wore the same clothes he'd had on at the shop a few days ago. From the smell, I was sure he hadn't changed since then.

"Where's my phone?" Lennard demanded. "And my wallet. I need it." He lowered his hand to let me answer.

"I don't have them." For the second time in one night, I'd been jumped. How did this keep happening?

"Then where are they? I know they're not at the shop."

Was I bleeding? Dizzy, I reached back and gingerly prodded the spot that hurt. My fingers came away wet. I held my hand in front of me and stared at the blood.

Lennard's eyes widened. He cursed and shrank back, putting some space between us. "I'm sorry. I shouldn't have—" He scrubbed a hand over his face. "I don't want to hurt you, okay? I just want my things. Just give me my things."

"I don't have them," I said again, then hesitantly added, "I . . . gave them to the police."

His mouth slackened. Even in the meager light from the porch, I could see the color drain from his face. "No, you didn't," he said, sounding more like he was trying to convince himself than interrogate me. "Tell me you didn't."

"I did."

The sound of a wounded animal pressed through his teeth. He folded his hands over his head, anguish carved into every line of his face. "Do you know what you've done? The great one makes no exception. I'm out of time."

"Who is the great one?" I asked, confused but distracted as I glanced over his shoulder, toward the road and the neighbor's house in the distance. Could I run? Would I make it? If I screamed, would anyone hear me? "I don't understand."

"It doesn't matter," Lennard said. Then to my surprise he started to cry. Thick tears streaked down his face. He bent forward, sobs bursting from his lips. "It's over. I'm done."

Perhaps I should've shouted for help, fought, or tried to run. But a strange sympathy had taken hold of me.

He pointed a finger in my face. "You were supposed to help me!"

"I really am sorry," I said, trying to calm him down.

Was he this scared of being caught? Did he think, now that the police had his phone and wallet, he couldn't keep hiding? Looking at his condition, I couldn't believe he'd want to continue living as he had the past few days.

"Aren't you tired?" I asked him. "Don't you think it's time you come clean?"

He shook his head. "You don't understand."

"I understand that it's hard to do the right thing. And I know you're scared. That's okay. It's natural."

Over his shoulder, a pair of oncoming lights appeared—a car approached. Muriel, probably. I didn't want to scare him off just yet. He seemed to be listening to me, taking in my words. Considering them. Maybe I could convince him to turn himself in.

It was strange: I'd been in two altercations that night and the one with the suspected murderer felt less threatening.

"You've done bad things, Len."

"I know," he whispered, so soft I almost missed it.

"And I think you also know what you have to do. Yes, it will be scary. But I promise, it'll be okay."

His gray eyes bore into me, desperate and unbearably sad. I got no anger or malice from him. Only fear and grim resignation. My breath hitched and I was struck by a sudden realization.

I'd gotten it all wrong.

We all had.

Lennard Bisson might not have been a good person. But he was not a murderer.

The headlights finally found us, catching us in the glare of the high beams. Len flinched like he'd been slapped. I tried to reach for him, but he was already retreating, sprinting away.

"Wait!" I shouted.

This was wrong, all wrong. He needed to stay and explain.

The car stopped and the driver's side door flew open.

"Selina?" Muriel sprang out. "Selina! What's happening? Are you okay?" A second later, she had me in her arms, crushing me to her. "Are you hurt?" She pulled back to look me over, fear etched on her face.

Behind her, Janice emerged from the passenger side. "What the hell is going on?"

I couldn't answer, still stunned. My heart thundered in my chest. Lennard moved quickly, nothing but a shadow now. He entered the forest, melting into the darkness.

Muriel let out a shriek. She'd found the blood on the back of my head. "What happened, Selina? Tell me what's wrong."

In my daze, I could only answer honestly. "I don't know."

CHAPTER
THIRTEEN

"And you're sure it was him?"

"Yes," Muriel confirmed before I could speak. "It was Lennard Bisson. The one in the newspapers. Isn't that right, Selina?"

"Maybe. I'm not sure. . . ." I shook my head, then winced as my skull throbbed.

Muriel clasped my shoulder. She'd barely left my side since bringing me to the medical center. It was at her insistence that the police came here to take my report rather than us going down to the station. When you owned more than half the commercial properties on the island, people tended to be accommodating.

The two officers spoke to us in the corner of the waiting room, the space conveniently empty at that late hour.

"He'd been hiding behind the bougainvillea bushes," I said, choosing my words carefully. A nauseous feeling rose in my chest. I had to force myself to focus. "When I got home, he jumped out. But it was dark and everything happened so quickly. Then Muriel found us, and he ran off."

"He was heading toward the forest," Muriel added, her words clipped with irritation. "We already told you what happened. Why are you still here, asking us the same thing over and over? You should be out there, searching for him."

"I understand, ma'am," Detective Clarke, the older officer, rushed to assure her. He had to be in his fifties at least, his black hair starting to gray at the temples. Despite his age, he had a baby face and a genial air of someone eager to please. "We're just trying to get as much information as we can in order to find him."

"Do you know why Bisson would specifically seek you out?" asked Officer Dannon. The short, thirtysomething-year-old seemed more immune to Muriel's status. Her directness drove most of the questioning so far.

I lifted my eyes to the ceiling as if thinking about it. The move made my headache worse, so I dropped it. "He rambled a lot of nonsense. He seemed . . . afraid. Thought he was being followed."

"And that's all?" Officer Dannon asked, scribbling away. All through the interview, she'd jotted notes on a small pad. At first, I'd mistaken her coolness for indifference, but when she looked up from the page, her gaze focused on me with a probing intensity and unconcealed skepticism. "If I remember correctly, the homes in that area aren't particularly close together, which implies that he specifically targeted yours. Why would he do that unless it was intentional? Unless he wanted to find you."

"How would I know what he was thinking?" I resisted the urge to shift in my seat. Any signs of nerves might be read as guilt.

My conviction to keep up the lie was fading fast. I should tell them. Admit that Lennard had been in the store. But then Allison would be so upset, and Muriel so disappointed. Plus, I didn't know how much trouble I'd get into for lying in the first place.

I already had a dicey relationship with the local police. Mummy's involvement in past cases had put some of them off, especially when she showed them up.

Then, after the attack on my parents, they'd interrogated me. Two large men sitting way too close, insisting I was lying. At one point, they almost had me convinced that I was. I'd never been so scared in my life. If Muriel hadn't shown up with a lawyer when she did, I might've said anything to end it.

"Can I show you a photo, Miss DaSilva?" Officer Dannon asked.

I looked at Muriel and she nodded. They probably wouldn't show me anything too gruesome with her right here. Not like last time.

"Yes," I said, and Officer Dannon handed me her phone. "Do you know what this is?"

The screen displayed a photo of a circular symbol. The same one I'd hallucinated in the cottage a few days earlier. The one from the scene of my parents' attack. Except this one had been drawn in chalk. Below it a few flecks that might've been blood stained the beige wall.

"Is that . . . ?" My words dried up as the implications sank in.

Where was this? Were those really flecks of blood? If so, whose? And why were they asking me about it?

"What is that?" Muriel plucked the phone from my hands. Her lips parted, her expression contorting with horror as she stared at the screen. "Why the hell are you showing us this? What is going on?"

"This was found in Kyle Gordo's hotel room." Officer Dannon's eyes raked over my face, searching for something. "I'm not sure if you remember, but it's very similar to the one found at the scene of your father's murder."

Yes, I remembered. Of course I did.

The symbol was not just similar; it was the same.

"What are you saying?" Muriel returned the phone, practically shoving it into Officer Dannon's hands. "You think there's a connection between that boy's murder and what happened to her parents?"

"We cannot say for sure, ma'am," Detective Clarke said.

"That's why we're asking," Officer Dannon added. A hint of accusation curled around each word as she asked me, "Do you know what this symbol is? Or why it would be at the scene of both crimes?"

My mind reeled with possibilities. Did Lennard know who'd murdered my father? Was he involved? I wished that I'd run after him tonight. I should've chased him down and demanded answers.

Ever since my parents' attack, I'd been navigating a labyrinth blindfolded. And now, when I thought I might've already faced the worst of it, a whole new level unfolded. I was plunged into the darkness all over again.

"Miss DaSilva?" Officer Dannon prodded.

I blinked, snapping back to the present. My head throbbed. "No. I don't know what it is."

"Are you sure?" she pressed. "The marking appears to be occult in nature. And it's no secret that your mother was involved in . . . unconventional practices."

"Excuse me?" Muriel seemed to swell with indignation, rising from her seat. "Now, listen, I don't know what lies you may have heard. Selina's mother was a renowned psychic." Her voice grew louder with each word. "She devoted her life to helping people and ensuring justice. You have no right to say—"

"Miss Muriel." The center's receptionist gingerly approached us. "We're terribly sorry, but we do have to ask you to keep it down. We have sleeping patients—"

"Me?" Muriel's tone sharpened. Her grip on my shoulder tightened. "With the amount of money I pump into this place, I should be able to say whatever I like, as loud as I—"

"Muriel." I touched her hand to get her attention. "My headache. It's getting worse. I don't think the painkiller is working."

She glared at the receptionist. "Well? You heard her. Can't you get her something?"

"Oh." The receptionist blinked. "No, I can't—"

"Then find someone who can!" She threw her hands up, exasperated. "Get Dr. Henry. Tell him we need him." Her attention returned to the officers. "No more questions. Selina has a concussion, for heaven's sake. What were you thinking, showing her something like that? She should be resting."

"Ma'am," Officer Dannon said. "We just have a few more points that need clarification. We need to know—"

"Selina?"

We all turned toward the entrance. Edward stormed into the room.

He approached us, his wide eyes never leaving my face. The wild, panicked air he carried reminded me of his performances for clients at the shop. Perhaps not as hollow, but just as melodramatic.

"What are you doing here?" I asked, confused.

"Janice told Allison, who told me what happened." He dropped into the unoccupied seat beside me, ignoring everyone else. "Are you okay?" He grasped my hand. "Why didn't you call me?"

"It's late," I said, pulling back, putting a little space between us. Public displays of affection made me cringe. I understood he'd been worried, but obviously I wasn't on my deathbed. "I'm fine. They've already checked me over."

"Thank goodness for that. But you're my girlfriend. You can call me whenever. It doesn't matter how late it is."

Detective Clarke cleared his throat, mercifully cutting Edward off. "As it's been established, time is of the essence. Could you please clarify where you were earlier this evening? You said you were dropped off at the bus stop. By who exactly? Was it a taxi? We may need to ask them if they saw anything."

"It was my son who dropped her off," Muriel answered before I did. "Gabriel Pierre."

My heart dropped. "How did you know?"

Muriel frowned as if puzzled by my question. "Because he called me. He said you were supposed to text him to confirm that you'd gotten into the house. When he didn't hear from you, he called me to check in."

Oh no. I'd totally forgotten. I started to reach for my phone, then realized that I didn't have it on me. I'd left it and my purse in Muriel's car.

"Gabriel dropped you off?" Edward asked slowly, each word heavy with confusion. "Why?"

Crap. This was exactly what I'd wanted to avoid. I turned to face him, my expression a picture of nonchalance. "I had a few errands to take care of. We ran into each other. Since it was dark, he gave me a ride home."

His brows knitted. "Why didn't you call me? I could've—"

"Sorry," Detective Clarke cut in. "What did you say his name was?"

"Gabriel Pierre," Officer Dannon said, frowning, her pen unmoving.

"You can find him working at the newspaper." Muriel's lips thinned at the mention of Gabriel's place of employment. "I'm sure he'd be willing to answer your questions."

"Miss Muriel." Dr. Henry entered the room. Upon spotting the officers, he stumbled to a halt. He adjusted his glasses, squinting at the scene as if trying to make sense of it. "You . . . uh, wanted to speak to me?"

"Yes," Muriel said. To the officers, she added, "That's enough for tonight. Selina needs rest. No more questions."

Neither officer appeared happy with this dismissal, but they left.

After they were gone, Muriel and the doctor discussed my medication. Muriel wanted the dosage raised, while the doctor politely explained why that wasn't possible.

Edward and I sat together, no longer touching, a noticeable space between us.

"What errands?" he asked, after a few minutes. His casual tone rang hollow.

"Nothing important. Just a few store-related things I had to drop off."

"Right," he said, his disbelief palpable.

———

An hour later, Muriel and I were back at the house. I prepared for bed, an unsettled buzzing beneath my skin. Instead of drinking my nightly cup of tea downstairs, as I usually did, I took it up to my room.

I sat against the headboard, sipping, the warm cup clasped between my palms.

Muriel knocked on my door and poked her head inside. "Are you sure you're okay with being alone tonight? You had quite the scare."

"I'm okay," I said, setting the empty cup on the bedside table.

"If you're sure. I am here if you need me. Your mother would never forgive me if I let something happen to you." With a small smile, she added, "And I'm also quite fond of you myself."

"Thank you," I said, hating that I'd made her worry. "Really. I swear. I'm okay."

"Okay." Muriel nodded, then watched me for a second longer, as if taking a second look to reassure herself. She flipped the switch and the room darkened. "Good night, love." She pulled the door in but did not shut it completely. A sliver of light from the hall cut across the floor.

Outside the window, the outline of a sparse plum tree swayed in the wind, the gnarled branches like emaciated hands clawing at the air. Sleep came upon me, tentative at first, like a wild dog nudging at helpless prey. Finding no resistance, it devoured me whole.

———

Mummy and I stood in the garden at the cottage. She had her watering can again. The maggot-infested red sludge poured from the spout. It seeped into the soil, rotting the plants.

Selina!

I lifted my gaze from the poisoned garden. He stood at the nearby window, staring out at us. His wound gleamed with blood and exposed tissue.

Most people didn't know that my father hadn't died instantly. Sometime after the attack, he'd woken up. The wound damaged the part of his brain that controlled reasoning, but the pieces relegated to routine and movement still functioned for the moment. Without understanding why, he got out of bed, slipped on his boots, and walked into the kitchen. He made a cup of instant coffee and stood at the window but did not drink. Then, in the bathroom, he washed his hands. Blood smears marked his movements, a trail for investigators to follow later.

Finally, he returned to the bedroom, the scene unimaginably gruesome, though he wouldn't have known it. Some instinct told him to sit on the floor beside my mother. That's where they found him.

I approached the window. Daddy smiled at me, his teeth stained red. One eye crinkled with mirth, while the other was embedded too deep in his head. Through the window, he handed me a pair of new sneakers. In a blink, they were laced up, on my feet.

We'd done this experiment before. I'd walk a specific path, and when I returned, he'd take samples from the soles of the shoes, examine the dirt and other particles, then guess where I'd been.

Sneakers on, I walked into the rainforest, though every cell in my body urged me not to leave my parents. I took the path that led to the lookout. The twenty-five-foot drop into the sea was a popular spot for teenagers and tourists. Despite several warning signs posted in the area, they'd jump, then make the half-mile swim to the beach.

It was dangerous. A local rite of passage. Jump a little too far in the wrong direction and you'd hit rock instead of water. That, plus the current and choppy waters made it difficult for people who weren't strong swimmers.

Gabriel had made the jump once. I'd backed out at the last second.

As I walked the path, the sun hung low in the crimson sky. Trees lined either side of me, the people hidden among them quiet, their dark silhouettes still behind the trunks and leaves. They said nothing, their silence anticipatory, like they knew something that I didn't.

Finally, the path opened up, ending at the cliff. Lennard waited for me at the edge. He stared at me, his eyes luminous and hateful. His skin appeared sallow and sagging, like melting wax. He wanted me to see this—whatever it was.

I wanted to run, but I could not leave, drawn toward him as if compelled by an invisible force. A string of fate tied us together. A link formed long before he'd walked into the store.

I stopped, standing before him, mere inches of space between us. A sudden fear swept through me, and I grabbed his arms, convinced he'd jump. He didn't flinch, as if he'd expected it.

When he opened his mouth to speak, he choked and coughed. Up came the stream of blood and maggots and chunks of rot. I closed my eyes too late. Some of it hit me, burning hot and acidic.

I woke up screaming and swiping at my face.

CHAPTER
FOURTEEN

Muriel tried to get me to stay home from work the next morning. Instead, I downed a few pain pills and proceeded with my usual routine, determined for things to return to normal as soon as possible. But when I got to the store and saw the people gathered around, I knew I'd made a mistake.

"Selina!" Allison caught me at the door. She tugged me inside, gingerly stepping around the broken glass. "I should've called you, but so much was happening, I forgot."

She wasn't the only one. After Lennard's surprise appearance last night, I'd forgotten all about the staged break-in. "What . . . ?" I gaped at the huge hole in the front display window, only half-feigning my surprise. "What happened?"

"It's bad. Really bad." She dropped her voice. "Don't say anything. The back room is still locked—"

"Hey!" An officer approached us. He held out an arm. "No customers. Not until we're done."

"She's not a customer." Allison gripped my arm. "Selina works here." With her chin held high, she tugged me deeper into the shop.

Souvenirs littered the floor, storage cupboards open, and containers overturned. My eyes snapped over to the safe. Another officer stood in front of it, examining the lock. Not just any officer—Officer Dannon from the night before. I stumbled and Allison steadied me.

"Sorry," I said, so confused. "What's going on?"

"It's bad. The police called me this morning. Somebody noticed the broken window and contacted them. They think *someone* broke in." She dipped her head and dropped her voice. "When I got here, the safe was open and empty."

"You think it was . . ." *Lennard.* I couldn't say his name. While her conclusion had been a part of my plan, this had not played out as I'd intended.

She nodded. "He must've broken in here after he attacked you."

Or, more likely, the other way around.

While Lennard held me up, he had mentioned something about knowing his belongings weren't at the store. At the time, I'd brushed it off. Now it made sense. He'd broken in, not found his phone and wallet, then come after me. When I'd busted the back door, he must've already passed through. Because I never ventured inside, I hadn't noticed the mess.

"I have no idea how the safe was open," Allison said, likely reading my alarm as shock. "I remember locking it before we left. But maybe I— Hey!" Allison pointed to the officer trying the knob for the back room. "That was locked. No one got in there."

"We have to make sure," the officer said.

"Well, I forgot the key at home, so it doesn't matter," Allison said.

The officer frowned, glancing at the door. His lips parted, about to say more, when another officer called out for assistance. Without hesitation, he returned to the front of the store.

"This is bad. So, so bad," Allison said. "At least now Len has what he wanted from the safe. He'll leave us alone."

Except that he hadn't gotten what he wanted. Because of me.

The image of his wide, fear-filled eyes flashed in my mind. A twist of guilt curled in my chest and I pushed it down. I shouldn't feel guilty for handing in his belongings. He might be a murderer, or at the very least he was involved somehow. He might've even had something to do with my parents' attack.

I'd done the right thing.

And yet . . .

"We've got to keep them out of the back room." Allison tugged on her braids. "They'll find the movie props, if we don't."

"Excuse me." Officer Dannon approached us. "Miss DaSilva." Though her expression remained flat, an unmistakable curl of distaste twisted around my name. "Interesting that I'm running into you. Again. You work here?"

"Yes," I said, finding it hard to focus on her questions while alarms blared in my head. "I help out."

"It's a shame what happened to the store. Do you have any idea why anyone would break in here?"

"Money?" I offered.

"The safe was empty," Allison chimed in. "I took the cash out yesterday. Nothing's missing, really. All this drama is unnecessary."

"I think I'll decide that," Officer Dannon said. "How many keys are there to the safe? And who has them?"

"Two keys and just me," Allison said.

"And the keys for the doors?"

"Again," Allison said, "just me."

"I see," Officer Dannon said. All the while, her focus never left my face. "And any idea why the intruder would need two points of entry—"

My phone rang. It couldn't have been better timing. I needed to get out of there, take a moment, and think. It wouldn't take a genius to link what happened to me last night to the store's break-in. Clearly, Lennard had been searching for me. This would only add to Officer Dannon's suspicions.

I pulled the phone out of my purse. Barely glancing at the screen, I said, "Sorry, I need to take this." Then I bolted out the back door. On the way, I passed a gloved officer dusting the handle.

They were taking prints? Panic snatched my breath before I remembered that, even if they did find anything, it was easily explained away.

I worked at the shop; I could have left fingerprints on the door at any time.

Seriously, I needed to calm down. And think.

"It's me," Gabriel said, when I answered the phone. "We need to talk."

"What—" I snapped my mouth shut and glanced at the officer a few feet away. He didn't seem to be watching me, but he could be listening.

As if hearing my thoughts, the officer lifted his gaze, meeting mine. I nodded in acknowledgment. Damn it. Walking away now might look suspicious. I had to watch what I said.

"This is not a good time," I told Gabriel. "The shop was broken into."

"Yeah, I heard. That's part of what I need to talk to you about."

"Oh." I drew a deep, steadying breath. The air was thick with humidity and the scent of wet dirt. Overhead, the sky drooped with miserable gray clouds. Today of all days, I'd have preferred the warmth of the sun against my skin, not the shadows pressing down on me. "Did you . . . give your friend the gift I gave you?"

"Yeah . . . I did," he said, picking up the meaning behind my coded message. "Look, it's not the best time for me to talk either. I'm at the office. Can we meet up later?"

"Where?"

"I've got an appointment with my new PT at the medical center this afternoon. I should be done by six. We can meet in your mother's room around then."

"I don't know . . ." It could be tough for me to get away. We usually closed at seven. Allison might find it suspicious if I asked to leave early.

"For heaven's sake, Selina. This is important."

"I realize that," I said through gritted teeth. I glanced back toward the store. The officer was no longer there. "Okay. I'll see what I can do."

When I returned to the shop, the officers were packing up and leaving.

"We'll be back later to follow up," Officer Dannon said. "If you do notice something has been stolen, or think of any more relevant information, please contact the station." She shot me one last look before joining the other officers in their retreat.

I stood beside Allison. "What happened now?"

"Not sure. Suddenly, they had to go." She crossed over to the front door and locked it—a pointless act, considering the huge hole in the window. "Maybe they finally found him. I'm not about to question a miracle." She spun to face me. "Okay, you start dismantling the props. I'll call the guys to come help us move them."

She reached into her pockets, pulled something out, and tossed it to me. I caught it, then looked down. The key to the back room sat in my palm. Of course she'd had it on her the whole time.

"You want to move them now?" I asked.

"We have to. We're lucky my father hasn't shown up yet, but he will. By then, all the movie props must be gone."

———

"The ocean called to Sam. He could not resist. Death tracked his steps like a most loyal hound, closer than it had ever been. He stayed the course, never wavering. In his hunt for the truth, he remained short-sighted, all logic and fear obstacles as easily overcome as the rocks beneath his feet.

"If only he'd looked ahead and listened beyond the sea's siren song, he might've seen the stranger lurking, or heard the wails of warning from the lost souls who perished before him."

"Sounds like Sam's in trouble."

I lifted my eyes from the page to find Gabriel standing in the open doorway. He held a bouquet of striped lilies, the flowers' burnt-orange color vibrant despite the washed-out hospital lighting. He'd brightened the room before even stepping into it.

I shut the book. "No, Sam *is* trouble."

Gabriel's brows inched upward. My tone had been a little more confrontational than I'd intended. But I'd been on edge the whole day;

my anxieties over Lennard, the police, and the store exasperated by a throbbing headache. It had only worsened with every passing hour.

"What are you reading?" he asked.

Seeing him in workwear was a bit jarring. I was so used to him in faded T-shirts and mud-stained shoes. When we were younger, he was always running, swimming, jumping off things—too active to bother with clothing that couldn't be carelessly ruined. He filled it out well enough now, though, the pale blue button-down flattering against his dark skin, the fit snug across the breadth of his shoulders.

"It's the new Samantha Lake." The second installment in the third series by Mummy's favorite author. I lifted the book so he could see the glossy hardback cover. She wrote sweeping Gothic mysteries that spanned familial generations.

He squinted at the cover. "Very new. I don't think that's out yet."

"You can borrow it, if you want." I rested the book on my lap. "I think Mummy must've signed up for some sort of subscription service. The latest ones keep coming in the mail."

Gabriel crossed the room. "Hey, Aunty," he said, pausing at my mother's bedside for a moment. Then he continued toward a small mahogany table that stood beside the window. "Patients in a coma can hear, right? I'm sure she appreciates you reading to her."

"Probably not," I admitted. "I've read three books to her so far. Every time, I stop about twenty pages before the end." I couldn't help but smile at his wide-eyed bewilderment. "I told her that if she wants to know the endings, she has to wake up to find out."

He shook his head. "That's . . . either brilliant or absolutely evil."

"I prefer to think of it as motivation."

"Whatever you need to tell yourself. I just hope you're ready to face the consequences when she wakes up." He removed the plastic hydrangeas from the glass vase on the table, replacing them with his bouquet.

I used to bring Mummy fresh flowers, too. Almost daily. She always seemed so at home among plants, whether it was working in her garden, or on rambling walks through the rainforest. It felt right that she should have some color—some life in the bland sterility of the hospital room where very little changed.

But then the flowers would die. And the routine of removing the remains had turned into another reminder of time passing. After a while, I stopped.

My smile slackened, then slipped completely. "The problem isn't her hearing. It's that her brain can't process what I'm saying. She doesn't know that I'm reading to her. She doesn't even know I'm here."

"I don't know about that." Gabriel faced me, finished with the lily arrangement.

For some reason, his energy was softer this evening. I appreciated it after the hellish day.

"Do you remember that time you tried to run away from home?" he asked. "We were about nine or ten. You and your mom were fighting—"

"And I came to your house." I had no idea where he was going with this. "Yeah. I remember."

He smiled—the first honest smile that he'd offered me since his return. Something in my stomach flipped in response. Until I realized, the smile wasn't truly for me, but rather for the memory.

"We hid you in one of our guest rooms," he said. "My parents were oblivious. We thought we'd gotten away with it. Then, in the middle of the night, your mother suddenly showed up. She found you and dragged you home."

"Yeah. Nearly scared me to death." She'd been so mad.

"Selina, she knew exactly which guest room you were in. As soon as Ma let her into the house, your mother went straight for it. No one had to tell her." He shrugged with an air of discomfort. "I don't know how your mother's gift works. But maybe, the same way she knew where you were then, she can tell that you're here now."

I glanced over at my mother.

Maybe.

Maybe not.

Hope was dangerous; I didn't want it.

"That's a nice thought," I said. "And I would like to think lugging through these melodramatic tomes is worth something. But in this book, the main character, Sam, is so annoying. He's constantly making the worst decisions. I'm ready to give up."

Gabriel lifted a shoulder in a half-hearted shrug. "Seems realistic to me. Most times, you don't know you've made a mistake until you're already in it. Sometimes not even then."

I eyed him, sensing some hidden meaning in his words. "Are you saying you never make mistakes?"

"I do. But I know when to stop. Some people can't help digging themselves in deeper."

"Wow." I snorted. "Tell me how you really feel."

"Well, what do you want me to say, Selina? You hid evidence, lied to the police, and possibly protected a murderer? And all for what? To help Allison, who treated you like trash for most of secondary school?"

So much for his softer mood. Already, we were arguing. This was a bad idea.

"Allison has changed," I said.

"Has she?" He tilted his head. "Because it seems like what she's asking you to do is incredibly selfish, which is very in line with the Allison I remember."

"You don't know how tough her father is on her."

"Maybe not. But I can tell you, whatever punishment she'd get, it wouldn't be obstruction in a murder case. He'd never allow it. Do you really think Chief Montgomery would go to the same lengths to protect you, too?"

"We've handed over the phone and wallet." I tried to explain my reasoning. "So it doesn't matter."

"Of course it matters!" He ran a hand through his hair, agitated. "The police already know you're lying. That's what I wanted to tell you."

"They do?" Well, I couldn't say I hadn't seen it coming. But if I weren't already sitting, I would've had to. "How do you know?"

"Cherice—Officer Dannon—is the friend I told you about. She said the only reason they haven't come after you yet is because all their resources are focused on finding Bisson."

"But—" I choked on my words, too stunned for coherence. Of all the people for him to be friends with, why did it have to be Officer Dannon? She'd been hostile toward me from the start. "This isn't fair. I haven't hurt anyone!"

"I know." The certainty in his tone mollified me. A little. "You're right. It isn't fair. But you know how the people here are. How they've treated you."

Yes, I did know. And I knew he did, too.

Because, in those dark days, when my family had been cast out and kicked down, when my classmates chased me with taunts and the wickedest words they'd learned from their parents, he'd been right there, running beside me. Facing it with me. That had been one of the reasons we'd decided we needed to get off this island.

One of the reasons I'd done everything I could to make sure he still left St. Virgil, even when I couldn't.

"I didn't come here to argue," he said, sounding defeated. "I just wanted to warn you about the police. And now you know." He headed for the door.

I jumped out of my chair. The book slipped from my lap, thumping against the floor. Gabriel turned at the noise. I caught up to him, grabbing his hand to make him stay.

Simultaneously, our attention dropped to his hand. Or, more precisely, my hold on it. I didn't know who was more surprised by the touch. Quickly, I let him go.

"Wait. Please," I said. When he didn't move, I took that as a sign to proceed. "Did Officer Dannon tell you about the symbol?"

"What symbol?"

"Last night, the police showed me a symbol that was found in the recent victim's hotel room. It was the same one drawn at the scene of my parents' attack."

His brows inched upward. "No, she did not tell me about that. It hasn't been shared with the press yet either. That would explain why they're so suspicious of you."

"And that's not all." I retraced my steps to the chair, pulled my father's notebook out of my purse, and held it out to him. "There's also this."

Earlier that afternoon, I'd gotten lucky: Allison had decided to close the shop early. After removing the props, all she wanted to do was hang out and decompress. I told her I had a bad headache to get out of it. Didn't even need to lie.

I'd had more than enough time to go home, grab the notebook, then get to the medical center.

"I found it hidden on my bookshelf in the cottage. Daddy put it there. I think he meant for me to be the one who found it in case something ever happened to him. It's a bunch of notes and articles about Maeve Downs and Elizabeth Alleyne."

"Your father worked on their cases?"

"He did for Maeve, but not officially for Elizabeth. Not that it matters, because he was a crime scene analyst. He examined the scene, then passed his findings to the investigators. It wasn't his job to figure out who did it or why, just the how. This is beyond anything he should've been working on."

Gabriel took the notebook and flipped right to the back.

"What are you doing?" I leaned closer to see what he was looking at.

"In a mystery, if you want answers, you go to the end." He turned to the last used page. Two long strings of numbers haphazardly scrawled across it. "Well, that's not as helpful as I thought it would be."

"But look at this." I took the notebook back for a few seconds, searching until I found what I wanted. "Look at the date on this article he clipped. It's only a couple of days before he was killed. He was still collecting information long after the cases had been closed."

"You think he might've found something the police missed? And whoever was responsible found out—so they killed him?"

"I don't know," I said, though I was relieved that we seemed to be on the same wavelength. "But after last night, seeing that symbol again, I can't help but think . . ."

"Your mother was right." He glanced over to the bed. "She was convinced Ken was innocent."

"Maybe," I hedged. "I wouldn't be surprised if Daddy was searching for some way to restore Mummy's reputation."

Gabriel returned his attention to the notebook. "Okay, let's say he did find something. What did he find?"

"That's why I need your help."

Gabriel lifted his eyes to meet mine. "Me? Why?"

"Because you've got connections to the police and resources at the newspaper. And because . . ." I shrugged. "I trust you."

He stilled, as if this surprised him. I hated the idea that he might think otherwise, but the softness creeping into his expression made me nervous, like I'd revealed something I shouldn't have. Like we were inching into forbidden territory. A boundary needed to be reestablished.

I cleared my throat and added, "If nothing else, I was with you when my parents were attacked, so I know for sure you didn't do it."

"Right." His jaw clenched and he dropped his gaze again. He flipped through the notebook pages, too fast to read anything. "So, what you're saying is—you want us to figure out what your father may have discovered, which might lead us to the people who murdered him. Which could then lead to answers about the recent murders. *And*, consequently, clear your name and help repair your family's reputation?"

"I know it's a lot."

"That's an understatement. I don't even know where we would start looking into this."

"Not *we*." I winced. This was the hard part—the part where I might lose him. "I want *you* to look into it."

"Me?" he said slowly, as if hoping I'd jump in to correct him. "But not you?"

"Gabriel, I can't—" A stabbing pain stole the rest of my words. It felt like a knife plunged through my left eye, angled upward. The doctor warned me there might be headaches after my concussion, but I hadn't been prepared for this. It felt like my skull was being split in two. I tried to breathe through it.

"You cannot be serious." Gabriel closed the notebook, too wrapped up in his anger to notice I was barely listening. "All this because you don't want to be seen with me? You're that afraid of what Edward and the others might think?"

"That's not it," I said through gritted teeth.

"Okay, then explain it to me. Give me one good reason why you wouldn't want to look into this yourself."

I couldn't answer. He wouldn't understand.

Up until a few days ago, I'd been building a stable, comfortable life, surrounded by people who were undeterred by my family's history. Then Lennard showed up, these murders happened, and now the darkness seemed closer than ever. I couldn't risk getting sucked back in or I might never find my way out.

"Right," he said, after a lengthy silence. "Well, if that's everything, I think it's time for me to leave." He tucked the notebook under his arm, about to take it with him.

"You're going to do it?" I asked. From his reaction, I'd thought he would refuse.

"Of course I'm going to look into it. But not for you. For her." He tipped his head toward my mother. "She and your father didn't deserve what happened to them." He reached for the doorknob. "Honestly, Selina, I never thought I'd be more disappointed in you than I was in those last days, when you did everything you could to push me away. But I think this might be worse."

His words punched the air out of me. There was no way he could've known. And yet, it seemed that he did.

"That's not what happened," I said. A weak defense.

He left, gently shutting the door behind him. I almost wished he'd slammed it instead. Then I could have been angry. Then I could have a reason to go after him and tell him off for making too much noise in a hospital. But I just stood there, quietly devastated.

After a few seconds of silence, my headache faded. I snatched the vase of lilies off the table and took it into the bathroom. I stuck it under the sink. It was just like Gabriel not to think that the lilies needed water. He was all grand ideas and big pictures, and never details or practicality.

Pain exploded, the headache rebounding with startling severity. A familiar spicy scent burned my nose. I bowed my head and closed my eyes, blocking out all light. When I reopened them, Daddy's reflection stood behind mine in the mirror. His skull was still cracked, minced brain matter exposed, blood leaking down the side of his face. I covered my mouth but failed to stifle a scream. The vase shattered on the tiled floor. Glass, water, and flowers everywhere.

When I spun around, he wasn't behind me.

My back hit the edge of the sink. I checked the mirror again, my hand pressed against my mouth. My reflection stared back at me, wide-eyed and desperate.

I scrambled out of the bathroom. How could this be happening? He'd been right there. I'd seen him. Even now, the spicy scent lingered in the room. I recognized it as my father's favorite cinnamon gum. This time, he'd appeared far more vivid than at the cottage, almost tangible. Whatever was wrong with me seemed to be getting worse.

It had to be the painkillers. Or a symptom of my trauma. Or stress. Or maybe the head injury, which I'd read could have unpredictable effects on the brain. Hallucinations weren't an impossibility. It could also be the other thing. But Muriel had confirmed that *seeing things* wasn't a part of the gift.

And yet, despite my rationalizing and reasoning, a chill skittered across my skin. I knew what I had to do.

I threw the door open and sprinted out of the room. In the hall, I nearly collided with Dr. Henry, then dashed past him. Gabriel had just left the lobby when I caught up to him.

"Forget what I said. I'll help. I'll do it."

It seemed to take him a second to process my appearance. I must've looked as frantic as I felt. "You want to?"

"Yes. I need to."

Gabriel frowned. "You *need* to?"

"Yes." I straightened my posture, trying to look confident despite my breathlessness. "Are you going to tell me no? You said that I should."

"I'm not telling you no, Selina. I'm confused. You just told me—"

"Forget what I said. I need to know what happened that night. The truth." Then perhaps I'd stop seeing these awful things.

I did not believe in ghosts, but I did believe in the insidious effects of guilt. Hadn't I seen enough affected clients to recognize it in myself? It ensnared them in the past, causing them to believe in the impossible, like their dead husband standing beside their bed.

I wanted to move on. But clearly, there was a part of me that could not let go. Not yet.

"You were right," I said. Waiting for other people to find the answers certainly wasn't working. If this was my only chance to make things right, then I had to take it. "I need to do this for my parents. They deserve better."

He scrubbed a hand through his hair. "I've got whiplash, but if that's what you want, of course you can help."

"Thank you."

The images that haunted my dreams were now bleeding into my waking moments. If I ever wanted to settle into a new life, I had to stem the overflow. I had to face the darkness and give a name to the unknown terrors. Maybe if I proved the culprit was nothing but flesh-and-blood human, I wouldn't be afraid anymore.

Then I could finally let go.

"Don't thank me," he said, turning away. "This was your idea. Plus, I learned a long time ago, no matter what I say, you're going to do what you want anyway."

CHAPTER
FIFTEEN

Two days later, Muriel announced the avocados were ready for picking. We'd been planning for this since weeks ago, when the very first blooms appeared in the grove. Our two-person harvests had become a semiregular activity. Over the time I'd lived with her, there'd been soursops, sapodillas, oranges, and rosy-pink shaddocks. We'd carted home buckets full of ruby-red governor plums and pomeracs, handfuls of which never made it to the house, too tempting not to be eaten immediately.

The remaining fruits were harvested by workers, boxed, and sold to groceries and roadside vendors. One of the many businesses that fell under Virgil Enterprises.

I'd welcomed the mindless, familiar activity. It never occurred to me that this time Janice might want to join in.

"I couldn't believe it!" Janice said. Her relentless complaints filled the peaceful pocket of time tucked into the hour after dawn. "The one bottle of moisturizer costs seven hundred dollars. It spilled all over an eight-hundred-dollar dress. That's fifteen hundred dollars of damage in one go. Now, tell me why the airline shouldn't reimburse me for it? If their clumsy baggage handlers can't properly handle baggage, that's their problem."

"I'm so sorry, sweetheart," Muriel said sympathetically. "Can you get another?"

I ached to point out that it was her problem for not properly sealing her absurdly expensive moisturizer, but I held my tongue. Instead, I plucked another of the pear-shaped fruits. Turning it over in my hand, I inspected the rough green flesh, then carefully placed it into my bucket.

Unlike me, Muriel had been overjoyed that her daughter tagged along. With Janice at school for most of the year, and Gabriel's estrangement, Muriel had made no secret of the fact that she missed her children.

"I did put in an order for a new dress," Janice said. "But last night, the vendor emailed to let me know the delivery will be delayed. It'll arrive after the anniversary party. Which is just my luck. I shouldn't even be surprised."

Muriel set her bucket down and used a hand towel to dab the sweat from her face and neck. "You have other dresses you can use."

"I can't wear a dress people have already seen me wear before." Janice reached up and tugged on a too-young avocado. She yanked and yanked, shaking the branch, until the fruit snapped free. She tossed it into her bucket.

"A little gentler," Muriel said. "If it's ready, you just have to give it a little twist." She demonstrated how to pick the fruit to her daughter, who wasn't paying attention.

My phone vibrated in my pocket. A message from Allison.

Shop closed today. Don't come in.

That didn't sound good.

Her father had shown up at the shop, as she'd predicted. But by that time, we'd had all the stolen movie props removed. Allison explained away the rest of the items in the back room as the decor for a themed tea shop. She said she'd hoped to surprise him with the business idea.

Chief Montgomery had listened to this explanation with a stern-faced silence. He'd barely looked at me and said little. By the time he'd left, I couldn't tell if he'd bought it. I suspected, whatever his thoughts, he didn't want to voice them in my presence.

I messaged Allison back.

Everything ok?

Her reply was quick.

Replacing window and door today. Busy now. Talk later.

Something still felt off. But a day without work presented an opportunity. I messaged Gabriel.

Hey. Free today if you want to meet up.

"You know what you should do?" Muriel was saying to Janice. "You should try Miss Heather's shop. You might find a dress there. Unless you want to take the ferry over to the sister island?"

Janice wrinkled her nose. She sidestepped a protruding root, heading right toward a patch of stinging nettle. I opened my mouth to warn her, but she stopped in time.

"Well, I suppose I don't exactly have much of a choice," she said. "I'll see what Miss Heather has first. Hopefully, she's got at least one dress that was made in this decade."

My phone chimed. Gabriel had messaged back.

Meet me at the Amber at noon.

At the Amber? As in the hotel right down the street from the shop? What if Allison saw us there together? How would I explain it to her?

Almost as if hearing my silent freak-out, Gabriel texted again.

The service entrance around back.

Oh. That should be fine, then. I replied: Pick me up?

This time his response took a little longer.

Not today.

"Selina?" Janice said, with a touch of exasperation.

I looked up to find them staring at me expectantly. "Sorry, what?"

"The party?" Janice said. "Are you and Edward color-coordinating your outfits?" She held up her hands, as if to ward off a comeback. "I know it sounds cheesy. But it could be cute if done right."

"Uh, no." I glanced at my phone, unsettled by Gabriel's most recent reply. "I'm not even sure what I'm wearing yet."

Janice smirked. "Who is texting you so much? Is it Edward? Speak of the devil."

I tucked my phone away. "Yeah." Whatever. So long as she didn't know it was Gabriel, it didn't matter.

"Why's he bothering you this early?" Janice smirked. "You must have him down bad." She pulled out her phone. "You know what? I'll text him. Let him know he needs to chill. No one likes a guy who's too desperate."

"Wait—don't." Crap. Why did she have to be like this? "It was actually Allison. She wanted to let me know that the shop was closed today."

Janice arched a brow. "Okay . . ."

Muriel looked over at us. A small frown marred her face.

I shifted my bucket to the other hand, embarrassed to be caught in a lie. "Since it looks like I have the day off, I'll go visit Mummy."

"Again?" Muriel asked, drawing closer. "You've been visiting her a lot lately. Is everything okay?"

"Yeah. I'm just missing her more than usual." I shrugged. "You know."

"Yes, of course." Muriel pulled me into a side hug, her perfume choice for that day fruity and heavy, like red wine. "I understand completely."

I knew that she did. Sometimes, I felt so alone in my grief, but I hadn't been the only one who'd lost loved ones. Muriel had her best friend ripped away, and her husband just a few years before that.

Janice tilted her head to the side, watching us. "I have an idea," she said suddenly. "Why don't we go dress shopping together, Selina? Allison can come, too."

Muriel clapped her hands together. "That sounds like a fantastic idea."

"Actually . . ." I hesitated. Spending more time with Janice sounded like an awful idea. "I might wear something I already have."

"No worries," Janice said, shrugging. "Just an idea. I thought it might be fun. Let me know if you change your mind."

Great. Now, I sounded like the mean one.

"Oh, look at that," Janice said, distracted by an abnormally large avocado. She hurried over to it.

"How are you, really?" Muriel lowered her voice, even though Janice had moved beyond earshot. That morning, Muriel wore a yellow-and-white sundress, a matching hair scarf tucked under a wide-brimmed hat. Sturdy gray gardening gloves protected her hands. "Have you been sleeping okay?"

I grimaced, embarrassed. "Did I scream again last night?"

"Yes. Janice was still out, so I knew it had to be you."

"I'm sorry." Over the past few days, my nightmares had intensified. The dream—meeting my parents at the cottage, then Lennard at the cliff—did not change, but each time it felt a little more real. Last night, I could practically smell the rotting plants and taste the acrid blood Lennard coughed in my face.

"Don't apologize for that," she said. "You've been through so much. We all have." She adjusted her hair scarf, then drew her hat a little lower. "I think it's important that we stick together. Which is why I would love it if you gave Janice a chance. Nothing would make me happier than seeing you two girls getting along."

I tried to hide my cringe at that comment, but it must've slipped through.

"Yes, I know she can be difficult sometimes. But she's been through a lot, too." Her voice dropped to a near-whisper. "After my husband went missing, both she and Gabriel took it hard. I tried my best. Gave them everything they could want. For Janice, it was things. For Gabriel, it was space. I'm afraid I've made a mess of both. At least she still wants to be around me."

Muriel glanced away for a moment. "Do you know Gabriel hasn't visited me since his first day back to the island?" When I shook my head, she said, "I think I pressed him too hard about VE. Now he's barely talking to me. He won't even consider coming to the anniversary party."

"That was never his thing, though," I offered in a slight defense, though I could not say for who.

She gave me a small smile. "Yes, I'm aware that, in the past, he'd stay at the party just long enough to show his face before running away. Never knew for sure where he spent those nights." She raised a manicured brow. "I don't suppose you'd know anything about that, do you?"

"No idea," I said. Despite my attempted flippancy, my skin burned with embarrassment.

She laughed, but very quickly her humor died. "I wish I could convince him to come this year, even if it's just for a few minutes. Then the governor would see our family still intact. Still together. Even if it's for one night." She shrugged. "I suppose that's not really an option for us."

"I'm sorry," I said.

"Don't apologize, love. It's not your fault."

But it kind of was. Gabriel wasn't just staying away from the house because of his mother. He was also staying away because of me.

"At least I have Janice," she said, shooting her daughter a small smile.

My heart twisted, resolve faltering in the face of her palpable hurt. She'd done so much for me. More than I could ever repay her for. What was one favor?

"Hey, Janice!" I called out. "Count me in for dress shopping." Maybe schoolyard grudges didn't need to persist beyond graduation. Edward, Allison, and Muriel had all asked me to give her a chance. A few hours with her wouldn't kill me.

Janice blinked, seemingly surprised, before a smile blossomed across her face. "Sure. I'll set it up."

"Great!" I said, and hoped my enthusiasm sounded sincere.

Muriel beamed, seemingly delighted either way.

I'd never considered how many people must be employed by the Amber. The kitchen alone seemed to house a village. When the door opened, I had to take an involuntary step backward, the bustle and heat overpowering. Cooks and servers darted in every direction. Wares clattered. Pots sizzled and steamed over blazing fires.

No one paid attention to us as we passed through.

A few seconds earlier, a young man with patchy facial hair met us at the service entrance. He wore a navy-blue security uniform, his thick neck and stout frame giving him a distinctly rectangular shape. Without a word, he ushered us inside, his steps quick, as if he was aware of some impending threat that we weren't privy to.

We followed him through the storage room and the kitchen, then cut around the perimeter of the busy dining room. The recent murders didn't seem to have deterred many guests, almost every table occupied. We stopped at a set of silver elevators. As we waited for one to arrive, the guard shot me a furtive glance.

Gabriel made the introductions. "Alexander, this is Selina. Selina, Alexander."

"Yeah, I know." Alexander stared ahead.

Instantly, I was on edge. What did he know exactly?

Alexander tugged on his sleeve. "You didn't tell me you were bringing anyone with you."

He sounded upset. Was it because Gabriel brought someone? Or because that someone was me?

"Is that a problem?" Gabriel asked.

The elevator arrived and we stepped inside. The doors slid shut. Alexander's eyes finally met mine in the reflective doors. "Maybe not," he said. "Considering the strange things that happened in that room, it's not a bad idea to have someone like her around."

Ah. Got it.

Gabriel bristled, shoulders squaring. "What's that supposed to—"

"Tell us what happened," I cut him off.

Alexander dropped his gaze. "When we get to the room, we'll talk."

Gabriel shifted his feet, impatient. He wanted my attention, but I ignored him for the moment. He might have been offended by Alexander's attitude, but I knew an opportunity when I saw it.

We exited on the eleventh floor, our footfalls muffled by carpeting. I shivered in the air-conditioning. As we passed the closed doors, I occasionally caught the sounds of life behind them.

Alexander stopped at room 1165. After a glance back the way we'd come, he used a key to unlock the door and rushed us inside. Once we were in, the door closed, he let out a loud exhale, like he'd been holding his breath for a long time.

"This is it," he said in a near-whisper. "We need to keep it down. No one's supposed to be in here."

"Are the police still collecting evidence?" Gabriel asked.

"Since they've cleaned, probably not." I nodded toward the two single beds. They'd been made with fresh white sheets. The scent of chemical cleaning products lingered in the air.

"I don't know," Alexander said. "Management just told us no one is allowed inside. I'm taking a real risk bringing you in here."

"Which we appreciate." Gabriel handed him a folded bill.

Alexander stuffed the cash into his pocket before I could get a look at how much it was. "Thanks. I appreciate the contribution to the therapy I'll need once this is all over." He tried to laugh, but it started listless and broke off abruptly.

"What happened here, Alexander?" I said, using the serene voice I'd perfected over many months of psychic sessions.

Alexander scrubbed a hand over his mouth. "It started with complaints from the room below. Loud footsteps. Dragging furniture. My coworker Randy was patrolling at the time, so I came up here to deal with it. We were the only two on duty that night."

While he spoke, I drew closer to the right-side bed, certain the symbol in Officer Dannon's picture had been drawn just above it. Now there was nothing. They'd cleaned it—and the blood—off.

"I arrived at the door," Alexander said. "And I was about to knock, when, suddenly, I heard a scream. A horrible sound. Like someone in terrible pain." His voice shook. "It was the worst sound I've ever heard."

"I'm so sorry," I said. "That must've been awful."

"It was. It really . . ." He sighed. "So I radioed Randy. Told him to get up here and bring the key. All the while, the noises continued. I kept knocking, trying to get in." His Adam's apple bobbed as he swallowed. "Sometimes, I wonder . . . if I'd just brought the key up here with me . . . if I'd just gotten into the room sooner . . . But I didn't think . . ."

"It's not your fault." I backed away from the bed and turned to face him.

"Yeah," Gabriel said. "No one expects something like that to happen."

"But I should have known it might be something strange." His nose wrinkled in an expression of anger and disgust. "Weird stuff happens in this hotel all the time. Whispers and odd noises. Everyone knows not to go into the basement alone. Things disappear down there. *People* disappear down there. Like, you know what happened to the guy who built this place, right?"

"Of course," Gabriel said.

"No," I lied. Several versions of the local legend circulated around the island. It could be useful to know which one he believed. Not to mention, it seemed like Alexander had been holding too much in and needed to talk.

"The man who designed this place," he said, "Reid Morgan. He disappeared while it was still under construction. The rumor is that someone murdered him, and the reason they never found his body was because it's hidden in the walls of this building. This hotel was cursed even before it opened."

I nodded to show that I was listening. Understanding.

He'd relayed the classic, vanilla story. Other versions spiced it up by pointing to Morgan's wife or the hotel's owner, Ian Amberson, as the killer. Some suggested there was no murder at all. That Morgan created a maze of secret tunnels within the hotel walls, then crawled inside one day, got lost in his creation, and never found his way out. They said he was still in there, rattling around, forever searching for an exit.

"I used to be skeptical about the stories, until that night," Alexander said. "While I was waiting in the hall, Randy on his way with the keys, I heard someone inside this room. They spoke to me."

"What do you mean?" Gabriel asked.

"I mean just what I said." Alexander's shoulders curled in a self-conscious gesture. "After the screaming, everything had gone silent. Too silent. So I leaned closer. And that's when I heard it. A whisper, right on the other side of the door."

"Kyle Gordo had his throat cut," Gabriel said. "How could he speak? Unless this was before . . ."

Alexander swallowed. "I don't think it was Kyle talking. I think it was someone else. *Something* else."

"What did the voice say?" Gabriel asked.

I found myself leaning in, needing to know.

"Open the door," Alexander said. *"Don't turn on the light."*

CHAPTER
SIXTEEN

For a few seconds, none of us spoke. The temperature of the room seemed to dip in the wake of Alexander's enigmatic words. I suppressed a shiver.

"What happened next?" I prompted him.

"Randy arrived," he said. "By then, some of the guests had come out of their rooms to see what was happening. One lady tried to help me, because I'd tripped like a fool. I was still on the floor when the door opened. The room was dark, but the light from the hall fell over him."

"Kyle Gordo?" I asked.

"Yes. He was hanging over the edge of the bed, like he'd been trying to drag himself out of it. His neck was cut, blood everywhere. On the walls. On the floor. The way he was facing, his eyes open—it was like he was looking right at us."

"Was he still alive when you found him?" Gabriel asked.

Alexander shook his head. "He . . . wasn't the first dead body I've ever seen. When I was about thirteen, my friend and I were walking to school one morning. We found a body lying in a drain. We thought it was a mannequin at first. He didn't seem real." He swallowed. "What I mean to say is—you can tell when they're gone. He was dead."

A brief silence trailed his words. I could not help but picture a young version of Alexander and his friend, and the fear they must've felt.

Alexander sniffed and cleared his throat. "Anyway, when we finally got into the room, it was empty. No murder weapon. Nobody else but the victim."

"How did the murderer get out?" I asked. The door to the hall seemed to be the only viable way in.

"I overheard the police talking." Alexander folded his arms, his biceps straining against the unyielding material of his uniform. "Maybe they've changed their minds since then. But, at the time, they thought that the murderer must've left before I arrived. They told me the shouts and sounds came from Kyle Gordo. That I must've been mistaken about the whisper. But I know what I heard. The voice came from in here. Right through that door."

The walkie-talkie on Alexander's holster crackled to life. A voice distorted in the static came through. "Alexander . . . at the desk. No one on cameras. What . . . Over."

Alexander cursed and turned his back to us. "Alexander here. Took a bathroom break. I'll be right back." He faced us again. "We've got to wrap this up."

"Can we have a few more minutes to look around?" Gabriel asked. "We can stay on our own if you need to get back. We'll be careful."

Alexander wrinkled his nose. I could see the no coming before he said it.

"You're right, Alexander." I let my gaze drift across the room. I pressed my hand against the cool wall. "There is something wrong with this place. A malevolent presence. I can feel it. But it's hidden under all these layers of energy. So many lives have touched this space. If we had more time, I could filter through and do a full reading."

Alexander watched me, a wariness in the downward tilt of his mouth. "You really think you can help?"

"I believe so. There are things that the officers would have missed. But my mother taught me ways of finding them. Of hearing them."

"The police didn't believe me about the voice. But I know what I heard."

"I believe you." I approached him slowly, carefully, and rested my hand on his arm. Initiating physical contact was always a risk. Some people would not react well to it. But instinct told me that Alexander needed something more substantial than verbal reassurance.

"I can tell you're a good person, Alexander." I held his gaze, ignoring the burn of Gabriel's glare on my back. "You faced an awful situation and have taken on the burden of knowing a truth that the police do not believe."

Alexander's lips pressed into a tight line, trembling slightly.

"But I'm here now," I said. "Let me take this burden from you. We'll find out what happened."

"Alexander!" the voice blasted through the walkie-talkie.

Alexander jumped, turning away from me, scrubbing a hand over his face. "I'm on my way," he shouted into the walkie-talkie. To us, he said, "You have ten minutes. That's it. Leave through the same door you came in. By the time I check back here, you better be gone." He yanked the door open and left the room without looking at us.

The second the door shut, Gabriel asked, "What the hell was that?"

"That was me buying us a few more minutes. You're welcome." I crossed over to the window to inspect it. The tiny push-out only opened a few inches. Far too small for an adult to slip through. Not to mention we were several floors up and a straight drop down to asphalt. "I, too, accept tips, if you're handing out more cash."

"No, that was something else," Gabriel said. "That was . . ." He couldn't seem to find the words, but the revulsion in his tone said enough. "How exactly would you know he's a *good person*? You just met him."

"Everyone wants to believe they're a good person. I was telling him what he wanted to hear. It's the easiest way to get a person to like and trust you." I crossed over to the beds and knelt on the carpet. I checked the space under one, and then the other. Nothing.

"For someone who despises her mother's reputation, you're quick to use it when it suits you."

Oh, he had no idea.

"It worked, didn't it?" I yanked open a slim closet. It stood against the wall perpendicular to the door. "I don't get why you're making a big deal about it. Alexander clearly knew who I am. All I did was play into the expectations he already had."

"Expectations that you hate."

"Yeah, well, sometimes it's easier to swim with the current than against it."

"That makes no sense. It is always easier to swim with the current."

I paused to look at him. "Do you have to be so pedantic?"

His lips twitched in amusement. "You know how I feel about a lazy metaphor."

I snorted, then returned my attention to the closet. It held a few shelves, an open safe, and a fold-down ironing board. Theoretically, a person could have hidden in here, then snuck out after the body was discovered. But that seemed incredibly risky. Surely, security would've checked the room, and this would be one of the most obvious places to search.

"Look, I know it's dicey," I said. "But Alexander feels guilty about not getting into the room sooner. And he's embarrassed that the police didn't believe him about the weird whispering. All he needed was for someone to believe him. Was it such a bad thing to say what he wanted to hear?"

"Yes."

I flinched at the venom in his tone and turned to face him.

Gabriel hadn't moved from where he stood. "You don't believe him any more than the police did. At least they weren't trying to deceive him."

Wow. Okay.

Now I knew for sure that I'd made the right decision not to tell him about the fake psychic sessions. He'd never understand.

"Are you saying you *do* believe him?" I asked.

"Yes."

I gaped at him for a moment, before snapping my mouth shut. "Of course you do." I didn't know why I was surprised. He believed anything.

"*But* I don't think it was a ghost." Gabriel's lips curled into a grin that was a bit too smug and far too attractive. "He did hear a voice. But I doubt the person was talking to him."

"How?"

"Come on, Selina. We've seen this before. Remember the Curious Capers? Book five?" He shook his head when I continued to stare blankly at him. "It's a locked-room murder."

I shut my eyes, overwhelmed by disbelief. "Gabriel . . ." He was drawing information from a children's book. "You can't be serious."

"Oh, but I am. And in a locked-room murder, there are three common solutions. The first is that the witness is in on it and lying, which we can scratch off. I mean, I believe Alexander."

I did, too, so I didn't object.

"Second is that the murder occurred earlier or later than we think. This seems to be the police's theory. But, again, if we believe Alexander, we can scratch that off as well. Third, and the one I think is most likely, the murderer somehow got out of this room without being seen."

"How?" I demanded, unimpressed by his storytelling lesson. "No one could've hidden in here or slipped past a hall full of people. Unless there was some other way—"

Gabriel's smile widened. Our thoughts aligned, finally on the same page.

"You can't be serious," I said, even as I glanced around the room again, searching for something I'd missed. "Reid Morgan's secret tunnels? Those are just ghost stories. Rumors at best."

"Come on. How else would the murderer leave without anyone seeing them?"

Many years earlier, Gabriel's father spent a year living at the Amber. At the time, Gabriel and I were too young to fully understand how close his parents had come to splitting, everything clearer in hindsight. It helped that we'd been enchanted by the hotel—Gabriel's father's suite on the fourteenth floor far more spacious and luxurious than the matchbox we currently stood in.

When Gabriel had visited his father, he'd bring me along. We'd spend hours exploring every inch of the room, searching for an entrance to the tunnels.

"Back then we'd only looked in my dad's suite," Gabriel said. "Maybe we had the wrong room." He approached the open closet. "Come, look at this. I saw it when you were flirting with Alexander earlier."

"I wasn't *flirting*."

He ignored me, pointing near the back of the closet. Faint indentations marred the carpet. "Do you see that?"

I bent over to have a closer look. "You've got to be kidding me."

"When the voice said *open the door*, they didn't mean the door to the hall. They were talking about a secret passageway."

I knelt on the floor. "I'm impressed. You lost me a little with the Curious Capers, but you turned it around in the end."

"Thank you," he said. "And for my next trick . . ." He pushed on the wall.

Nothing happened.

"Hold on . . ." He tugged on the ironing board, twisted the metal rod for hangers, then dragged his hand along the edge of the frame. "Give me a second."

While he poked at various items, I examined the back of the closet. I don't know why, but some instinct prodded me to shove the lower wall as hard as I could.

It swung open, exposing the dark passage inside.

CHAPTER
SEVENTEEN

I cleared my throat to get Gabriel's attention.

He released a nearby light fixture and frowned, looking incredibly disappointed. "Of course you found it first. As usual."

I knew immediately that we were both thinking of the treasure hunts his father used to plan for us, when we were children. Mr. Pierre would hide an object in a room or the yard, and Gabriel and I would compete to see who could find it first. I almost always won.

"Oh, did I ruin your big moment?" My tone dripped with self-satisfaction. "I'm sorry."

"No, you're not. We both know you enjoy it."

I laughed, and his answering smile ignited a pleasant hum beneath my skin. I'd forgotten what it was like to have my mind read—to be so aligned that we knew what the other was thinking about without it being said. It was far more exhilarating to be understood than play the eternal enigma, constantly holding a piece of myself back.

No. I shook the thought away. That wasn't fair to Edward.

I returned my attention to the small door, pushing it a little wider, meeting the resistance of a spring-loaded hinge. If I let go, it would slam shut.

Shifting onto all fours, I peered inside. "It's too dark. I can't see anything."

"Here." Gabriel activated the flashlight on his phone and handed it to me.

I took it and aimed it through the opening. A person would have to crawl through the door, but the space behind the wall opened up—high enough to stand but narrow enough to make me nervous. The gray walls appeared to be outfitted with exposed brick and pipes, and there were wooden beams above. A short ledge gave way to a descending staircase on the right.

"There are steps." I retracted from the entrance to look at him. "That would explain how the murderer got out. And all the disembodied voices and strange sounds in the walls." Nothing supernatural about it.

"Right," he said, straightening up. He started unbuttoning his shirt.

"What are you doing?" I demanded as he proceeded to strip off his shirt, revealing a thin white undershirt and a lot of rich brown skin. He had more scarring than I'd realized, including a line over his left shoulder that appeared to be surgical. I had the wild impulse to press my lips against it, which prompted me to look away.

"I'm taking my shirt off, obviously," he said. "In case it gets dusty in there. I've got to go back to work after this."

Okay, but he could've given me a warning. It was just his shirt, no reason to be this flustered, and yet my skin burned with mortification. I almost pointed out that his pants would get dirty as well but decided it might be better that I didn't.

"I'll go." He shook the shirt out and left it on the bed. "You wait here and keep the door open. Now, before you argue with me—"

"Okay."

He snapped his mouth shut. "Okay?"

"Yeah." I had no problem with that. "Confined spaces aren't my favorite."

If I didn't know better, I'd say he looked disappointed. "Thought you'd argue with me about who gets to go inside," he said. "This feels too easy."

I rolled my eyes, exasperated. And mildly amused. "I mean, you don't have to go in there if you don't want to."

"This is a secret passageway, Selina. There's no way I'm not going in. This is a dream come true."

A few seconds later, he crawled through the opening. Immediately, he started sneezing. "How's it going?" I handed him his phone. "Still living the dream?"

He mumbled something that I missed, then sneezed again.

"What do you see?" I asked.

"Dust," he said. "And . . . more dust."

"Apart from that."

"It's a spiral staircase. Seems to be in good condition. I'm ninety-nine percent certain that I'm not going to fall through to a painful death." A worrisome *crack* filled the passage. "Ninety-eight percent."

"Please, be careful," I begged, almost wishing that I had put up an argument to go inside. Almost. "I highly doubt they've been upkeeping this place. Whoever 'they' may be."

How many people did know about this? Were there other passages? Why had it been built in the first place?

I pulled out my phone. Using the flashlight, I kept an eye on Gabriel until I couldn't see him anymore. As the minutes passed, I grew more and more nervous, straining my ears, listening for some sign of him down there.

I crawled forward, stopping about halfway through the entrance. One hand held my phone, the other I used to balance on the stone floor. A musty heat permeated the air. Instead of shining the light down the stairs, I examined the space around the panel door.

To the left, what I'd assumed to be a solid wall did have a small square opening. It could've been a vent of some sort. I shone my light into it and saw no end. A small person might just fit in there, wriggling along their stomach, their hands tightly clamped at their sides. With one of my feet pressed against the panel to keep it open, I crawled deeper into the passage to get a better look.

A hand reached out of the vent, its fingers curled over the edge, jet-black and hairy.

No, not fingers. Legs.

A spider.

It darted out and scurried up the wall. I screamed and dropped my phone, backing away from the vent. The panel slammed shut without my foot to hold it, sealing me in darkness.

"Selina!" Gabriel shouted. "What's wrong?"

No, no, no . . .

I reached for the panel door, running my hands over the sides, feeling for a handle. The edges fit smoothly into the wall, no place to pry. Nothing to grip. Along my skin, I felt the skitter of imaginary legs running along my arm and up the back of my neck. Tangling in my hair. I shook and patted myself down.

"Selina? Answer me!"

The spider wasn't on me. Not yet, anyway. "I'm okay!"

With shaking hands, I patted the dusty floor until I found my phone. When I did, I lifted it, the freshly cracked screen lighting up. I shone my light around the area, muttering a string of curses, searching for something—*anything*—that could trigger the small door to let me out. I couldn't find anything. Not even the spider.

"I'm coming down!" I called out. There was no way I'd stay up here with that thing lurking around.

While I hurried down the narrow stairs, the dull thumps of Gabriel's footsteps grew louder. After a few seconds, we met.

"What are you doing in here?" he asked. "I thought you were waiting in the room."

I squinted against the glare of his flashlight. "There was a spider."

"A spider?" His voice dropped with dry incredulity.

"A big spider."

"Unless the spider was big enough to toss you in after me, you're going to need to give me more than that."

"Can you lower your light first? I feel like I'm in an old Hollywood movie interrogation." When he did as I asked, I explained what happened, growing more embarrassed with each word. "It was an accident, okay? Let's keep moving. The more distance we put between me and it the better."

"I don't understand. How can you be afraid of spiders when you spend so much time in the rainforest?"

"There's a difference between seeing one out there and getting trapped with one in a closed space."

"We aren't trapped." His voice softened. "We have our phones. I can call Alexander for help. But if I do, he'll try to get us out as soon as possible. I want to see where this leads first."

"I'm not sure that's a good idea." I glanced back the way we'd come. No one knew we were in here. What if something happened to us? Or our phones stopped working for some reason? My battery already sat at a discomforting 20 percent.

"Come on," Gabriel assured me. "It'll be fine."

I hesitated for a moment, then relented. With the spider back there, I didn't have a choice. The only way out was down.

And so, we went. Gabriel illuminated the way forward, while I swept the walls and the area behind us, looking for clues but also ensuring that we didn't have any eight-legged stalkers.

Sweat bloomed across my skin. My curly hair lifted in the heat. It felt like a heavy blanket smothered the air, making the enclosed space feel even smaller. Even Gabriel kept tugging on the collar of his undershirt in an attempt to cool down. The fine hair at the back of his neck plastered against his skin.

"You're not claustrophobic, right?" I asked, perhaps a little too late.

"No. But if you're wondering if I have a fear of being trapped down here and starving to death, the answer is yes."

"Don't be ridiculous," I said. "You'd die from dehydration long before then."

He let out a bark of startled laughter.

"It wasn't *that* funny," I muttered.

"Not that," he said. "I just remembered my shirt. Alexander's going to find it when he checks the room."

"I left my bag, too," I realized.

"What's he going to think? The both of us gone and our things are just there? Will he assume that the ghosts snatched us?"

I pressed my lips together, fighting back my laughter. But it was too late. All I could do was picture Alexander gingerly lifting the cotton shirt, staring at it with wide-eyed horror. "Snatched you right out of your shirt?" I said, and broke.

"We shouldn't laugh," Gabriel said, gasping for breath. "We're terrible people. Plus, the guests outside might hear us through the walls."

"Yeah. They're out there thinking, *Wow, those ghosts sure sound like they're having a great time.*"

"Stop it," he said, but neither of us did for another minute.

The part of my brain not dying of amusement noted how strange this was. Not being trapped in a secret passage—though, that was admittedly unusual—but laughing like this. With Gabriel, of all people.

Despite myself, I felt a flush of pleasure. I used to bend over backward, pulling out every joke, every trick, just to hear his laughter. It was embarrassing, honestly. But back then, I hadn't even noticed or cared.

When we mostly sobered, we started downstairs again. Now and then, one of us would break, setting off the other. As time passed, though, the staircase twisted on and on, almost dizzying as it ceaselessly unfolded. Our humor faded.

"This feels like more than eleven floors," Gabriel said.

I agreed, though it was difficult to tell for sure. "My phone's battery is low." The flashlight was draining it faster than usual.

"Turn it off for now. We'll be okay using mine."

I didn't like the idea of having less light, but I hated the thought of completely draining my battery even more. The second I swiped the flashlight off, the wall of darkness around us pressed in closer. It rested like a weight against my back.

"Why couldn't you pick me up this morning?" I asked, mostly to fill the silence.

"Had a bad night last night," he said gruffly. "My arm was hurting more than usual. It's okay now, but I didn't want to risk driving this morning."

My chest clenched with concern. "Does that happen often?"

"Sometimes. Mostly during the night."

"How——" I started, then broke off the question.

"How what?" He glanced over his shoulder. "How bad is it?"

"Yes. But I wasn't going to phrase it like that."

"You almost didn't ask at all." His steps slowed as he spoke. "It could have been worse. Or so the doctors tell me. Most of the damage was to my axillary nerve and deltoid muscle. If I take it easy, there's just a dull ache and some numbness. Every few days I'll randomly get an intense shooting pain, but it passes. The day-to-day stuff is usually no problem, but you won't catch me cartwheeling or deep-sea swimming anytime soon."

"I'm sorry," I said.

"Why?" he asked. "It's not your fault."

Except, in a way, it was.

He never would've gotten onto that plane if it wasn't for me. I'd pushed him into the breakup, made him so upset that he'd felt the need to leave for university early.

"It's an adjustment," Gabriel continued, unaware of my internal self-recrimination. "But it's part of my life now and I'm learning to live with it. If anything, I'm just glad to be here. In an actual *secret passage*." The awe in his voice inspired a twinge of fondness in my chest.

This was a huge mistake.

I hadn't been lying when I said that I did not trust anyone as much as him. But I'd also never loved anyone as much as him. All too easily, I could see us falling back into our old ways, which could not be allowed.

Gabriel would be leaving St. Virgil in a few weeks. Dredging up old feelings would only cause problems. A year ago, he'd almost given up university to stay here with me—something I couldn't let happen then, and I wouldn't allow it to happen now.

When all was said and done, I couldn't leave St. Virgil, and the last thing he needed was a reason to stay.

As soon as this makeshift investigation ended, I would reestablish the distance between us. Our breakup might have been painful, but I'd do it again. I'd do it a hundred times, if it meant that he'd have a chance at the life he always wanted. A life he could not have with me tying him down to this island.

"Do you have a photo of the symbol?" he asked, breaking the silence. "I want to try looking it up online later."

"I can draw it out for you," I offered, trying to shake my lingering despair. I needed to focus on the present. On this investigation. "I think it might be a sigil, though."

"A what?" he asked.

"It's a symbol used in rituals. It represents a magic user's desired outcome, like designating sacred spaces or invoking entities. Like spirits, demons . . ." I waved my hand dismissively. "All that stuff."

"Demons?"

I give him a flat look, though he wasn't facing me to see it. *"Anyway,"* I said pointedly, "I've been searching for the symbol online and in books for the last two years. I haven't found an exact match yet. At least I hadn't until Officer Dannon showed me that picture."

"You're sure it was the same symbol at both scenes?" he asked.

"Yeah. Positive."

When the police questioned me, after my parents' attack, they made me look at pictures from the scene. While most of that day remained a blur in my memory, those photos were burned into my brain.

"I honestly thought the symbol didn't mean anything," I said as we picked up our pace a little. This did feel like way more than eleven floors. "My theory was that the murderer only put it at the scene to mislead people. They wanted everyone to think that my parents' attack had something to do with the occult. Because apparently my mom's the devil or whatever."

"Maybe," he agreed. "It could also be that whoever's behind the recent murders just copied it. They might want to link them with your parents on purpose."

"Why would someone want to do that?"

"To throw people off." He shrugged. "I might be overthinking it."

"Well, I do have a running list of suspects for my parents' attack, whether it's related to the recent murders or not."

"Like Marlon Alleyne?"

"Yeah." I grimaced, remembering Mr. Alleyne's angry eyes and sour breath on my face. "He's number one. Along with Brent and the rest of their family. They blame Mummy for Elizabeth's murder."

"And, as recent events would suggest, they're not afraid to get physical." He paused, then added, "Although . . ."

"What?"

"Nothing," he said. "Who else is on your list?"

I could tell he had something more to say, but I let it slide for now. "Then there's Detective Nickolas Legrand."

"A police officer?"

"Former police officer. He oversaw Maeve Downs's and Elizabeth Alleyne's cases. He blamed Mummy for Ken's acquittal in the first trial. He was one of the officers who interrogated me after my parents' attack."

Gabriel's lips curled with distaste. "I remember him. He questioned you without an adult present. Ma made a big stink about it. Wasn't he suspended from the service?"

"He was. Then he got mad about the suspension, had a very public argument with Chief Montgomery, and got fired."

"Good riddance."

"Agreed. All thanks to your mom. She stepped up for me." I almost ended it there, but then I remembered my conversation with Muriel that morning. "Since I've moved in with her, she's done so much for me. I try to be good company, but she still seems a bit lonely. Just this morning she mentioned how much she . . ."

My words dried up as I became conscious of a clicking noise behind us. I stopped and glanced over my shoulder, my vision useless against the prevailing dark.

"How much she what?" Gabriel asked.

"Misses you," I finished, only to startle when the clicking happened again. The eerie, unpleasant sound chilled my blood.

"I'll bet," Gabriel muttered, continuing downstairs, taking the light with him. I hurried to catch up. The clicking grew louder, now followed by a heavy slide, like something dragging on the walls or on the floor. The rhythm was too irregular to be mechanical.

"Do you hear that?" I asked.

"What?"

"A clicking noise?"

"You mean our footsteps?"

Click, drag. Click . . . drag . . .

"No."

If the sound was footsteps, they weren't ours.

He sighed. "We must be near the bottom by now. I've got to get back to the office."

"Are you seriously telling me you don't hear—"

"Wait." Gabriel stopped. "I think this is it. Yes, look!" He lifted his phone a little higher. The light skimmed along the stairs, hit a corner, and climbed up a wall. A dead end. He focused on another crawl-sized cut-out. "This must be the exit."

"Great. Let's go."

Click . . . drag . . . Click . . . draaag . . .

How could he not hear that? Unless it was another hallucination.

But this wasn't like seeing my father in the mirror. When I'd seen him, yes, I'd been afraid, but mostly I'd felt disappointment, and an unbearable sadness that cut right through me.

Now, in addition to my fear, I felt anger and hunger so sharp it could bite clean through flesh. Rip muscle from bone. This awful, ceaseless starvation was all-consuming, pressing into my stomach and carving me out.

Gabriel stooped down to inspect the door. The clicking and dragging picked up speed.

"Just push it," I said.

Gabriel did, but the door stopped about an inch wide, meeting some resistance. He readjusted his stance, then pushed again. "Something's blocking the other side."

"Push harder."

"I got it," he said before giving it a hard shove. This time, it opened. A cacophony of falling objects followed. He stuck his head out. "It looks like some kind of cleaning closet. I knocked over a pile of detergent containers."

The clicking grew louder, reverberating off the walls, so much closer than before. I felt the echo of each drag like nails across my skin. "We need to get out."

"Let me go first to make sure it's okay," he said.

"Fine." I didn't want him in here with whatever that was either. If only he'd move faster. The darkness behind us felt heavier, burdened with the unseen.

When Gabriel crawled out, he took the light with him. With the last barrier removed, I was consumed by the inky black. Something shifted behind me, moving, running. Almost here.

The instant Gabriel cleared the space, I darted out after him. I slammed the panel shut behind me and held it there.

Gabriel turned his phone light on me. "What the hell?"

I couldn't speak, heart in my throat. I knew what I'd just experienced wasn't real. Very likely a side effect of my concussion and the meds that lingered in my system. And yet, I couldn't take my back off the door. I couldn't move, terrified that at any moment it would fly open, unleashing the unseen horror.

"I'm . . ." I cleared my throat. If I told him about the concussion side effects, he might exclude me from the investigation, thinking I needed to rest. Or, worse yet, he might believe it wasn't the concussion at all. "I'm a little more claustrophobic than I realized."

"Why didn't you say something?" He held out a hand to help me up.

I hesitated, listening for a few seconds. When I was sure the sounds behind the door had stopped, I accepted his hand, drawn upward on shaking knees. His fingers enfolded mine in a warm, gentle hold. It felt like a lifeline in the dark, drawing me back to safety.

"Are you okay now?" he asked, close enough that I could smell the traces of his cologne on his skin.

I stepped away, slightly dizzy. "Where are we?"

"Let's find out." Gabriel opened the closet door, then traced his light over the outer room. It was bigger than I'd expected. Cardboard boxes, cleaning supplies, and old furniture were stacked on top of one another. Exposed pipes and wiring lined the walls. What appeared to be a giant water heater hummed in one corner.

"I think it's the basement," he said.

"The one where people disappear?" I laughed, jittery as the adrenaline continued to wear off. Light filtered around the edges of a door across the room—our way out, I guessed. I crossed over to it, frustrated when Gabriel didn't follow. Instead, he returned to the closet.

"What are you doing?" I went after him, terrified that he'd reopen the passage.

"I think I saw something earlier. I just need to check."

I found him inspecting the area around the panel. "Do you see any way to open it from this side?" he asked. "Unless I'm missing something, this only goes one way. How did the murderers get into the room?"

"They could've propped it open ahead of time," I suggested, though I saw no reason why we couldn't discuss this outside. In the light. "Or they used another passage."

"You think there are others?"

"Maybe," I said. "The only thing I do know is that this proves the murderers weren't ghosts. Or demons. Nothing supernatural about it."

"I . . . wouldn't close off the possibility just yet."

"What? Why?"

"Come. Look."

I joined him, my stomach sinking with each step. His flashlight illuminated a spot low on the wall. As I drew closer, I saw what he saw. Just under the panel, a very familiar symbol had been outlined in white chalk.

CHAPTER
EIGHTEEN

We reunited with Alexander, retrieved Gabriel's shirt and my purse, then showed the rattled security guard the hidden opening to the passageway. Alexander agreed to tell the management about it without mentioning us. He didn't want anyone to know we'd been in the room any more than we did.

While Gabriel returned to work, he let me wait in his apartment. I spent the early afternoon researching and resisting the urge to snoop through his things. He'd collected a surprising amount of information on the recent murders, some of which I'd already known, but quite a lot that had not been reported in the papers.

Kyle Gordo was an Australian living in London. He'd recently signed a contract with an international modeling company. He kept a well-curated Instagram and a professional website, but no other social media. Friends called him a career-driven workaholic. He never withheld an opinion or money, simultaneously spoiled and overly generous.

The second victim, Chord Grayson, was eighteen years old, born and raised in LA. He'd become a social media celebrity after amassing millions of followers over the last year. His mother and his friends were currently on the island, heavily involved in the search for Lennard. Both Chord and Kyle died of blood loss.

Kyle showed defensive wounds on his hands, but Chord had none. The police suspected that they had been drugged first. Incapacitated to make it easier for the killer or killers. But they awaited confirmation from the toxicology results.

Then there was Lennard Bisson, the main suspect. He'd worked part-time at a café in Florida. What I'd assumed was family money had likely come from the abrupt sale of the home he'd inherited from his parents. He had no living family, but a persistent girlfriend who'd made several social media appeals for him to contact her. According to her, he'd just left their home without any reason one morning. I wasn't surprised to find she was the same auburn-haired girl from the photos on his phone.

All three guys came from different places and moved in different social circles. They had nothing in common. If it weren't for Len and Kyle sharing a room, it might've been difficult to connect them at all.

By the time Edward called me, I'd resorted to going through my father's notebook again, sure that I'd missed something.

"So we're color-coordinating now?" Edward asked, his laughter crackling through the phone. "I didn't realize we were one of *those* couples."

"What?" I flipped to the last page. Whether or not Gabriel was right about finding answers at the end of the book, if Daddy had written these numbers, then they must've meant something.

"According to Janice, that's our plan for the party," he said. "I also heard you two are going dress shopping together. My favorite color is light blue, by the way. Like a clear afternoon sky. Peaceful and delicate."

"I don't think either of those words has ever been used to describe me." My fingers dragged across the page as I counted ten digits in the first number, and seventeen in the second. My father's handwriting was so bad that I had trouble deciphering some of it. The third digit of the first number could've been a four or a nine. Unless it was a seven.

Edward laughed. "Perhaps not, but my parents would love it. Which reminds me, about the dinner—how's tomorrow night?"

"Tomorrow night?"

"For the dinner? Remember, we talked about you meeting my parents?"

"Right. Yeah, that sounds good." I tilted the book sideways, trying to see if that helped. Without thinking, I muttered aloud, "Six, two . . . *four*?" It had to be.

"What? Are you listening to me?"

"Sorry, I'm just a little distracted. Trying to read this number." Belatedly, I threw in, "It's for Muriel." It was a clumsy cover, but I didn't want him asking questions. "The handwriting is confusing."

"A phone number?" he asked. "Six-two-four is an area code for the sister island."

"No, it's not . . ." Wait. Was it?

I rewrote the digits, spacing them out as a typical phone number. When it worked, I stared at the page, speechless. It took me a while to realize Edward was still talking.

"I've got to go," I interrupted him. "Call you later."

"But tomorrow night—"

"Dinner with your parents," I confirmed, and hung up.

A few hours later, Gabriel returned to the apartment. By then, I'd practically memorized my father's notebook, read through all the notes, and combed through most of the victims' social media. Chord's pages took the longest due to the sheer volume of content he'd put out.

"It's a phone number," I said, the second Gabriel walked in.

He stalled in the doorway, seemingly taking in the scene. I waited for his reply, confused, and trying to view his apartment from his perspective. I had made myself comfortable, my shoes off. Hair loose. Perhaps sitting on the bed crossed a line, but the desk chair had been far from comfortable, and he'd been gone for hours.

"Gabriel?" I pressed.

He cleared his throat. "Yeah, sorry." He shut the door and dropped his duffel bag on the desk. "What were you saying about a phone number?"

I lifted the notebook. "On the last page. The first number. I called it and you'll never believe who it belongs to." Without giving him a chance to guess, I blurted out, "Carla Paul."

"Who?" He unzipped his bag and retrieved his phone.

"The lawyer who represented Ken Thomas."

He plugged the phone into his charger, then froze. "So, we were right. Your father must've found something that proved Ken didn't do it. That's why he contacted Ken's lawyer."

"*Or* it could've been another step in his investigation," I pointed out. "Daddy could've been trying to see what information the lawyer knew about the case."

"I'm pretty sure that's not how lawyers work. They can't just give out information about their client's cases."

"Okay," I said, slightly frustrated. "But you're making some huge assumptions."

"Not assumptions." He knocked his fist against his stomach. "A gut feeling."

I rolled my eyes, clearing up the mess I'd made of the bed. "Can we please try to stick to something more substantial than *feelings*?"

"If you insist. But the only person who'd know for sure is Carla Paul. What did she say when you called?"

"Nothing. She wasn't available. I left a message, but the person I spoke to was kind of rude and dismissive. We may need to call back."

"That's disappointing." Gabriel went to the set of drawers and pulled out a T-shirt and a pair of jeans. "But good job figuring it out. Is the other number a contact, too?" He took the clothes into the bathroom and shut the door.

"No," I said, lifting my voice so he could hear me. "It's too long." After organizing the notes into piles, I set them on the desk. "There's something I've been wondering about, though."

"What?" he called back.

"How did they know about the secret passageway? Think about it."
I stood in front of his small mirror and scooped my hair into a pony-tail. It was a slapdash job without a brush and product. "Kyle was rich and could've afforded a nicer suite, so he and Lennard must've specifically requested that room. That means they already knew about the passageway."

"Now who's making assumptions?" he said.

"It's not an assumption. It's a deduction."

"Now you're the one being pedantic."

I glared at the door. "Are you going to use everything I've ever said against me?"

"Not *everything*." He emerged from the bathroom wearing faded jeans and a worn black T-shirt that looked soft to the touch. It took me a second to remember what I was talking about.

"What I'm saying is . . . according to everything I've read, this was Kyle, Chord, and Lennard's first visit to the island. They have no rela-tions living here. No ties to St. Virgil at all. So, how did they know about the passageway in the first place?"

"It would make sense that there's at least one local involved. I've suspected we were dealing with a group of people for a while now."

"You never mentioned that."

"It's just a working theory." He retrieved his phone and stuck it into his back pocket. "What if the symbol is related to this group? Like a calling card they use to identify each other. Or to summon something they believe in."

"And the victims were a part of the group?"

"Possibly. Or they could've just been unlucky. Used as part of some sort of ritual."

I didn't like that idea at all. "But how would my parents fit into this?"

Gabriel snatched his keys off the desk. "Well, I doubt they were a part of the group. Not if your father was investigating them."

Though his words made sense, he seemed to be overlooking one important point. Even if my father had nothing to do with it, we couldn't rule out my mother. "Do you think—"

My phone rang, interrupting my question. We both looked over to the desk, where Edward's name lit up my screen. I crossed the room, snatched it up, and silenced it. "I'll call back later," I mumbled, then went about retrieving my shoes.

"Why?" he asked with a casualness that rang hollow. "I don't have a problem with you taking the call now. Do *you* have a problem with taking the call now?"

I sat on the edge of the bed, lacing up my shoes, my silence as incriminating as anything I could say. Maybe more so.

"You haven't told him about any of this, have you?" he asked.

I winced, fumbling the laces. What did he want me to say? Of course Edward didn't know. He would never be okay with me spending this much time with my ex-boyfriend. And I couldn't even explain why to Edward without revealing our investigation. It wasn't that I didn't trust Edward with the details; I just preferred to keep this part of my life away from him.

"Amazing." Gabriel's anger tasted sulfuric, like the air around a used match. "At least you're consistent."

"What's that supposed to mean?" I demanded, sitting up.

He walked out of the apartment without answering.

———

Twenty minutes later, we were in his Jeep, heading east, toward the handful of villages scattered throughout the more rural side of the island. It had been ages since I'd driven this way. All the changes surprised me. Until recently, the pothole-ridden roads had been bracketed by farmlands, wild brush, and the occasional cluster of tin-roof houses. Now smooth asphalt cut through several commercial development sites, each in various stages of completion, the Virgil Enterprises sign plastered across many of them.

"Are you going to ignore me the whole way there?" I asked, pushing back the loose strands of hair that whipped against my face.

"I'll speak if I have something to say." He turned the Jeep onto a dirt street. Long grass crowded either side of the road.

As we drew closer to the village that I used to call home, my anger at Gabriel tangled with old memories and anxieties. With each passing second, I grew more firm in my resolve that I should not be here.

Hell, I was beginning to think that I shouldn't have gotten involved in this investigation at all.

If anything, my situation had only gotten worse. Gabriel was mad at me. The hallucinations persisted—the freaky clicking and dragging sounds of the hotel tunnels forever engraved in my memory. And now, to top it all off, I couldn't shake the suspicion that my mother had been involved in her own attack.

Did she know who this group was? Had she been a part of it?

Soon enough, we entered the village of Whimshaw. Multicolored houses lined the road, each one separated by wire fences or wooden gates. Some had small gardens or trimmed lawns. As we passed, dogs barked after the Jeep. Curious residents watched us from their covered porches.

Did they recognize me? It wasn't too long ago my family had left.

We parked next to the church my father used to attend. The one that strongly suggested he stop coming after his marriage, some of the other parishioners no longer comfortable with his presence.

Crabwood trees covered the cemetery tucked beside the ornate building. Brightly colored flowers—both real and fake—adorned some of the graves, while other plots were unkept, folding back into the wild. In this area, it was understood that your land needed to be constantly reestablished, or else it would be taken, either by the forest or someone else. And even then, due to circumstances beyond your control, it could still be lost anyway.

Gabriel cut the engine and got out. When I didn't follow, he finally looked at me for the first time in what felt like ages. "Aren't you coming?"

I shook my head. "This was a mistake. I shouldn't have come here."

Gabriel gripped the edge of the door with his hand, his body sagging with exasperation. "This was your idea. You wanted to talk to the former detective."

"Legrand will never talk to me." Because of me, he'd gotten fired. We'd be lucky if we weren't run off his property immediately. "We should just go."

Gabriel hung his head, silent for a long moment. "No," he said, straightening up. "I still want to ask him some questions. I'll tell him I'm doing a story about the *unjust* circumstances of his firing or something like that."

"If that's what you want. I'm not leaving the car."

Gabriel said nothing, his jaw clenched tight. He silently restarted the car, lowered the windows, then tossed me the keys, before walking away.

I watched as he crossed the road, headed toward a blue one-story house. Patterned ventilation blocks underlined the galvanized roofing. When he rang the bell on the gate, the wooden door opened. A young woman in a graphic-print T-shirt and denim shorts walked out to meet him. After a few seconds of conversation, she let him inside.

I reclined my seat a little, prepared to wait. But as the minutes passed, the day's heat permeated the Jeep, roasting me inside. The wind that filtered through the lowered windows made little difference.

A group of preteens stepped out of the church—two girls and three boys. They noticed me, whispering to each other as they passed. I recognized their emerald-green-and-white uniforms. I'd attended the same school not too long ago.

Through the side mirror, I watched as one of the boys turned around to look at me. While the rest of his group walked on, he remained. With his hands at his sides, his posture pin-straight, he reminded me of a soldier, unnaturally still.

As I stared, waiting for him to do something, a jagged laceration bloomed across the side of his forehead. Skin broke, blood spilled. The features of his face morphed into something more familiar. I twisted around, the seat belt cutting into my torso. With trembling, fumbling hands, I undid the buckle so I could get a better look—

But no one was there.

Loose leaves tumbled across an empty street. The children were gone, if they were ever there at all.

When I turned back to the mirror, my father's face filled the reflection, so close that I could see the gouged skin and the crusted blood around his wounds. I screamed and jerked back, falling across the seat. I closed my eyes, trying to blot out the image, but I could still smell the cinnamon.

He lingered beside the door, a heavy presence. When I finally worked up the courage to open my eyes, he'd moved, no longer beside the car. He was cutting across the cemetery, heading for the tree line. I knew exactly where he was going.

Compelled by a force I could not name, I got out of the car and followed him.

CHAPTER
NINETEEN

One minute I sat alone, the next Gabriel was there with me. He gently shook my shoulder, calling my name. I lifted my gaze to meet his.

His expression briefly brightened with relief before clouding with concern again. "Are you okay?"

I glanced around, honestly not sure. The sky had darkened, cloaking us in pink twilight. I was sitting in the center of the foundation that was once my home. The charred carcass had long been cleared away, tufts of grass and weeds sprouting from cracks in the cement. With no one to care for it, the traces of our old house had almost succumbed to the flora surrounding it. Soon it would be like we'd never been here at all.

Gabriel bent to meet my eye level, his concern a gentle brush across my face. "What are you doing?"

I didn't have an answer for him. Nor did I remember the trek out here, my last memory following Daddy across the grave-lined path. I froze, gripped by the terrifying realization that I'd lost time.

"Is something wrong?" Gabriel asked.

Yes, obviously. I manifested a hallucination of my father and followed it into the forest, and I couldn't even remember doing it. But I could not tell him that. As freaked out as I was, if he knew something was wrong with me, he wouldn't let me help investigate.

Then again, maybe that would be for the best. I couldn't be sure anymore.

Slowly, I exhaled, assessing my surroundings again, trying to make sense of my actions. Why was I here? My subconscious must've wanted to see it, though I did not know why. It was strange returning to this place, so many memories simultaneously unraveling.

I hadn't been here since it happened. Never really wanted to come back.

"Did I ever tell you, on the night of the fire, I saw them?" I said without thinking. Perhaps it was a symptom of my anxiety, but the words spilled out. "People were hiding behind the trees, watching us as we left the house. My parents didn't notice them, but I did."

By the time we'd returned home, the place had been engulfed, the flames licking the sky. The fiery glow was visible for miles.

"Our neighbors just stood there," I said. My eyes focused on a spot beyond Gabriel, toward the forest. "They watched it burn. No one called emergency services. No one tried to help. The officer in charge told me it was something called the bystander effect. Supposedly, when there are a lot of people around, any one of them is less likely to help because they all assume someone else will."

I didn't believe that back then any more than I did now.

The police never made any arrests. After a quick investigation, all they had for us were stiff platitudes and the advice that we should relocate. Muriel offered us the cottage and that was where we decided to stay.

"You never told me," he said.

"I didn't tell anyone."

Though I'd never thought the neighbors would resort to arson, when I'd seen them, hiding in the trees that night, I knew they were up to no good. But I'd said nothing, consumed by a bitter certainty that their retaliation had been inevitable.

"I'm scared," I confessed. "What we're doing—what if we find something that shouldn't be found?"

"What do you mean?"

I half-heartedly gestured toward the area where the house once stood. "When this happened, I blamed Mummy, though I knew it wasn't fair. I wanted her to admit that she was wrong about Ken, but she wouldn't. And Daddy had defended her, like he always did, even though she had ruined our lives." My breath hitched as I remembered the ugly words I'd slung at them. "We were arguing about it right up to the day I lost them, and I've hated myself for it ever since."

I raked my hand through a tuft of grass, manipulating one of the blades so it wound around my finger. "What if we find something that shows that Mummy did have something to do with the attack? That she is the reason that Daddy's gone and she's lying in a hospital bed?" I lifted my gaze to meet his. "She's the only family I have left. I don't want to be mad at her anymore."

Gabriel knelt in front of me. "I don't know what we might find—if we do find any answers at all—but one thing I do know is that your mother loved you and your father. I don't think she would've purpose-fully put either of you in danger."

I drew a deep, steadying breath. "I hate that I have these doubts about her." Just like those mean-spirited islanders who said my mother deserved what happened to her. That she was paying the price for consorting with the supernatural. I never wanted to think like them.

Gabriel glanced away, toward the trees. The leaves shivered in the wind. A flock of parakeets squawked as they sailed overhead. Gradu-ally, I grew twitchy in the silence, increasingly self-conscious about all I'd said.

"What are you thinking?" I finally asked.

"That you make it very hard to stay mad at you."

"What?" I wasn't sure if I should be offended, after all I'd shared.

"You have a very real reason to not want to be here." He faced me, not quite meeting my eyes. "And yet you are here, digging into your past. A past that I'm sure you'd much rather forget. I'm sorry for not realizing sooner how hard this must be for you."

I stared at him, words knotted in my throat.

"In my experience, not knowing is so much worse than any truth," he said. "But that's a decision you need to make for yourself. If you want out, I understand. I can continue looking into this on my own."

He lifted his eyes to meet mine. While his offer seemed sincere, I knew I could not let him do this on his own.

I exhaled, steeling my resolve. "No. I don't want to be a bystander that does nothing again." And I doubted my subconscious would let me, even if I wanted to. "I want to help this time."

I just didn't know if I could handle another fire. I'd lost too much already.

Gabriel smiled—a *real* smile. At me. For me. "Okay," he said softly. Then a bit louder, he repeated, "Okay!" He rose to his feet and held out a hand. "Come on, it's getting late. We don't want to get caught out here after dark."

I took his hand, ignoring the spark that ignited on contact. Once I was on my feet, I quickly let go. After a quick look around for my handbag, I realized that I'd left it in the car. "How long has it been since we got here?"

"About an hour. A quarter of which I spent looking for you."

"Sorry," I said. "I shouldn't have abandoned you to deal with Legrand on your own. It's just that, coming back here, everything felt so intense. It messed with my head."

"It's fine," Gabriel said. "The interview went about as well as it could, considering he's dead."

I froze. "What?"

"Yeah. For a few months now."

"I didn't know."

"Me neither. But *I* was in a foreign country receiving extensive medical treatment at the time. What's your excuse?"

I shot him a flat look. "Don't be a smartass. How did he pass away?"

"Heart attack. His niece Neela is living in his house now."

"Neela?" I repeated as we set off through the trees, along the shortcut that led to the cemetery. "You were talking to his niece for forty-five minutes?"

"Yeah." He shrugged. "She was friendly."

"Friendly?" I swiped at a mosquito that landed on my arm. "What do you mean *friendly*?"

He rubbed the back of his neck, the way he did when he was nervous. "You know—friendly. Like we chatted for a bit."

Ah. So *friendly* as in flirty. It would explain his nervousness. Gabriel had never quite known what to do with a compliment or blatant admiration.

The slight guilt in his downturned gaze wasn't necessary. We weren't together. But I did wonder if it might've been better if I had gone with him. Not because I was jealous, but if he was going to get this flustered, it could've affected his objectivity.

"Okay, but was any of this friendly chat useful?" I asked.

Gabriel bit his lip and seemed to consider it. "I suppose it would depend on your definition of *useful*."

"Gabriel!"

"It's not my fault she was a chatterbox. She kept going on about being new to St. Virgil and asking me the best places to get this and that done. It doesn't seem like she knows much about her uncle's life, much less his cases. All that is to say, I think we can rule him out. At least when it comes to the more recent—" He stopped and grabbed my arm.

I stumbled to a halt. "What?" I asked, then followed his line of sight.

We'd cleared the trees, halfway across the cemetery, the Jeep now visible. A small group had gathered around it, watching us approach. They appeared restless, one of them carelessly twirling a brushless broomstick. Somehow, I doubted they just wanted to say hi.

"That's not good," I said. While I thought my reappearance might cause a little stir, I hadn't expected a full confrontation. "Do we need a plan?"

"We'll go say hello." Gabriel started forward again. "And tell them to get the hell away from my car before they scratch the paint."

I followed. "Like anyone would notice a scratch on that old thing?"

"I would notice and that's what matters." Lowering his voice, he added, "Try not to start something, please."

"Who? Me?"

He didn't answer, turning his attention to the group in front of us.

I did vaguely recognize most of the guys and the one girl present. Brent was the only one I knew by name, though. He'd dressed for the occasion, ready to intimidate in a billowing red shirt, unbuttoned to reveal a threadbare undershirt. From the way he approached us, he seemed to be the appointed leader of the bunch.

"Evening," Gabriel called out. "Something I can help you with?"

"I think I should be the one asking you that," Brent said. "You're the ones trespassing."

I squinted at him, then made a show of glancing around. "*Trespassing* on a public road? I don't think that word means what you think it means."

Beside me, Gabriel sighed.

The lanky guy swinging the stick pointed it at me. "Shut up, witch."

"Why?" I asked. "Afraid of what I'll say?"

"All right," Gabriel said, shooting me a quick glare. "We didn't come here to make trouble."

Brent folded his arms. "Then why are you here?"

"We came to speak to someone," Gabriel said. "And we have. So now if you'll step away from my car—"

"Speak to someone?" Brent laughed. "Over there?" He nodded toward the trees through which Gabriel and I had come. Toward my family's land. His gaze slid toward me, a smug curl to his lips. "No one lives over there. Not anymore."

I chuckled softly. Beneath my breath, I muttered, "That's what you think."

"What is that supposed to mean?" Brent asked.

"Nothing," I said. Clearly, Gabriel's peaceful approach wasn't getting us any closer to the Jeep. I decided it was time to try handling this my way—by freaking them out.

Lanky Guy narrowed his eyes at me. "Why are you laughing?"

"Because you're so short-sighted." I kept my tone light, crackling with amusement. "All of you are. You burn what you see and you think that it's gone. But what about the roots? Did you ever consider what happens when the roots remain?"

I smiled. Lanky Guy shivered and tried to hide it.

"Relax, Skip," Brent said. "She's talking nonsense to mess with us."

"Maybe not," the girl said, eyeing me. "I've heard rumors. She's been selling potions out of a store in town. She's a witch, just like her mom."

"I don't care if she's been levitating in the middle of Main Street," Brent spat out. His thunderous expression prompted Gabriel to stand between us. "As far as I'm concerned that fire wasn't enough. If there was any justice, your mother would be rotting in jail next to the man who killed my cousin. I only hope that the night they got her she felt half the fear that Elizabeth felt."

My breath caught in my throat, but I fought to keep my expression placid. In that moment, fear or remorse would only be seen as weakness.

Brent was a wildfire. A rage scorched through him, the relentless kind of anger that could eat a person alive and singe everything they touched. Just standing this close to him, I could feel the blaze of unsated fury against my skin and hear the pain in his words. And I realized with sudden, burning clarity—he did not attack my parents.

If he did, he wouldn't still be this angry. His uncle wouldn't be confronting me in front of a bar. It seemed so obvious now.

Had I not been clouded by my own anger I might've seen it earlier.

"Go," Brent said. "We don't want you around here. Or did the fire not make that clear enough?"

It was clear. Very clear.

"We would leave," Gabriel said, through gritted teeth, "if you would get the hell away from our car."

Brent stepped aside, the others following suit. Gabriel opened my door and waited until I was inside before going around to the driver's seat.

"Get moving!" Lanky Guy—Skip—whacked the back of the Jeep with the stick.

I flinched. Gabriel twisted around to look at him, absolutely livid. Even though I'd mentally crossed the Alleyne family off my suspect list, that didn't mean I couldn't still mess with Brent and his friends.

"Hey!" I called through the open window. "Your name is Skip? As in Skip Aubrey?" The first name seemed unique enough. I doubted it was a coincidence.

"Yes." Skip's brow furrowed. "Why?"

Got him.

"I know what you've done, Skip," I said, very conscious that all his friends were listening. "Sneaking into your mother's house, even after she kicked you out. I've seen you squatting. Eating her food. Stealing her money."

Miss Aubrey hadn't mentioned any missing cash, since it wouldn't fit her soucouyant theory, but I thought it likely. From Skip's dumbfounded expression, I'd say I'd hit the nail on the head. If he didn't feel shame before, he certainly did now.

"Should I tell her the truth, Skip?" I asked, tilting my head to the side. "If I were you, I wouldn't give me a reason."

Gabriel had the good sense to drive off then. I managed to hear the girl ask Skip, "What's she talking about?" before the rest of their conversation was lost in the distance.

"What was that?" Gabriel demanded over the roar of the engine and the wind wiping at our faces.

"What? I was just messing with them."

"Not that," he said. "I know you too well to expect anything else. I meant—what did that girl mean when she said that you've been selling potions out of your shop? Did she mean the souvenir store?"

Uh-oh. In the corner of my eye, I could see him snatching glances at me. Shame settled like a weight in my stomach. I wanted to sink right through the seat and disappear.

"Selina," he prompted when I took too long to answer. "Tell me."

"You're not going to like it."

"I don't doubt that," he said. "Tell me anyway."

———

The ride back to the house was rough. Gabriel remained silent for most of it, not a word or even a glance to indicate that he was listening to me. I explained everything about the shop, the back room, and the fake psychic sessions. How Lennard had paid for a reading, the botched cleansing ritual, and the way Lennard had fled.

The whole time I spoke, I'd watched his stony profile, checking for his reaction. I didn't notice the bus stop until we'd passed it.

"You can drop me off—" I said.

"After what happened last time?" he finally spoke. "No, I'll leave you at the gate. Make sure you get inside."

"It wouldn't have made a difference last time. Lennard would've waited until you were gone."

He shot me a glare. Probably not the best time to poke at his logic when he was already pissed.

"You lied to me," he said.

I couldn't deny it. "Only because I knew you would react like this."

"Like what? Upset that you lied? That you've been scamming people?" For a moment, his jaw worked, seemingly speechless. "I . . . I can't even process this level of hypocrisy. This is the same thing you've been mad at your mother for doing for years."

I knew he wouldn't understand. "Yeah. And I still don't believe in it."

"That's exactly my point," he said. "You're so judgmental. You look down on anyone who believes in anything you can't prove. But somehow, you're perfectly okay with making money off it?"

"I know it looks bad, but—"

"How else would I look at it? It's one thing if you believed. Because then you'd be careful. Who knows what kind of problems you could've caused because none of it meant anything to you."

"But I *was* careful," I said defensively. "No one has gotten hurt."

"As far as you know."

What did he want me to say? "I told you all the important parts. The fact that Lennard thought he was being stalked by an invisible monster wasn't relevant."

"Just because you don't believe it doesn't mean it isn't relevant!" Gabriel pulled up to the gate of the house. He haphazardly parked the car and let the engine idle. He reached over to open the glove compartment, his arm grazing my knee.

I jumped, startled. "What are you doing?"

He ignored me, riffling through the contents of the compartment.

"Gabriel—" I started, but he grabbed a folded yellow paper and dumped it into my lap.

"Read it. Go on."

After a second of hesitation, I unfolded the paper. *"Psychic Readings by Miss Claudia . . ."* I read the title and recognized the flyer. "Are you serious? Why do you have this?"

"I thought it might come in handy one day."

"Why? I'm a hundred percent positive Miss Claudia is about as fake as I am."

"Yeah. You know that, but would he?"

"What?"

Gabriel snatched the flyer and held it up. "Did it ever occur to you that if Lennard came to you for help, he might've tried somewhere else, too?"

Oh.

Gabriel dropped his hand, the paper crumpling in his grasp. "We've wasted time. We could've been looking into this." He sat back, head turned toward the window.

Outside, the night was still as the weight of the argument sank in. The silence it left was terrifyingly hollow.

"What is going on with you?" he asked. "Yes, I hate this fake psychic business, but the part that's truly pissing me off is the lies. Why didn't you tell me?"

"Because I knew you wouldn't understand." And, whether I wanted to admit it or not, I still cared what he thought of me.

"Selina, we've known each other forever. We've seen each other at our worst, and I still loved you anyway. Just because we broke up doesn't mean all that disappears. It doesn't mean that I wouldn't at least try to understand."

"Well, how was I supposed to know that? You've been so mad at me since you got back."

His lips twisted in a grimace. "Yeah, I have been. I'm sorry. That's on me. Between my arm and all these changes, I've got some things to work out. But I thought you were doing better. Done with your self-destructing."

"I wasn't—"

"Yes, you were. And I think you still are."

I swallowed, my throat tight with a knot of emotion. "You don't get it. People, when they hear my name, they have one of two reactions. It's always the same. They either hate me or they fear me. So, I chose their fear."

And for it to work, I had to use a bit of deception.

"I know you want me to say that I completely regret it, but I can't. Lying to people is wrong, I know, but it's the only way I don't feel totally defenseless. Like back there with Brent and Skip. At least when they're afraid, I know they're less likely to try to hurt me."

If they were afraid, then I didn't have to be.

Gabriel was silent for a long time. I looked up at the house and glimpsed a curtain falling shut on the second floor. Someone had been watching us.

"I should go." I opened the car door.

Gabriel stayed me with a gentle touch on my arm. "I meant what I said. All of it hasn't disappeared. I am here for you. Even if I don't understand."

"As a friend?" Because that was all I could give him. "Can we be friends?" I asked, not a proposition, but a genuine question. Was friendship between us even possible?

A million emotions seemed to cross his face, settling into something wary. "We used to be."

It wasn't an answer. But I didn't have one either.

CHAPTER
TWENTY

I sat beside the cliff, the sun directly above, the light so bright it was almost blinding. I squinted through the glare, the world as visible as an overexposed photo. There was no breeze. No sound.

A sickly sweet scent permeated the stagnant air. It reminded me of the old stray cat that got trapped under our school building. For days, we'd heard it moving around the crawl space under the floorboards, scratching, and wailing. We tried to lure it out, but the scared creature only retreated deeper into the building.

One day, the noises stopped. We hoped it had found its way out. Then the smell came, and we knew.

Slowly, I rose to my feet, my limbs as stiff as boards, my bones cracking as they unfolded. I returned to the path. A familiar flame lily plant had sprouted in the middle of it. It should've been at the cottage. Not here, where it could be damaged. Unprotected. I needed to move it.

Some part of my brain registered the missing shadows, but for now, I ignored it.

I gripped the stem and pulled. It did not budge. After readjusting my hold, I tried again, pulling with all my strength. The earth around it flaked, then cracked. A fist was clasped around the end of the stalk. It broke through the soil. I let go and the lifeless hand fell open, palm-side up to expose the roots lodged inside, branching out like veins beneath the pallid skin. A black spider tattoo marked the inside of the wrist.

I jerked awake. The heavy sheets enfolded me like a cocoon, the air conditioner gently humming. The light from the hall filtered through my open bedroom door. The shadow of a person stood beside my bed.

I kicked out, my screams mingling with theirs. I scrambled backward until I hit the headboard.

"What the hell is wrong with you?" Janice shouted, clutching her stomach. "I was trying to help."

Muriel ran into the room. "Selina?"

"He's dead," I told her. "In the ground. I saw him."

"What are you talking about?" Muriel drew closer to my bedside. "Who?"

"Lennard. He—"

The dream released its hold on me, the drop back to reality dizzying. I looked around, gasping for air, trying to catch my breath.

"What happened to you?" Muriel asked her daughter.

Janice slunk over to the window seat, still clutching her stomach. "She *kicked* me."

"What were you doing in my room?" I demanded, tossing off my covers. My clammy skin chilled in the cold air.

"I was going to wake you up," Janice said, through gritted teeth. "You were screaming. *Again*. Maybe Ma can keep ignoring it, but I can't. Some of us don't like being woken up at three o'clock in the morning, every day, feeling like we're in the middle of a slasher movie."

"It was a nightmare," I said. It wasn't real. It was only a dream.

"You said Lennard is dead?" Muriel said. "Do you mean Lennard Bisson? The one who attacked you?"

"He . . ." I started, then shook my head. As the seconds passed my fear dissipated, unease filling its place. I took in Muriel's worry and Janice's hurt. What was wrong with me? God, I'd actually kicked her.

"I'm sorry," I told Janice.

"Whatever." She sounded strained. I noticed her hands shook. Had I hurt her that badly?

Muriel's thoughts seemed to run parallel with mine. "Janice, how bad is it? Do you need to go to the hospital?"

Janice lifted the edge of her pajama top and inspected her bared stomach. "No bruising." She let go of the material. "I think it's okay. Just give me a second."

"If you're sure," Muriel said, wringing her hands. "What if I made us some drinks to calm down? Selina, I could make your tea? Janice and I could have cocoa?"

"Isn't it way too late for that?" Janice said, a bite to her tone. "We're getting up in a few hours anyway."

Muriel blinked. "Yes. I suppose so."

"I could use some water," I said in an attempt to mitigate the awkwardness. Even though I didn't really want anything, I could see that Muriel needed something to do. "If that's okay?"

"Of course, love," Muriel said with a small smile. "I'll be back in a minute."

After Muriel left, I remained sitting against the headboard. I would've tried to distract myself with my phone or a book until I settled down. But I couldn't do that with Janice right there.

She returned my stare, unconcealed irritation in her regard.

"Are you okay?" I asked.

"Yes." Janice sat up, wincing. "But no good deed, right?"

I shrank against the headboard. "I didn't mean to hurt you."

"I'm sure there are a lot of things you don't mean to do," she muttered, shifting and exhaling slowly. Her expression hardened. "I saw Gabriel drop you off tonight."

Every muscle in my body tensed. If I wasn't already fully awake before, I would've been now.

"You two have been spending a lot of time together lately," she said. My expression must've betrayed my shock because she added, "Was it supposed to be a secret?"

I knew this would happen eventually. Someone would find out. And yet, my limbs still went numb. "He's helping me with something. It's not a big deal."

Janice stood, still holding her stomach. "What about Edward? Do you think he'd think it's *no big deal*?"

My spine stiffened. Was that a threat? "What is your problem? Why do you hate me so much?"

Her brows lifted in a way that reminded me of her brother. "I don't hate you."

"Yes, you do. You have ever since we were children."

She snorted. "Wow. I find it incredibly unfair that you hold what I did as a child against me, when you seem to have forgiven everyone else."

I shook my head. "No, you— Clearly, you still hate me. Even now."

"No. Now I'm afraid of you." She dropped her voice to a sharp whisper. "Afraid of what you can do to my brother. You're going to hurt him again and he's just going to let you."

That was not what I'd expected.

"We're not together," I reminded her. "He broke up with me."

"So? That doesn't change the fact that after you two broke up, Gabriel was a mess. And then he nearly *died*."

I flinched. "I know."

"Do you?" she asked. "Because he's been given this second chance at life. He doesn't need you messing it up again."

"*I know*," I repeated, holding her gaze to show that I meant it. "I don't want to hurt him."

"That doesn't mean it won't happen anyway. Even if you don't mean to do it."

I dropped my eyes to the bed, clutching at the loose sheets. "We aren't getting back together." My words were slow and deliberate. Each one felt like pulling teeth. "Gabriel has been helping me. That is all."

When I lifted my gaze, Janice's hazel eyes searched my face. I held my breath, frozen under her blatant assessment. I did not know what she found, but the tension in her shoulders eased.

"I want to believe you, Selina," she said, backing away. On the threshold, she stopped. "For the record, I'm not going to tell Edward. Even though he is my friend and you're putting me in an awkward situation."

My skin burned with embarrassment. "Thank you," I said softly, surprised and deeply grateful.

"Don't thank me. Seriously." She shifted her feet. "I haven't always made the best decisions either, so I get it. Mistakes happen. But if you want my advice—you should be the one to tell Edward."

"I will tell him."

"Then do it soon," she said. "Before he finds out from someone else."

Later that morning, we ended up at Miss Heather's. Though it was a Saturday, the port more active than usual, the shop remained relatively empty. I had no problem with that since Janice seemed set on putting on a show, trying on every dress that fit, and a few that didn't.

"What do you think about this one?" She dragged the curtain aside and sauntered out of the fitting room.

I lifted my eyes from my phone and nearly choked on shock. She spun around to show off the body-hugging black dress. Some sort of flashy gold tinsel hung from the skirt and the deep V-shaped neckline. I had no words.

Our shopping excursion had been going surprisingly well so far. By some miracle, Janice was being nice to me. Or at least she'd been treating me better than usual. Our 3 a.m. conversation seemed to have birthed a new unspoken understanding between us. We both wanted to see her brother happy, and we agreed that wouldn't happen with me.

With this conflict locked away, we could just be ourselves, and I was beginning to see the charm in Janice's blunt personality. I didn't want to insult her taste and ruin this newly formed camaraderie, but there was no way that Muriel would ever let her wear something so awful.

She blinked, her smile slipping. "What? You don't like it?"

I floundered, trying to find a diplomatic answer.

She burst into laughter. "I'm just messing with you."

I chuckled, too, relieved.

"Yeah." She turned her back to the row of full-length mirrors. "Could you imagine Ma's face if I wore this to her party? Actually, no. Let me not think about it. It'll make me want to do it for the laugh. You know, I might buy it anyway, just so I can whip it out on the right occasion."

"Definitely," I agreed, though I could not think of a single occasion that would warrant it.

"I hope you don't mind," she said, shimmying, the tinsel shaking behind her in the mirrors. "While I was in the fitting room, I invited Allison to join us."

"You spoke to her?" I'd been trying to contact Allison all day. Apart from a text telling me not to come to the shop again, she'd completely ghosted me. When I'd spoken to Edward that morning, he had mentioned that she'd been acting weird, but even he didn't know what was up.

"I sent her a message," Janice said. "She's nearby anyway."

"What did—" *Allison reply to you?* I started to ask, but in the act of turning my head, I noticed the row of Janice's reflections, all of them mimicking her movements, except one. It had turned its head, staying perfectly still, staring at me through the glass.

I dropped my gaze to my phone screen, hands shaking.

The hallucinations had been popping up all day. I'd been getting better at ignoring them. Nothing had been as disorienting as the one in the secret passageway the day before. Mostly it was little things— glimpsed movements out of the corner of my eye. Wayward reflections, unnatural shadows, and warped faces. Like little glitches. I blinked and they were gone.

I knew it wasn't real. As long as I remembered that, I'd be okay.

When I lifted my gaze, all six Janices were once again in sync. She frowned at me. "You good over there?"

I smiled and hoped it came off as reassuring.

"Is there anything I can help you girls with?" Miss Heather approached us. She'd been hovering in the background for a while, waiting to swoop in at polite intervals. Her question had been directed toward Janice, and only Janice. She could barely look at me, nervous from the moment I'd walked in. As if, at any second, I'd bring up our psychic readings or her incense addiction.

"Yes," Janice said. "Can you bring the white dress for me again? That one should be *appropriate* enough. Right, Selina? Might as well."

"Definitely," I agreed, though I couldn't remember which dress she meant. In the last hour, she'd tried on so many. Luckily, Miss Heather seemed to know precisely what she'd meant.

I'd made my selection relatively quickly. An emerald-green dress with a cinched waist, scooped neckline, and loose skirt. My favorite part was the gorgeous lace that ran across the shoulders and down to the wrists.

"Hey!" Janice called out. "Finally."

Allison threw the glass door open and marched inside. She didn't acknowledge Miss Heather, making a beeline right for us.

"Check it out!" Janice shimmied. "What do you think?" Her tone crackled with amusement, ready to rope Allison in on the joke.

Allison didn't even look at her. She stopped in front of me, aggressively close. "Do you know where I've been this whole morning?" Before I could even process the question, she answered, "Being interrogated by Officer Dannon. Do you know why?"

My stomach dropped. Even though I had a pretty good guess, I shook my head.

"What's going on?" Janice joined us, her steps small and careful in the tight dress.

Allison's glare never strayed from me. "I was just telling Selina the bad news. My store is closing. For good. She'll have to find a job somewhere else."

What? The word clogged my throat.

"Really?" Janice laid a comforting hand on her friend's arm. "I'm so sorry. I know how much work you put into that place. What happened?"

Allison dropped her voice. "My father found out that I'd withheld information from the police. And after what happened at school, this was the last straw. At the end of the year, he's sending me to live with some second cousin in Inverness. Do you know where Inverness is, Selina?" She drew closer to me. "*Scotland*. Do you know anyone in Scotland, Selina? Because I sure don't."

"I didn't tell the police anything." I backed away from her. "But what did you think would happen? Lennard attacked me and the store was broken into. People were going to figure it out."

"But how did they get his phone and wallet?" She stepped forward. "Daddy said that someone *anonymously* handed it in. That was you, wasn't it?" Again, she answered before I could. "I know it was. Because I've been thinking about that day of the break-in, running it back in my head. I know I locked the things in the safe. But I also know if anyone can manipulate a situation, it's you."

I flinched, stung. I opened my mouth to protest, but she cut me off.

"Don't even bother lying to me." Her voice hitched. To my surprise, tears pooled in her eyes. "I feel like such a fool. I've seen you trick people almost every day for months, but I never thought you'd do it to me. I thought we were friends." She sniffed, blinking rapidly. "What's that saying about trusting hornets? I shouldn't be surprised that I got stung."

"It's scorpions," Janice said, taking her side. Literally standing beside her. They faced me, this impenetrable wall of friendship that predated my inclusion. There was never any space for me at all. I was a fool to think otherwise.

Fine. If Allison wanted the truth, I'd give her the truth.

"Yes, you're right. It was me." I folded my arms. "What did you want me to do? Someone had to hand them in."

Allison pointed a finger in my face. "You admit it!"

"Yeah. And I don't regret it either. People were dying, Allison. And we were withholding vital evidence because you were too scared of getting yelled at by your father—a father who'd do anything to shield you from real consequences anyway. Do you realize how warped that is?"

"I didn't just get yelled at. I got banished!" Her tears flowed freely. "Don't you realize what you've done? You ruined my life."

"Don't say that." Janice embraced her friend, blocking me out. "Let's strategize. We'll figure it out. I'm sure we can come up with something." She looked at me over her shoulder. "Selina, if you've already gotten what you wanted, I think you should go."

Right. I could see no place for me here. Too bad this had to happen just when Janice and I finally started getting along.

At the register, I paid for my dress. Miss Heather said nothing, stony-faced as she took my money. Even after all the sessions over the past few months, I could barely elicit acknowledgment from her in public. Dealing with her frosty attitude after the blow-up with Allison, I was beginning to wonder what was the point of trying. No matter what I did, I always ended up on the outside.

Miss Heather bagged my dress and shoes. I took them from her, blinking back tears, silently daring her to say something.

Speak! I almost shouted, beyond frustrated.

Her thin lips flattened, stretching until they cut from ear to ear in a too-wide smile. I stared, transfixed, as her mouth fell open, a wet, gaping wound in the center of her face. Her blackened tongue writhed like a slug coated in thick slime. I clutched the bag to my chest, terrified, stumbling backward as she scrambled onto the counter. Her elongated fingers extended toward me. I dodged her grasp and sprinted outside.

The sun blazed down on the port. The ferry had recently docked. I dove into the crowd of tourists coming and going in every direction.

As I pushed through, their faces warped in a sea of too many. Light-headed, I dropped my eyes to the bleached pavement and breathed. People passed around me, an unrelenting current, their shadows trailing after them. Where my shadow should be, there was none. Was this a dream?

I closed my eyes, dizzy. So faint, I wondered if I was even there at all.

Someone bumped my shoulder. Solid. Tangible. Not a dream.

I was here. At the port. Something was wrong with me, but I needed to get ahold of myself. I opened my eyes. Focused on the wall of one of the shops, I slowly made my way toward it, out of the direct flow of people, careful not to look too long at anything or anyone else.

When I got there, I stopped and called Edward. He didn't pick up. I tried twice more, but he never answered. Had Allison told him what I'd done to her? Was he mad at me, too?

Against my better judgment, I looked down. Still no shadow.

Whatever was happening to me, I knew I shouldn't be alone. Before I talked myself out of it, I called Gabriel. Janice might hate me for it, but she was already pissed. What difference did it make?

He answered on the second ring.

"Can you hear me?" I asked.

"Not really. It's loud."

I retreated farther from the crowd, clutching the phone to my ear like a lifeline. My only tether to reality. I ducked into a nearby souvenir store. Unlike Allison's place, this store was bright and colorful, every surface so shiny it might've been polished that morning. The sour-faced man behind the counter watched me warily. I ignored him.

"Is it better now?" I asked Gabriel.

"Yes. What's going on?"

"Where are you?" Even within the walls of this brightly lit store, something was off. I felt it, a light but tangible awareness, like dozens of spiders crawling over my skin. I did not want to be alone.

"I am speaking to Miss Claudia right now," he said. From the formal tilt to his tone, I knew the medium in question was within his immediate proximity. "She has been channeling my uncle Samuel. He wants to let me know that he is at peace."

Gabriel did not have an uncle Samuel as far as I was aware.

"Can you come pick me up after?" I asked.

"Aren't you at work?" He sounded a little bitter about it.

"Please."

Gabriel must've caught the desperation in my voice. He was only silent for a moment, the rustling sound of movement in his background. "Tell me where you are."

CHAPTER
TWENTY-ONE

A popular travel publication once called the Cobalt Café restaurant one of St. Virgil's best-kept secrets. I'd never read past the title of the article, but I'd assumed they were being ironic. Famous for their three-peas pelau, the place was never empty, especially during lunch, when it seemed the entire town descended upon it.

Gabriel and I took the last available table at the edge of the patio, near the banister that overlooked the sprawling bay. The sun glared down at us—a scorching, all-encompassing spotlight. Despite the heat, I preferred to see everything.

No swimmers had breached the rough sea, most people likely flocking to the calmer waters on the southern side of the island. Only a pair of women lounged on blue canvas chairs, a lone child digging in the white sand.

"Why are we here?" I pulled out my chair and sat.

"You're not hungry?" He snatched up the one-page menu, flipping it over. "That's fine. You can watch me eat."

I gave him a quick, flat look, which he missed while skimming the menu's contents. My attention could not rest on one thing for too long, lest it change into something it shouldn't. The throbbing pain behind my left eye was now constant, accompanied by a hint of nausea that made the thought of food—however well-praised—unappealing.

"Are you ready to tell me what's wrong?" he asked. When I didn't answer, he sighed. "Fine. Then ask me about my meeting with Miss Claudia."

"How was your meeting with Miss Claudia?"

"Very interesting."

"Let me guess. One day you'll meet a tall, dark stranger?"

He smiled, lowering the menu. "Doesn't everyone at some point?"

I picked up the metal fork, setting it beside the matching knife. "I told you she's fake."

"Well, I certainly hope so. She told me to be careful of large bodies of dark water—which is deeply concerning, considering we live on an island." The amusement faded from his tone. "She also said that she never saw Lennard. It was a waste of time."

"No, it wasn't." I glanced toward the sea, squinting against the glare of the water. "It was a good idea. I should have told you the truth earlier. It just never occurred to me that he might seek out someone else." I toyed with the carved napkin holder.

"You're twitchy." Gabriel set down the menu. "Tell me, what happened this morning?"

Where to start? "Well, you won't believe this, but I was shopping with your sister. We were actually getting along."

"Wow."

"I know, right? But then Allison interrupted. She found out that I handed in Lennard's belongings. Some words were exchanged, not all polite. The store is over. Her father is sending her to Scotland. And now she hates me."

"I'm sorry."

I rolled my eyes. "You could at least try to sound like you mean it."

"My heart is irrevocably shattered by this news," he said in the flattest monotone I'd ever heard.

"Now, was that so hard?" I bit back a smile. "All jokes aside, I am sad to lose the job. Unless I plan to depend on your mother for the rest of my life, I'll need to find something else to do on this blasted island."

A yawning gap of free time unfolded ahead of me, the future terrifyingly unclear. Edward might be all I had left. If I hadn't already lost him.

I checked my phone. He still hadn't replied.

"You know you could leave this blasted island," Gabriel said. "Which was the plan, before you decided to throw it away."

"Don't," I warned him. I wasn't anywhere near the best headspace to rehash our reasons for breaking up.

"I'm not." He kept his tone light, but I didn't believe that hadn't been his original intention. "But if you insist on staying here, I doubt Ma would mind if you did depend on her forever. She certainly has the money for it."

"It doesn't matter if she minds. *I* mind."

He shrugged.

I leaned forward, pissed by his dismissiveness. "Do you have any idea how much she misses you? How much she worries about you? I know you have your reasons for staying away, but if you ever did want to return home, I know she'd welcome you back, without question."

He shook his head. "It wouldn't be *without question.* There'd be conditions. There always are. She has them for you, too, even if you don't see them. Just look at how you're defending her now. Would you still be doing that if she wasn't taking care of you? If you didn't feel like, on some level, you owe her something?"

I bristled, sitting back. "Muriel has never once implied that I owed her anything."

"Of course not. She wouldn't have to. My mom is more subtle than that. She thinks love and loyalty can be bought. Clearly, she already has yours."

"That doesn't even make sense."

"Doesn't it?" Gabriel set his elbow on the table. "Think about the way she runs the company. You've seen all the developments popping up. All the changes to the island. They tell people all the work VE is doing is to help increase tourism. It'll make the island more attractive and modern."

"Which it has."

"But they promise that the changes will benefit everyone—and it's not true. Think about it. Who owns the hotels? All the stores near the port? All the places the tourists stick to? It's the big corporations like VE. Soon, small businesses and family-owned restaurants won't have the space to exist here anymore."

I started to object, then stopped. He wasn't entirely wrong. "Look, I don't know how the company works. But if you hate the way it's being run, why not try to change it?" For all his complaints, he wasn't offering any solutions. "Why not accept your mother's job offer and fix it from the inside?"

"You can't fix a machine as big as VE. Either it breaks you or you become a part of it. Look what it did to my father. It was supposed to be his passion project. A way to invest his money and improve life on St. Virgil. In the end, it crushed him."

"Gabriel . . ."

"It did. It made him miserable. Even when things were good, when profits were higher than ever, it still wasn't enough. He still . . ." Gabriel's voice cracked and glanced away.

My fingers curled into fists as I resisted the urge to reach over and take his hand.

A waitress in a white shirt and black apron stopped beside our table. "Afternoon!" She tapped a pencil against a tiny spiral-bound notebook. Her eyes darted between us. "Ready to order?"

"No," I said.

"Okay!" She retreated quickly, probably sensing the tension. It might've been funny under different circumstances.

Gabriel picked at the edge of the tablecloth, shifting in his seat. "Virgil Enterprises killed my father, Selina. It's poison. To my family. To this island. I don't want any part of it."

I reached for his hand, unable to stand the distance any longer.

"Then don't join the company. You don't have to do anything you don't want to do."

He lifted his eyes to meet mine. "If I stay here, I'm afraid that it will happen anyway. Whether I want it to or not."

And there lay the crux of our problem. He needed to leave and I had to stay. I'd thought pushing him away would make the breakup easier. It turned out to be the hardest thing I'd ever done.

"Hi again!" The waitress returned, and I retracted my hand. She tipped her head to the side, exposing the intricate zigzag pattern of her cornrows. "Are we ready now?"

When Gabriel didn't answer, I said, "No, not yet. Can we have some water in the meantime?"

"No problem." She lingered beside our table, biting her lower lip.

"Something you want to say?" I prompted.

Her eyes widened. "Yes! I should've realized you'd pick up on that. Sorry, I just want to quickly thank you. My father's arthritis has been getting so much better since he started using your tea. Yesterday he returned to his boat for the first time in months."

Recognition fell into place like dominos. First, I remembered her face, then placed it across from me in the back room. Then came the details of that session, and finally her name. "Asha, right?"

"Yes!" She beamed and the enthusiastic energy she already emanated intensified.

"I'm glad to hear he's doing better," I said. Adding the stinging nettle had been the right choice. I'd have to put that in my notes when I got home.

"So am I," Asha said.

From the corner of my eyes, I checked Gabriel's reaction to hearing all this. He still seemed somber but otherwise unaffected. While I didn't think he'd out me as a fake in front of Asha, I knew he disapproved.

"I stopped by the shop yesterday to get more," Asha said. "But it was closed?"

"Yes. Closed for good, unfortunately."

She pouted. "Oh no. But you've been so helpful. What are we supposed to do now?"

Though I didn't want to discuss this in front of Gabriel, I didn't want to leave Asha's father without help. Especially since the tea was working. "If you want, I can drop off some here, at the restaurant, when I have the time."

"Really?" Her face lit up. "Thank you!" She tucked her notepad under her chin and pressed her palms together in a gesture of gratitude. "You're a lifesaver. I work here every day except Mondays. But, even if I'm not here, you can leave it at the counter for me."

"Sure," I said.

She lifted her chin and the notebook fell into her waiting hands. "I'll go get your water. You can have sparkling, on the house. Be right back."

I watched her hurry off, a little in awe of all that energy. "I don't even like sparkling," I said, making a mental note to parcel out the tea ingredients when I got home. I returned my attention to Gabriel.

"I thought the sessions at the shop were fake?" he said.

I frowned, confused. "They are."

He scrutinized me for a moment longer before looking out at the beach.

After a few beats of silence, I did the same, letting the sound of the rolling tide wash over me. The two lounging women had left. Only the digging boy remained.

"I know it's not your thing," I said. "But you should still come to the anniversary party. If nothing else, it's tradition."

"No, tradition is sneaking out of the party to find you." He dropped his voice, his lips curling in a grin. "Do you remember the last one? When we met at the beach?"

I rolled my eyes, trying to appear unaffected, but my body warmed at the memory of soft lips, slow kisses, and hot hands exploring previously uncharted skin. I cleared my throat. "My point is—it would mean a lot to Muriel if you came."

"And what about you?" His gaze focused on me with a thrilling intensity. "What would it mean to you?"

I looked away.

On the beach, the young boy wasn't there anymore. Lennard had replaced him. His skin was unnaturally pale, almost translucent under the glare of the sun. His long arms arched over his head, scooping away the sand, the excess wildly flung out behind him.

"Selina?"

"Yeah?" I plastered on a smile. "What were we—" I broke off, distracted as Lennard burrowed deeper into the sand. There was something uncanny about his movement, his arms long and rubbery. "Gabriel. Do you see anyone on the beach right now?"

"Right now?" After a beat, he answered. "No. It looks empty."

I suspected as much.

Ignore it, I reminded myself, even as my headache worsened.

Lennard stopped digging. He lifted his face for a moment. Even across the distance, I knew he was looking at me, making sure he had my attention. Then down he went. Headfirst, he crawled into the hole, his lean body twisting as he disappeared into the earth.

"What if Lennard *is* dead?" I gripped the edge of the table. "What if we're too late and he's already gone? He's hidden in the forest somewhere, and that's why no one can find him?"

Gabriel's chair grated against the tiled ground, prompting me to look at him. He'd leaned closer. "Where is this coming from?"

"I don't know." I hadn't meant to say it all aloud. "It's just . . . that night. When he stopped me in front of the house . . ."

"When he attacked you?"

"It wasn't an *attack*." The word sounded too malicious.

"What would you call it, then? He gave you a concussion." Gabriel searched my face, his eyes narrowing with suspicion. "Is there something else you're not telling me? Why are you defending him?"

"I'm not defending him." My feelings were more complicated than that. "I'm worried about him."

Gabriel's expression softened. "It makes sense. What you went through was terrifying. We didn't know he'd be waiting for you at the house. I should never have left you at the bus stop that night."

"No. I'm not worried *about* Lennard hurting me. I'm worried *for* him. I think he might be in danger."

Gabriel's brows shot toward his hairline. "Because of his invisible monster?"

"He was so scared, Gabriel."

"And I would be, too, if I committed two murders."

"That's just it. I don't think that he did."

"Why would you think that?"

I bit my lip. What could I say?

I had no concrete reason. Lennard hadn't claimed he was innocent, but he'd never confessed to murder either. If anything, his behavior that night proved that he was capable of violence, even if he did seem to regret hurting me afterward.

"Was it like . . . ?" Gabriel started, but seemed to think better of it.

I knew what he meant anyway. "My latent psychic abilities kicking in? No, it was the way he acted. We need to find him." My words—my entire body—shook. Gabriel reached over to hold my hand, as I had earlier.

I let the warmth and weight of his touch ground me for longer than I should have. His thumb caressed my skin in small circles, his affection tangible. I wanted to give in to it, fold like the tall grass bending toward the will of the wind.

I pulled my hand away. "Gabriel . . ."

"Sorry. I didn't mean . . ." His fingers curled before he retracted his hand from the table. When he spoke, his voice was so soft, I almost missed it. "It isn't easy for me. Sometimes I forget."

I knew what he meant. I felt the echo of it humming through my body. The memory of what it felt like to touch him, to hold him, buzzed beneath my skin. Since there was nothing that I could say to make this easier for us, I stayed silent.

He spoke, not meeting my eyes. "If Lennard is working with a local, as we suspect, it's possible they're hiding him. That could be why he hasn't been found. He could still be alive."

"Maybe," I said. Or maybe not.

Gabriel let out a heavy breath. "For now, let's continue to try to figure out where he might've gone for help. Are there any other psychics on the island?"

"Other?" I repeated.

"You know what I mean. Or spiritual advisors. Healers. Magic users."

"Apart from you?" Asha stopped beside the table, a chilled bottle of water and two glasses balanced on a tray. She winced. "Sorry, I didn't mean to interrupt, but I couldn't help overhearing. You looking for a second opinion or something?"

"Or something," I agreed. "Why? Do you know anyone?"

"I'm not sure if this is who you're looking for, but there is a woman who practices Obeah in my old village. Or at least that is what the people in the village said. All our parents used to warn us children not to bother her. We couldn't even look at her house if we passed it, not that most of us dared to get anywhere close enough."

"What's her name?" Gabriel pulled out his phone and started taking notes.

"They called her Mother Nia. I moved many years ago, but I think she's still in Patience. You have to cross the river and turn onto the street with a silk cotton tree. It's the very last house. If you think you've gone too far, you haven't gone far enough. Trust me, you'll know it when you see it."

"Patience?" Gabriel repeated. "That's north, right? In the valley. That's a long drive." While St. Virgil was not big, the roads to the north were winding. Driving from one end of the island to the other was not so simple.

Asha nodded.

"If we leave right after you eat," I said, "we can probably make it there and back before nightfall." Even though I needed to talk to Edward, and fix things with Allison, this was more pressing.

"Thank you," Gabriel told Asha. "Seriously. You've helped us big-time."

For the first time, Asha's smile was less than beaming. "Ah, one thing. If you are going to find Mother Nia, could you do me a favor?"

"What is it?" Gabriel asked.

"Don't mention who told you about her. You know. Just in case."

CHAPTER
TWENTY-TWO

"**W**e should've waited to come in the morning," Gabriel said. A drizzle of rain smattered the windshield. I gripped the door for balance as the Jeep bounced and crunched over dirt and gravel. The air smelled of wet foliage, the brush encroaching on both sides of the road. Strange visions continued to plague me in the form of small faceless figures darting between the trees. They watched us, tracking us into the valley.

"We can't waste any more time," I said, rubbing my aching head. Lennard needed to be found.

He glanced at me. "Do you know something that I don't?"

"What would I possibly know?" I said, a bit harsher than necessary.

Gabriel flipped on the windshield wipers. They dragged across the glass, muddy streaks momentarily clouding the view ahead. A few buildings perched on the mountainsides, including the abandoned monastery, an old fort, and a handful of mansions for the rich and reclusive. A famous writer was said to have a home somewhere out here.

"Tell me about the tea," Gabriel said. "The one you made for the waitress. If the sessions were fake, why did you help her?"

"Why wouldn't I?" The fact that he'd doubted that I would stung. Had I so completely poisoned his opinion of me? "She asked for help with her father's arthritis, so I made her a tea from stinging nettle."

"Okay," he said. "And when Brent and his friends cornered us, you told Skip something about his mother? What was that about?"

I winced. "That was a little petty of me. I knew that Skip had been breaking into his mother's house and stealing from her. Miss Aubrey came to me, convinced it was a soucouyant. Because, obviously, what else could it be? I gave her a charm that would only work if she'd change her locks."

"To keep him out." He laughed. "Okay, I get it now. But I still don't understand why. You said you wanted them to fear you, but then you help them anyway?"

"Yeah. If nothing I gave them worked, everyone would stop buying the act. Don't get me wrong, a lot of times, the placebo effect does wonders. But if I get a chance to test my herbology skills, then why not?"

"So you helped the elderly fisherman with his arthritis just to maintain your evil reputation." His tone sounded too sarcastic to be asking a question.

"Yes," I answered anyway.

"Sure."

"Don't do that." I knew what he was thinking. Instead of outright condemning what I'd done, he was trying to justify it. A part of me ached to accept his rose-tinted view of my actions. But it wasn't right. I was so clearly in the wrong. "I've been lying to them."

"I'm not saying it wasn't a bad idea." Gabriel slowed the Jeep. "But maybe you're not the villain you're making yourself out to be."

Or maybe I was, and after all this time, he still refused to see it.

Finally, we arrived at the river. The bridge creaked and groaned under the weight of the Jeep. Only one car could cross the narrow length at a time—not much of a worry in this low-traffic area. Through the window, I watched the railings slide past, the red metal of it faded and tainted by patches of rust and moss. Below us, the river snaked on both sides. A caiman slipped off one of the banks, disappearing into the muddy water. Another faceless figure lurked behind the long grass.

After the bridge, Gabriel turned onto the first street. It was marked by a huge silk cotton. It wasn't hard to see why this type of tree starred in so many local legends. With its gnarled branches and large buttress roots, it looked like something out of a folktale—people even believed jumbie spirits lived inside them.

The pressure in my chest mounted as we neared our destination. My knowledge of Obeah was limited. As a child, I'd heard warnings not to pick up abandoned coins on the street and tales about dead animals found with items stuffed into their mouths. Even though our social studies textbooks discussed the problematic demonization of African-derived religious practices, the word *Obeah* still provoked fear and disdain.

Mystery surrounded it. Only those who practiced knew how it worked. For others who believed but did not know, there existed an unseen terror. An inability to defend themselves if the eye of a wrathful user turned its gaze upon them.

The sky grew darker with every second. We passed a few small houses, fields of grazing cows and goats, and then a long stretch of uncut brush. Small yellow flowers bloomed on vines that clung to trees. I'd forgotten the name, but I recognized the invasive parasites, beautiful in their destruction. Their petals carpeted the roadside.

As the road curved, a galvanized roof slid into view.

"End of the road," Gabriel muttered. He stopped the car. "This must be it."

It had to be.

I stepped out, the drizzling rain cool against my skin. The house was one-story, compact, and shut up tight, every window and the front door barred by burglar-proofing. The remains of a wire fence lined the side of the house, what was left burdened by the encroaching vegetation. Plants were everywhere, the house itself half consumed by vines, seemingly on the edge of giving in to nature completely.

I hesitated beside the car. "I've been here before."

Gabriel stopped. "What?"

An eerie awareness, as tangible as a finger pressed into the back of my head, prompted me to turn around. In the empty lot across the road, long grass stood as tall as a grown man. The leaves swayed. Their rustling sounded like breathy voices, an exchange of a thousand whispered secrets.

"You've been here before?" Gabriel stood in front of me. "Do you know Mother Nia?"

"I think . . . maybe, my mother did."

He nodded, seemingly as rattled by that information as I was.

But we were here and I needed answers. "It's okay. Come on."

Together, we climbed the stairs, our footsteps heavy against the aged wood. Potted and hanging plants dominated the front porch. An older woman sat on a small wooden chair in the farthest corner, almost hidden in the shadows of a bamboo palm and a monstera bush. Her hair was wrapped in a scarf, her dress a simple wraparound.

I froze and grabbed Gabriel's arm. His steps faltered beside me.

"Why would you come here?" she asked. A metal bowl with raw pigeon peas rested in her lap. The line of her gaze fell somewhere to the left of us. "Foolish."

"I'm sorry?" Gabriel asked, confused.

"Not you, child," she said. "The one next to you. The one who think she know everything."

"Me?" I asked.

She sucked her teeth. "You think I don't know who you are? Or you don't remember?"

"No, I remember. A little. I recognize this house with all the vines. I've been here before. At the time, you were burning paper at an altar."

"Yes, I was. Among other things." Her lips curled with wry amusement. "Your mother used to come running to me every time she needed help, as so many do. The last time was because of a mistake she made. She believed someone she shouldn't. She wanted my help to see even more clearly."

At the mention of a mistake, my mind instantly went to Elizabeth and Maeve. Had she come here because of Ken Thomas? Was it possible that Daddy wasn't the only one looking into the old case? "When was this last visit?"

Her expression soured and I had the feeling that I'd said the wrong thing.

"I didn't like your mother," she said bluntly. "Josephine had a gift. I don't deny that. But I never liked the way she showed off. It is better to be humble and appreciative. You invite that many eyes into your life, you don't know whose attention you'll attract." She sniffed. "At least your mother knew not to step out of her lane. Never messed with things bigger than herself. Looks like she never taught you to do the same."

"Bigger than what?" I shook my head. "I don't understand."

"No, you don't." She grabbed the armrest and used it to push out of the chair. The loose peas and shells rattled in the bowl. "If you did, you wouldn't be here, would you?"

"Ma'am." Gabriel held up his hands in a staying gesture. "Please. We just have a few questions. There's a man named Lennard Bisson on the island. Have you been contacted by him? We have reason to believe he might've come to see you."

"And why should I tell you anything?"

"We'll pay," he offered.

She laughed, shuffling over to the front door, her slippers sliding against the floor. "If the little witch want to make spell and charm, go on, then. Let her face the consequences."

"You won't help us?" Gabriel asked.

"Boy, you're lucky I even letting you leave here just so. I should be teaching you a lesson. Make sure you never play up in this business ever again." Her gaze returned to somewhere beside me. "But it looks like somebody else already taking care of that."

My blood chilled. "What is that supposed to mean?"

Gabriel rested a hand on my arm. "Selina, let's go."

"No, what do you mean somebody else is taking care of it? I want to know."

The woman smiled. "I think you already do."

"Come on," Gabriel urged.

She opened the security gate and the door behind it. I shook Gabriel off and grabbed the gate before she could shut it. "What's wrong with me?" The hallucinations, the exhaustion, the persistent feeling of dread—if she had a reason, I needed to hear it.

The door shut in my face.

I slammed my fists against the wood. "If you know, tell me!"

Gabriel tugged my arm. I wouldn't budge, ready to knock and shout until she came out and answered my question. His arm wrapped around my stomach, and he pulled me away from the door.

"Selina, what are you doing?"

I twisted out of his hold. "I need her to tell me."

"Tell you what?"

"Tell me . . ." I faltered. Tell me *what*? That I'd been haunted by things I didn't believe in? Things I knew were not there. Even now I could see someone in the field, their delicate, dark fingers parting the long grass across the road.

Gabriel's eyes were wide with worry. All at once, the fight sapped out of me.

"I've been seeing things," I admitted, the words tumbling out. "Strange things. Lennard dead in the rainforest. My father. People that aren't there."

"Like ghosts?"

"No. Like hallucinations. Something's wrong with me. Even now, I can see someone behind you. I know she's not real."

"Not—" Gabriel whipped his head around. His grip on me slackened.

A woman emerged from the field, her long black-and-blond braids hanging down to her waist, a nose ring glittering in the light.

"Hey!" Gabriel called out.

The woman pressed a finger to her lips. She pointed to us, then down the road, before retreating into the grass.

"Wait, you can . . . ?" *See her?* I almost said, but I let the words float away as exhaustion and regret washed in.

"Come on," Gabriel whispered to me. "We'll talk about this later."

I followed, a little dizzy from emotional whiplash. Gabriel could see her? She was real. I'd told him everything, and now he knew.

The woman waited for us at the side of the road, just after the Jeep. A cotton bag hung over her shoulder. On a closer look, she appeared older than I'd first thought, in her late forties or early fifties. As we approached, she hunched over, as if trying to stay out of sight from anyone at the house.

"Who—" Gabriel started, but she shushed him.

"Keep it down." She glanced toward the house. "I heard you talking to Mother. You're here about Len, right? The one who's been in the paper?"

"Yeah, do you know him? Was he here?" Gabriel stepped toward her, which only prompted her to retreat farther into the grass. He froze. "We just want to ask a few questions."

"Not here," she said. "I live down the road. The gate with the ceramic toad out front. Meet me there."

After that, she backed into the grass and disappeared.

CHAPTER
TWENTY-THREE

We found the ceramic toad easily. It squatted in front of a retractable iron gate, its painted black eyes greeting us with a menacing stare. Apart from that, the peach-colored house behind the gate seemed fairly normal, if slightly bigger than the others in the area. When Gabriel parked the Jeep, a large rottweiler sprinted toward us. It jumped against the gate, barking wildly, likely notifying anyone inside of our presence.

"I'm not sure this is a good idea," he said, after cutting the engine. "Trusting this random person who appeared out of nowhere. This is how horror movies start."

I stared out the windshield. Rain drizzled against the glass. "She called him Len. That's how he introduced himself to us when he came into the store. Not Lennard. Len."

"So, she must've met him."

"It certainly seems that way."

I folded my arms, feeling oddly vulnerable after my admission and Mother Nia's reprimand. I knew the fake psychic sessions were wrong, but I only felt the full weight of that now. What if the hallucinations were a punishment? Consequences for interfering in something I didn't understand?

No. None of it was real.

Why was it becoming harder to remember that?

"Selina . . ." Gabriel's careful tone set me on edge. "What you said back there, about seeing things— How long has this been going on?"

"A few days," I admitted. "The doctor did say that I might experience some side effects from the concussion and the medication. . . ." I ignored the voice in my head reminding me that the first time I saw my father was before the concussion. And that I'd already stopped taking the medication.

"If you think it's because of the concussion, have you told the doctor?" The pinch in his tone suggested that he already knew the answer. "Or my mother? Or anyone?"

"It's not—"

"Don't say it's not a big deal. Of course it is." He dragged a hand through his hair. "Every time I think we're on the same page, there's another layer of secrets you've been hiding."

"Well, excuse me for not bearing my entire soul to you. I don't *have* to tell you anything, even if you were still my boyfriend, which you're not."

Gabriel flinched.

Instantly, I felt awful. "I didn't mean—"

A hand slapped against my window, startling us. The woman's face appeared through the rain-speckled glass. "Come on," she said.

With her head ducked, she ran around the front of the Jeep. After tugging the handles of her bag over her wrist, she reached through the gate and unlocked it. All the while, the rottweiler jumped and licked at her arms. The second the gate opened, she held on to the dog collar, stepped back, and waited.

"She wants us to go into the house," I said unnecessarily. Her intentions were obvious, but I wanted to break the awful silence that lingered between us.

Gabriel got out first. Then I did, too. We hurried through the gate, past the woman and the excited dog. The rain intensified with every passing second. By the time we ran up the stairs to the covered porch, we were soaked.

The woman joined us a minute later. The dog wasn't with her. Her face broke into a smile as unexpected as it was revelatory. Where she'd been intimidatingly stern before, she now appeared warm and friendly.

"You have interesting timing." She shook the rain from her hair and swiped it off her skin. "But everything does work out, yes."

"Who are you?" I asked, worried we were skipping this important part.

"Toni." She smiled over her shoulder, opening the door, which was unlocked.

"Gabriel," he said. "And this is Selina. You said you had some information on Lennard Bisson?"

"I do." Her words were almost lost under a blast of thunder. "Come in. We'll talk."

She entered the house, shucked her slippers, and left them beside the door. Gabriel toed off his shoes easily, but I had to untie mine. While standing on one foot, I nearly lost my balance. Gabriel held out an arm. I took it, grateful, until I noticed the angle of his body and the way he tried to maximize the distance between us.

"Thanks," I said. Shoes off, I let him go.

He shoved his hands deep into his pockets.

"Come on!" Toni came back for us. "Follow me."

We did, rounding the corner, then crossing an artfully cluttered living room. Not a single piece of furniture matched, and yet it all fit together. Carved wooden bookshelves stood among a pleather couch, sleek glass tables, and wicker chairs. Paintings of seascapes hung beside vintage movie posters. A huge crystal vase held dried bamboo stalks, and a mahogany table was lined with a collection of frog figurines. The air smelled spicy and earthy, like fresh seasoning.

"Jaya!" Toni called out, entering the adjoining kitchen. "Look what I brought home for dinner."

Like the living room, the decor in the kitchen was another mashup of sophisticated and quirky that somehow made sense. Even the woman who stood at the sink seemed to be an extension of the place, her straight black hair in a single braid to her waist, her dress some-what shabby with age but more elegant than expected for a night in.

The woman—Jaya—looked us over. She wiped her hands on a dish towel and then set them on her hips. "When you said you were picking something up at your mother's, I thought it was flavoring pepper, not more mouths for dinner."

Her mother? As in Toni was Mother Nia's daughter?

Now that I looked for it, I could see a resemblance in the set of her eyes. In the shape of her mouth.

"I got that, too." Toni set the cotton bag on the counter and kissed Jaya.

Jaya narrowed her eyes, seemingly unimpressed. "They are dripping on my floor."

"Ah, yes. I'll get some towels." Toni rushed past us. "You two wait here."

We stared at Jaya, who stared back.

Gabriel cleared his throat. "You don't have to worry about dinner. We won't be long."

"Yes, you will." Lightning and thunder punctuated her declaration. "With the weather like this, you kids aren't going anywhere. This area is prone to landslides. If you try driving in that, more than likely you'll end up buried or sliding into the river." She reached for the bag and dumped the red and green peppers onto the counter. "Now, tell me, how do you feel about curried goat, dhal, and rice? Are you allergic to anything?"

"Food colorings for her," Gabriel offered. "Only certain kinds of penicillin for me."

Jaya gave him a flat look. "I think we should be fine, then."

I dropped my voice, leaning closer to Gabriel. "I don't think it's a good idea for us to stay here."

"We can't drive back," he said. "I don't know about you, but I don't want to end up in that river."

"I wouldn't recommend it," Jaya chimed in.

"Here you go." Toni returned with towels. She handed one to me and another to Gabriel. A third she draped around her own neck.

I wiped my cheeks and arms. "Are you Mother Nia's daughter?"

"I am," Toni said. "But let's talk in my office and leave Jaya to her art. Believe me, once you taste her curry goat, you'll see what I mean. The thing is a masterpiece."

Jaya sucked her teeth and returned to her cooking.

Toni led us into another room, this one a little more spacious, the view from the large windows obscured by the torrent of rain. Hundreds of books lined ceiling-high shelves, a long ladder leaning against a corner. She stood in front of a massive wooden desk and pointed to a plush couch on the opposite side of the room.

"Holy hell," Gabriel whispered, awed. He drifted aside, distracted by the bookshelves.

"Go on," Toni told me. "Have a seat. Don't mind you wet."

I sat on one end of the couch, right beside a small stuffed frog. Its body was a reddish-brown color with thin white stripes.

"Oh," Toni said, crossing the room to pick it up. "Sorry, I forgot I left her there. Do you recognize it? Phantasmal poison frog. Not to scale, obviously. The real one is exceptionally tiny. Fascinating creatures."

"And poisonous," I said. It felt like that was the aspect of the animal most worth mentioning. "I've read that scientists are trying to use the poison to create a nonaddictive painkiller."

Her eyes lit up. "Really? I did not know that. You are clever, aren't you?"

I shifted, a bit embarrassed. "I'm just interested in that sort of thing. I wanted to study pharmacology or botany at university, but . . . it didn't work out."

"Yes, I know," she said. "I am sorry."

I blinked, confused by her answer. How would she know?

Before I could ask, Gabriel pointed to a stack of books on her desk. They all had the same title and were very familiar. "Are you a huge Samantha Lake fan or something?"

She followed his gaze and laughed. "These are my author copies. My editor sends me about two dozen of every first edition."

"Author copies?" His eyes widened. "*You're* Samantha Lake?"

"That's me. It's the pen name I use for fiction. My real name I reserve for my academic work."

"My mother loves your books," I told her. "She collected all of them. The new ones still get delivered to us."

"Oh good." She smiled. "You got them. I wasn't sure if I should send them to a different address."

I sat up. Wait. "*You* sent them to us?"

"I had to. I promised your mother."

"You knew my mother?" I asked, feeling several steps behind in this conversation. "How?"

"We went to school together. After we graduated, I wanted to be a novelist and she helped me with my first book, reading and critiquing it. Basically, she'd earned free copies for life. Admittedly, it's been over a decade since I last saw her. The writing keeps me busy. And I'm a bit of a hermit. Wouldn't bother leaving the house at all if I could."

"I had heard a famous author was living up here," Gabriel said. "But I thought you'd be in one of the mansions in the hills."

"And what would Jaya and I do in a big house like that? No, we have a yard for Ziggy, and all the room we need here. And, though my mother would never admit to it, she likes that we stay close to her."

The mention of Mother Nia brought us back to the most pressing topic at hand. All the questions I had about her and my mother would have to wait until later.

"Did Lennard visit you?" I asked. "Is that how you know him?"

"Wait. Before we start." Gabriel pulled out a piece of paper, unfolded it, and handed it to Toni. It was the photo of Lennard from the newspapers. "Just want to make sure this was the guy you saw."

Toni tucked her stuffed frog under her arm and took a good look at the photo. "Yes, that is him." She handed the paper back to Gabriel. "About three days ago, he was sitting right where you are now."

I looked down as if there would be some evidence of this on the couch.

"My mother had the same reaction to him as she did to you." Toni set the frog on top of the desk so that it faced us. Almost like a fourth member of the conversation. "She chased him off. Told him that she wanted no part of it."

"No part of what?" Gabriel asked.

"That's what I wanted to know. So, I asked him over, then offered to help, if I could."

Gabriel asked, "Did you help him?"

I sat forward, a buzz of anticipation beneath my skin.

She seemed to absorb our sudden alertness with wry amusement. "That remains to be seen. But I did try."

"Do you practice Obeah, too?" I asked, trying to work out the kind of help she might have offered.

"I do," Toni said. "Although, I've come to incorporate other practices into my life as well, a fact which my mother greatly disapproves of. I can't blame her. There are so few Obeah practitioners left who truly know what they're doing. But then, I've always had a personal and academic interest in various African-derived practices. It's my area of expertise, along with the history of Caribbean folklore."

She crossed over to one of the shelves and plucked two hardbacks from the stack. She came over and handed them to me. The raised lettering on the covers read *Obeah, Hoodoo, and Haitian Vodou: African Spirituality and the Diaspora* and *It Waits in the Forest: Tales of Traditional Caribbean Folklore*, both by Toni Gray.

I tipped the books sideways so Gabriel could read them as well. Our eyes met and I knew we were thinking the same thing: She was the person we'd been looking for.

"Tell us what happened with Lennard," Gabriel urged.

"Well, he told me quite the story." Toni hopped onto the desk, sitting on the edge. "Strangely enough, it all started online."

CHAPTER
TWENTY-FOUR

There'd been a time when Lennard Bisson didn't believe in love at first sight. Then he saw Isabelle smile, and in that second, his world shifted. She became his new center of gravity, the point around which he revolved.

She wasn't the most beautiful person he'd ever seen. Not even the most attractive in the café. But there was something about her. Something in the gentle arc of her neck, the way she moved her hands as she talked, the sultry rasp in her voice—it all spoke to him in a language that was both familiar and foreign, comforting and exciting.

Before he knew what he was doing, he'd left his table and joined hers. The introduction went smoothly, the conversation took off, and the blind date he'd meant to meet was long forgotten.

Their first year together was tough. For a while, she was hesitant to engage in anything too serious. They were both finishing up their last years at different high schools, the problem of distance eventually solved when they got into the same university. The school was her first choice, not his. He never told her.

When they finally started dating, his friends were as delighted as he was. Everyone loved Isabelle. Her dimpled face and bubbly personality easily disarmed most strangers. She loved posing for photos—big smile, hip cocked, two fingers extended in peace. But Len preferred the pictures when she wasn't posed, not so self-conscious. No makeup.

Dressed down. When she kicked back on the couch, too focused on her laptop. Or late at night, when her features softened, slack with sleep.

She didn't love him as much as he loved her. He knew that. They stood on uneven ground from the beginning. It didn't matter, so long as she stayed, and he did everything to make sure that she did.

But as the years passed, it got harder to maintain. The more perfect he tried to be, the further she pulled away. It got worse after she caught him outside her house one night, uninvited. He made excuses, reassurances, promises. He even spent two paychecks on a gold necklace, the pendant depicting their entwined initials. She never wore it.

One night, he'd been venting in an online forum—anonymously, of course. The notification for a DM caught him off guard. He vaguely recognized the account as someone who'd been floating around the forum for a while. They'd never interacted.

You might be interested in this, they'd said.

Lennard didn't know what possessed him to click the link. Perhaps the alcohol or self-pity. It took him to another forum, one he'd never heard of before. One that could not be found through any search engine. Only a select few could access it. The things the users talked about—magic, rituals, creatures that granted your wildest dreams—were all too fantastical to believe. At first.

Then Isabelle canceled their third date in a row. He'd called a few times, then went to her house. She met him at the door, crying and begging for space. She wouldn't let him inside.

He returned home, rattled and desperate. After all these years, everything he'd done for her. Anything she'd ever wanted. He'd been selfless from the start. Did she think she'd ever find someone better? Someone who'd love her more than he did?

Wading through a haze of anger and hurt, he logged back in to the forum, found the thread he needed, and took notes. Some of the items proved to be harder to find than others, but the forum members were eager to help.

When he finally collected everything that he needed, he waited for sunset, drew the markings, and spoke the words. Sitting on the cold floor, he kept his eyes tightly shut. He summoned Isabelle's image and held it in his head. Her face was so beloved and familiar that he could easily picture her sitting across from him. Her lips curled into that smile he'd fallen in love with.

But as he continued to say the words, she blurred, shifting until, somehow, he was looking at an image of himself. As if a mirror had been erected in the middle of the room. He opened his eyes for a second. To clear his mind. To refocus on Isabelle. But when he shut them again, all he saw was himself, sitting much nearer now.

He did it again and it happened again. His image even closer. Still smiling.

When he opened his eyes this time, he held them wide. He could not move, afraid to blink. The room cooled, goose bumps rising along his arms. His eyes stung as seconds passed, tears pooling, blurring his vision. But he kept them open.

When he finally blinked, it wasn't voluntary. It wasn't what he'd wanted. The reflection sat right in front of him, its hands outstretched, reaching. . . .

Isabelle called him the next day.

She asked him out for lunch. They needed to talk.

Lennard went expecting the worst. In the history of the universe, *needing to talk* had never been a good thing. He took his time, every step toward the café weighed down by misery. It slowed his pace. He arrived twenty minutes late.

She wasn't mad. Not at all.

Instead, she greeted him with a smile, her upturned face a beacon of love, almost as bright as the gold necklace she wore. Their initials rested against her chest. For the first time, he knew, they were truly standing on even ground.

He thought about that day often. It made the tasks a little easier.

They started small, at first. Leave some food here, drop some money there. Steal this phone. Break into that house. The requests meant nothing to him, all random. Sometimes it took a little effort, but nothing he couldn't accomplish.

Besides, he didn't have a choice. It was this or his life. And now that he was happy—*truly happy*, he told himself—he'd do anything to keep it.

It worked. For a while.

It wasn't until he found himself crouched in the corner of a bedroom, breath held, knife in hand, praying that he did not hear footsteps on the blood-soaked floors that he realized a line had been crossed. In that moment, he could not recall Isabelle's face, only the mutilated horror lying six feet away. He made it out of the house and two streets over before he vomited in a drain.

The next request came a few days later, somehow even worse. He refused to do it.

It did not like that.

The demands multiplied, compounding like interest. He could not comply. It would ruin him. It already had.

He searched the forums for some solution. A loophole. An escape. Deus ex machina. He'd been far from the first to regret what he'd done. If only he hadn't loved so much. If only Isabelle had been less.

But now she was no longer the girl he'd fallen in love with. Lately, she was always reaching for him, touching him, drinking up his every move. She'd shed every part of her life that didn't involve him, all traces of the confidence and charm that had drawn him to her in the first place gone.

Leaving her proved to be easier than he'd expected. He simply slid from the bed while she lay soundly sleeping. He knew she'd be devastated in the morning, her dependency suffocating.

He bounced from country to country, consulting anyone who might help him. He drank potions. Chanted spells. Collected charms, talismans, and amulets. All the while, the requests kept coming. It kept following. Waiting.

Then, finally, someone posted on the forum, sharing exactly what he needed. They claimed to know how to survive. An island in the Caribbean where strange things occurred. If the impossible could happen anywhere, it would be there. The best part was that he wouldn't have to go it alone. There were others in his situation. They were traveling to the island as well.

With his days numbered, Lennard booked the flight. It drained most of his money. To his relief, one of his new friends floated him some cash and offered to split a hotel room.

Lennard took the trip, desperately hoping it would not be his last.

CHAPTER
TWENTY—FIVE

"Lennard wanted a way out," Toni said. "He'd traded one year of his life in service to the creature in exchange for one wish. If Lennard did not complete his tasks by sundown of the last day of that year, then the creature would reap Lennard's life as compensation."

"You keep saying *creature*," Gabriel said, oddly sedate for having heard the story she'd just told us. "What is it exactly?"

She paused for a beat, then asked, "Have you heard of a buck?"

"No," Gabriel said.

"Yes," I said, a hidden memory unlocked. "When my grandmother was alive, she used to tell me bedtime stories about them. But that was too long ago." I tried to recall exactly what she'd said, but I'd been very young at the time. My earliest years had intersected with my grandmother's last.

"It's a character of folklore," Toni said. "The origins have been traced back to West Africa, though the legend as we know it now came from Guyana. The creatures can grant wishes for their owners—like immense wealth and innumerable worldly pleasures—but the owners must provide it with food and shelter. If the owner fails to live up to their end of the bargain, the buck will ruin their life or kill them."

"Sounds Faustian," Gabriel said.

"It does," Toni agreed. "There are similar legends found throughout cultures all over the world. This creature that haunts Len—whatever it is—it's something similar and very old. As old as humans themselves. It derives its power from appealing to the most basic human desires. Money. Love. Great power. It's about wanting something so much you'd trade your soul for it."

Gabriel jumped off the couch, the investigative reporter wheels in his brain starting to spin. "It makes sense." He paced over to the window in a display of animated energy. "Lennard traded his life for love. Kyle Gordo recently signed a big modeling contract. Chord Grayson's social media blew up over the last year. It all fits." He stopped and turned to face Toni. "Wait—was it the creature that killed Kyle and Chord? Because their year was up and they didn't complete their service?"

"I'm not sure," Toni said. "Len did not talk too much about the others. Nor did he mention how much time he had left. Though, from the way he was acting, I got the impression it was not much."

I thought of my session with Lennard, the things he'd said he'd seen and his overwhelming fear. "You told us you tried to help him? How exactly?"

She blinked as if surprised by my skepticism. "As far as I could see, there was only one solution."

"And what is that?" I pressed, gripped by a whole new level of fear. I had to keep reminding myself none of this was real, but each successive reminder weakened in resolve, just a little less effective.

"It's simple, really," Toni said. "But I can't say if it will work or not. You have to understand, a creature like this has the power to manipulate reality because reality can be manipulated by their power, you follow?"

"Not even a little," Gabriel said.

"I'm saying it is *because* it is."

"Whatever happens is meant to be," I muttered, recognizing the same circular logic my mother used.

"Yes." She pointed at me. "But, at the end of the day, a deal is a deal."

"I'm so lost," Gabriel said.

"Like all deals," Toni said, "there are terms that must be met on either side. They are clear. The creature must grant the wish and Len must complete all his tasks. If he does not meet his end of the bargain, he dies. *However*, if the creature does not fulfill its part—"

"Then the deal will be void," I finished, understanding.

"Okay, I think I get it," Gabriel said. "But just in case, can you explain this to me like I'm five?"

"If whatever Lennard wished for didn't come true," I said, "the creature would not have fulfilled its end. The deal would break."

"*But,*" Toni said, "according to Len, the creature did fulfill his wish, and he had no hope of reversing it." She shook her head. "It's a shame. That's why, when you make these deals, you must be very careful with your wording."

"So that's it, then," I said. "No loophole."

"There is another way he could survive, I suppose," Toni said. "Len could finish his tasks, whatever they are."

My heart sank. I felt torn between sympathy and disgust. The more I learned about Lennard, the more he repulsed me, controlling and manipulating the emotions of someone he'd loved in such a way.

Maybe he'd only gotten what he deserved. Maybe he should not be saved.

And yet, I couldn't dismiss his fear.

Was this what Mummy felt during Elizabeth's and Maeve's cases? For years, I was convinced that she'd made the wrong decision. Ken Thomas had been a creep and a stalker, and even if he hadn't done the murders, his behavior had been abhorrent. I had not understood why Mummy stuck her neck out to defend someone like him. But I was beginning to understand the complexity of her choice. It wasn't so easy after all.

Wait. No.

What was I thinking?

Yes, Lennard might be in danger, but not from some magical creature.

I'd gotten too wrapped up in Toni's story, like falling into the pages of one of her books, thoughtlessly suspending disbelief. But I was not one of her characters. Not like foolish Sam, who'd been fatally naive. I knew better. I could not—*would not*—chase imaginary monsters.

I stood. "This is ridiculous. Gabriel, you can't possibly believe what she's saying. A creature that grants wishes? That reaps souls?"

"You asked me what I told Len," Toni said. "This is what I told him."

"So you wasted his time, too?" I looked at Gabriel. "She's making this up. She's a fake. Just like Miss Claudia and me."

"Selina—" Gabriel started.

"No," I cut him off, backing up toward the door. "How can you sit there and listen to this, much less believe it?"

Toni frowned. "Why is this upsetting you so much?"

"Because we are wasting time. Len needs help. What if he's in danger? *Real* danger? We should be out there searching for the truth."

"Searching for the truth?" One of Toni's eyebrows arched. "Though you've already decided what it isn't. Or do you know the truth and you don't want to admit it?"

"No," I choked out, my throat tight. With both of them facing me, it was hard not to feel ganged up on. Them versus me. Absurdity versus reason.

Toni sighed. "Your mother—"

"I am not my mother! Whatever she had, I don't have it."

"Selina," Gabriel said, "you must realize, some of the things you know . . . the way you can read people . . . yes, some of it is observation, but—"

"Don't," I warned him.

"Some of it shouldn't be possible," he finished anyway. "Like that day, all those years ago, when you tried to run away from home. When you were in our guest room. Before your mother even entered the house, you hid under the bed. Like you knew she was near."

"It was a coincidence," I said.

He shook his head. "I was with you, remember? We were sitting on the floor, playing cards, and suddenly, you got this look on your face. I saw the second you knew."

No, that wasn't true. Was it?

"I must've heard her, or . . ." A pressure started to build in my chest, suffocating me. "If this *is* real, and I have the gift, then why didn't I know something was wrong? Explain that." I looked to Toni since she apparently had all the answers. "Explain to me why, on the night of my parents' attack, I felt nothing. No visions, no premonitions. I snuck out and left my father to die, and I didn't know a thing. How does any of that make sense? What's the logic in having a gift if I couldn't save them?"

"Selina—"

"No. I can't listen to this." I turned and left the room, nearly colliding with Jaya, who was on her way inside.

"Careful!" She steadied the tray in her hands. A little of the iced juice in the jug sloshed over the rim.

"Sorry," I said a bit too loud.

"No harm done." She lifted her gaze to my face. "Are you—"

"Where's the bathroom?"

She pointed it out, and I wasted no time barging inside. I shut the door and rested my back against it. A large circular mirror hung over the sink, the edges of it molded to the terra-cotta-colored walls to appear like it was bricked in. I tried to calm down, drawing deep breaths.

A familiar scent filled the enclosed space. Cinnamon.

"No." I shut my eyes tight because I did not want to see. "Not now. Please." Seconds passed in silence. I never peeked.

After a while, the scent faded.

CHAPTER
TWENTY–SIX

The rain continued into the night. The weather forecast predicted thundershowers until morning. My phone died and I hadn't brought a charger. I used Toni's landline to call Muriel to let her know that I'd be taking shelter with some friends in Patience until the storm passed. She didn't like it, though there was little she or I could do about it.

"It's really raining out there," Gabriel said, rolling out the duvet on the floor. "Sounds like it's going to bring down the roof."

I sat on the couch next to him, watching for the lightning as it lit up the windows, then bracing for the thunder that followed.

Since the scene in Toni's office, he hadn't brought up Lennard or the buck. That was not to say he and Toni hadn't been discussing it. Before and after dinner, they'd huddled together, their voices low. Jaya kept me company in the meantime, seemingly okay with my silence. She asked no questions, which I appreciated. I had a lot to think about.

When it got late, they set us up in the living room. Gabriel insisted that he take the floor so I could have the couch. Toni gave us some T-shirts and sweatpants to sleep in. The borrowed clothes fit me fine, but the T-shirt was noticeably too tight on Gabriel.

"I'm guessing you're not in the mood for scary stories?" he asked.

I gave him a flat look.

"Here we go." Toni entered the room, two pillows in hand. She tossed one to each of us. "I'm going to bed now. If you need anything else—anything at all—just shout. Jaya is a very light sleeper. She'll come help you."

Jaya—somewhere outside the living room—loudly sucked her teeth.

Toni laughed. "Good night, kids."

After they left us, Gabriel fluffed his pillow, then lay down. I stayed where I was, sitting up. After a few minutes, I felt a tug on one of my toes. I looked down to find him watching me.

"The roof's not really going to fall in, you know," he said.

Perhaps not. But that didn't mean I could sleep. After everything we'd heard that day, I didn't know how he could either. More than anything, I feared my dreams, sure I was in for another round of nightmares.

I still had no idea what to believe or how my parents were involved in all of this. More than anything, the uncertainty bothered me. For so long I'd put my faith in provable, measurable, testable facts. Believing anything else felt like ripping out part of my identity—a vital piece of what made me, *me*.

But it was getting harder to see any way around it.

If I tentatively gave in to the notion that the creature was real, then that opened a whole slew of questions, like: How powerful was this creature? Could it hurt me? Did my mother know about it? Had either of my parents made deals? Or had they somehow crossed the people who did? Was that why they were attacked?

I hated to think it, but my mother did love the fame that came with her abilities. For a while, she had been flying high before it all came crashing down around us. How far would she have gone to get it all back?

"Do you remember that weekend at Blueside?" Gabriel asked suddenly. "When we got caught in a storm? This reminds me of that night."

It took me a second to reorient my thoughts, but now that he'd mentioned it, I could see the similarity, too.

We'd been about fourteen at the time. Our mothers had rented a villa from one of Muriel's friends. Janice had brought Allison and they stuck together. That left Gabriel and me on our own, as usual.

On our second night there, a tropical storm struck the island. It knocked out all the power. We were right in the worst of it. The windows vibrated with the thunder. The walls of the villa, perched on the seaside, took a beating from the spray of the waves as they crashed against the rocks just below.

For a while, I had tried to keep a brave face while utterly petrified. Janice and Allison saw through my mask, teasing and trying to scare me. The three of us were meant to share a room, but I refused to stay with them, afraid of what prank they'd pull on me as I slept. I thought of telling my mother, of sharing her room instead. But if Janice and Allison ever found out, I'd never hear the end of it.

My last resort was sleeping on the couch. I hadn't expected Gabriel to already be there. He said the noise was too loud. "If I'm going to be up anyway, I might as well enjoy the show."

I sat in the space beside him. Just being near him was a comfort.

Thunder cracked and I flinched, shutting my eyes tightly. When it passed, Gabriel spoke to me, his voice low. "Keep your eyes open." He pointed to the pitch-black window "It'll be worth it. I promise."

The next time, I kept my eyes open. I watched as lightning forked through the dark sky over the raging sea. A stunning display of nature's power, as beautiful as it was terrifying. He held my hand, an anchor in the chaos.

We weren't together then, still on the precipice between friends and more. But between one clap of the thunder and the next, I'd irrevocably fallen for him.

"You were so calm that night," I said now, breaking my silence. "I was terrified the whole time."

"Me too," he said matter-of-factly.

I frowned down at him. "No, you weren't."

"Yeah, I was. But I was trying to impress the girl I liked. Of course I couldn't act like it."

I poked his side with my toe, ignoring the fluttery feeling in my stomach. "You're such a fool. You didn't need to do that."

He shrugged. "It made you feel better, didn't it?"

I lay down, turning onto my side to face him. We stared at each other, our bodies aligned. Instead of looking away, I stayed. The rain got louder, intensifying. The moment stretched between us, fragile and reckless. I wanted to touch him.

"I'm going to ask you something," he said. "You don't have to answer if you don't want to. But why is it so hard for you to open up to the possibility that we might be chasing something supernatural?"

My first impulse was to pull away, but I couldn't raise the energy. Perhaps it was the late hour, the steady beating of the rain, or the way he was watching me, but I couldn't. "You mean why can't I throw away everything I believe in and fully embrace something absolutely terrifying?"

Gabriel sat up so we were face-to-face. My breath stilled at his nearness.

"Denying it won't make it any less real," he said. "It's still there."

His eyes were soft and filled with far more care than I deserved. I wanted to drown myself in it. Maybe, if I did, then I could feel *something* other than this fear that continuously lurked on the edges of every waking moment.

Without thinking, I shifted. Resting on my elbow, I leaned forward. But before our lips met, he turned his head.

I retreated.

How had I miscalculated so badly? I'd thought . . . Some of the things he'd said . . . Maybe . . .

"I'm sorry." I flipped onto my back. "That was a mistake. I shouldn't have done that."

"No, you shouldn't have." Anger hardened his tone.

I turned my face into the couch cushion, burning with embarrassment.

He let out a sharp breath. The wooden floor creaked as he shifted, then seemed to settle. I squeezed my eyes shut, as if blocking it all out would help stay my spiraling shame. If only I could take the moment back. I would much rather live with the possibility that he might still want me than know for certain he no longer felt the same.

When he spoke again, it was so soft that the words were nearly lost beneath the storm.

"The only ones to blame for what happened to your parents are the people who hurt them," he said. "If you could've helped them, you would have. But more than likely, if you'd stayed in that cottage, you would've been hurt, too. Maybe you regret that you weren't there at the time, but I don't. Not if that meant that you wouldn't be here now. I think your parents would say the same."

Heart in my throat, I looked over at him. He had his back to me. Even after I'd messed up, he still offered comfort.

He really was too good for me.

I lay back down, curling into the cushions. Eventually, I fell asleep.

CHAPTER
TWENTY—SEVEN

Winston had one job. He took the goats to graze, every Saturday and Sunday.

During the week, while he attended school, his father and older brothers shared the responsibility. The weekends were left to him. While Winston's friends slept in or hung out, he awoke before sunup, prepared the animals, and led them to an open field three miles from their property. There, he left them until evening, and then returned them home in the dark.

The walk took over an hour, leading them along the roadside, then skirting the edge of the rainforest. Sometimes, it took even longer if the goats gave trouble, which they usually did. He'd grown numb to the yells of irate drivers. It was pure luck they hadn't caused an accident yet.

Curly in particular proved to be a problem. At five months old, the toffee-colored kid was a menace. A true escape artist. Burning with endless energy, running, jumping, and wandering off at every opportunity. One time, Winston had made it all the way home, only to realize Curly wasn't with them. At some point during the walk, he'd slipped his rope. Winston's parents had never let him hear the end of it.

That Saturday morning, Winston hadn't had the best start. He'd woken up later than usual, though it was still dark. In the kitchen, his mother greeted him with a sour expression. He scarfed down his roast bake and salt fish, then hurriedly prepared the goats, but by the time he reached the road, the sun had already risen. It heated him from above, while the hot asphalt cooked him from below.

Cars blew past. He tugged on the ropes, trying to keep a steady pace. He had seven of the goats with him that day, including Curly, who'd been unusually docile. He didn't trust it.

Winston thought of everything and nothing, so bored he could've cried at the unfairness of it all. Music wasn't an option, proven to agitate the skittish animals. He had asked his parents to buy him earbuds once, but they refused before he even finished the request.

"Don't even bother with any of that," they'd said. "When you're on the road, you mind the goat and watch for cars. Just focus on what you're doing."

Even at fourteen, they still treated him like a child.

Halfway to the field, a fancy silver car pulled up beside him. One of his friends, Reggie, stuck his head out the passenger-side window and called out to him.

Winston called back, then bent his head to see who was driving.

Danny. He should've realized from the car. Only one boy he knew had money to drive something like that. While Winston didn't hate Reggie's cousin, he didn't like him either. The guy was three years older than them, with a serious superiority complex. He'd lime with their crew, then make smug remarks about them being immature.

"Danny got the new PlayStation," Reggie told him. "We going to lime at his house. Come, nah."

Winston ducked his head again to check Danny's expression. Danny looked ahead, unreadable. Not the most welcoming, but not objecting.

Winston *really* wanted to go. He'd heard about Danny's huge house, the pool, and a big-screen TV that covered an entire wall. He desperately wanted to see it.

"Can you pass back for me in an hour?" he asked them. "I need to drop off the goats first."

Reggie retreated inside to discuss it with Danny. While Winston waited, Curly veered off the road, extending his rope as far as it would go. Winston tugged, reeling him back.

Reggie stuck his head out again, his lips stretched into a grimace. "We going to the grocery now to pick up some things. Passing back in about twenty minutes. We could pick you up then?"

Winston would never make it to the field and back here in twenty minutes. He needed something quicker. Somewhere close by.

"Yeah," Winston said. "I'll be right here. Twenty minutes."

After the car drove off, Winston moved quickly. He led the goats away from the side of the road and through the trees. He had a spot in mind. A small clearing just ahead, the area marked by the remains of an old Spanish cedar tree. It had been cut after lightning struck the bark, splitting and setting the insides of the trunk aflame. The huge burnt stump now stood like a gravestone, a marker of its long life.

Winston tied the goats to a pair of leaning coconut trees. He made sure the rope had enough length for them to walk about and reach shade. He'd go with the guys, then be back for the goats this evening. His family would never know he'd never made it to the field.

Winston returned to the road and waited. He prayed he didn't smell like goatskin and sweat. Reggie and Danny picked him up and he squeezed into the fancy car, beside the cases of drinks stacked in the back seat.

Danny's TV did not cover the whole wall, but it was still impressive. They played for hours, only breaking for food and the bathroom. Danny gave them full access to the kitchen and told them to take whatever they wanted from a pantry full of snacks and a fridge stuffed with every brand of soft drink. Danny was smug when he won, then sour when he lost. Winston was about to call him on it when he caught sight of the darkening sky through the window.

He checked the time, saw the missed calls and messages from his parents, and his heart dropped. Not only was it later than he'd realized, but those were rain clouds blotting out the sun. The island was under a storm warning.

Winston panicked and cursed and begged the guys to drop him back where they found him that morning. They refused to leave until the game finished. Winston insisted until they gave in. He suspected this would be his last time invited over, but he didn't care. Now his neck was on the line. All he could think about were his parents' angry, disappointed faces. They already expected the worst of him.

By the time they dropped him off, it was raining. Winston ran toward the clearing, his phone ringing with calls from his parents. He ignored them to avoid explaining his situation.

The bleats greeted him before he arrived. Two of the does had entangled their ropes around each other, probably startled by the storm. Freeing them took longer than it should have, both animals wriggling and moving, countering his progress. It wasn't until he got them separated that he realized his count was off. Curly's rope lay on the grass, the kid nowhere to be seen.

A yell broke from his lips, part panic, part frustration. His skittish audience milled about, agitated, and soaked. He walked one way, then the other, checking the time, then looking at the sky. He could not return without all of them. Not after what happened last time.

Winston retied the ropes, his wet hands slippery and shaking, then scanned the ground for tracks. A trail of scat lay at one end of the clearing. He followed it. From there, he took the path of least resistance, hoping Curley would've done the same.

Not too long later, he came across a swamp. The banks were crowded with mangrove and beach apple trees. The threat of Curly falling into open water was bad enough, but if he'd known the poisonous fruits were so close by, he never would've left the goats here. A few beach apples could bring down a grown man. He didn't want to think what it could do to a young goat.

"Curly!" he shouted in one direction, and then the other. He strained his ears, listening over the rain. Minutes passed and his worry morphed into fear. His mother would have his hide, if she knew he was alone this deep into the rainforest. He knew the stories. He'd been warned about the creatures that prowled through the trees, stalking unsuspecting wanderers with ill intention.

Of all the legends, douens terrified him the most. The creatures looked like young children, faceless except for a mouth, their feet turned backward. They mimicked voices, like those of parents calling for children in the night. The children, hearing their names from multiple directions, chose which one to run to. Those that made the wrong decision were never seen again.

"Curly!" he shouted again, praying he would not hear the echo of his own voice. He'd never heard of a douen going after an animal, but you never knew.

His clothes were soaked; his arms and legs stung from sharp blades of grass and branches dragging across his skin. Cold and afraid, he wanted to go home, almost ready to give in, resigned to whatever his parents' reaction might have been—then he heard it. Curly's bleats, calling out to him. He took off, running toward the sound.

It didn't occur to him that he might be the child lured by an echo, that he was making a choice, until he was almost upon it. Fear punched his chest, radiating outward. He skated to a stop, sliding in the mud.

Thunder cracked. The bleating continued, insistent. Close. His heart raced. With shaking hands, he reached for the low-lying branch ahead, drawing it aside so he could see.

Curly stood on top of a large rock, turning in circles, agitated like the rest of the herd. Winston approached cautiously. The goat startled at the sound of him, freezing. Winston rushed forward, afraid that Curly would bolt. He tripped, falling on his face.

He flipped over and froze. A man was lying next to him.

Winston shot up, backing away. Later, he'd realize he must've tripped over the man's legs. The body curled in a fetal position, both hands retracted at its side. A bruised rash covered the skin around the mouth.

The gray eyes were open and lifeless, staring up at the stormy sky.

CHAPTER
TWENTY-EIGHT

When I woke up, the rain had stopped.

It took me a second to remember where I was, and why I was there. The living room felt airless. Cold and still. In the weak light that filtered from the hallway, I sat up and inspected the unfamiliar surroundings. The pile of blankets on the floor sat empty. Through the foggy glass windows, I spotted Gabriel's blurred shape standing on the patio. I got up to join him.

Only when I stepped outside did I realize my mistake. I should've worn shoes—the ground was wet. Gabriel didn't seem to mind; he was barefoot, too. He had his back to me, his hands braced on the railing, the view beyond the patio cloaked in absolute darkness. I meant to ask what he was doing, why he was out here. But he spoke before me.

"Do you remember the first time we kissed?" he asked.

I did. It happened on an extraordinarily hot afternoon, the kind of heat that seemed to stretch time and inspired exhaustion after you made the slightest movement. He and I had taken shade under a flamboyant tree, the red flowers blooming.

"You laughed it off as a joke," he said. "Then you didn't talk to me for a week."

I let go of the door. It clicked shut behind me. Why would he bring this up now? The shame of my rejected kiss still lingered against my skin, a prickly sensation. Was this a lead-up to a further letdown? Did I want to hear it?

His fingers tapped against the banister. "You told me it was because you were scared. You didn't want to ruin our friendship. But that wasn't the truth, was it?"

"It was." I didn't like how he kept his back to me. But maybe it was the only way he could get the words out.

"The only truth?" he pressed.

"Yes." I stepped closer, the water cold against my bare feet. "And you were too good for me. Always have been." I surprised myself. The admission flowed from my lips, thoughtless. "I was worried that one day, you'd finally turn on me like the other islanders. You'd realize that you wanted nothing to do with me."

He finally turned around, the shadows melding his features into something severe. "Is that why you wanted me to leave? How does that make sense?"

I folded my arms, as if erecting a barrier between myself and this conversation. "I don't want to talk about this."

"I do." He approached me. "How can you not? Sometimes it feels like all I think about, all these questions rattling around in my head. Why would you let me go? Why wouldn't you come with me? I can't get these feelings out, Selina." He grabbed my face with both hands, his palms icy cold against my cheeks. "I know you feel the same. I know you do."

"Gabriel . . ." I whispered, faltering under the weight of his intensity, his passion. His wide, pleading eyes were like arrows aimed at the softest, most vulnerable parts of me.

When he kissed me, it was a shock and a release, need tangling with resignation. I gave in to it immediately, wanting to melt into him with everything I had. But under the pressure of our lips, his skin caved like thin paper. His body, so neatly pressed to mine, felt like ice.

I pulled away, my hand covering my mouth.

"What's wrong?" he asked.

I backed up, a strange sensation prickling at the back of my neck. A warning.

He closed the gap. "You didn't have a problem earlier when you tried to kiss me." He tipped his head to the side. "I don't understand. What do you want from me? The whole reason we broke up is because I had to leave, right? Well, now I'm here. Isn't this what you wanted?"

"No!" This wasn't what I'd wanted. He was supposed to escape this place. Live the life he'd always wanted.

"Don't lie to yourself," he said. "You always knew one day I'd leave you. It was inevitable. But that doesn't change the fact that, deep down, you're angry that I didn't choose you. You wanted me to be stuck here. Just like your mom. Just like you."

I shook my head, backing away from him again. I didn't want to hear this.

"Why not?" he asked as if answering my thoughts. "It's the truth, isn't it?"

"What do you want me to say?" My back hit the wall. I reached in the direction of the doorknob and grasped air. A quick look revealed that there was no door to be found. I had nowhere to run.

"I want the truth. I want you to admit that it didn't matter whether we stayed or left. In your heart, you know, no matter where you go, no matter what you do, it won't change the fact that you—Selina DaSilva—are not good enough for me. You're rotten from the inside out."

And then it was no longer Gabriel standing in front of me.

It was me.

I screamed.

A breath later it was on me, its overly sweet breath hot against my ear. "You can't lie to me, Selina. I know everything about you. All your hopes, your doubts, your desires. All your best and worst memories. Every thought you've ever had; every feeling you've ever felt. Every person you've ever loved. I know what makes you laugh and the fears that keep you up at night."

"Shut up!" I pushed against the creature that looked and sounded exactly like me. "Let me go!"

"I will. Once we understand each other." It grabbed my face. "You need to stop interfering in my business." Its nails dug into my cheek. "I don't think you understand how easy it would be for me to pick you apart piece by piece. Or just break you all at once. It's as simple as snapping my fingers."

I struggled, but it held me in a grip of unnatural strength.

"Do not make me angry, Selina, or the next body that washes up on the beach will be very familiar."

All of a sudden, I could hear Gabriel—the real Gabriel—calling out my name. He sounded too far away.

A wicked smile graced its lips—*my* lips. "Like him, for example."

Horror pierced through me. "Don't touch him."

"Then don't give me a reason. This is my one and only warning."

It snapped its fingers and disappeared.

A second later, Gabriel was shaking my shoulders. I screamed and pushed him back. The sound of the storm returned at full blast, like the dial on a speaker turned all the way up. We were on the ground. In the rain. I was soaked.

Gabriel held out his hands. He meant no harm. "I heard you screaming," he said, raising his voice over the rain. "What were you doing out here?"

I glanced to the side and spotted the door, only a few feet to my left.

"Why did you come out here?" he asked again.

I reached for him, my fingers trembling. His skin was cool but not cold. His cheek was firm beneath my touch. This was real. This was Gabriel.

He rested his hand over mine, worry etched into every feature of his expression. He might've asked again if Toni and Jaya hadn't thrown open the door. We turned our attention to them and their flurry of questions.

CHAPTER
TWENTY—NINE

In the morning, Gabriel woke me with the news, his phone in hand. "They found Lennard."

I sat up, squinting against the morning light that streamed through the windows. The rain had stopped. The sounds of chirping geckos and birdsong floated in from outside. After borrowing another set of clothes from Toni, I'd lain awake, finally dozing off close to dawn.

In my exhaustion, it took me a second to process what Gabriel was saying. And a few more seconds to read the grimness of his tone.

"He's dead?" I asked.

"Poisoned by beach apples."

"In the forest." Not a question. I knew.

"It looked like he's been there for a while." Gabriel searched my face.

In the light of a new day, I couldn't hide. He must've realized I had no intention of denying the undeniable anymore, because he ducked his head, his body sagging with obvious relief.

"Are you ready to talk about what happened last night?" he asked.

Do not make me angry, Selina, or the next body that washes up on the beach will be very familiar.

I swung my feet off the couch, setting them on the floor. "I told you: I was sleepwalking." I might no longer be denying the supernatural, but there were still things I couldn't talk about with Gabriel.

"Sleepwalking?" Gabriel rested his phone down on a nearby table and sat beside me. He sounded skeptical and I couldn't blame him. I didn't believe me either. "Since when do you sleepwalk?"

I stood, my eyes on the floor. Exhaustion crashed over me. Immediately, I wanted to sit back down.

"Hey," Gabriel whispered, a desperate note of concern in his tone. "Are you really okay?"

My eyes burned with the threat of tears. I hated that I kept lying to him. But, whereas before I'd held back to protect myself, this time I had to protect him.

This was all my fault. I'd brought him Lennard's things and showed him my father's notebook. I'd asked for his help and brought this nightmare upon us.

"There's more," he said. His words were hesitant. "The way they found him . . . He had a note in his pocket. He confessed to murdering the others. It looks like he might've done this to himself."

"No, that can't be right."

Toni walked in. She wore a pink shawl over a white linen shirt and long jeans. "Good morning, sleepyhead. Feeling better after your midnight outing?"

"Sorry," I mumbled, ashamed.

She shrugged like it was nothing, still excessively chipper, even at the early hour. "After checking on my mother this morning, I took a ride down to the bridge. I'm happy to report both are in good condition. You can drive back, no problem."

After a breakfast of whole wheat bread, sardines, and tomato choka, Gabriel and I retrieved our clothes from the dryer and got dressed. We said our goodbyes and thanked Jaya. Toni walked us out. She wore a pair of thick rubber boots that squelched with every step.

"Before you go, Selina," Toni said, unlocking the gate, "can I speak to you? Alone."

Gabriel watched us, wary. He had a handful of books tucked under his arm, including a signed copy of the new Samantha Lake. "We should be getting back," he said.

I didn't know if he was more worried about what I might say to her, or what she might say to me. Either way, he clearly didn't want trouble.

"Only for a second," she pressed, holding my gaze. "Please."

I nodded my agreement, then said to Gabriel, "I'll be right back."

Gabriel hesitated for a moment, before climbing into the vehicle. I walked away from the gate, past the large frog statue. Toni followed. We strolled along the dirt roadside, the ground soft beneath my feet. The air was heavy with the scent of wet foliage. Once we were far enough from the house, I stopped and faced her.

She glanced back the way we'd come. Gabriel was watching us through the windshield of the Jeep. "He's very protective of you," she said. "It's sweet."

"What do you want to talk to me about?" I refused to engage in small talk. If this was about my *sleepwalking* last night, I'd rather she just said it. We'd been in Patience long enough.

"We have quite a bit in common, you know," she said.

I folded my arms. This still felt like small talk, but maybe if I played along, she'd hurry up. "How so?"

"Our mothers. Mine is a known Obeah woman in these parts. Growing up as her daughter, it was a problem for me. The other children at school were afraid. They never invited me over to their houses. Their parents told them to stay away from mine." She smiled. "Except for your mother. She was different."

I held up a hand, interrupting her. "You claim to be my mother's friend, but how is that possible? I don't know you. And don't say it's because you've been busy."

"I *have* been busy," she protested.

"For eighteen years?"

"You don't remember; I was around when you were young. Your

mom and I would spend hours talking about my latest book idea, while you crawled around our feet."

"And then? Where did you go?"

Her shoulders slumped. "It's a bit complicated. It seemed that Josephine wanted to keep this part of her life—the parts that cannot be so easily explained—away from you." She kicked a pebble, and it rolled off the road, disappearing into the grass. "And I, a little offended by her distance, did not do much to maintain the friendship."

"She wanted to keep me away? Why?" Even as I asked the question, I knew the answer. "Because she thought I was ashamed of her."

She offered me a thin-lipped sympathetic smile, which was confirmation enough.

Guilt lodged like a block in my throat, making it hard to breathe. My voice strained as I tried to speak around it. "She must've been so mad at me. I was awful. I don't blame her."

"Oh, no." She waved her hands. "I don't think she was mad at you."

"She *was* mad." My heart ached, like a vise tightening around my chest. It was one thing to suspect and another to know. "She was disappointed in me. I didn't inherit the gift. I never fully believed her. And now those awful things I said were the last words I'll ever speak to her."

"Breathe, Selina," Toni said, her voice surprisingly stern. She squeezed my shoulders until I met her gaze.

I didn't realize I couldn't breathe until she mentioned it. Suddenly, there wasn't enough air.

"It's not like that," she said. "Your mother was not disappointed in you. I know."

I shook my head, careful to keep my back to the Jeep. The last thing I wanted to do was worry Gabriel. He'd come running over here. "You can't know for sure."

"I do," she insisted. "She called me, a few days before . . . it happened. Out of the blue, after years of silence. My first thought was *Oh, now you're a pariah, you want to talk to me again?* Not very nice, I suppose.

But it's how I felt." Toni dropped her hands and her gaze followed. "She told me we had to talk. And she said it in *that way*. You know what I mean?"

"Yeah, I know." I sniffed, blinking back the tears. Mummy did that sometimes. Even if she didn't know why, she felt compelled to do something. To strangers, it might have seemed like she gave in to random impulses. But even if her actions didn't make sense in that moment, they would later.

"So, we start chatting," Toni said. "It's small talk. She tells me how she's been; I tell her how I've been. We talk about your father, Jaya, you. She brags about the foreign schools you want to apply to. She's so happy that you're going to be a scientist, like your dad." Toni smiled, her eyes glassy. Distant. Like she was replaying the moment in her head. "It goes on like this for a while. The whole time I'm waiting, bracing for the important part. But then it ends. We hang up and I'm left there, wondering, *What was the point?*"

Toni broke, tears pooling in her eyes. "I didn't understand then. But, I think, the reason for the call was so that I can talk to you now. So I can tell you that you meant so much to her. That she admired you for following your dreams, even though they were so different from her own. That, even though you weren't on the best terms, she was very much proud of you."

"She was?" I whispered around the emotion clogging my throat.

"She *is*." Toni tilted her head to the sky and let out a somber, self-conscious chuckle. She swiped her tears away. "You want to hear something awful? I haven't visited her at the center." The hunch of her shoulders betrayed her shame in the admission. "I don't think I can see her like that. But, knowing her, I don't think she'd want me to remember her like that either."

"I've been reading your books to her," I offered.

She barked out a wet laugh. "That's very sweet of you."

Sweet wasn't the right word for me, but I didn't correct her.

"Is this my fault?" I asked. "Would all of this be happening if I'd believed her sooner? Believed in her powers? Could I have stopped it? Saved them?"

"No," she said firmly. "You cannot think like that. This creature knows how to protect itself. It's tricky. Deceitful. It far predates me and you." Possibly sensing my doubt, she ducked her head to meet my eyes. "I understand why you had doubts. For ages, I wasn't receptive to my mother's teachings either. It wasn't until I was older that I understood.

"Our ancestors knew what they were doing. They held on to their beliefs and used them to find strength, power, and comfort in difficult times. It's that strength that fought wars and won rebellions. It can be used for good or bad. As always, it depends on the person practicing it."

Finally, I came to the question—the one that had been eating at me for days. Even now, I hesitated to ask it. "Do you think . . . ? Did my mother make some kind of deal? That's why this is happening?"

"No," she said with so much confidence, I believed her. "Your mother would never. She was too aware of the unseen dangers around us. More than anyone, she understood the need to be careful."

I inhaled sharply. It felt like my first real breath in ages. The relief made me dizzy.

"But listen . . ." She pulled her shawl tighter. Her expression sharpened with concern. "If my mother is right, it means someone has marked you."

All my relief evaporated. "What should I do?"

"Be careful," she repeated. "Listen to your instincts. And remember, belief can be extremely powerful. It may be your only source of strength in a time when you'll need it most."

O n the road back to town, we mostly remained silent. Gabriel and I had a lot to process. Despite my darker thoughts, the sun inched higher, warming the air and drying the freshly washed earth. Only when we'd almost reached the house, he brought up the topic I was desperately hoping to avoid.

"Tomorrow, I'm going to call Ken's lawyer's office again. I'll tell them that I'm contacting her on behalf of the newspaper."

My heart dropped. "Why?"

"Because if it sounds official, Carla Paul may not blow us off this time. I'm sure your father was onto something. There must be a reason her phone number was in the notebook. We just have to find out what it is, and if it relates to the creature."

Do not make me angry . . .

This is my one and only warning.

"No!" I blurted, then forced my fears down, my voice flat. "I mean, why bother? Lennard's dead. We can't save him. There's no point in looking into this anymore."

"What?" he demanded.

"I'm saying maybe we should let it go."

"Are you serious? You want to give up?"

"There's nothing to give up. It's over."

He glanced over at me, his disbelief palpable. "Did you forget why we were doing this? You wanted to know what happened to your parents. Don't you care about that anymore?"

"Of course I care." My fingers clenched, nails biting into my palms. He would hate me for this, but it had to be done. Finding answers wasn't worth losing him. "But I just don't see where we can go from here. Any information Lennard had he took with him. We've hit a dead end."

"So what? We sit back and let the police close the case? Because that is what they're going to do. They have their murderer, their confession. They're going to blame everything on him."

"And what do you suggest we do about it?" I asked, getting irritated. Why couldn't he let it be? "Do you want us to go to them and explain that it's not Lennard's fault? That he was tricked into a deal with a supernatural creature? They'll laugh us out of the station."

Gabriel exhaled harshly. He looked pissed, but he had to know I was right.

"We have to let this go." *Please*, I silently begged him. I might not have been able to prevent my parents' attack or the plane crash. But, this time, the danger had come to me in the night with a warning. I would protect him.

"How am I supposed to let it go?" he asked. "How can you? Do we spend the rest of our lives acting like we don't know about this creature and the things it makes people do? Sure. Okay. I'll go back to the newspaper and you—what? Return to scamming people with Allison and Edward?"

"Stop it," I said. "Leave Allison and Edward out of this. They aren't the problem."

"Of course you wouldn't see them that way. To you, Edward and Allison are the solution. They're going to give you the status and validation you always wanted."

Oh, so we were doing this now? I knew he'd be mad, but I didn't expect this. "You don't know what you're talking about."

"I never understood it," he said. "The people here treat you like crap, and you're still so desperate to fit in. That's why, even during your fake-psychic revenge, you still tried to help them. To make them like you. Tell me the truth—do you even like Edward?"

"Stop the car." I didn't care that we were within sight of the house. I didn't want to stay another second with him. "You can't ask me that. We're not together. *You* broke up with *me*."

"Because you wanted me to," he said. "And because it hurt to watch you grieving and punishing yourself for something you had no control over. Nothing I did helped. Sometimes it felt like I was only making things worse."

His words knocked the air out of me. Was that how he'd felt? My plan had been to push him away, but making him believe he'd made my life worse hadn't been a part of it. Especially when, for so long, he'd been the only piece that felt right.

Gabriel parked in front of the open gate. He cursed and cut the engine. "It would be one thing if you were happy with him. *Them.* But I don't think you are."

"In your unbiased opinion?" I grabbed my bag, opened the door, and jumped out. It was becoming clear, the only way to get him to drop the investigation was to make him think I didn't care. "I told you, the day you got back, a lot of things had changed. Has it ever occurred to you that you don't know me anymore, much less what makes me happy?"

"Selina, wait!" He got out, left the driver's door open, and rounded the front of the car to meet me. "I'm sorry, I shouldn't have said that. Of course you know what you want. What makes you happy." He blew out a breath, frustrated.

I didn't understand him. What was the reason for all this? He'd rejected my kiss. Made it very clear that he didn't want me anymore.

He stepped closer. "After everything, you must know that I still—"

"Hey!"

I startled, turning toward Edward's voice. He stormed toward us from the direction of the house. Allison and Janice poured out the open door behind him.

"Get away from her!" Edward said.

I rushed forward, getting between them. If I'd been paying more attention, I'd have seen Edward's car parked beside Janice's.

"Edward, please calm down." I caught him, using my body as a barrier.

"Give me one good reason why I should," Edward demanded. "All night, I've been trying to call you. I come here this morning, worried. And you turn up with him?"

"Let's talk inside," I said.

Edward tried to step around me, but I blocked him again. Janice and Allison watched us from the steps, totally unhelpful.

"Gabriel was just leaving." I looked over my shoulder, silently pleading with him to listen.

Gabriel didn't take the hint, glaring at Edward. His jaw was clenched. Defiant.

"Leave, Gabriel," I said firmly. This mess was mine to clean up. His presence would only make it worse.

Edward vibrated with fury, straining against my hold. He could have broken through if he'd wanted to. I suspected my presence, more than my strength, restrained him. Looking at the scene, it would appear I'd chosen him.

"Please," I begged Gabriel. "Let it go."

The words seemed to cut through Gabriel's walls, cracking the foundation. His resolution crumbled, the stages of the fall visible in his expression. First came anger, then hurt. Then, finally, resignation.

He returned to his car and left.

It was only then Janice decided to intervene, sprinting down the drive after him. "Wait!" she shouted, but it was too late. She whipped around and pointed in my face. "I can't believe you."

If any goodwill had been left between us after Miss Heather's, it was gone now.

"I told you something like this would happen," she said.

To be fair to her, she did.

While she retreated into the house, I returned my attention to Edward. "Let's go inside." I pressed my hand against his shoulder, leading him through the door.

In the entrance hall, he shook me off. "Where were you all night?"

"My battery—" I started, but he didn't let me get further.

"You completely forgot, didn't you?" He rolled his shoulders and leveled me with a glare. "The dinner with my parents. Last night."

Oh no. I had totally forgotten. "Edward, I'm so sorry. We got caught in the storm." It was a weak defense, but the only one I had. "We stayed together, but nothing happened." I should've told him about the rejected kiss, but it would only make him angrier. He might go after Gabriel when it was my mistake.

"Do you have any idea how embarrassed I was?" he said. "Everything was set up. We were all there, sitting, waiting, and I couldn't get ahold of you. We'd even arranged for catering. A three-tier red velvet for dessert."

I was allergic to red velvet. But from the look on his face, I could tell this wasn't the time to mention it.

"All night, I worried about you," he said. "And this whole time, you were with *him*."

Shame curled in my gut. "I know this looks bad."

"Bad?" Edward barked out a dry laugh. "You told me I had nothing to worry about."

I did say something like that, only a few days ago. It felt like so much longer. Too much had happened. I didn't even feel like the same person.

Edward drew away from me, hands on his head. "Gabriel still wants you, Selina. He's not even trying to hide it." He turned back. "Tell me you understand why I'm upset."

"I do."

"It's not fair to me."

"It's not." I swallowed, guilty. "I'll apologize to your parents. Explain what happened."

"No, you won't."

Oh. I froze like startled game, afraid that if I moved, I'd be dealt the killing blow.

So this was it? The end. I should have seen it coming. And yet, even knowing that I deserved it, I felt a vicious spark of panic. It made me want to grab onto him and cling to this last vestige of normalcy. Everything had been so easy before the murders. There were no invisible monsters and less fear. I wanted to go back to that.

"I made a mistake." My voice shook as I fought to temper my desperation. He would lose all interest in me if I begged. Instead, I approached him with false confidence, holding his eyes, locking his focus so he had to listen. "Give me one more chance. I know I can do better. For you, I can be better."

He searched my face, his brown eyes probing. Each passing second of uncertainty felt more excruciating than the last. I didn't know what he was trying to find, his silence unnerving. I stuck my hands into the pockets of my jeans, about to withdraw in defeat, when his hand cupped my cheek.

"One more chance," he said.

I leaned into his touch. "Let me prove it to you. And to your parents."

"At the anniversary party."

"Okay," I agreed quickly. "At the party. We'll have our reintroduction. I'll impress them so hard they won't know what hit them."

The corner of his lips twitched in the beginnings of a smile. "I'm sure you will." His amusement eased the worst of my worries. "You're very good at that." From the angle of his bent head, I thought he'd kiss me then. He dropped his hand instead. "At least, you are when you remember to be."

I said nothing as he headed for the open door.

"I need to go," he said. "I'm still mad. Let me cool down before I say something stupid."

He slipped through the door and headed for his car. I didn't stop him, watching from the doorway. All things considered, it could've gone worse. I'd gotten one more chance; I couldn't blow it.

My life had been knocked off course thanks to Lennard Bisson, Gabriel's reappearance, and our half-baked investigation. Now that I'd corrected my path, everything would be set right. The creature would leave Gabriel and me alone, and everything would go back to the way it had been.

The memory of Gabriel's face before he left—his look of betrayal—flashed across my mind, my resolve almost faltering. I hoped he'd forgive me one day.

Confused, tired, and desperate for a shower, I headed back into the house. Allison met me a few steps inside. She frowned, looking over my shoulder as Edward's car sped out the front gate.

"He was my ride," she said.

I stopped beside her. Allison's hands folded behind her back, her bony shoulders hunched. She looked nervous in a way that didn't suit her.

"Did you want something?" I hesitated to ask, not overly eager for another fight.

"I came to talk to you," she said. "I know it's a bad time, but . . . it's about the shop. And what I said earlier."

I couldn't deal with this now. "Allison—"

"No, let me say this. I know I was wrong. I understand why you gave Lennard's things to the police. It wasn't fair for me to ask you to withhold evidence. You did the right thing."

I stared at her, shocked silent.

"Janice and I talked about it," Allison said. "She helped me see the situation from your perspective. I'm sorry for putting you in that position."

"Janice helped you see that?" Of all people? I never expected her to take my side.

"Yeah." She gave me a small, tentative smile. "She can be reasonable on the rare occasion. I'm glad she was in this case. I didn't appreciate how privileged I am. That there are worse things the chief of police can do to a person than take away your phone for a few days."

"What about the shop?" I asked. "And Scotland?"

"The shop is over. And Scotland . . . who knows? Maybe it's for the best. I did want to get away from my parents. This could be a fresh start for me."

After a beat of hesitation, she held out her arms. "Are we okay?"

I accepted the hug. "We're okay."

CHAPTER
THIRTY-ONE

I pulled the dress over my head, careful not to get makeup on the fabric. It slid over my shoulders and down my body. The material fell like liquid, soft against my skin. Reaching over my shoulder, I zipped the back, then adjusted the lace sleeves. All the while, I was very conscious of my freshly done nails, trying not to mess them up.

The day of the party had arrived. Expectations and nerves ran high. I'd underestimated the amount of time it would take for me to get ready, guests already arriving downstairs. A line of cars formed along the road in front of the house.

I'd made a huge mistake visiting my mother that morning. Not the act of visiting, but my timing. Dr. Henry had been waiting in her room, standing beside her bed. He wanted to speak to me again. After our last talk, which amounted to nothing, I hadn't bothered to brace myself for what was coming. I should have.

"You are eighteen?" he'd asked. "Is that correct?"

"Yes," I'd said, confused.

He had regarded me through thin wire-frame glasses. "As it stands, Miss Muriel is your mother's court-appointed guardian. Do you know what that means?" When I'd nodded, he said, "And are you aware that you are old enough to change that? As your mother's only living blood relative, you can challenge her position and take on the decisions for your mother's care."

"Okay . . ." Where was he going with this?

"While it's clear that Miss Muriel has the best intentions, she has repeatedly ignored my professional advice."

I hadn't understood. "What advice?"

His lips pressed into a thin line, as if reluctant to let the words out. "I don't think it comes as news to you that it is highly unlikely your mother will wake up. After two years, we've seen no change. In fact, after the most recent round of tests, I'd say the possibility is nonexistent."

And then I'd understood. My head swam with a dizzying lightness. I breathed through it, somehow still standing. "You think we should let her go?"

"I think Miss Muriel's decision to keep her on life support is motivated by grief, understandably. You need to think about what is best for your mother. What would she want? How would she feel about living the rest of her life this way?"

I had no answer for him.

"You have time to think about it, of course," he'd said, standing. "I just thought you should be aware of the situation as it stands. If you have any questions about how to go about seeking guardianship, let me know. I can advise you."

———

Hours later, his words replayed in my head. I still had no answer.

With the dress in place, I stepped back and regarded my image in my full-length mirror. I adjusted my silver necklace. Like so many times over the last few weeks, I waited for some horrid image to appear behind me. For my face to contort or the reflection to move independently. In a strange way, I'd grown used to the visions. It was becoming easier to see through them. Distinguish what was there and what was not.

There had been no sign of the creature, though. It seemed to have stuck to its word. I stayed out of its business and it left me alone. Not so surprising considering its penchant for bargains.

All my research on the sigil had been deleted, and my father's notebook stashed behind other books on my shelf. Most importantly, I hadn't contacted Gabriel. He'd tried calling a few times and messaged me to please talk to him, until I hit block. I'd caught a glimpse of him once as he left the newspaper offices. I'd been waiting in the flower shop across the road for that very reason. I had wanted to make sure he was okay and, perhaps, sate that foolish part of me that needed to see him.

I exhaled, the bodice cutting into my torso. I didn't remember it being so tight, nor the emerald green so vivid at the store. The dress was undeniably gorgeous, but the cut was far bolder than might've been wise. Tonight, my plan was to fit in with these guests, not stick out.

"I am happy," I stubbornly told my reflection. Gabriel's words from earlier still needled at me. Certainly, the girl in the mirror looked like she should be ecstatic.

In a few minutes, I'd be attending the most exclusive party, on the arm of my handsome boyfriend, wearing a dress far more expensive than anything else I owned. And yet, I felt one snipped string away from that perfect image collapsing completely.

"I am happy," I repeated, this time louder, as if raising the volume would make it true.

Then I remembered my mother. And Dr. Henry's advice. My smile dropped, hopelessness swelling like a balloon in my chest, suffocating. I almost fell apart.

Someone knocked on the door. Without waiting for an answer, Edward poked his head inside, giving me only a split second to pull myself back together. I smiled in greeting, but it felt weak.

"There you are." He halted in his tracks. He looked surprised but not in a good way. "What are you wearing?"

Crap. I knew it was too much. "I guess it's a bit—"

"I thought we agreed you'd wear light blue."

"What?" I blinked at him, speechless. Completely lost. When did we agree on that?

"You really—" He stopped to close the door, then continued. "You really don't listen to me, do you?" He pointed to the light blue shirt under his blazer. "We're supposed to be coordinating."

"I'm sorry," I said, searching my memories. I remembered he'd said he liked the color, but I didn't remember agreeing. "Is it a big deal?"

"It's not about the color," he said through clenched teeth. "It's that you didn't listen to me." He pressed a hand to his forehead and stepped away. "Color coordinating is exactly the kind of cutesy move that my mother would love. Now we can't even use that."

"We don't need it." I tugged on his sleeve so he'd face me. "I promised to impress them, and I will."

His gaze raked over my face. "Well, you are beautiful," he relented.

I tried to be assured by his compliment, but it had felt almost mean. Like something he held against me.

"Thank you," I said, stepping away from him. "Can you give me a few more minutes? I'll meet you downstairs."

"Fine," he said gruffly. Just before he stepped out, he turned back. "Tonight's important, Selina. One more chance. Don't embarrass me."

———

The first floor was packed with people in dark suits, shiny shoes, and dresses of every color. Gemstones dripped from ears, adorned necks, and circled wrists. The light from the chandelier refracted off carefully cradled glasses. The music that played held vaguely familiar melodies—the blandest covers of popular songs, all the fun of the originals removed. Servers in gold waistcoats and black ties held up silver platters loaded with drinks.

Muriel met me at the bottom of the staircase, drawing me into a loose hug. Tonight's perfume reminded me of the wildflowers in the field next door. She beamed, resplendent in a deep purple dress, a black shawl made of glittery material draped across her shoulders. She was the perfect blend of glamour and sophistication. Standing next to her, I felt gaudy in my green lace. I wished I'd asked for her opinion on my dress before I bought it.

"You look perfect," she said, like she was reading my mind.

"Really?" I asked, hoping it was true.

"Absolutely," she said. "And so much like your mother, sometimes, it's startling."

Oh. My hope dimmed. She wasn't seeing me, she was seeing Mummy, her opinion on the matter tainted.

A waiter passed and Muriel stopped him. She grabbed two flutes of champagne and handed one to me. I took it from her, grateful for something to do with my hands.

Edward approached us. "There you are," he said for the second time that evening. He sounded exasperated, like I was something he kept losing. "Miss Muriel, you look stunning as usual."

"Thank you, Edward." Her words were friendly but distracted as she searched the crowd.

"Do you mind if I steal her for a moment?" he asked.

"Go right ahead." She strained her neck, her focus in the direction of the front door. "I think the governor just arrived. Let me go welcome him."

Edward laced our fingers together and led me away. I glanced over my shoulder to see Muriel greeting an older man with graying hair and long features. He wore a black suit that was well tailored to his lean frame. From his puffed posture and lifted chin, he gave off the impression of great self-importance.

"Are you ready?" Edward whispered in my ear, dragging me back to the moment. Before I could brace myself, he planted me in front of his parents. They stood in the center of the living room, where the couch usually sat. For the party, most of the furniture had been removed or set aside to create an open space.

Edward's mother smiled upon seeing me. Chief Montgomery was more reserved, which was unsurprising given the fact that he'd been icy and reticent in all our past meetings. It was perhaps too optimistic to think that he'd warm in a less professional context.

As Edward indicated earlier, his mom was indeed a fan of color coordinating, the hints of coral in his father's outfit matching her dress exactly.

"Selina, good to see you." His mother beamed. She looked me over, seeming to approve. Thank goodness. To her son, she said, "You were right, she cleans up very well."

Cleans up? Her choice of words gave me pause. Still, for the sake of politeness, I forced out, "Thank you, Mrs. Montgomery."

"Please, call me Letty. Mrs. Montgomery makes me feel so old." Her eyes darted toward her husband expectantly, like that was his cue, a second stage of a long-running joke. Whatever was meant to be said, he didn't pick it up. She cleared her throat and pressed on. "It's awful that Allison's shop is closing, isn't it?"

"It is," I agreed, confused by her phrasing. Why did she say it like she wasn't the one to pull the plug? Like they weren't sending their daughter to Scotland?

"What are you planning to do for a job, then?" she asked. "Now that you're available."

"Mom." Edward sighed. "You don't have to bring this up now."

"It's just a question." Her eyes never left my face. "Selina?"

This was starting to feel like an interrogation. I glanced at the chief of police, his stony stare still on me. Fine beads of sweat broke out along my skin. It was less than a minute, only one question, and I was already floundering. "I haven't decided yet."

"We are looking for more help at the real estate agency," Letty said, "if you're interested."

"Mom!" The pitch of Edward's voice heightened with exasperation. "I told you not to do this."

Letty laughed. "I'm just putting the offer out there."

Edward squeezed my hand. "Although, it would be fun working together, wouldn't it?"

Letty waved her hand, her thick gold bracelet catching the light. "Oh. She wouldn't have a front-facing job like you. Not right away. But we could build up to it. Over time." Even though her smile never faltered, I detected a hint of condescension. Or perhaps I was too sensitive and she truly meant to be generous.

Edward squeezed my hand. "That doesn't sound too bad, does it?"

I made a vaguely affirming noise and sipped from my glass.

It was perfect. A respectable job, working with Edward. A chance to improve my reputation and prove my worth to his parents. If all went well, I wouldn't need to depend on Muriel anymore, and I'd finally have that new life that eluded me for so long.

It should be perfect. Everything I wanted.

And yet, the idea of working for Letty held no appeal. At least, at Allison's shop, I could still work on my herbal experiments and—in a roundabout way—help people. By joining the real estate agency, I'd become a part of the corporate machine that Gabriel warned me about.

While we'd driven across the island, I'd seen the new developments slowly but surely consuming St. Virgil. How long would it be until it consumed me as well?

"Actually," I said, the words thoughtlessly spilling out, "I'm thinking of going back to school."

"You are?" Edward asked.

"Yes." Under his attention, my burst of confidence faltered. "Maybe."

"You never mentioned this."

"It's just a thing I've been thinking about recently."

"Oh, which school are you looking at?" Letty asked.

"I'm not sure yet."

Letty frowned. "You know, if you don't want to take my job offer, you don't have to make an excuse—"

"No, no!" I rushed to assure her. "I'm just . . . considering my options."

A brief silence trailed my words.

I knocked back the rest of my champagne. When I looked up from the glass, I was greeted by Edward's disapproving frown. Yes, I was very aware I was messing up, but I didn't know how to fix it. Like a car barreling toward disaster, I figured the best thing to do was pump the brake.

"Excuse me," I said, drawing away. "I see someone I need to speak to."

It took a little bit of strength to untangle my hand from Edward's. He didn't want me to go, but I needed a moment to steady myself. If I kept going, at this rate, I'd completely alienate his parents before the first round of drinks was done.

Usually, I knew exactly the right thing to say. I didn't know where the impulse to go back to school came from.

I crossed the living room, almost through the back patio doors, when Allison, dressed in a lovely pink-and-gold pantsuit, snagged me by the shoulders. She pulled me into a group with Janice and Nathan, the three of them huddled beside an antique marble-top table.

I greeted them, distracted. A quick check confirmed that Edward had stayed with his parents, likely running damage control. I went to sip from my drink, disappointed to find the glass empty. Tonight was a total failure. Why did I ever think I could fit in here?

"That dress is gorgeous on you," Janice said with a smug smile. She flipped her long ponytail over the shoulder of her white dress. She swirled her drink, the pearl bracelet on her wrist matching the pins in her hair. "I told you it was perfect."

Nathan shrugged. "The lace is okay, but why isn't it shorter? We need more skin."

"There is something very wrong with you." Janice smacked his arm.

"Just something? Not everything?" He lifted his glass in her direction. "Glad to see I'm rising in your estimation."

While the others laughed, I mapped out a path to the patio. Only a few feet and a handful of people stood between me and freedom.

"What the hell?" Allison said suddenly. "Janice, who's that with your brother? She looks familiar, but I can't place her."

My heart leapt into my throat. We all turned our attention to the direction of her gaze. I leaned forward to see, my chest tight with bittersweet anticipation.

A few guests stepped aside to reveal Gabriel, his hair freshly cut, mind-meltingly gorgeous in a sharp three-piece suit. Khadija strutted in on his arm, her A-line black dress more suited for an office than this party, but she somehow pulled it off with a pair of strappy heels and dangly silver earrings.

Janice snorted, her eyes darting toward me for a moment. "Oh, that's his landlord's daughter. Maybe he brought her in exchange for a few dollars knocked off his rent."

They broke into another round of laughter, unnecessarily cruel. An ugly part of me wished I could be so dismissive. Questions about Khadija and Gabriel's relationship ignited a storm in my head.

I'd begged Gabriel to come to the party. But now that he was here, it felt like a slap in the face.

Why would he bring her?

"You okay?" Allison whispered into my ear. At first, I thought she meant about Gabriel, but she went on. "I saw you talking to my parents. I know they can be intimidating."

Oh. For a minute there, I'd forgotten about her parents. First that disastrous conversation, and now Gabriel and Khadija's appearance. All that layered on top of my concern for my mother, and the pervasive fear of the creature's threat—suddenly, the lights, the music, and the chatter felt like too much.

"I need some air," I whispered to Allison.

"Of course," she said, unlatching her arm from mine. "Do you want another drink?"

Janice—who'd caught our exchange—plucked the empty glass from my hand and swapped it for her full one. "It looks like you need this more than I do."

I accepted it gratefully and finally made my way outside.

Cool air greeted me on the patio. The backyard was even more elaborately decorated than inside, the lawn adorned with covered tables, sculptures, flowers, and fairy lights. I followed the railing toward the side of the house, which appeared to be empty.

Tonight was supposed to fix everything—repair my relationship with Edward, impress his parents, and prove to everyone that I wasn't just my mother's daughter. This was supposed to be the beginning of the rest of my life. Without the darkness. Without the investigations. Without the baggage of the past. And yet, now that I stood at the border of respectability, I hesitated to cross over, suddenly conscious of what I'd have to leave behind.

I took a sip from my drink. Then, in a burst of frustration, I gripped the railing and said the words meant to fortify me: "I am happy."

"Lucky you," a voice leaked from the shadows.

Startled, I spun on my heels to face it.

Officer Dannon leaned against the wall of the far corner, almost hidden. She wore a black pantsuit and a red silk blouse beneath.

"Thought I was alone," I said, catching my breath.

"Evidently," she said.

The scent of cigarette smoke lingered in the air. Though I couldn't see one on or near her, it would explain what she'd been doing out here.

"How convenient that I'd run into you," she said. "I have been meaning to talk to you for a while now."

My blood chilled. "Should I get a lawyer?"

"Why? This isn't an interrogation. Just a chat."

"And why should I trust you?" I folded my arms, glancing toward the open patio doors. Would walking away make me look guilty of something? Did I care if it did? "You've made it very clear that you don't trust me."

"Can you blame me when you keep lying?"

I shifted my feet. She did have a point. And Gabriel had advised me to come clean at the next opportunity.

"Lennard's things," I said. "The phone and wallet. I'm the one who asked Gabriel to hand them in."

"Yes, I know." She straightened off the wall. Stepping free of the shadows, she revealed the markers of exhaustion on her face that she couldn't hide with makeup. "Gabriel is a good kid. I was the one who handled his father's case. At the time, he had a lot of questions. He's been through a lot." She stopped in front of me. "Which is why I hate that you've dragged him into this mess."

"What?"

"Tell me, how do you DaSilva women do it? How do you convince smart, rational-minded guys to believe in your psychic crap?"

"Excuse me?" I couldn't believe what I was hearing.

"I worked with your father," she said. "He was something special. The work he did in forensics helped so many. He was smart. Funny. An all-round admirable man." She smiled, and I could not help but wonder if her admiration had been purely platonic. "He could've—and should've—continued doing great things. But your mother had to ruin it all, dragging him into her web of lies."

"You're wrong about my mother," I said, my irritation mounting. "She tried her best." After everything I'd seen and learned over the past few days, getting a glimpse of life through my mother's eyes, I knew it to be true. "All she ever wanted to do was help. She wasn't perfect, but she did try."

"She let a murderer go free to kill again."

"Oh, *she* did? I didn't realize she was queen of St. Virgil. That she controlled all the courts, the judges, and juries." I lifted my chin, unrepentant. "Tell me, are you out there harassing all of their children, too?"

All my mother, father, and I ever wanted to do was help people. All St. Virgil did in response was hurt us. Well, I was done with it.

"Your mother influenced their decision," she said, just as stubborn as me. "That makes her responsible for the consequences."

"Is she?" I asked. "Because my father—the one you so admire—believed she was right, too. Up to his last day, he was looking into Elizabeth's case. And you know what? He found something."

Her glare faltered for a second before it rebounded. "You're lying. And even if he was looking into it, it was because he'd been tricked by your mother."

"I can prove it," I said. Then hesitated.

Even if I did show her the notebook, it would only prove that he'd been investigating, not that Mummy was right. She needed something substantial. "Contact Carla Paul. Ken Thomas's lawyer."

She snorted. "And why would I do that?"

"Because my father did." It occurred to me that, even though the lawyer's office blew off Gabriel and me, they'd have to answer to a police officer. "He had evidence that proved that Ken was wrongly convicted."

A wild leap. But I took it. What did I have to lose?

The curl of her lips betrayed her amusement. Perhaps she'd caught onto the fact that I was bluffing. She stepped around me. "In that case, I think I will give her a call."

She walked away, reentering the house. I felt a rush of vindication, a pleasant humming in my blood. Finally, I'd done something right. I'd stood up for my parents and myself, making no excuses, and it felt good. So, *so* good.

I realized my mistake too late.

In the dark glass of the window in front of me, my reflection smiled. The corners of my lips were a little too sharp, the shape a little too wide. My entire body went numb.

I'd forgotten. I did have something to lose.

"I told you." It raised a single elongated finger. "Only one warning."

CHAPTER
THIRTY–TWO

One second, I was staring at the creature in the glass. The next, my own terrified expression. A flash of emerald green drew my attention to a nearby window. My image darted from one glass to another, along the wall, then through the open patio doors, sprinting into the house.

Oh God. Gabriel.

I followed it inside, chasing the nightmare. No one else seemed to notice the chill in the air or the snatches of an image that looked so like me racing across every glass and polished surface.

I collided with someone, stifling a scream at the last second. It was a stranger. I stuttered out a distracted apology. The man, so alarmed by my reaction, skirted around me, muttering unkind words under his breath. I barely registered the attention I'd drawn, spinning in circles, sloshing champagne everywhere as I searched the room.

I couldn't find the creature anywhere. But I knew it was there, hiding beneath the chatter and light and music.

"Hey, you." Allison grabbed my arm. "Why don't you come with me." Her high-pitched tone betrayed her concern. "We're over here. Why don't you settle this debate for us."

We returned to the marble-top table. Only belatedly, I realized, not only had Edward joined their group, but so had Gabriel and Khadija.

For a few seconds, Gabriel's gaze locked with mine. While his expression appeared stony, the fire in his eyes betrayed that he was far from indifferent.

I needed to warn him. But how would I get him alone?

Edward took the spot beside me, arms crossed, still as a sentinel. While Gabriel couldn't seem to look away from me, Edward couldn't look away from him. Though the others did their best to lighten the mood, the tension was undeniable.

"What do you think, Selina?" Allison asked. When I looked at her blankly, she quickly clarified. "By withholding the food for the first few hours, is Muriel being sadistic?"

"I'm just saying—it's not right." Nathan recklessly gestured with his full glass. "Clearly, she enjoys our suffering."

"Please," Janice said, rolling her eyes. "You're not going to starve from one late dinner."

To my surprise, Gabriel chimed in. "I think my mother's very aware that a large subset of the attendees only come for the food. By withholding it, she ensures a full house for at least a few hours." He punctuated his joke with a charming grin.

The others laughed, but it struck me as wrong. It seemed like Gabriel was actually trying. He certainly looked the part, his hair combed, suit on, like he'd come to the party tonight with the intention of playing the role of the good son for Muriel.

He was doing exactly as I'd asked, but it unnerved me.

"No joke," Khadija said, adjusting one of her earrings. "The second they bring out the food, I'm jumping on it. I might even smuggle something home for Adrian. He loves anything with shrimp."

Janice snorted behind her glass before taking a sip.

Gabriel playfully knocked against Khadija's shoulder. "If the finger food's not enough, we can pick something up on the way home."

The smile Khadija gave him made me want to rip something. Instead, I went to take another sip of champagne and realized the glass was empty again. I waved down a waiter and snagged a fresh one.

"I'm not so bothered about the food," Janice said. "As long as they've got drinks, I'm happy. Right, Selina?"

I paused, the glass to my lips. Her words processed, and I lowered my hand, slightly embarrassed that she'd drawn attention to my drinking. The overhead light caught my liquid-filled glass.

Inside, my watery reflection smiled with an abundance of needlelike teeth.

I flinched and fumbled the glass. It fell, soaking part of my dress and the carpet. Allison stepped away, avoiding the splash zone. There was a bit of commotion as I dove to retrieve the flute. Edward, in his rush to help me, stepped on it, breaking it apart.

"Well, someone reached their limit for tonight," Nathan said, laughing.

Edward yelled for a waiter. Gabriel offered me a white handkerchief. Flustered, I took it from him and dabbed at the wet spot on my dress. I glanced around the room, trying to anticipate where the creature would appear next.

"Here," Edward said, sticking a stack of napkins in front of my face. "Use this instead. You don't know where that handkerchief has been."

"It's been in my pocket," Gabriel said dryly.

"We don't need it." Edward snatched the handkerchief from my hand and tossed it. Gabriel caught it right before it hit his face.

Sensing trouble, I stepped between them and held out my hand. "Don't—" I started, but my words died as my focus shifted to the lace of my sleeves. They were moving, snaking like vines over my skin.

No, no, no . . .

This couldn't be happening now.

"What are you even doing here?" Edward asked Gabriel. "I was under the welcome impression you weren't coming tonight."

"I wasn't," Gabriel said. "Then Selina talked me into it."

"What?" Edward raised his voice.

Nathan snorted. "I didn't realize we were getting live entertainment this year."

"Shut up." Allison elbowed him. "Selina, are you okay?"

I vaguely registered that we were drawing too much attention, but my focus remained on the vines as they slid and burrowed beneath my skin. Leaves sprouted. Flowers like small bloodred amaryllis bloomed and died, their decayed remains stuck to my arms, creating the grotesque illusion of open wounds.

"We need to talk," Edward said, grabbing my hand. He yanked me backward, the move so sudden, I lost my balance. I fell.

And fell.

And continued falling.

Finally, my back crashed into a bed of overgrown brush. We appeared to be in the forest somewhere. Large trees blotted out the night sky. The vines—now much thicker—wrapped around my limbs, trapping me where I lay.

The nightmare stood in front of me, my borrowed face cast in shadow. *"We need to talk,"* it said, its version of my voice mimicking Edward's. "What do you think he wants to say? It didn't sound good to me."

"What do you want from me?" I choked out, breathless. My back ached from the fall; my heart hammered against my chest. I wriggled and pulled, trying to break free.

"I already told you what I wanted," it said. "You're the one who broke our deal."

"I never made a deal. Never with you."

"Are you sure about that? I already know what you want. The things you desire. One boy or the other. Freedom. Safety. I could send you to any university, guarantee any career. Make you successful beyond your wildest dreams."

"Never," I repeated, stressing the word.

"What about your mother?"

My heart stuttered. The creature's smile widened as if it heard it, or caught some other tell. For a second—only a second—I wondered, *What if?*

Then I remembered the fear in Lennard's eyes. The terror that chased him from one country to another, only to end in his death. "No. I don't trust you."

"Why? Do you doubt that I can do it?" It sounded amused. "I can. A part of your mother's still there. Just . . . distant."

I ignored it, pulling and kicking, relieved when the vines around one arm started to snap. My plan did not extend beyond standing up, but anything was better than lying on the ground, painfully vulnerable.

It stooped beside my feet. "I know you want to wake her up, more than anything. And you should. Do you want to know what her last conscious thought was?" It dropped its voice as if sharing a secret. "She didn't know you'd snuck out. She thought you were still in your room. Her last thought was a bloodcurdling fear that the people hurting her would hurt you. And that fear is still there, living in her head. In her heart. In her bones. She'll never know otherwise."

"No," I said, one arm loose.

"Yes," it said, crawling over me. "It's been gnawing at her soul for the last two years as she dies so, *so* slowly."

"No!" I tugged one last time, breaking free. I shoved the thing off me, the upward movement propelling me back to the living room. Back to the party. I sat there, on the floor. Guests circled around me, a collage of horrified expressions.

I wasn't the only person on the ground. Edward, in a similar position, sat across from me.

"What the hell is wrong with you?" he demanded. "You pushed me."

"I didn't . . ." My words fell away as I looked around, the true weight of what happened crashing down on me. Gabriel knelt beside me, on my left. Allison, on my right.

"What happened?" I asked everyone and no one.

"You fell," Gabriel said.

"And screamed," Allison said. "Edward tried to help you up and you shoved him off."

"Are you okay?" Gabriel hooked his arm underneath mine. "Do you think you can get up?"

I did. But a twinge of pain in my lower back made it difficult.

"There's something wrong with you!" Edward scrambled to his feet, while Gabriel and Allison helped me up. "Everyone warned me. I should've listened. But I thought I could fix you. Obviously, this was a big mistake. We are done."

"Hey!" Gabriel said, adjusting his hold around my waist so that I could lean against him. "Shut up. Can't you see something's wrong?"

"You shut the hell up." Edward got right in his face. "Do you know what your problem is—"

Edward's father yanked him back by his collar. Chief Montgomery's voice was low and cold. "Look at where you are. Think about what you are doing. Haven't you already humiliated us enough tonight?"

Edward shook with rage, but he dared not move while his father had him. As Gabriel, Allison, and I crossed the room, the glare he leveled our way burned with loathing.

Allison patted my back. Gabriel supported me. We cut through the crowd, the chatter picking up again. As we passed Muriel and the governor, she didn't meet my eye, clutching her glass to her chest. I knew that I'd let her down.

That hurt more than anything.

CHAPTER
THIRTY-THREE

They took me to my room and set me on my bed. Allison rested her clutch on the floor, knelt, and unbuckled my shoes.

Gabriel hovered beside me. "Do you need something? Anything? Water?"

"An exorcist?" I finished, then broke into laughter. Like a snowball rolling downhill, it picked up steam, growing into something large and uncontrollable. Soon I was gasping for breath, my lungs aching, tears in my eyes.

Allison shot Gabriel a look, concerned and, possibly, a little scared.

A phone chimed. Allison cursed, leaned back on her heels, and dug into her clutch. She pulled out her cell. "It's my mom." After reading the screen, she looked up at me, her eyes wide and apologetic. "They want me downstairs. We're leaving."

Her *we* included Edward. Though I knew there was no coming back from tonight, I wasn't prepared for the punch of hurt, that perfect life I'd wanted slipping away.

"I understand," I told her. "I'm okay now."

It was a lie. I felt far from okay. All I wanted to do was curl under the covers and disappear.

Her phone chimed again and she flinched.

"Go ahead," I insisted.

After a beat of hesitation, she rose to her feet. She shot Gabriel a narrow-eyed look. "You'll take care of her," she said, more of an order than a question.

Gabriel raised a brow in response. After she left, he said, "I may have been wrong about her."

"I told you," I said, though I couldn't work up the energy to be smug about it.

He shut the door and collected my shoes. I watched him cross my room, all smooth lines in his dark suit. The only flaw was a few strands of hair that had sprung loose from whatever gel he'd used. He opened the closet and placed my shoes inside.

I'd made a mistake. Though I had planned to protect him, I'd actually left him defenseless. He had to be warned.

"I wasn't sleepwalking. That night at Toni's house."

He froze, his back still facing me.

"It's real," I said. "Toni was right. I've seen the creature. It spoke to me."

Slowly, he turned around. "Was that— What happened just now—"

I nodded, my throat tight.

"And it happened before. That night at Toni's house?"

I nodded again.

His lips parted, seemingly stunned for a long moment. Finally, he approached the bed and sat beside me. "I don't understand. Why didn't you tell me? Right after it happened? It's not like I wouldn't believe you."

"I knew you would. That wasn't the problem."

"Then what was it?" His shock melted into irritation. "I knew something was wrong that morning. Suddenly, you wanted to stop looking into what happened to your parents. It didn't make sense."

"It threatened me. Told me to stop investigating."

Gabriel cursed under his breath. "You must've been so scared. But you still could've told me. Maybe we can find a way to make sure it can't hurt you."

"No, not me." I grasped the comforter, tugging at it nervously. "It threatened to hurt *you*."

"Me?" He blinked. "That's why you—" He jumped to his feet and crossed over to the window, as if needing to put space between us. This little imposed distance terrified me.

The creature was right. I'd been terrified that he would want to leave me one day. That's why I'd tried to push him away first.

"How many times are you going to do this?" he asked, tugging at his collar, undoing the top button. "You keep making these decisions that affect both of us without telling me."

I stared at him, baffled. "I wasn't going to let it hurt you."

"But it hasn't hurt me." He gripped the edge of my work desk and lowered his head. "Just tell me what happened."

This time, I told him everything, even the parts about the weird visions. While I spoke, I watched as his shoulders stiffened. He was doing his best to hide his alarm, but I could see it. By the time I was done, he'd shucked his jacket and migrated from standing at the window to seated on the edge of my bed. I lay on my side, facing him, the skirt of my dress fanned out across the duvet. The music downstairs had grown louder, the party hitting its peak.

"I think it was lying," he concluded.

I blinked at him, my eyelids heavy from exhaustion and champagne. "What?"

"It threatened me through you. But nothing happened. I'm okay. Why wouldn't it do something? Unless . . . it can't." Gabriel's investigative reporter instincts began to take over, compiling the evidence. "Take what happened downstairs, for example. It was mad, but it didn't harm you. You did hurt your back, but that was because *that guy* pulled you too hard. Everything else was an illusion."

I snorted. "That guy," I repeated. With the amount of venom he'd injected into the two words, he'd made them sound harsher than any insult. "You really hate him, don't you?"

The corner of his lips tugged into a reluctant grin. "Have I been too subtle?"

I shook my head.

"Good," he said, then looked toward the window. He straightened his back. "It's getting late." He stood, went to the door, and cracked it open. "Sounds like the party is still going strong down there."

I sat up, worried that he might be ready to leave. "Are you going now?"

He paused with his hand on the knob, looking back at me. "Do you want me to?"

"No." I didn't want to be alone.

What if the creature came back? What if it never left, lurking in the shadows, waiting for a vulnerable moment to strike? Even though Gabriel didn't believe it could hurt us, what if it just hadn't yet?

"Can you stay with me?" I asked.

He hesitated at the door. I was sure he was about to tell me no. Instead, he said, "Will you be okay for a few minutes? I should have some clothes left in my old bedroom. If I'm staying the night"—he tugged on his shirt collar—"I'd rather change into something else."

I swiped a hand over my skirt. "Yeah, I should change, too."

"I'll be right back," he promised, then slipped out of the room.

I climbed out of bed. Whatever I'd hurt in my lower back twinged. I lifted my arms and twisted my body, trying to stretch it out. It didn't help. Without wasting any more time, I yanked the dress off, perhaps a little too rough. Something ripped. It didn't matter since I had no intention of ever wearing it again.

All the while, I kept an eye on my surroundings. A flash of movement in the mirror snagged my attention. But when I looked, nothing was there.

By the time Gabriel knocked, I'd changed into an oversized shirt and shorts, taken off my makeup, and was about to crawl back into bed. He stepped inside, and I couldn't help the bubble of laughter that broke from my lips. His gray T-shirt was plain, but his pants had a pattern of Christmas wreaths on them.

"It was my only option," he mumbled, charmingly embarrassed. He barely looked at me before snatching one of my pillows and setting it on the floor.

"Don't," I said, shifting to the inner side of the bed. "We can share." It was one thing when he'd insisted at Toni's house. There had only been the small couch, which he did not fit on anyway. But here, there was room, and he was still recovering. "If you want. I don't mind."

"Uh, yeah." He rubbed the back of his neck. "Okay. We can do that." He picked up the pillow and set it on what was now his side. Then he sat, resting his back against the headboard.

While he did this, I settled my head on my pillow and watched him.

"Oh, the lights—" He started to stand.

"No, leave them on. But you can lock the door. I don't want some random guest walking in."

"Right." He got up, flipped the lock, and resettled against the headboard. His back was pin-straight, as tense as a taut string.

This was awkward. Tension rolled off him in waves. He wouldn't even look at me.

"Are you still mad that I didn't tell you?" I guessed.

"Livid," he said. "Probably will be for a long time." He sighed, scrubbing a hand over his face. "It's not that I don't understand why you did it. I might have, too, in your shoes. It's just—I hate when you make decisions for the both of us without telling me. It's not protecting me, it's hurting me. If that plane crash taught me anything, it's that bad things can happen anywhere at any time."

"But they happen more often around me."

He frowned, finally looking at me. "What?"

"Edward was right," I said. "There is something wrong with me. I'm a poison, tainting your life. I'm always holding you back, dragging you down. At school, people wouldn't talk to you because of me. You almost turned down a great university to stay with me. Then, even when I tried to do the right thing—when I made you leave—it almost killed you."

His eyes widened. "Is that what you've been thinking all this time? Selina, you weren't holding me back. The reason I considered deferring university was because I was grieving for your parents, too. What happened to them was so . . . vile. And so much was going on. I thought I might need more time."

Oh. I'd never thought of that.

It was horrible of me, but I hadn't truly considered how the attack might have affected Gabriel. I'd been too wrapped up in my own pain at the time. But he'd grown up around my parents, particularly my mother. Of course their loss would've hurt him, too.

"And as for you *making* me leave," he said, "I knew what you were doing. We'd had that fight before."

"That fight was different." Worse than before.

He shook his head. "No, it wasn't. You were hurting and I didn't know how to help you. It felt hopeless. So I—" He inhaled deeply, as if bracing himself. "So I gave up."

He looked devastated by the admission. It hurt my heart.

"Hey." I tugged on the end of his T-shirt so he'd look at me. "I didn't give you a choice. I made it impossible for you to stay."

"Of course I had a choice," he said. "Just like it was my choice to book that ticket. To get on that plane."

He lifted his hand, then hesitated. The movement reminded me of the day he'd returned to St. Virgil, when he'd found me fleeing the cottage. But unlike that day, this time, he didn't drop his hand. Instead, he brushed my hair out of my face.

"Recovery gave me a lot of time to think," he said, his voice raspy. "For the first few months, all I could do was dissect every choice I'd made, trying to figure out what went wrong. How I'd gotten there. What if I'd flown on a different day? Packed a good-luck charm or touched the outside of the plane before boarding? What if I'd just stayed with you?"

The tips of his fingers trailed along my hairline. His touch was soothing, igniting a pleasant thrill beneath my skin. I leaned into it greedily. Longing curled like a lazy animal in the pit of my stomach, desire only tempered by exhaustion.

"Thankfully," Gabriel said, "the facility I was in didn't just have excellent physical therapists but psychological ones, too. They helped me understand that sometimes bad things happen. They're random and awful. All we can do is try to make good choices when we can, and accept that some things are out of our control."

I stared up at him, trying to keep my eyes open. But between his soothing caress and my exhaustion, it was becoming difficult. Even though I knew the creature could still be watching, that there'd be consequences for my actions earlier that night, for the first time in weeks I felt safe enough to let my guard down. It was a feeling I'd only ever gotten around him. Somehow, I'd forgotten.

"You are not poison, Selina. There's nothing wrong with you. Bad things have happened *to you*. You've been figuring out how to cope."

"I am sorry for trying to make you leave," I said, skirting on the edge of sleep. "From the day you did—even before then—I've missed you."

His smile was the best thing I'd ever seen, like daybreak after an endless night. "I missed you, too."

CHAPTER
THIRTY-FOUR

I woke up screaming, panicked.

Sunlight spilled through the window. Gabriel was just about to sit on the bed. He stilled, watching me warily as I recoiled, curling against the wall. "You were dreaming," he said. "I'm sorry, I only left you for a few minutes."

Remnants of the dream lingered like ice against my skin. My memory conjured up the creature as it had been that night at Toni's, when I'd reached for someone who I'd thought was him, only for a nightmare to reach back. It took all my courage to hold out my hand. Seeming to understand what I needed, he took it.

"Are you okay?" he asked.

I nodded, staring at our clasped hands, worried that I might be pushing it. Asking him to stay might have already been too much. Was it just friendship he wanted? If so, where did the boundaries lie? It was hard to gauge without more information. Even before our first kiss, we had been especially close.

"I'm okay," I told him. "It's just that, when it touched me, it was so cold. You're warm, so I know you're real."

"What happened?" His grip tightened. He sat, the bed beneath us dipping slightly. "Did it show up again? Was it trying to scare you?"

"No, it was a nightmare. I've been having them for weeks. Sometimes it starts at the cottage with my parents, but then I go to the lookout. Every time. No matter what else happens. That's where I end up."

"Do you think it means something?" he asked, then frowned. "Wait. Do you mean the *jump-off*?"

I glared at him. "It's called the lookout. No one is supposed to jump off it. Even if you and some other fools like to act otherwise."

He laughed. It was a welcome sound. With each passing second the nightmare lost its grip, leaving just us.

His grin wavered a little. "Well, as it is, I can't make the swim to the beach. So you won't have to worry about me doing that for a while." He rolled his injured shoulder and winced.

"Is your arm hurting?"

"A little," he said.

"Please tell me you weren't sitting up all night." I lifted my head. "What time is it?"

"Late. After ten. I didn't want to wake you." He scratched his jaw, a hint of stubble growing in. He was sleep-mussed and gorgeous. "Sorry for leaving you just now," he said. Then, as if he felt he needed to explain, he added, "Bathroom."

"Did Muriel see you?" While I knew she'd love nothing better than Gabriel spending more time at the house, I couldn't guess her reaction to him staying the night in my room.

"I haven't seen or heard anyone all morning," he said.

On one hand, I was relieved. On the other hand, that meant that Muriel hadn't felt the need to check on me at all. If she'd knocked, one of us would have heard.

"Muriel must be so mad." I flopped onto my back and covered my eyes. "I've embarrassed her in front of the new governor." Flashes of the night before came back to me. Edward's anger. Muriel's disappointment. The guests' shock. "She told me how much she needed to impress him. How important it was for the business."

"I get that." Gabriel brushed the hair out of my face. I'd forgotten how tactile he could be. "Maintaining a good relationship with the powers that be is always a good policy. Especially if VE is pushing forward with the resort project."

I lowered my hands to look at him. "She did mention something about the resort project. It's not going well."

"Yeah, I'm not surprised. They've been eyeing Crimson Bay as the location for St. Virgil's newest luxury hotel."

"No way." I sat up. That couldn't be right. "Crimson Bay is public property. Open to everybody."

"Not if my mom and her company get their way." He laughed a little, apparently amused by my reaction. "Look, if you did mess up the deal last night, then you probably did St. Virgil a huge favor. It would've been like the medical center controversy all over again."

I couldn't believe it. Privatizing Crimson Bay—closing off a place that was not only breathtakingly beautiful, but a part of the island's rich history seemed unthinkable. While I hated the thought of disappointing Muriel, I was shocked by this act of callousness. And, not only that, but she'd almost made me a part of it. She'd encouraged me to get Gabriel to attend the party, so she could use him to play into the image of her happy family.

It reminded me of what Edward had said about fixing me. The night before, I'd been too embarrassed to fully parse what he'd meant, but I was beginning to understand. He also hadn't checked on me last night. He seemed to care more about his reputation, and impressing his parents, than making sure I was okay.

My eyes stung with the threat of angry tears. I felt like such a fool.

"Selina?" Gabriel sounded concerned.

"Yeah. I'll be right back," I muttered, crawling out of the bed. "Bathroom."

I needed a moment alone. I felt raw, the shame too fresh.

I stepped outside, the silence in the hall eerie. Maybe it was just the contrast between the bustle of the night before and the stillness of that morning, but it felt so complete, almost deliberate. I could not help but think of a horror movie, when the sound dropped away, right before something jumped out of the dark.

Halfway down the hall, a door snicked shut, startling me. I glanced back to find no one. Perhaps I was being paranoid. But perhaps not. After what I'd seen—and now knew—nothing could be easily dismissed. The creature had never appeared to me during the day, but I could not trust the sun's presence to protect me.

Quickly, I did what I had to do, then returned to my bedroom. I only relaxed once I'd shut the door behind me.

Gabriel looked up. He was sitting on the edge of the bed. "All good?"

"Yeah. It's just so quiet out there."

"The party is definitely over."

I felt a twinge of unease. He'd probably want to go now. Return to his apartment.

"Oh no, Gabriel!" I'd just remembered who he'd come to the party with. "What about Khadija? Please tell me you didn't ditch her."

He laughed. "Are you only just realizing this?"

"Gabriel, tell me you didn't," I begged.

"Don't worry. Before I changed clothes last night, I explained the situation to her. She got her food, then a ride home."

"And she was okay with her date disappearing on her?"

"It wasn't a date," he said.

I narrowed my eyes. "It looked like a date."

"Oh, did it?" He grinned. "Interesting."

My mouth fell open. "Gabriel, did you bring her to make me jealous?"

He leaned away from me. "My answer will depend on if it worked and how mad you would be if I said yes."

"How mad I would—" I grabbed a pillow and whacked him. Laughing, he fell back and tried to roll out of my reach. I crawled up the bed and smacked him again. "Does this give you an idea of how mad I am?"

This time he did manage to snatch the pillow and toss it away. I went to grab another, then remembered—"Oh! Your arm." I sat back on my heels, regretful, but he was still laughing.

"I'm fine," he said, sitting up. "You didn't hurt me."

He certainly didn't look hurt, his eyes crinkled, a massive smile on his face. His laughter was delicious. I wanted to taste it. The spike of adrenaline from our playfight hummed in my blood, making me twitchy. Needy.

Without thinking, I kissed him. Belatedly, I remembered his earlier rejection and moved to pull away. To my surprise, he made a noise of discontent and chased my lips. He cupped the back of my head, pulling me closer.

Gabriel tasted of spearmint and home, achingly familiar, but tinged with a new recklessness, a sharp-edged desperation knocking the air from my lungs. Somehow I ended up in his lap, straddling his thighs. I melded against him, my heart hammering, thoughts unraveling.

When I pulled back to breathe, he held on, burying his face in the crook of my shoulder.

"I don't understand," I said. "You didn't want to kiss me before."

"You had a boyfriend before." His warm breath tickled my skin, making me shiver. "I didn't want to do something you'd regret, then use to hurt yourself later. Believe me, there's no reality where I wouldn't want to kiss you."

Oh. I supposed that made sense.

"But we still shouldn't," I said, my hands contradicting my words. They wandered across the breadth of his back. My fingers tangled in his T-shirt. "It's too soon. I was just with Edward, up until last night."

"Who cares?" He lifted his head. The tip of his nose, then his lips trailed up the sensitive skin of my neck. "I don't care. You don't care. What's his name might care, but he can buzz off as far as I'm concerned."

I laughed, then inhaled sharply. His lips had stopped at the corner of my jaw. He was playing dirty, breaking out the old tricks that were guaranteed to make me squirm. My objections—and most other thoughts—melted out of my head.

Why did I care what other people thought anyway? All this time I'd been trying to fit in, shake off my family's image. But last night proved it would never happen. Even if I tried, I'd never truly be one of them, and I was beginning to realize that I didn't want to.

I tugged on his hair, pulling his head back so that he would look at me. "We do need to talk, though," I said, but almost changed my mind at the sight of his kiss-bruised lips.

"Do we have to?"

"Yes." I kissed him quickly, then refocused. "We need to be clear about our intentions."

"I don't know, I feel like I'm making my intentions very clear."

"Gabriel—" I started, then bit back my smile so I wouldn't encourage him. From his grin, I could see I'd failed there.

"Selina, why do you think I'm in St. Virgil for the summer?" Our faces were so close, his eyes crossed a little as he focused on me.

The question seemed a little random, but I answered anyway. "Because of the internship. And you wanted to spend time with your family before you start university."

"The internship is a good opportunity," he agreed. "But I could've tried to find one at another, more prominent newspaper on the sister island. And, as it's been proven, Ma and I tend to get along better from a distance."

I stared at him, waiting for further clarification. Surely, he couldn't mean what I thought he meant.

Gabriel smiled at my shocked silence. "I was hopeful." He tucked my hair behind my ear. "For me, it's always been you. Ever since we were fourteen years old, sitting through the storm in that villa. When I thought that the world could be ending outside, and the only place I'd want to be is next to you."

Something inside me cracked open, overflowing with far more affection than I'd known I could contain. It almost felt like too much.

"Sometimes I think you can't possibly be real. You're too perfect. It makes me feel twice as bad when I mess up."

"Trust me, if you heard half the thoughts I'd been having about Edward, you'd know that I'm far from perfect. But I am very real." He wrapped an arm around me, pulling me into a hug. "After all, I am warm, aren't I?"

He was. I hugged him back, soaking it in.

Then he went for my neck again. I pushed him back, laughing. "We were having a sweet moment."

"We are. It's just—do you have any idea how gorgeous you are? Last night, I could barely look away from you."

"Really? Because you just looked pissed to me."

"Oh, I was." The amusement dropped from his voice. "If you don't want to be with me, Selina, tell me. Don't lie and shut me out. Every time you do, it hurts."

"I'm sorry. Never again." I punctuated the promise with a kiss. And then another. And then a third, which lingered and deepened. The edge of desperation wore away, something slower, more purposeful taking its place.

Gabriel's phone rang from my desk.

"Ignore it," he said, his hot hands sliding up the back of my T-shirt.

As soon as the ringing stopped, it started again.

I shifted off him. "You should see who it is. If they're calling again right away, it might be important."

Gabriel muttered something disapproving, but he still got up. He checked the screen, then answered. "Hey, Khadija. Can I call you back? I'm—" He frowned. "What? Slow down. I don't understand." As he listened, his posture straightened.

I crawled to the edge of the bed, worried by the change in his expression.

"Okay, I'll be there soon," he said. "Just hold on for me." He hung up. "Adrian's missing."

"Khadija's brother?" I vaguely recalled the boy with the ice bucket.

"Yeah. He didn't come home last night and he's not answering his phone. That boy is *always* on his phone. She's worried that if she goes to the police alone, they won't take her seriously."

I could see why they might dismiss it. He had only been missing for a night. But I figured that Khadija, more than anybody, would know if something was wrong with her brother.

"I left my suit in my old room. I'm going to get it." Gabriel took a step toward the door, then hesitated. "You should change, too, and come with me. After last night, I don't want to leave you here alone."

I didn't want to be alone. But more than that, I didn't want to leave the house.

Even though I was beginning to realize how little impressing the citizens of St. Virgil mattered, it didn't mean I was ready to face their scorn already. The embarrassment of last night was still too fresh. I needed time to rebuild my defenses before I stepped out.

"You go help Khadija," I said. "I'll stay here."

He shook his head. "I don't think that's a good idea."

"I'll be okay. I'm not alone. Muriel and Janice are probably around here somewhere." When he didn't look convinced, I added, "You can't be with me all the time."

"Is that a challenge?" He closed the space between us to kiss me. When we parted, he rested his forehead against mine. "Come with me."

I smiled at his obvious reluctance to be apart. "I'll be okay."

He sighed and stole another kiss. "Fine, stubborn. But keep your phone charged and near you. Call me if anything happens." He opened the door, pausing on the threshold. "And remember what I said last night? About the creature?"

"That it can't hurt me?"

"Yeah, but—it felt the need to scare you. As far as I can see, the only reason it would do that is if it saw you as a threat. That means, on some level, it's scared of you, too."

CHAPTER
THIRTY–FIVE

watched Gabriel leave from my window. He hurried around the side of the house, having used the back door to avoid his mother. I watched as he darted out the front gate. Then, rather than make a break for it, he turned, his attention drawn to my window, like he knew I'd be watching.

I lifted my hand in a small wave. He smiled, walking backward. The fool did not seem to care that he might trip, ridiculous and reckless. He would not look away. I mouthed, *Turn around*, and spun my finger in several circles before he finally did.

His Jeep was the only car still parked on the street, conspicuous enough for worry, but far enough from the house to hope we'd gotten away with it. As he drove off, the fluttery feeling faded as the eerie silence of the house pressed in. All the lightness of the morning seemed to evaporate.

I knew I should not stay in the room alone, but facing Muriel felt like a herculean task. I put it off as long as I could.

An hour later, I changed into a loose blouse and a pair of jean shorts. While combing my hair in front of the mirror, my eyes fell upon the silver necklace. The ghostly white of the pearl pendant stood out against my brown skin. Now that Edward and I were over, should I give it back? Or keep it? Either way, it didn't feel right to wear it.

I set the comb down, unclasped the necklace, and took it off. Without it, I felt strange. Lighter, but also vulnerable. I opened my jewelry box, dropping it into one of the compartments. The space next to it, where my mother's chain should be, was empty.

A quick search through the rest of the box proved to be fruitless. With a sinking horror, I realized that I couldn't remember what I'd done with it. My last memory of it ended in the kitchen, during my talk with Muriel, just after Edward had taken it off.

After a minute of panicked riffling around, I spotted something shiny behind my desk. I reached for it. To my disappointment, it was just a cut of wrapping ribbon. I retracted my hand, knocking my elbow and shaking the desk. My experiments rattled. A few small bottles tumbled off the edge. The lavender oil cracked open, spilling on the floor. Immediately, the scent infused the room.

I gathered the bottles quickly and set them back on the table. I had to breathe through my mouth to dilute the power of the lavender. It was a relief to find the other bottles sealed tightly, some of the ingredients difficult to acquire or dangerous. The snake eye seeds in particular might've caused trouble on both fronts.

My hand stilled. I stared at the tiny bottle, half-filled with orange powder.

I'd stopped using snake eye after it failed to help Mummy wake up. But with my recent conversation with Dr. Henry still lingering in my brain, I couldn't bring myself to put down the bottle. Did I want to try again? Or was it time to face the inevitable?

Someone knocked on the door, yanking me out of my reverie. The knob turned before I could answer. "Yes?"

"It's me!" Janice called out.

Just before the door swung open, I stood and stuffed the bottle into my back pocket, not wanting Janice to start asking questions about what I was doing. "Yes?" I repeated, flustered.

"Ma has called for a family meeting." She leaned against the doorway, rolling her eyes. "In the kitchen. Your presence is required."

My stomach sank. "Can you give me a minute?"

"Okay," she said, then didn't move, glancing around my room. "What's that smell?"

I reluctantly walked toward the door. It was clear she had no intention of leaving. I'd have to sort this out later. "I'm ready. Let's go."

She leaned off the wall and started down the hall. I followed a few steps behind her.

"It's a shame Gabriel didn't stick around," she said. "He could've joined us, too."

I stumbled to a halt.

She glanced back, the amusement in her tone not reaching her eyes. "Don't worry, Mummy didn't see him."

But Janice had? And she was okay with it?

Janice continued downstairs without breaking pace. After a beat of hesitation, I continued after her.

In the kitchen, Muriel sat at the dining table, an open newspaper in front of her. "You're up," she said as we entered. "Good. We need to talk."

I sat across from her. Janice headed for the pantry. Muriel paid no attention to her, making it clear who this family meeting was meant for. I braced for the worst.

The newspaper crinkled as Muriel folded it and set it aside. Beneath her usually immaculate makeup, I spotted hints of exhaustion. She did not want to have this conversation any more than I did. "Do you want to explain what happened last night?" she asked.

I did not.

"Honestly, Selina." Muriel pinched the bridge of her nose. "I expected better. You may be old enough to drink now, but you must know your limits. Did you ever think about how your behavior would reflect on us? What would your mother say if she'd seen you last night?"

I thought about it for a moment, then answered honestly. "If my mother were here, she wouldn't have let me go to the party in the first place."

"Excuse me?" Muriel demanded.

Laughter floated over from the pantry. Janice emerged with an open bag of potato chips. She took the seat to my left.

"I'm sorry, Muriel," I said, wishing that we didn't have an audience. "The last thing I ever want to do is embarrass you. I take full responsibility for messing up last night. But if we're going to bring up my mother, let's not pretend she wasn't who she was."

"Who she *is*," she sharply corrected me. "Don't say *was*."

Maybe if I hadn't been so offended by the resort project—and if I hadn't recognized the kernel of truth embedded in the creature's taunts the night before—I might've let it go. But, after all that happened, I could no longer deny what I'd tried to avoid for too long, partly to sate my own guilt but also to keep Muriel happy. I hated to disappoint her again, but this could not go on forever.

"I spoke to one of Mummy's friends recently." My gaze dropped to the table. It was hard to look at her, knowing she'd hate this. "She's never visited Mummy in the center. She told me that Mummy wouldn't like to be seen that way. I think she was right."

"Which friend was this?" Muriel asked.

I shook my head. "Her name was Toni, but that doesn't matter."

Janice stood, her chair dragging against the floor. She must've realized this conversation wasn't for her because she left the room, taking her chips with her.

I lifted my gaze. "I've spoken to Dr. Henry. He filled me in on some things."

Muriel went very still, all the energy draining from her face. "What did he say to you?"

"He told me about Mummy's latest test results. I know she's not going to get better." My voice strained against rising reluctance, but I'd come too far not to push through. "He told me, because I'm eighteen now, I can be my mother's medical guardian."

"Did he?" Muriel's lips barely moved as she spoke, her tone frostier than I'd ever heard it. "Now, why would he do a thing like that?"

"Please don't punish him for telling me the truth." I reached over, placing my hand on top of hers, hoping she'd understand and not hate me. "You knew Mummy. You know how easily she went stir-crazy. She would hate being trapped indoors for a few hours, much less stuck in a hospital room for two years."

"You don't know what you're saying," Muriel said.

"I think I do." We were holding on to Mummy to assuage our grief and guilt. It wasn't what she would've wanted. "Don't you think it's time we let her go? Let her return to the earth that she loved so much. Let her finally be free?"

Muriel snatched her hand away and stood. She marched away from the table, passing the island counter. "You would be making a mistake." She pressed her hands against the edge of the sink, her attention on the small window ahead. "So long as you live under this roof, and depend on my money, I will not allow it."

Her words punched through my chest. I knew she'd be upset. I did not expect the ultimatum.

"Then I'll leave," I said. The idea burst from my lips, impulsive and vague, but with each passing second, they became more concrete.

Why shouldn't I leave? That had been the original plan. Perhaps I shouldn't have said it until I'd spoken to Gabriel, but he'd been firm in his desire for us to leave St. Virgil together far longer than me. With Mummy laid to rest, there was no reason I should be here as opposed to anywhere else.

Muriel grabbed a glass from the rack and filled it in the sink. "No. You are not going anywhere."

"Agreed," Janice said from behind me.

Tingles of awareness flared on the back of my neck. Muriel turned and I caught a flash of her expression. Her too-wide eyes that might've been comical in another situation.

Before I could react, Janice stabbed me in the arm. The prick of the needle felt like the sting of a large insect. A bite beneath the skin. I jerked away, too late to prevent more than half of the contents of the syringe from flooding my system. I screamed.

"Janice!" Muriel's glass slipped from her hand, shattering on the floor.

Janice dropped the syringe, wrapped her arm around my stomach, and pulled me to her. I lashed out, my elbow connecting with something soft. Janice grunted and let go. I did not wait to see her reaction, scrambling out of the kitchen, sprinting for the front door. I yanked it open, light flooding the hall.

I intended to run, but my vision swam. All the energy seemed to sap out of me, my body dragged down by an all-encompassing heaviness. I collapsed on the last step, face-planting onto the gravel.

"Janice, what did you do?" Muriel caught up to me. She settled me on my back, the sharp little stones digging into my skin. "You didn't need to do this for me. I could've handled it."

Janice strolled down the stairs. Strands of her dark hair lifted in the wind, giving her a frantic appearance that contrasted with her cold demeanor. "Not everything has to do with you, Ma." Part of the syringe peeked out of her clenched fist. "I'm doing what I have to. What I would've done sooner, if Gabriel hadn't spent the night with her."

Why was this happening? I felt strangely detached, like a spectator watching a play—but one where Muriel, Janice, and I were the actors. My vision blurred at the edges.

Muriel raised my head, propping it on her lap. She dusted off the gravel and pushed the hair back from my face. "What were you thinking? You could have killed her."

"That's the point."

"What?" Muriel shook her head, blinking back tears. "No! You told me not to worry. You were done."

Janice knelt beside me. I tried to shrink away, move, resist. Nothing worked, a disconnect between my thoughts and my body's ability to move. Even my tongue lay too heavy in my mouth.

"I told you I was *almost* done," Janice said, her lips retracted with revulsion. "But then that ungrateful ass, Lennard Bisson, decided to take care of himself before I could. He was supposed to be my last kill, but he messed it all up."

What was Janice talking about? Lennard was her last *kill*?

"How could you let this happen?" Muriel said, horrified. "Janice, today is your final day."

"I didn't let——" She exhaled loudly, then lowered her voice. "I didn't *let* anything happen. After Lennard poisoned himself, I obviously couldn't kill him. Thankfully, the great one has shown mercy. I've been given one last chance to complete my service with a new task. But it must be done today."

The great one? I thought back to the night Lennard confronted me outside the house. He'd used those same words to talk about the creature.

As I fought to stay focused, every blink a battle, two terrifying truths became clear: Janice had made a deal with the creature. And Muriel knew about it.

"You should have told me what was going on sooner," Muriel said. "I could've helped you."

"I don't need your help. I'm handling it." Janice thrust her hands in my direction. "This is me handling it!"

No. She couldn't mean what I thought she meant. That I was her final task?

Her final *kill*?

But it was the only thing that made sense. Why else would she wait until her brother was out of the house? Why else would she drug me?

My mind reeled, the sensation of panic weirdly muted by whatever she'd injected into me. I needed to run, but I couldn't, my body growing heavier and heavier. It felt like at any moment, I'd sink through the ground.

Gabriel was right. The creature couldn't hurt me, but it could order someone else to do it. I'd been so focused on a supernatural threat that it never occurred to me that the danger would be human—that it would come from people I'd lived with and known all my life.

Janice flinched and raised her head. "Someone's coming down the road. We need to bring her inside. Now!"

My consciousness drifted for a moment. When I returned, I was being moved, hauled into the house by my hands and legs. It seemed that they were trying to hide me from someone. Perhaps someone who could help? Maybe Gabriel came back?

I screamed. The sound was gurgled. Nonsensical. Trapped beneath a heavy tongue.

How could this be happening? Muriel was like a second mother to me. She loved me. She wouldn't let Janice go through with this.

"She needs to be quiet," Janice said, as they set me down. "Move aside."

"No, wait!" Muriel choked out a sob.

"What?" Janice hissed. "They're going to hear and come knocking at any moment, Ma. We can't wait."

"Just let me think . . ." Something dripped on my forehead and cheeks. Something wet.

Muriel's tears.

"You can't be serious." Janice's chilly nonchalance twisted into fury. "I am your daughter. *Me.* She's not. No matter how much you might wish it was the other way around."

"Why would you say that?" Muriel's voice shook. Her image blurred above me. "Of course you're my daughter. It has never been a competition."

"So you say," Janice said. "But now it's time to prove it. Here's your chance, Ma. You have to decide. It's her. Or me."

I fought the pull of the drug, trying to focus on Muriel. Begging her without being able to say a word.

"What's it going to be, Ma?" Janice asked.

Muriel's face contorted with anguish. Her hands, soft and shaking, brushed my hair from my face. "I'm sorry," she whispered. Another tear landed on my cheek. "I am so sorry."

My arm stung with another prick of the needle.

Finally, my eyes shut, one last time, like a curtain descending. The show was over.

CHAPTER
THIRTY-SIX

My cheek stung.

I opened my eyes in time for a leafy branch to whip against my face. My body bounced. I was upside down. Someone held me over their shoulder. Slowly, the reality of my situation sank in.

My memory returned in vivid, horrifying flashes: The fight in the kitchen. Muriel's tears on my cheek. Janice drugging me.

"Do you really need her alive?" a male voice asked. It took me a second to place it as Dr. Henry's. He was the one carrying me. "Actually, don't tell me."

Janice laughed.

I could hear but not see her. The crunch of their footsteps and panting breaths mingled with the rustling, whistling sounds of the rainforest.

"You don't want to know?" she asked.

"It's better that I don't. I shouldn't even be out here doing *this*."

"Don't blame me. Blame the coward who deserted me at the last second. Besides, does it make a difference? You're already in too deep."

"Do you have to sound so gleeful about it?"

My stomach churned, only partially inspired by being held upside down. The coward? Was she talking about Muriel? And why was Dr. Henry—of all people—helping Janice?

"This is sick." Dr. Henry seemed to echo my sentiments. "As soon as this is over, I'm done. I don't care what your mother says."

"That's funny. It almost sounds like you believe what you're saying."

"This is madness! The longer she stays alive, the more likely we'll get caught."

By *she* did he mean me? Where were we going? How much longer did I have before Janice fulfilled her task?

"Well, that's my mother for you," Janice said. "Her conscience has a habit of reappearing at the most inopportune moments. A total hypocrite. Wouldn't you agree, Selina?"

My heart dropped.

Janice leaned into my eye line, smiling.

Dr. Henry flinched and slowed. "She's awake?"

"For a little while now, I think." She cupped my chin and dug her thumbnail into my skin. Pain bloomed in my cheek as she drew blood. My heavy tongue could not form words, the protest a high-pitched vibration in my throat.

"What are you doing?" Dr. Henry turned, trying to see, unintentionally yanking me out of Janice's hold.

"Checking," Janice said, straightening up. "She still can't move."

"But she will eventually."

"Then we shouldn't be wasting time, should we?" Janice sounded upset. "Can't you walk any faster?"

"No. Do *you* want to carry her?"

"If I could, I wouldn't need you, would I?" she asked. "If it were up to me, I would've gotten this done hours ago. But between my inane brother—and the annoying party organizers, who refused to leave the house before they'd picked up every last piece of their equipment—I'm kind of screwed for time. So, when I say walk faster, you don't make excuses—you walk faster!"

"I don't have to take this." He stopped. "I'm a doctor. Graduated top of my class. You keep talking to me like that, I'll put her down, and you're on your own."

"Aw, the super-smart doctor feels disrespected? Too damn bad. If I don't get this done before sunset, everything falls apart. All our secrets come out, and everyone will know you've been helping my mother keep Josephine sedated. I do wonder what they'll charge you with. Does keeping a patient in a fake coma for two years count as medical malpractice? Fraud? Kidnapping?"

Sedated? Fake coma?

A hot rush of anger burned through my body, brutal and violent. My mother was in a *fake coma*? All this time, she'd been okay?

Dr. Henry had tried to get me to take her off life support. What if I'd agreed sooner? Would he have killed her?

My muscles tensed; my fists clenched like a coiled snake preparing to lash out. I wanted to hurt him. Claw at his eyes, rip off his face. Mummy had been trapped in that bed all this time. He could've made me . . .

Wait. My fists clenched.

I could move.

Quickly, I relaxed my hands and made my body as limp as possible. Hopefully, the doctor hadn't felt any of that.

My body thrummed, blood boiling with unsated fury, but I needed to be still. It was the hardest thing I'd ever done, but while I could move now, the drug still had me unsteady. I had to wait for the right moment to try to get away.

"Shut up," Dr. Henry said with alarming vehemence. "You're a fool like your mom. Why drag this out? You have Selina drugged. Kill her now and get it over with."

My breathing hitched. Wait—no! I wasn't ready.

"I can't. Believe me, I would if I could, but it must be done a certain way. And right now, you standing here and complaining is only wasting more time."

"Oh for— Fine." He started moving again. "Whatever."

Janice inhaled and exhaled loudly. "It's okay," she muttered, seemingly more to herself than anyone else. "All will be well. The great one has a plan. I have faith. I am protected."

"What are you—" He sucked his teeth. "Never mind. I do not want to know."

"This is the spot," Janice said after a few more minutes of hiking

The doctor dumped me onto the ground with very little care. Pain shot up my tailbone and ricocheted through my spine. It took everything I had not to curl into a ball and reveal the drugs had worn off. Instead, I collapsed, my head rolling to the side. My back slumped against one of the six-foot-high buttress roots that extended from the trunk of the largest silk cotton tree I'd ever seen.

I did not know how much time had passed, but the light had taken on the orange glow of late evening. Now that I could see my legs, I confirmed that my bare feet were also taped together.

"Hey, Doc," Janice said in a cloyingly sweet tone. She stooped in front of me. "I forgot to ask—is it safe to mix that stuff you gave me with snake eye seeds?"

My eyes widened involuntarily.

She noticed and started smiling. "Yes, Selina. I added some to your champagne last night." Her attention never left my face, as if drinking in my distress. "Thought it might be fun to mess with you. Make you lose your mind at the party in front of Edward's parents and the new governor. I got the idea when you were playing around with the seeds in the shop."

I laughed to myself. Sure, the snake eye seeds had probably made things worse, but little did Janice know that I barely needed the help to make a complete fool of myself—my visions had done that all on their own.

Janice lifted her shoulder in a careless shrug. "Plus, who knows? Maybe your weird behavior at the party might help explain why you went missing today."

I kept my face blank. The last thing I wanted to do was give her the satisfaction of seeing my fear, even as it stole my breath.

"Does the reaction to the seeds matter?" the doctor asked, sounding exasperated. He wore distressed jeans and a T-shirt, looking younger than he did in his scrubs. "You're going to kill her anyway."

"I told you—it must be done the right way."

"In that case, I'm not sure. It might explain why she's already awake. Either way, I'm done. I need to get back to the hospital."

Back to my mother?

"Don't hurt her." The words slurred out of me without thought.

Both turned to look at me.

"She can talk," Janice said, more of a grim statement than a question. She held out an open palm to him. "She'll need another dose."

Dr. Henry gaped at her. "I didn't bring it with me. It's in the car."

She threw her hands into the air. "Then what am I supposed to do? We don't have time to hike back to the car and—" She squeezed her eyes shut. "It doesn't matter. It'll be okay. It'll be okay." Despite what she said, there was an undeniable bite to her tone. Any control she had seemed to be unraveling.

When she reopened her eyes, her gaze refocused on me. "No problem. If she tries anything, I've got this." Janice reached into her bag and pulled out a knife. Fear curled in the pit of my stomach. Dodging a syringe was far easier than a blade.

"Great." Dr. Henry's voice pitched higher, a touch hysterical. "Good luck with that." He returned to the path, never looking back. His steps were quick, as if he couldn't get away fast enough.

"Pathetic," Janice muttered.

I panicked, watching him go. What would happen back at the medical center? Would he hurt my mother? I still hadn't fully processed that she wasn't in an actual coma. That would have to come later. For now, I needed to focus. I needed to save her.

I needed to save myself.

"Stay." Janice pointed the knife in my direction. While she turned her attention to the bark of the tree, I tested the muscles of my feet, successfully wriggling my toes. The tape around my ankles was loose, I could probably wrench it off if I had the time, but Janice stood too close. She'd be on me before I got anywhere. What I needed was a plan.

Janice recklessly tucked the knife under her chin, then riffled through her backpack. She pulled something out. It was chalk. She started drawing on the trunk. A tremble in her hand betrayed the fact that she was more rattled than she tried to project. I would be, too, if I thought I only had minutes left to live.

Hell, I probably did only have minutes left, if Janice had her way.

Panic hit me like a first sip of coffee. It went right to my head. I was on my own, my hands and feet taped together, defenseless in the middle of the forest. No phone. No idea which way to run to safety.

I forced myself to breathe. I knew I needed to stay calm, but it wasn't easy. All I had to do was stall until sunset: Janice's deadline. Then she'd succumb to whatever the creature had in store. Silently, I took stock of what I had on me. It wasn't much. Just a hair band, shorts, and a T-shirt. Nothing in my pockets but— *Oh.*

"Why did you bring me here?" I asked her. "The doctor was right. This is a waste of time."

Janice snorted. "I didn't realize you were so eager to die." She patted the trunk. "We are here because of this."

I looked up. The silk cotton's leaves were sparse, but large branches stretched outward. It stood at least eighty feet high, dwarfing all other trees around it. Some people wouldn't even touch the silk cottons, fearing they'd contract some form of bad luck or be possessed by the jumbies that lived inside them. It seemed that Janice had no such fear.

"The police think Lennard killed the others," Janice said, still scribbling with the chalk. "When your body turns up, it might kick up a full investigation all over again. The best thing to do is play into the islanders' superstitions. Make them think you did this to yourself. They already think your family is involved in some kind of demonic cult. The addition of the feared silk cotton tree will make your case untouchable."

"That seems like a stretch. The police won't be scared off by superstitions."

She snorted. "Shows what you know. Strange things happen on St.

Virgil all the time. People disappear and die under weird circumstances. Most of it never makes the newspapers. In fact, the weirder the details, the less it's reported. That's why they were so quick to accept that Lennard killed the others and close the case. The last thing they want to do is scare away those tourist dollars."

"I still don't think you'll get away with it."

She shrugged. "It worked for your nosy parents. After their attack, all we had to do was circulate a few rumors about occult involvement and the police backed off quickly. If only Ma could let go of your mother. And you." Her lips curled. "I told her taking you in was reckless, but she wouldn't listen."

The fear that had once enveloped me receded, curling inward, set ablaze by unparalleled loathing. All this time, I'd been afraid of the uncaught attackers and they'd been living under the same roof as me. "So that symbol you're drawing now—is that nonsense, too? All part of the occult coverup?"

"No." She exhaled harshly. "This is unfortunately very necessary."

Despite my resolve, I felt a spike of alarm following her words. But I needed to keep her talking. "Like killing Lennard was necessary? He never murdered anyone, did he? That was all you."

"Are you just figuring it out?" She laughed. "Judge me if you want. At least this way their deaths meant something. Those faithless fools were incorporated into my service. Another way for me to prove my devotion. Not to mention what I did to them was far more merciful than the end they were facing."

"How generous of you," I said dryly. "Though, from what I heard, Kyle Gordo's death did not sound merciful."

"That's because Kyle had a bad reaction to the drugs. He screamed bloody murder in that hotel and nearly got us caught. At least it had the side effect of scaring the crap out of Lennard and Chord. After that, they believed anything I told them." She sucked her teeth and flung the chalk away. "This isn't working! It's fading right off. Screw it."

She snatched up the knife and moved to carve into the tree.

"Don't!" I shouted. "Stop. I wouldn't do that."

She froze, the blade poised to dig into the bark. "What?"

"You must never cut into a silk cotton tree. If you do, you'll set free the jumbie spirits that live inside it."

This was a bit of an exaggeration. Technically, the legend claimed the malevolent ghosts would be released if the tree was cut *down*. But I was willing to take the chance she'd still believe me. If nothing else, it had slowed her progress.

"Trust me, you don't want to mess with those," I said.

Thunder rumbled overhead.

Her lips twisted into a sneer. "You're so full of crap." She lifted the blade and stabbed the bark, defiantly holding my gaze as she did. "Those superstitions aren't real."

Her certainty floored me. Laughter broke from my lips, a bit hysterical as my emotional bandwidth stretched beyond its limits. "How can you of all people say that? Look at where you are—what you're doing. You're in the middle of a ritual right now."

"Because the great one is real," she said, working the knife deeper into the bark. "The great one protects. Provides. All that other stuff about jumbies and forest spirits is nonsense. Make-believe."

"I think at this point, it might be safer not to discount anything." I held my breath, willing her to pause at my words for even one more second.

"And that is just one of many reasons why you have always been such a damn fool."

Her blade continued scratching at the tree. Thunder cracked, filling the excruciating pause in our conversation. She seemed to be making progress. I needed to slow her down again.

"You really do hate me, don't you?" I said. When she didn't answer, I added, "Last time I asked you that—the night I kicked you in my bedroom—you lied to me. Somehow, you made me believe I was wrong. Like I'd misjudged you, even though you've been mean to me for years."

She shook her head, still focused on the symbol she was carving.

"I guess, I believed you because I wanted to. Because I wanted to think that things between us could be better."

Thunder clapped again, so loud that it shook the tree at my back, resonating deep in my bones. Precious seconds were slipping through my fingers.

"I've never understood why," I said, raising my voice, no longer able to hide my urgency. "What did I do that was so bad? I've always been so nice to you."

That did it.

Her head dropped; her hand stilled. "Are you serious?"

"Janice, I have only ever tried to be your friend."

"No," she said, approaching me. "All you ever wanted was Gabriel. It didn't seem to matter that you almost ruined his life *multiple times.*" She leaned close. "And after everything we did to get him healthy and back here, you have him ready to throw it all away again."

She lifted the knife. I flinched as the cool blade slid against my skin.

Now that we were close, I could see the wild panic in her eyes. She was angry and afraid. On the edge of unraveling.

"You were right," she whispered. "You are a poison."

My heart stuttered, a deep fear validated. A private moment violated. "Were you eavesdropping on us? Listening at the door like a creep?"

The blade pressed harder, and I knew I was going to die. Her hatred for me emanated off her skin. Her emotions were a storm of anger, fear, envy, and hurt. She would not let me live. Not at the cost of her own life.

If this was the end, I had one question. "How much does Gabriel know?"

"Oh, forget about my brother already!" she shouted, spittle flying into my face. "He'll miss you for a bit. But once you're not parading in front of his face all the time, he'll get over it. Edward will move on, too. They may have been convinced by your fake, oh-so-mysterious facade. But they're fools who can't see the truth. You're just a scared girl who has nothing, is nothing, and will always be nothing."

I exhaled slowly, the blade biting into my skin.

"I know you think you've been distracting me," she said. "But the symbol is done. All I needed was a little blood." She withdrew the knife so I could see the specks of red that dotted the shiny blade. "Now we can get started."

I recoiled. She seemed to be enjoying this—having me at her mercy. But perhaps I could use that.

I licked my lips, my mouth as dry as the Sahara dust that tinted the evening sky. "You're right."

A flash of surprise crossed her face before it blunted with forced ambivalence. "About what?"

"I am scared. And I do lie. I was a bad daughter and a terrible girlfriend. You have always been pretty, rich, and perfect, so I doubt you'd understand how hard it's been for me to fit in. Just look at what happened with Muriel. Of course she chose you over me. I never stood a chance."

To my relief, she did not move, too focused on what I was saying. She ate up every word, which wasn't surprising. I was telling her exactly what she wanted to hear.

That didn't mean there wasn't some truth in it.

For so long, I'd tried not to be my mother's daughter. I'd rejected it. Distanced myself and made fun of it. I wanted so badly to be someone else—someone like Janice. Someone Muriel would approve of. Someone the island would accept.

"The truth is," I said, "I never will fit in here. Not like you."

But Janice was very wrong about one thing. She said I had nothing. That wasn't true. I had my mother. Even though our relationship was complicated, and we argued the last time we spoke, I knew she loved me. Both of my parents did. While I might have been lost, still trying to figure out who I was and what I wanted to do with my life, I was not nothing. Witch, demon spawn, liar—I would no longer let her or anyone else define me.

And, if there was one thing I did know about myself, it was that I was a damn good herbalist.

"Breathe deep," I said, then threw the open bottle of snake eye powder into her face. I turned my head, but some of it still blew back on me.

Janice cried out, tripped backward, and dropped the knife. She fell onto the ground, scrubbing her eyes. I wasted no time, grabbing the knife, and sawing through the tape on my feet. The blade was alarmingly sharp, so it didn't take long. Unfortunately, achieving the angle needed to free my hands proved to be much harder.

Janice cursed and swiped at her face. She stumbled, trying to stand, recovering too quickly.

My time was up. I scrambled to my feet. With my hands still taped together, I sprinted through the trees.

CHAPTER
THIRTY-SEVEN

Adrian's mother warned him about la diablesse, the creature with the cow foot and corpse-like face hidden behind the illusion of a beautiful woman. She appeared in the night, strolling along a dark streetside or in the middle of an overcrowded room. She selected a man and sweet-talked him into walking her home. The man eagerly followed, too awestruck by her beauty and his good fortune to worry about direction or distance until he found himself so deep in the forest that he could never find his way out.

Adrian believed her. He'd heard too much about the strange and supernatural in St. Virgil to brush it off.

When he asked what happened to these men, his mother only patted his arm and said, "Just remember, never let your desires lead you past common sense."

But this was back when his mother still held long conversations. When she could sit up for more than a few minutes without needing a rest. Before their bar started facing stiff competition from the establishments on Main Street. Before his father decided he couldn't be a caretaker and left.

Running track, which had always been his escape, turned into a literal way out. His sister used to run for the joy and the accomplishment. He did it for the business, the sponsorships, the endorsements, the prize money. All the lucrative possibilities.

Motivated like never before, Adrian ran ten times faster and worked a hundred times harder, but too soon the catch became apparent. The best gear, the top trainers, and the biggest opportunities required money—the same money he wouldn't be so desperate for if he already had it.

The first solution came skulking through the alley behind the bar. Adrian recognized the older boy from school. The guy was under the drinking age, but he offered to pay twice as much as a case was worth. Adrian snuck the bottles out of the stockroom, slipped the amount to cover the cost into the till, and pocketed the rest. Later that night, at a party, the guy told another guy, and word spread. For a few months, Adrian's little side business was set.

Then Khadija caught him and put an end to it. For some reason, she felt the need to play third parent, running the bar and his life with equal resolve. She didn't understand, her vision too limited. She couldn't see the bigger picture. Their way forward wasn't the bar. It was him.

The second solution, when it appeared, was so different from the first. For one thing, his belladonna did not skulk. She entered the scene like a heroine in a movie, descending the back staircase, her manicured hands gingerly sliding down the banister. Adrian's breath caught in his chest as he tracked her every move, the click of her pink strappy sandals imprinted in his memory.

She spotted him and tilted her head, her glossy straight hair sliding over her shoulder like silk. *Is my brother here?* Adrian reluctantly admitted he was not, his words tangled between his teeth, hesitant to do so because she'd leave.

But she didn't go. Not right away.

This was the first time they'd talked. It lasted over an hour. Though they stemmed from different backgrounds, approaching different milestones, their iron-willed determination to make more of their lives connected them.

Adrian knew she only saw him as a friend at best, a second younger brother at worst. But he liked being around her, the focus of her attention, enfolded in her sugary perfumed scent. He held her compliments close, near to his heart where they kept him warm. Her unwavering belief in his talent further fueled his desires. More than ever, he *wanted*.

When another opportunity appeared, he jumped on it. His friend's uncle, who worked at a factory outlet on the sister island, acquired high-end sneakers at a discount. The plan was to resell a dozen pairs on St. Virgil at a huge markup. All the uncle wanted was a cut of the profits. And, of course, the money to acquire and ship them the merch. Adrian sent every dollar he had left, then never heard from the uncle again. His friend offered no help or explanation, having been taken in as well.

Without enough money for daily transport, Adrian started missing or showing up late for practice. His coach berated him. His teammates isolated him. He was on the edge of losing his position as team captain.

Adrian complained to his belladonna. He did not hold back, railing against the system, and the unfairness of it all. People with money would never understand. When he belatedly remembered her family's wealth, he tried to apologize, but she waved him off.

She told him her family secret.

Her father had been a terrible businessman: too soft, too altruistic. He gave away more than he made, dragging their family to the brink of ruin. It got to the point where her mother had to make a deal to save them.

"What kind of deal?" he asked.

She smiled, a sly upward tilt of glossed lips. "Help me and I'll show you."

It started small: Take this, move that. Hide a bag. Never look inside it. Hike to the northern mountains and collect snake eye fruit. Shadow her brother and the DaSilva girl, and report back to her.

She said it was a test to see if he was worthy. For if Adrian could not handle this, then he did not have what it took to serve.

Adrian wasn't an idiot. He knew she wasn't telling him everything. But he'd seen what the creature could provide, and if this was the price for a fortune—to save himself and his family—he was willing to do anything.

At least he had been. Before the night when it all fell apart.

She came running at him, sprinting through the alley. A wild panic blazed in her eyes. His first instinct was to save her. His belladonna should never cry. She always seemed so immaculate, so unbreakable. So perfect. He wanted to gather her in his hands and put her back together again.

"I need your help," she said.

Without question, he followed her through the alleys, leaving town. Into the forest, they walked, deeper and darker, the canopy filtering the moonlight. He hesitated briefly. A prickle of memory, a feeling of wrongness tickled his subconscious, and slowed his steps.

"Come on, please!" she said, begging. Her body trembled from the cold. From fear. "He's figured it out. He knows what my task is. I need to find him now, before he ruins everything."

Adrian's feet started moving before he knew what he was doing.

When they found Lennard Bisson, he was still warm but already dead. Janice's scream collided with a rumble of distant thunder, ominous and angry. Adrian felt like he was seeing her for the first time.

Later, after he dragged the body behind a rock—but before they'd returned to slip a false confession into the dead man's pocket—he remembered the story of la diablesse. He wondered at what point he'd passed good sense, so deep in the trees he did not see a way out.

Adrian did not sleep for days. When Janice called and texted, he did not answer. Finally, she cornered him behind the bar, calling him weak, a traitor, unworthy. She compared him to his father, her father, and all those who could not do what needed to be done.

"What happened to your father?" he asked.

"He tried to undo what had already been done and died for it."

When Janice smiled, the glamor was gone. He was afraid.

The night before her last day, Adrian knew Janice would be desperate. She'd tried to call him so many times, he turned his phone off. Just to be safe, he ran away, seeking shelter in the old fort. That was where they found him.

Hungry, sleep-deprived, and desperate for it to be over, Adrian started talking.

CHAPTER
THIRTY—EIGHT

I crashed through the brush, running for what felt like hours. Time and distance seemed to stretch and retract. I was stuck in an interminable moment where everything happened too quickly and lasted forever.

My eyes burned, my vision blurring from snake eye powder and drizzling rain. Branches clawed at my skin and tore my clothes. The rain had soaked the tape and slicked my skin, allowing my hands to slip free. I clutched the knife, pointing it away from my body, afraid I'd accidentally stab myself. Or that it would fall and land in Janice's hands again.

"Selina!" Janice called out, far closer than I'd realized. "Stop!"

To scream might bring help, but it would lead her right to me. I needed to find someone. Get to the road. Or hide. I now understood that sunset might bring a revelation—the creature would take her or it would not—but running out the clock might not be enough to save my life. Should she survive, she still had to get rid of me. I knew too much.

"You'll never make it out of this forest!" she shouted over the rain.

I might've on a normal day. I'd grown up among these trees. After a while, I could've figured a way out. But today was not normal. I was being chased by a murderer, my energy already waning. The drug I'd been injected with slowed me down, while the snake eye started messing with my senses. I tried to shake it off, but dark shapes flittered in my periphery.

The sounds of the forest amplified tenfold, every snapping twig as loud as a gunshot. The colors pulsed and brightened, extraordinarily vivid. I could smell them, breathe them. A clap of thunder reverberated in my head, bringing me to my knees. I pressed my hands over my ears, a stabbing pain behind my eyes.

I needed to get up. To keep moving. But the raindrops felt like hail against my oversensitive skin. The shower turned into a stoning. The scent of cinnamon tickled my nose, eventually overpowering everything.

Go, Selina. Run!

When I opened my eyes, the forest had changed. It was more vibrant and far more alive than I'd realized. My focus narrowed. I knew exactly where I was. I'd been here before.

Two distinct paths branched out before me. One would lead toward the road and possibly people—a challenge to reach before Janice caught up, but possible. The other path was shorter, irrational, and risky. It had been laid out to me over the course of many nightmares and required more faith than I'd ever put into anything.

Go!

I leapt to my feet and ran. The back of my T-shirt snagged in Janice's fingers, the fabric slipping through before she closed her fist.

I could hear her, *feel* her, right behind me. The darkening sky pressed in on us, every passing second sealing us within its deadly limits. The gaps between the trees morphed into tall, faceless silhouettes. Like spectators at a race, some rooted for me to win, others for me to lose. Some watched, indifferent, while others hungered for the sight of blood.

My father was among them. And my grandmother. A line of ancestors unfurled to the very first, who was brought to St. Virgil against their will, and had since come to call it home.

When I arrived at the lookout, the last light of day bled into the ocean. The sea was turbulent and dark, terrifying in its immense size and unseen depths. The white sands of the bay stretched along the coast, the beach empty. A few anchored boats bobbed on the rolling waves in the distance.

A blow landed in the center of my back, shoving me face down in the dirt and stone. The knife flew out of my hands and skittered out of reach. I knew every cut and bruise that stung now would hurt like hell later. If there even was a later.

"Stop!" I tried to flip over, but Janice pressed her knee into my back, pinning me under her weight. "It's too late. Look!" I tried to point toward the sun, which was slightly visible behind the clouds. It dipped toward the horizon, the space between the water's edge and the luminous yellow circle rapidly diminishing.

"No!" Janice screamed, tripping on snake eye, caught in a frenzy of fear and driven by the need to survive. "I'm not dying today." Her pupils were alarmingly dilated. She was no longer capable of seeing reason. "Stay still," she said.

Her weight shifted as she reached for the knife, and I took the chance to flip over. She lost her balance, tumbling off me. She dove for the knife again, and I leapt on top of her, grasping at her shoulders, her hair, her clothes—anything to hold her back. She slipped away from me.

"Stop!" Gabriel picked up the knife before she reached it.

Janice and I froze in surprise. I recovered first, twisting her hand behind her back and pinning her to the ground.

"Toss it!" I called to Gabriel.

Without missing a beat, he threw the knife. It sailed through the air, disappearing over the edge of the cliff. The sound that burst from Janice's lips wasn't human. Her entire body seemed to keel under the weight of it.

"Why?" she demanded, her voice hoarse. "You always do this! You always pick her. You never take my side."

"Not if it means killing someone." Gabriel gawked at her. "What is wrong with you?"

"She made a deal with the creature," I told him, my voice a painful rasp. "Your mom—"

"I know," he said somberly. "I just came from the house. Ma was a mess, drinking and crying. She told me what happened."

Janice lifted her head and tried to shake me off. "You're pathetic, you know that? Mummy's little angel. Too weak, too nice to get your hands dirty. Ma wouldn't even tell you about the creature because she knew you couldn't handle it. You've never had what it takes to do what needs to be done."

Gabriel ignored her. "Selina, are you okay? Are you hurt? Can you get up and run to the road?"

At the thought of running again, my body grew heavy. My words came out in rough bursts, like a sputtering car engine. "I can't— I'm not—"

"It's okay." He held out a hand. "You'll be okay. Get over here. Behind me. Janice, do not move."

"Or what?" She sprung up the second I shifted off her. She lunged for me.

Gabriel grabbed her, holding her as she struggled. I rose on shaky feet, every single muscle aching. My soaked clothes felt far too heavy.

"Selina, go!" Gabriel shouted.

"No." I staggered one way and then the other. My back to the forest, I searched for balance in a world that seemed to swim in front of my eyes. "I can't leave you with her. What if she tries to hurt you?"

"Hurt him?" Janice broke into choppy laughter, the sound fake and grating.

"It's okay now, Jan." Gabriel's voice shook even as he tried to sound reassuring. "We'll get you help. It'll be okay."

"Don't you get it?" she asked, still laughing. "No one can fix it. I'm done. Over. It's coming for me now."

"Why would you do it?" Gabriel asked her. "Nothing could be worth the deal. No amount of money."

"I didn't have a choice! You were dying."

Gabriel froze. "What?"

Janice broke his grip, turning her back to the cliff to face us. Her lip was bruised. Wet tendrils of hair stuck to her face. "I volunteered to make a deal for you! After the crash. So Ma wouldn't lose her precious baby boy. So I'd finally do something right in her eyes."

Stunned by her admission, all I could do was stare at her. Gabriel had almost died around this time a year ago. No, not *around* this time. It would've been exactly a year ago.

"What was the deal, Janice?" Gabriel demanded.

It seemed clear to me what she'd asked for, but maybe he needed to hear her say it aloud.

She exhaled sharply, nostrils flaring. "I asked that you'd survive your injuries. I had to be specific with my wording, you see. It's very tricky like that."

"But I'm still injured?" Gabriel said. "My arm—"

"So it wasn't perfect!" Janice shouted. "The point is, you didn't die. I did everything—*everything* right. And it was never enough."

Gabriel backed away from her, as if he could put distance between himself and what he didn't want to hear. "You did this because of me?"

"That's right," Janice said, sniffing. "You're alive because of me. And now you have to choose. Her or me?"

"Don't listen to her," I begged him. "She made her choice. You don't owe her anything."

"Her or me, Gabriel!"

But he didn't appear to be listening to either of us, a terrifying blankness to his expression. He seemed a million miles away.

"Do you want to know what the worst part of selling your soul is, Gabe?" Janice drew a breath only to choke. She smiled bitterly, blood staining her teeth. "When the great one comes to you, it looks like you. It wears your face and says the vilest, most disgusting things.

Makes you do the vilest, most disgusting things, until you start to hate yourself. Until you can't even look at yourself in the mirror anymore."

I gaped at her in horror. She was even more far gone than I'd realized.

"Gabriel?" I called again, worried. I knew he would be sympathetic toward his sister, but he should not trust her. "Gabriel, please—"

Janice lunged for me.

Gabriel caught her around the waist, then dragged her backward. It happened so quickly. They were there. And then they were gone. It took me a second to realize that he'd hauled her over the edge.

On shaky legs, I peered into the rough gray sea. No sign of them on the rocks, which meant they'd made it into the water.

Why the hell would he do that? Had he meant to drown her? It seemed wildly out of character for him, even if she had meant to hurt me. Besides, she was a strong swimmer. He could not swim.

That's when it hit me—Janice had asked that Gabriel survive his wounds, but he was still wounded. Toni's solution to the bargain was to break it. Gabriel couldn't swim with his injury. Especially today when the seas were rough.

Of course he wouldn't choose between us. He would sacrifice himself instead, making the original deal null and void.

I'd never made the jump before, too afraid. This time, I dove right in.

My heart flew into my throat, the water rushing up to meet me. Feet-first, I plunged into the dark icy waves, sinking beneath the surface. Immediately, instinct took over. I kicked and stroked, swimming upward, until I broke the surface. I looked around, furiously treading, straining to spot some sign of them, but the rain and the choppy waves made it difficult. It took all my energy to stay above water.

A hand grabbed my ankle and yanked me under.

I inhaled water, choking, and spitting. My throat burned. I kicked and kicked, but her grip was like a vise.

My eyes opened, the salt water irritating. Looking down, I could just make out Janice. I reached down, trying to pry her hands off me, my movements sluggish and clunky. My lungs screamed with the need for air.

A dark shape emerged from below us, growing bigger. Drawing closer. My mind conjured images of sharks, saltwater crocodiles, and giant tentacled monsters that were once a myth recently proved real. But it did not move like any animal I'd ever seen. It unfurled like smoke. Like a drop of black ink in a glass of water. My heart seemed to stop, so tightly gripped by terror. I could only watch as it rose toward us.

Janice didn't seem to notice at first. Then it touched her, and her face contorted in a scream, bubbles blooming from her mouth. The dark plume coiled around her body. A sharp yank dragged us deeper. And deeper. My senses returned and I started kicking again. This time, I broke free, propelling upward. In my last glimpse of Janice, the darkness enveloped her head, swallowing her completely.

When I surfaced, the sky had darkened. The sun had set.

I had no time to process what I'd seen or come to terms with the nightmare that lurked in the water below me.

"Gabriel!" I shouted, and scanned the water. I found no sign of him.

Panic threatened to pull my focus, but I shoved it down. I needed to concentrate. I'd ignored my instincts before. This time, I would listen.

After drawing a deep breath, I dove beneath the water and swam. All my doubts, all my fears vanished as I focused on Gabriel—his face, his smile, his goodness. Everything that made him, *him*. My certainty sharpened, and I followed that feeling until I found him.

I quickly brought him to the surface.

Among our childhood games, we'd pretended to be lifeguards, saving each other. I never thought I'd actually have to do it.

I did know enough to hold him from behind and swim backward, making sure his head stayed above water. *It's okay. . . . It's okay. . . .* I repeated in my head, not even sure he was breathing. Tears and salt water burned my eyes. The shore felt impossibly far away.

A shout cut across the water. I couldn't tell where it came from. I didn't even know if it was real. The buzz of a motor grew louder than the rain. A small fishing boat sped toward us. I tried to call out, water rushing into my open mouth. Thankfully, they'd already spotted us, arriving in seconds.

"Help him. Help . . ." I coughed and begged as they hauled Gabriel into the boat. One of the two guys started CPR while the other pulled me out of the water. They asked me questions, which I did not hear. I was too focused on Gabriel, who appeared unnervingly lifeless.

I willed him to move. To breathe.

"Please," I whispered.

Gabriel shuddered and coughed up water. One of the guys helped him onto his side so he wouldn't choke.

I couldn't believe it. He was okay. He'd be okay.

Exhaustion slammed into me like a speeding truck. It had been tugging at the edge of my consciousness for some time, so much stronger now that the need to survive and find Gabriel had been satisfied.

I barely registered Gabriel reaching out as my vision blurred. I let my eyes fall shut. All that I'd been holding back finally took me.

CHAPTER
THIRTY-NINE

"What is that?" I asked.

The doctor's lips tightened with barely concealed irritation. To be fair, I'd been asking a lot of questions. After everything we'd been through, I felt no shame in monitoring everything they used on Mummy.

"It'll ease her pain as she wakes up." Despite the older woman's exasperation, her tone was gentle. "Your mother has been heavily sedated for two years." She retracted the needle and set it aside. "We cannot say what complications may arise. We cannot even say for sure that she will wake up."

"I know," I said. The doctor had warned me already. But I could not help the buzz of anticipation humming beneath my skin.

"All we can do is wait and see," the doctor continued. "We don't know how long it will take the drugs to wear off. Speaking of which . . ." She approached my chair and crooked her finger in a now-familiar gesture. I lifted my face. She examined my eyes, frowning. "How are you feeling? Do you still have a headache?"

I shook my head. "I'm good."

Out of the corner of my eye, I noticed a faceless figure passing by the open doorway. I'd lost count of the number I'd seen since I'd been admitted the day before. The medical center was far more crowded than most people knew.

The doctor stepped back. "Okay, but let me know if it changes. You ingested a considerable amount of snake eye. We don't know how that may have affected your brain chemistry. Because the fruit is so rare, only a few studies have been done on its use."

I almost laughed. After all my experiments with plant material, I'd become an unintentional test subject. "I'll let you know if something's wrong."

Her skepticism wafted off her skin, lazily curling in the air.

My visions hadn't stopped. Maybe they never would. I didn't see a reason to mention it.

"Okay," she said, retreating. "I'll be back in a few minutes to check on her progress."

"And I'll be right here." At my mother's bedside. Just as I had been for the last eighteen hours. After Dr. Henry had been arrested—and a few other medical personnel from the center had been taken in for questioning—a handful of new doctors had been brought over from the sister island to replace them.

It turned out that, while I'd been unconscious, and then running for my life, a lot happened.

Khadija's brother, Adrian, had been found, hiding at one of the old forts. He'd confessed to helping Janice, though he'd never participated in the murders directly. She'd guaranteed him a gold medal in the Olympics and all the sponsorships he wanted. But before he made the deal, he backed out—a claim which confused the police officers but came as welcome news to Gabriel and me.

Meanwhile, Officer Dannon had gotten ahold of the lawyer Carla Paul, who confirmed that my father had contacted her. He'd discovered that Muriel had paid the witness to testify against Ken Thomas in Elizabeth's murder trial. The second set of digits in my father's notebook was the number to the bank account that Muriel used to transfer the money.

Since my father hadn't obtained the information legally, the lawyer couldn't bring it to court. Plus, after my father's death, and aware of the influence Muriel had on the island, Carla Paul was understand-ably terrified to share the information. That's why she dodged our attempts to contact her. If Officer Dannon hadn't pressed, she might not have shared it at all.

Muriel had been arrested, and Officer Dannon felt confident that the charges would stick, but I was in doubt. In my mind, Muriel was too rich, too powerful, and too well-connected. There was no proof she'd been involved in my parents' attack. And though we had proof that she'd paid a witness in Elizabeth's case, there was no evidence that she'd taken part in Elizabeth's death.

Janice might have confessed to me, but she was gone. Her body had yet to be found.

So far, Dr. Henry wasn't talking. Unless he decided to flip on Muriel, our only hope was that Mummy woke up.

I shifted in my chair, a twinge in my thigh muscles. After checking to see if there'd been any change with Mummy, and noting none, I got up to stretch my legs. I paced from one end of the room to the other. The scent of cinnamon stopped me in my tracks.

In the bathroom, I stood in front of the mirror, my father's reflection beside me. How strange it was to see him, now that I wasn't afraid. I stared and he stared back, his dark brown eyes so similar to mine.

"I'm sorry," I told him. "You loved us and you were trying your best. I understand now."

He said nothing, not that I expected him to. For all his gruesome injuries, he did not look like he was in pain. I took some comfort in that.

"Thank you for helping me," I said. "We'll be okay now. You can rest."

After he disappeared, the scent of cinnamon lingered for a moment. And then it was gone, too.

Someone knocked on the hospital room door. I retreated from the bathroom to find Gabriel hesitating on the threshold. He looked like a freshly scrubbed mess. When we'd spoken that morning, he'd told me that he had to oversee the police search of the house and then visit his mother. Now he was back and hovering nervously, like he wasn't sure of his welcome.

"Hi," he said.

"Hi," I said.

He shuffled his feet. "Are you still mad at me?"

It was a fair question. For most of last night and that morning, I'd given him the cold shoulder, livid that he'd chosen to make that jump.

Without a word, I leapt across the room and launched myself at him. To his credit, he didn't hide or retreat. Instead, he braced for whatever I threw at him. My arms wrapped around him in a crushing embrace.

The hours at my mother's bedside had given me time to think. Enough time for the awful possibilities of what could've been to melt my anger. I hated knowing that I'd almost lost him.

"I'm so mad," I said, pulling back just enough to kiss his lips, his cheeks, his chin. "Never do anything like that again."

His hand gently rested on my back, his body shaking. "I thought I could fix it. Save you both."

While I understood his motives—Janice was his sister after all—I didn't think anyone could've saved her at that point.

"I didn't want to jump," he said. "But it seemed like the only solution." His hand skimmed over my shoulder, down my arm. "I am sorry for what they did to you. More than I'll ever be able to say."

"Don't apologize for your family." I knew better than most how unfair it was to have someone else's decisions held against you. I couldn't do that to him.

"I hate that Janice hurt you because of me. That she's gone because of me." His voice hitched with sadness and regret.

"Don't do that," I said, ducking to meet his lowered gaze. "When you said it wasn't my fault that I couldn't stop my parents' attack, did you mean it?"

He frowned. "Of course I meant it."

"Well, if I was being unfair to myself, then how is it any different for you? As soon as you knew what was going on, you did try to save us."

"I know what you're saying makes sense," he said. "But I still feel . . ."

"I know." I rested my forehead against his. Knowing and feeling were different things. After everything we'd been through, it would take a lot of time and work for us to align them. "We'll figure it out."

We kissed again, the press of our lips light and unbearably sweet, fueled by love and reassurance. It sank into my bones, steadying me in a way nothing else could.

When we parted, I tugged him farther into the room.

"Wait with me?" I asked.

He glanced over to my mother, then ducked his head. I hoped one day, he'd look at her without guilt. I did not blame him for any of it and I knew my mother wouldn't either.

"Any changes?" he asked softly.

"No," I said. "Not yet."

We squeezed into the bedside chair, just managing to fit. I turned my body toward his, resting my head on his shoulder. He held my hand, his thumb stroking the tender skin of my inner wrist. I watched the rise and fall of my mother's chest.

"She told me everything," he said. "When I went to see her."

It took me a second to remember he'd spoken to his mother that morning.

"I feel like I don't even know her." His brow wrinkled. "She told me that she first heard about the legend of the buck while hanging around Toni and your mother, when they were teenagers. After that, she got fascinated with the idea and started researching it on her own."

"She knew Toni?"

"Apparently."

"I guess that makes sense." Why hadn't that occurred to me earlier?

It shouldn't have been a surprise. They were both friends with my mother. "So Muriel figured out how it worked and made a deal?"

"Multiple deals." His lip curled in open disgust. "Sacrificing Elizabeth Alleyne was one of her tasks. She covered it up by pinning it on well-known creep Ken Thomas. He was the obvious fall guy since he'd almost gotten convicted of something similar. She didn't anticipate the consequences it would have on your family, or that your parents would figure out what she'd done."

"So Maeve Downs's death really was an accident?" I asked, and he nodded. "Mummy was right after all."

"She was," Gabriel said softly.

"And Muriel is the one who attacked my father? Who killed him?"

Gabriel swiped a hand across his face, his expression tight with exhaustion and grief. "She knew all about the research he was conducting on his own, after Elizabeth's death. She knew he was close to figuring the whole thing out."

"And Mummy?" I asked, even though I already knew the answer.

"She was never supposed to be there. But in the end . . . my mom couldn't bring herself to kill her best friend."

I close my eyes, letting the full weight of his words sink in. I had already lost one mother, and now it felt like I was losing another. Like I had never known her to begin with.

Gabriel continued, his voice heavy and rough. "I asked her if my father knew what she'd done. She said that he didn't at first. He thought the company's financial turnaround was because of him. When he found out about the deal, he thought he could break it by . . . removing himself from the equation. She'd lied to him about her wording, though. His death made no difference."

His father had tried to sacrifice himself to void the deal and save his family, just like Gabriel tried to do. Thank goodness Gabriel's outcome hadn't been the same.

I opened my eyes to look at him. "Are you okay?" I couldn't begin to imagine what he must have been feeling.

"I think I might be in shock." His nose wrinkled and he let out a dry laugh. "Virgil Enterprises is mine now, and I don't know what I'm supposed to do with it!"

I wrapped my arms around him tightly, as if I could physically hold him together. "Whatever you choose to do, I'm with you."

He said nothing, his gaze distant. Mentally, he seemed to be somewhere else, a dark place I dreaded to let him go alone.

I kissed his cheek, trying to reel him back to me. "Thank you for saving me at the lookout. How did you know where we were?" I'd forgotten to ask earlier.

He blinked. "You told me."

"What?"

"When Officer Dannon and I got to the house yesterday, Ma told us Janice took you to the big silk cotton tree. But when we got there, we realized you were gone. The officers wanted to search the area near the tree."

I sat up. "But not you?"

"I remembered what you told me about your dreams. That you always ended up at the jump-off." His small smile still held a touch of melancholy, but it was an improvement. "I knew it had to mean something."

I was speechless. Somehow, he'd always had faith in me, even when I didn't have it in myself.

"Oh—before I forget . . ." He shifted, pulling something out of his back pocket. "I found this when the police were going through the house. It was on the floor in the kitchen. It's yours, right?"

He dropped it into my hand, my mother's gold chain pooling in my palm. Warmth bloomed in my chest as I stared at him in awe.

After clasping the chain around my neck, I sat forward. I reached for my mother's hand, just as she'd reached for mine so many times before.

One day, Gabriel might want to write this story. When he does, some people will not believe us. They'll try to find mundane explanations for all that happened, our strange experiences explained away by snake eye seeds, paranoia, and superstition. But we'll know what we've been through.

There were just weird and wondrous things about life and St. Virgil that I'd never completely understand. And that was okay. Because if seemingly impossible things could happen, that meant hope wasn't such a useless thing after all.

I squeezed my mother's hand.

My mother's hand squeezed back.

ACKNOWLEDGMENTS

A few years ago, if someone told me I'd be writing for Rick Riordan Presents, I never would've believed it. Seemingly impossible things really can happen!

First, I'd like to thank Rick Riordan. I am honored to have had this opportunity to write for RRP. You, your work, and this imprint are a source of inspiration for so many, including myself.

I remain immensely grateful to my agent, Wendi Gu, who continues to be a great advocate for me and my books. Sorry about the scary scenes! But thank you for reading them anyway.

A huge thank-you to my amazing editor, Rebecca Kuss, who believed in this project from the beginning. I'm so grateful that you understood the heart of the story, sometimes even more clearly than I did myself. And another big thank-you to Ashley I. Fields for your invaluable insights and encouragement.

Many thanks to the team at RRP / Hyperion: publisher Kieran Viola; copy editors Guy Cunningham and Jody Corbett; and managing editors Sara Liebling and Iris Chen. Thank you to Crystal McCoy in Publicity; Andrea Rosen, Michael Freeman, and Vicki Korlishin in Sales; Danielle DiMartino, Matt Schweitzer, Holly Nagel, and Ian Byrne in Marketing; Dina Sherman, Maddie Hughes, and Bekka Mills in School & Library Marketing; and Jordan Lurie for the Read Riordan website.

Special thanks to designer Phil Buchanan and artist Hillary D. Wilson for the spectacular book cover.

Thank you to the authors from my 21ders group for their advice and support.

Thank you to my mother for her unwavering belief that I can do this, even when I doubt myself. To my grandmother for teaching me the names of the flowers. To my Uncle Louis for guiding us through the forest and sharing the folklore.

Thank you to my wonderful family, the best people I know. I am so lucky to have you all in my corner.

And finally, to the readers—I hope you enjoyed uncovering some of the secrets and dangers hidden in the forest of St. Virgil. Thank you for reading.